THE FINAL MASQUERADE

ARIANA NASH

The Final Masquerade

Ariana Nash ~ ***Dark Fantasy Author***

Subscribe to Ariana's mailing list & get the exclusive story 'Sealed with a Kiss' free.

Join the Ariana Nash Facebook group for all the news, as it happens.

Edited by Jennifer Smith.

Proofread by Marked and Read.

Cover design by Bonobo Book Covers.

Content warning: (spoilers) this book contains devious fae, dubious consent, coercive rape, sex with multiple partners, suicide, and physical punishment.

Version 1 - December 2021

www.ariananashbooks.com

Chapter One

Five Years Ago

A gilded envelope slid under Latchly Hall's front door and landed on the hallway tiles like a gasp.

Brice glanced from his chair by the fireplace. The envelope had come to rest near the foot of the stairs. He blinked, then frowned, his thoughts slow to churn. What fool would risk the long ride through the forest on such a cold night to deliver a letter?

A dull ache throbbed behind his eyes. He massaged his temple, trying to ease the pain. His gaze slid accusingly to the empty bottle beside his chair, then to the empty glass in his hand. A second glass, still full, sat on the floor next to the opposite chair. His mother's glass. Of course, she wasn't there to drink it.

Guilt stabbed at his heart, forcing his gaze back to the letter.

Whoever had delivered the note hadn't knocked, so

perhaps Brice didn't need to do the gentlemanly thing and offer them shelter for the night.

Although he really didn't need more guilt weighing him down.

He set his glass on the table and staggered into the hallway. Still no knock. The messenger must have left.

He rested his hand on the stair banister, torn between retiring for the night and doing the right thing. What Brice needed was to crawl into bed and stay there until the days were warmer and the nights fleeting. Charon, his younger brother, could be the master of the house all winter. He chuckled at the idea, shaking his head. Charon was too frivolous, too much the dreamer. As Brice placed his boot on the stairs' first step, the envelope's glittering penmanship caught his eye. Its swirls and loops, inked in gold, lured his gaze around each letter like a hand taking his, leading him somewhere forbidden.

Brice LeChoix

Some part of him already knew what it was. And what it meant. But the wine had dulled his thoughts and the rest of him was already too numb to summon the rage the invitation's arrival would normally have ignited.

He'd expected it, hadn't he? An invite was as inevitable as the passage of the seasons. As inevitable as the untouched wineglass by Mother's chair and the guilt sitting cold in his gut.

The rage came then, scorching through him, burning away the alcohol, leaving him as sharp as a honed blade.

Flinging open the door, he waded into a blast of winter

air. Bitter wind swirled. Snowflakes kissed his face and melted into his clothes. A few steps ahead, trees stood like dark sentinels while the seemingly endless forest lay beyond. The cold stole his breath. He gasped and clutched his dressing gown tighter. Driving wind pushed in, forcing him back toward the warmth and light of the open front door.

Snow had driven against the house, banked under the windows, and buried the garden path. Where the snow should have shown the messenger's tracks, the divots revealed only Brice's retreating steps. But someone had come, someone had delivered the invite. Some-*thing*.

Damn them.

He stomped back inside, slammed the door closed, and scooped up the note, marching back to the fireplace and then tossing the wretched thing into the fire. Flames licked at the paper's curling edges. Black scorches ate his golden name from the inside out. The invite twisted, warped, and turned to ash. Brice stared, his own rage burning him up inside.

If the fae dared venture near Latchly Hall again, he'd burn them all to ash exactly as he had their invite.

Chapter Two

Present Day

Masquerade! candy-colored posters on every pole and market wall declared. *Dance the darkest night away... Forget your worries! Come join the Masquerade!* Traders chanted their wares, selling the finest of silks and fake jewels from faraway lands so the townsfolk could preen themselves in preparation, should they be lucky enough to receive an invite. Masks fluttered at every market stall, some elaborately adorned with feathers and pearls while others were the more mundane card and lace.

Brice jostled through the crowds, ignoring the furor. The townsfolk all lost their minds during the winter solstice to the point where he wondered if he was the only sane one left. They were good people, and all worked the long summer days so they might survive each harsh winter. He couldn't begrudge them their fun. He just wished they didn't rely on the fae to provide it.

After veering from the main street, he took a back alley shortcut, and maneuvering around snow-slushy puddles, he hurried toward the post office. Up ahead, Jeremiah, the local baker, loaded loaves onto his cart with the help of his shop boy.

"Master Brice!" Jeremiah called. "Esme sends her regards. Won't you stop by for supper—"

Brice tipped his hat and hurried on. "Another time." They were good people. They'd helped him and Charon when the worst had happened. He owed them a meal at least, but it should be him hosting them at the house, as was proper. But with no staff, the house was in no fit state to host a gathering. And neither was Brice.

Snow began to fall in earnest. The traders would soon pack up their wares and the crowds would hunker down inside their homes. Brice pulled his cloak's fur-lined collar against his neck and ducked into the post office.

Postmistress Patrice stood behind the counter with her back to him. A substantial woman in both physical stature and personality, she always had a smile for Brice. Of all the townsfolk, Patrice had known him the longest, ever since he'd hidden behind his father's tailcoat and looked up at her with big dark eyes, or so she'd constantly delighted in reminding him for the last twenty-five or so years.

"Ah, Master Brice, just the man. Now where did I put it?" Patrice patted her apron and rummaged through the stacks of parcels and letters threatening to topple off the countertop. "Ah!" She plucked a letter from under one of the many piles and handed it over.

He eyed the writing. Whoever had penned it had pressed deeply into the heavy parchment paper.

Brice LeChoix
Latchly Hall
Chamonet

"Looks official, don't you think?" Patrice inquired, silvery eyebrows raised above her thin spectacles as she leaned her plump figure against the counter. "Postmark says Massalia."

He couldn't imagine why anyone would be writing him from Massalia. Father's social contacts had stopped corresponding years ago, and Brice didn't have any social contacts of his own. He tucked it safely inside his coat and touched the brim of his hat. "Thank you, Patrice."

"I'd have had the boy bring it up to you, but them roads aren't getting any better and with the nights as they are—"

He waved her apology away. "No need." One letter wasn't worth anyone getting themselves turned around and lost on the old mountain roads.

"You know, it's good to see you. Some folks had wondered lately if you and Charon were still in that big ol' house—"

"Thank you again, Patrice." He opened the door.

"Brice."

Her tone pulled him up short. Few could stop him in his tracks quite like Patrice and her motherly tone. When he looked back, her smile was the pitiful kind, like those given to people who found themselves caught up in the cruel hands of fate. If she offered to invite him to supper, he might struggle to reply with a smile.

"On these cold nights, no folks should be alone. Why don't you drop by the inn for a drink?"

"I have to get back for Charon."

She heard the excuse for what it was. "The solstice is tomorrow—"

"I'm well aware." He closed the door too hard behind him and flicked his collar up, barring the snow from slipping down the back of his neck. The flakes had fattened in the short time he'd been inside and now filled the street, gusting on the occasional blast of wind. The onset of a storm had stolen the rest of the light from the day. He'd have to hurry if he was going to make it home before dark.

He passed by the inn, ignoring how the windows shone with warmth and cheer.

Reaching the hitching post, he mounted his mare and trotted her on in the direction of the valley roads that would eventually lead him home. The skies had been clearer when he'd left. If he'd known to expect a storm, he wouldn't have come at all. There was nothing to do for it now but bow his head to the wind and try to keep to the road.

He'd only made it a few miles before the snow closed in on all sides, blurring the path ahead with white. There was no way he could safely make it home. If the horse went down and he went with her, they'd both die in the cold. Better to lose a few coin for a night's board at the inn than his life.

He drew his horse to a halt and turned her on the path. A white blur darted from the trees. The horse startled and reared, and Brice slid down the saddle. He grabbed higher up the reins, but it was too damned late. Air slipped through his reaching fingers. His back struck the ground, knocking his breath from his lungs. His horse reared again, screaming at whatever creature had come for them. Her hooves punched the air and threatened to come down on Brice.

He rolled aside and scrabbled away from the terrified animal. Finding his feet, he managed to stand only to slip on the ice and fall again, tangled in his cloak.

The growl, when it came, bubbled through the sound of the screaming horse and Brice's pounding heart. He looked up and froze. The wolf was the size of a man, and a bigger man than Brice. Its ears lay flat. Its mouth bristled with pointed teeth. Brice was so close, he saw how its eyes were a crystal blue, the kind of blue found near the bottom of a frozen lake. Cold and distant. Unforgiving.

A shotgun barked, the boom spooking both horse and beast. His horse bolted into the whiteout and the wolf plunged into the trees, leaving Brice staring up at a cloaked figure atop a horse.

"You all right, Brice?" Charon asked, tossing back his hood. His mop of golden hair framed his freckled face while his cloak hid the rest of him.

Brice struggled to his feet again, careful not to slip. "What are you doing out here?"

"Followed you from town. Glad I did. That wolf had his eye on you." He tucked his shotgun back into its saddle loop and offered his hand with a smile. "Let's head back into town." His smile wilted some when he saw Brice's frown. "We'll freeze out here before finding your horse, if the wolf doesn't find it first."

He was right. There was no use stomping about in the dark and the cold. The night harbored far worse things than hungry wolves. Brice clutched his brother's hand and mounted behind him. He spurred his horse on, the jolt almost unseating Brice again.

Charon shouldn't have been out in this weather. Brice's teeth chattered from the cold. "Y-you're supposed to stay in the house."

"Be grateful I didn't."

"Charon—"

"Brice," he said. A blast of cold wind and snow froze any further argument between them.

By the time they reached the inn, the cold had soaked into Brice's bones. The heat and noise from the crowded inn lounge rattled his already frayed nerves. Most folks ignored them as they muscled on through, but some gazes lingered, curious. They'd be recognized eventually. Maybe if he kept his head down and stayed on the fringes, this would all be over without incident.

"Kris, somewhere we can get cleaned up and dry?" Charon asked the barkeep, a man in his late forties with a whiskered chin and salt-and-pepper hair tied back in a messy tail. Kris narrowed his eyes at Charon, reading his frost-nipped cheeks and ragged shirt beneath his cloak. A cloak that could do with some repair patches.

"Charon, boy, that you?" Kris's eyes widened. "By heavens! It's been how long? What happened to you both? Get caught in the storm?"

Brice opened his mouth to explain but Charon jumped in. "My brother fell from his horse. Damned wolf. Never seen one so big."

Kris jerked his chin at Brice. "You need to be careful. The old Lord LeChoix always said those woods weren't friendly."

"That's true. He did," Brice grumbled, digging around his jacket to unhook his coin pouch. He poured a few coins on the bar top. "Do you have a room for the night?"

"We're almost full with the masquerade an' all. I can fix you up in the attic if you like?" Brice nodded. "I'll get it made up right away." Kris clicked his fingers and summoned one of the serving lads, then sent him off to ready the room.

The weight of Charon's stare lingered. Brice blew into his cupped hands. If he didn't get out of his wet clothes soon, he'd never get warm. Charon was probably similarly cold and wet, although it didn't seem to gnaw at him like it did Brice. Charon had a way of shrugging off the worst of things while they seemed to cling to Brice.

Charon grinned. "With a bag of coin that fat you can pay for our drinks?"

Charon didn't know that bag of coin was all they had to get them through the month, and Brice had no appetite for that argument now. "Go ahead." He left Charon at the bar ordering drinks and found a chair beside the roaring fire.

Charon appeared minutes later, tankards in hand. He shoved one into Brice's numb fingers. "Get that in you."

He brought the tankard to his lips and followed Charon's gaze into the busy crowd. The townsfolk had piled into the inn to keep out of the cold. As the only meeting place in town, the Laughing Crow Inn also served as somewhere to socialize, keeping the long winter nights at bay. Given the size of the crowd, word of their appearance would be around the town by morning.

"You blend right in," Charon said as he slid his gaze back to Brice. Charon, on the other hand, had the soft good looks and charming smile that naturally captured the gaze of most everyone here.

"And folks can't help but see *you*," Brice said. His younger brother had always been the center of attention, even when they were boys. Brice was the heir, the one expected to carry the family name. Charon had no such responsibility. He'd light up any room he walked into whereas Brice had the opposite effect and seemed to suck all the life from a gathering. Of course, that had all been *before*. Now Charon rarely left the house. Overnight he'd gone from being the belle of the ball to a recluse alongside Brice. Still, it gave the locals something to gossip about.

As Charon eyed the crowd and sipped his drink, the lamplight reflected in his long-lashed blue eyes. He garnered more than a few looks, mostly from the women. *His Little Lord*, Father had called him, whereas Brice was the *disappointment*, the one who could never do enough. Resentment simmered between them, made worse these past few years. Charon had a freedom Brice would never have.

"We'll rest up and return home at dawn."

"To the prison," Charon mumbled.

"Charon—"

The serving lad interrupted and led them up the inn's winding staircase to the attic. A fresh fire hissed and spat in the small grate. A few sooty lamps lit the sloped ceilings, but it was warm and cozy and would do for a night.

Charon flopped onto the bed and locked his hands behind his head. "If I ask to go back to the bar, will you allow it?" He kept his gaze on the ceiling.

Brice shrugged off his cloak and frowned at the patches

of mud. The rest of his clothes hadn't fared much better. A tear gaped in his trouser leg. He'd have to fix it on their return to the house. His whole left side ached from taking the brunt of the fall and he was still struggling to get warm.

He shuffled off his jacket, placed it and his cloak over the chair beside the bed, and started on his shirt buttons as he crossed the room to the fireplace. He focused on unbuttoning his shirt instead of Charon's lingering question.

"That's a no." Charon sighed. "I saved you. If I'd listened to you and stayed home, if I hadn't been there, you'd have... well... You'd still be out there."

He was right. If Charon hadn't followed him, he'd probably be stumbling through the woods in the dark and the cold. Nobody would have found him. If the wolf hadn't killed him, the cold would have.

He stretched his hands near the flames, thawing his fingers.

"Are you really all right?" Charon asked, rolling onto his side and propping his head on a hand.

"Fine. I just—" Having Charon stay in the house was safe. If anything happened to him, Brice would have nothing left, and he couldn't bear that thought. He tore off his shirt and draped it over another chair to dry by the fireplace, turning his back on his brother's forlorn expression.

"I'm twenty-one, you know," Charon went on. "A man in my own right. I can do as I please."

Also true. But this was their life now. It had to be. "Get some sleep."

Brice braced against the mantel and bowed his head, soaking up the fire's heat. Closing his eyes, the wolf's icy glare was in front of him again. He opened his eyes and stared at the fire. His racing heart thumped. He'd come close to death, maybe looked it in the eyes. It was unusual for wolves to attack riders. The animal had probably been frightened, turned around by the storm. And frightened beasts lashed out.

"What's this?" Charon asked, drawing Brice from his thoughts.

"Hm?" Brice straightened to find Charon sitting on the edge of the bed, the letter from the post office in his hand. "It arrived a week ago. A rider sent word up the valley. It's why I came to town." He waved a hand, dismissing it.

"You should open it now, or it'll dry and you'll never pry the pages apart."

"Go ahead." He couldn't imagine it was anything of importance. Initially, the letters had flown in from all four corners of the land, offering condolences, inviting Brice and Charon to all the important gatherings. Brice had kept them all but replied to none, and soon the letters had stopped arriving. This latest one was probably a relic of someone's list of notable family names. They must not have known the LeChoix had fallen out of society and wealth years ago.

Charon's gasp was the first indication the letter was more important than he'd realized. Then his brother was up, striding toward him, his smile broadening into a grin. "An invite!"

Brice's racing heart turned to ice in his chest. He snatched the slip of paper from Charon's fingers.

Brice

The same swirling golden lettering, shining like sunlight. The letter hadn't come from Massalia at all. The postmark was a ruse!

The Masquerade awaits your—

Brice turned and flicked his wrist, launching the invite at the fireplace. It spiraled in the air, miraculously avoiding the flames, and fluttered to the floor.

Charon scooped it up. "Are you mad?" He laughed, turning on his heel to wave the invite at Brice. "This is an invite to the masquerade!"

"I know very well what it is." Brice's heart unfroze itself to beat like a warning drum. "Return it." He held out his hand, hoping his brother would see sense.

Charon clutched the glittering paper to his chest, blue eyes blown wide. He looked so very young again, his face full of wonder and hope. The little brother Brice would go to the four corners of the world for—do *anything* to keep safe. Including getting rid of *that* invite.

"Do you truly mean to burn it?" Charon whispered.

"Absolutely." Brice flicked his fingers toward his palm. "Charon."

"You can't!" Charon lifted the invite to his nose and breathed in. "Hm... like jasmine. An actual *invite*? I never thought I'd see one. To hold one in my hands..." He held the invite to the flickering lamplight and traced the elaborate writing's artistic design beneath his fingertips. The expression on his face was how Brice imagined a starving man might look when presented with a feast. For some, receiving an invite meant a chance to witness real magic, offering an evening of fantasy, a chance to visit a world where every hunger and desire imaginable was sated over and over. Rumors swirled every year of how a guest might find their fortune at the masquerade, of how a fae could bestow immortality on a lucky mortal, or of how the lonely might fall in love. Nobody cared to mention the guests who vanished or the rumors of how the vicious host could turn a mortal mad with a single unmasked glance. Those horrors were conveniently ignored or wilfully forgotten.

Charon looked upon the embossed piece of paper as though it offered freedom. His bespelled awe chilled Brice's heart. The masquerade was always and forever would be a trap.

"Charon, hand it over."

"You *must* go, Brice."

He stared at his brother. "You don't know what you're saying."

"It's bad luck to refuse."

Brice snorted and started forward. "I've refused five times before in six years and my luck is just fine. Hand it over."

Charon hid the invite behind his back and stumbled over his feet, bumping against a dresser. "Five times? Brice! The lucky only receive one in their lifetime. You *must* go."

He stopped in front of his brother and stared at the fool. It wasn't his fault. He didn't know any better. He didn't know *the truth*. "I must do no such thing."

Charon gasped breathlessly. "I've heard they're so beautiful, to witness their faces is to fall in love with them. They lavish attention on the guests, wine and food and... *other things*." Brice had heard the tales regarding those *other things*, but with little interest in sex himself, he'd hardly paid them any mind. Charon, however, wanted them but had been denied such pleasures. There were no staff to be frivolous with and no female visitors to distract him. Brice hadn't considered how Charon might be suffering in such an intimate way too. But the masquerade was not a safe place to indulge in such things.

"You might meet the host," Charon gushed. "They say if any mortal sees the host's unmasked face, they're cursed to forever dance for him. Isn't that nonsense just... *fantastic*?"

"Listen to yourself," Brice snapped. "Mother warned us of the fae. She kept a witch's stone above your cradle to keep them from switching you with one of their own! The fae are not harmless fun. They are wicked and dangerous. They—" He cut himself off before he said too much. *They drove her mad.*

Charon blinked. "They... what?"

Brice reached around his brother and grabbed the invite. "Never mind. No LeChoix will ever dance for the fae, nor will one ever attend their ridiculous ball again." He tossed the invite into the fire.

"You're a sour, jealous, coldhearted man. The same as Father."

Charon's words landed hard. Brice leaned against the mantel, buckling under their weight, but the blows just kept coming.

"He kept Mother locked up in that wretched house and you're doing the same to me. That invite could be the one good thing to land in our lives, our one chance at changing *everything*, and you throw it away. Well, fuck you, Brice. I'm not dying in that house with you, like they did!"

Brice turned on his heel, rage bubbling in his veins, but Charon's pained face and sorrowful gaze made the furious words fizzle to nothing on his tongue. It wasn't fair. Brice knew that. Life wasn't fair. "I'm trying to protect you."

Charon made for the door and flung it open.

"Wait!" Brice started after him but stopped at the top of the rickety old stairs and listened to Charon's boots hammer down its spiral. The last thing Brice wanted was to hurt him. There was no use taking their argument downstairs. He could let Charon have his fun in the bar this one night.

He let the sounds of revelry swallow those of his brother's retreating footfalls and backed into the attic room, closing the door on his brother and the rest of the world.

The solstice would be over soon, and the masquerade would vanish like mist on a summer's morn. Like it did every year. Things would go back to the way they should be. Charon would be safe at Latchly Hall, even as its walls fell down around them.

Chapter Three

BRICE WOKE to the sound of boots clomping on floorboards somewhere below and groaned into the pillow. A glimmer of sunlight illuminated the attic through its one small window. At least the snowstorm had passed. He threw the sheet back and looked for Charon beside him. He wasn't there. There were no clothes or boots either. He hadn't returned after their argument.

He lurched from the bed, tugged on his pants and boots, threw his jacket on over his shirt, and staggered down the stairs. The inn's staff stoked the fireplaces, stirring the embers to relight the kindling. Last night's crowds had long gone.

"Kris." Brice spotted the barkeep wiping down tables. "Have you seen Charon?"

"Not since last night. He racked up quite the tab, said you were good for payment?"

"Yes, of course." Brice's gut tensed. Damn him.

"He didn't return to your room?" Kris asked.

"No..."

"Check the stables," Kris suggested. "See if his horse is still there."

Brice hurried outside into the cold, but the stables were empty. He spotted a stable boy sweeping out the stalls. "The man I arrived with last night. Tall. Blond hair—"

"I remember 'im, sir," the boy said, setting aside his broom.

"Did you see him leave?"

"Aye, left at dawn."

Left at dawn? "Did he say where he was going?"

"Aye sir, said he was goin' home."

"All right. Thank you." Home. Of course. Where else was there to go? Charon had returned home at dawn, just as Brice had told him, taking their only horse because he was clearly still mad at Brice. Well, that was something, at least.

Brice returned to the attic room to retrieve his cloak, stopping only to cast a cursory glance at the ashes in the fireplace. A tiny corner of gold-embossed paper had fallen through the iron grate—all that remained of the masquerade invite. Brice would find Charon at home where he belonged, and this nonsense regarding the masquerade would be over and done with. At least for another year.

He paid the hefty inn bill and began the long trek home through the snow.

Latchly Hall had been built some two hundred years ago on the site of an old quarry, as though a giant had taken an enormous bite out of the steep forest-clad valley side and the LeChoix ancestors had decided to build a house in the scar. Old stories told of how the forest valleys around the house had once been resplendent in colored blooms, turning golden in the autumn and a verdant green in the summer, but Brice had never known the land to be anything but a dull gray-green all year round. As though the life had been sucked out of the land decades ago.

Brice trudged up to the front door, stamped caked snow from his boots, and shoved inside the grand hall. Not so grand now that they couldn't afford the hundreds of candles or oil lamps needed to fully illuminate it. The location was too isolated for gas lamps, and the new electric lights were far too expensive to install in Latchly Hall's many rooms.

"Charon?" His voice carried far up the ornate curving staircase and deep into the quiet. He began pulling off his gloves, taking a few steps in before pausing to listen. "Charon?" The emptiness of the house crawled across his skin. Charon wasn't here. *Nobody* was here. The house suddenly felt larger, colder, and hollow. As though it might swallow Brice whole.

After dashing outside, he stumbled through the snow toward the stables. Half the stable roof had collapsed under previous heavy snowfalls, but of the two stalls that remained, both were empty. Charon hadn't returned home. Either the stable boy had lied or Charon had, knowing Brice would waste time returning home to look for him.

A nearby snicker made his heart leap. His own horse plodded closer, having made its way back home after throwing Brice in the storm. "Hm, at least I'm not all alone." Brice grabbed the reins and led her into the stable yard.

Damn Charon. He knew better than this. Their argument was just words. He should be at the house. Why wasn't he? Brice would have passed him on the road had he been heading this way. Where else would he go?

With the horse stabled and fed, Brice returned to the house and lit the fire in the lounge for Charon's return, his anger rising with each new log he tossed into the flames. A glance at the window revealed lengthening shadows. Brice poured himself a glass of wine but didn't touch it. Instead, he sat at the table and stared at his full glass, waiting for the rattle of the front door and the thud of Charon's boots in the hallway.

It would be dark soon.

Today was the solstice.

The shortest day.

The longest, darkest night.

Charon would not leave Brice on this night. Any other, but not *this* night.

Unless...

Brice straightened and glared at the fogged window. The fire crackled in the grate behind him, spitting its displeasure at tasting wet wood. He turned, watched the flames dance, and closed his eyes. He'd thrown the masquerade invite into the fire. It *had* burned. He'd seen it burn.

But Charon's words, his accusations. *You're just like Father.* Brice had turned away from the fireplace. He *hadn't* witnessed the flames devour it. He hadn't seen the damn thing burn up into ash, and the fae had their ways of making sure their wishes were heard.

What if it hadn't burned, not entirely? What if Charon had returned to the room and fished it out of the grate while

Brice slept? If just a piece of it had survived, it could be enough to allow him entry to the masquerade.

No... Charon wouldn't... He was a fool, a romantic, a dreamer, but he knew to keep his feet on the ground, and he knew not to pander to the fae. Mother had warned them both...

Oh, but his anger had been real. His lusting for freedom, for laughter and dance and life. The things he'd been denied. That need of his was real. He'd looked at that invite like it might finally free him from this house, from their name, and from the nightmare they both shared. Free him from Brice.

"It's my invite. They won't let him in," Brice said to reassure himself.

But with Charon's charm, he'd easily talk his way in as Brice LeChoix, and no fae would care. One mortal fool come to dance for them was as good as the next.

"Charon," he whispered into the quiet. "Come home."

But only the house's heavy silence replied. The sun was setting. There was no time...

Brice had no choice.

He shoved from the table, knocking its edge. His full glass toppled over, spilling wine, but he left it dripping. Grabbing a lit candlestick, he ran up the stairs, down the dark landing, and into his father's room. The stale air smelled of old books and damp rugs. Brice set the candlestick down on a dresser, yanked open the cupboard, and pulled out the piles of clothes, revealing the traveling chest beneath. The embossed metal nameplate read *LeChoix*. An old memory struck again. As a boy, Brice had watched through a slit in the doorway as his father had reached into this same chest and plucked the magical prize from inside. A thing so beautiful, Brice had covered his mouth to hide his gasp and prevent Father from knowing he watched.

It would be inside. Waiting.

Brice dragged the chest from the cupboard onto the floor with a thump, flicked the latches, and shoved open the lid. And there it was. The masquerade mask, made of fine black silk laced with golden thread. So beautiful he was afraid to touch it, like the mask was something not meant for his rough hands. He reached in, fingertips hovering over the sculpted design. Father had caught him reaching for it once before and had flown into a rage so vicious Brice had forever flinched from him after.

His fingers curled around the silk tie and seemingly without thought, he lifted the mask from its bed and cradled it in both hands.

The masquerade calls, Mother had told him over and over. *Can you hear it, Brice? The fae have all the time in the world, but ours is finite. When they call, you must never answer.*

He'd vowed never to answer them. He'd cursed them until his tears had dried in the churned dirt of his mother's grave.

The mask looked back at him with its elegantly lined hollow eyes, and he wondered if the laughter he heard came from it or himself.

They don't like to be ignored. They'll take something of yours, taking your choice with it. Hope they never call, Brice. It is the only way to survive them.

Holding the mask in his right hand, he bunched the black dinner jacket it had lain on in his left hand and dragged it from the chest. A folded square of paper fell from the inside pocket where he'd hidden it one past year in a moment of weakness and spite. And there it lay, an innocuous piece of paper at his feet. Just like all the others.

Golden letters swirled and danced. *Brice,* they summoned.

The masquerade calls. Can you hear it?

A small laugh escaped him.

After all these years, after all his mother's warnings and all the nightmares, he was going to the masquerade.

Chapter Four

Moonlight glittered from the rows of dripping icicles lining the town houses' gutters and windows, their shimmering stalactites reminding Brice of the wolf's jagged teeth. He pulled his cloak tighter and rocked with the motion of his horse.

He'd spent much of the early evening asking after Charon at the late-market to no avail. In the flurry of excitement to buy the last masks or collect their tailored dresses and suits, the townsfolk were more interested in the masquerade than his missing brother.

His horse plodded through the street. A carriage would have been more befitting, but he'd sold it in the summer. As he rarely left the house, the carriage had seemed superfluous at the time. Being able to afford food through the winter had been far more important.

He tied his horse at the hitching post outside the inn and ducked back inside. The inn was quiet. Most folks were at home, either awaiting a last-minute invite or prettying themselves for the ball.

Kris raised his brows at Brice and continued to wipe down the bar. "Master Brice. Don't see you for months and then it's two days in a row? Did you find your brother?"

"No."

"Ah." Kris brought a folded note from his pocket and handed it over. The fine writing was instantly recognizable as Charon's.

I must go.
You know why.
C.

Brice sighed, folded the note back up, and tucked it inside his jacket pocket. Kris continued wiping the bar down, rubbing the varnished wood to a high sheen. The note hadn't been sealed. He'd likely read it too. With everyone abuzz with the masquerade, Kris would have guessed where Charon planned on going.

"I don't suppose you'll be buying a drink from me when you'll be getting them free at the masquerade tonight?" Kris asked.

Brice snorted. Nothing came free at the masquerade. He tossed a few coins on the bar. "Soup, if you have any?" He hadn't eaten all day and to arrive at the masquerade hungry would put him at a disadvantage. Resisting their gifts was the hardest part of all, so Mother had said.

Kris took the coin and returned moments later with a bowl of steaming broth and a slab of seeded bread. "You know, most would be thrilled to go." His gaze briefly caught on Brice's attire. He'd kept his cloak on, but its folds had fallen open when he'd reached for the bowl. Kris's eyebrow arched. "But not you?"

"Where was the note?" Brice asked, dunking bread in the soup and readily eating.

"On the floor by the bed. You must have missed it last night or lost it in the sheets."

Typical. Brice had been so desperate to find Charon at home, he hadn't thought to look for any kind of note in the room. He nodded his thanks and used a chunk of bread to swirl the soup.

A small crowd of women entered the inn, each of them dressed in their finest dresses, their cloaks concealing little. Snow melted in their bejeweled hair. Kris tended to the new arrivals while Brice ate.

"Brice, my goodness, is that you?"

He winced internally, dragged a smile onto his lips, and lifted his gaze to the approaching woman. "Sophia." Like the others, she was dressed in her finest evening wear. Pearls dangled from her ears—probably real. The Brodeur family was now the wealthiest locally. Her blonde hair had been artfully fixed in tight curls and clips. She was beautiful, both inside and out, but he'd known that since they were small. Remembering his manners, Brice took her offered hand and brought it to his lips in a cursory kiss. "You're most radiant this evening, Sophia."

"As are you, Brice." She rested an arm over the bar and leaned closer. Her blue eyes sparkled. "I haven't seen you for almost a year. If I didn't know you better, I'd take it personally."

"I'm sorry, I just... the house..."

Sophia's hand came down and rested on his. "I know. It's fine, really."

He mustered a smile. "You forgive too easily."

"Only with friends."

They'd been promised to wed. In another life, one in which the worst of things hadn't happened, Sophia would already be his wife. In many ways, the fact their arranged marriage hadn't come to fruition was one of the better outcomes from the past few years. He had nothing to offer her but a life in a crumbling house with a man who could never give her the love she wanted and deserved.

"I heard you had an invite?" she asked.

He smiled. "Of course you did." She had always been the first to trade in rumors.

"Well, there's nothing the townsfolk like more than news of their most beloved mysterious bachelor and his personal life."

He couldn't sneeze in the town without someone a mile away wishing him well. "I hate to disappoint, but I really don't have a personal life, or any kind of life," he said. Perhaps he shouldn't have spoken so freely, but Sophia was one of the few people in town he trusted absolutely.

She gave his hand a squeeze. "I think the masquerade will be good for you."

"I sincerely doubt that."

"I hear they are freer with their desires."

Brice donned his gloves, focusing on tugging them on instead of meeting her gaze. She knew his desires ran differently to most, in ways some might think unseemly for a gentleman. "Yes, well... I'm not going for that." Their marriage would have been at best a farce, at worst a disaster.

They had both known it. Unfortunately, Sophia's father hadn't. "Your father would not approve of us speaking—"

Kris collected his empty plate and bowl, briefly distracting Sophia's gaze. She had an uncanny skill for reading Brice's expressions—the real ones, those he kept hidden beneath those he openly wore.

"What my father doesn't know won't hurt him." She smiled and Brice couldn't help but smile in return. She'd always been terribly fun. As children, they'd often been the menace of the school class, along with Charon, who had often become the target of their jests.

"Tomorrow, after the ball, won't you visit? You and Charon?" The refusal was already on his lips when Sophia pressed a finger to them, stopping the words. "Please. Nothing formal. Papa won't be there. He's in Massalia. He won't be back for weeks."

He caught her hand and gently lowered it, noting the lack of a wedding band on her finger. The choice of men to wed in Chamonet were few and far between. It was likely her father was seeking a suitable fit outside the town. Such a match would take her away, probably forever. He should spend more time with her. He wanted to, but there was too much to consider. The house needed to be prepared for winter, and Charon... "I appreciate the offer."

Her face crumpled. "Brice, you cannot stay locked in that house forever. Consider it?"

Guilt squirmed inside. He'd cut her out of their lives like he'd cut everyone else out. It certainly wasn't her fault, but to her it must have seemed as though he'd vanished overnight, taking their lifelong friendship with him. "Very well, I'll consider it."

Her smile warmed her face. "Will I see you at the ball?"

He pushed the gloves tighter in place, focusing on that instead of the hope on her face. "I won't be staying long."

"Oh—"

He caught her hand. "Please, Sophia... be careful there."

She grinned, thinking him jesting. "It's just a ball."

Perhaps it was. Perhaps he was worrying over nothing. He hoped to be wrong. Most guests returned from the masquerade full of wonderful tales. "Don't let them..."

"Oh, Brice." She pulled him into a startling, sudden hug. "It will be fine, darling. And please," she whispered into his ear, "find yourself some cock, hm? Heavens knows you won't get any in this town."

He barked a laugh, even as color warmed his face. She always did know how to make him laugh. She chuckled and smiled innocently. "Such a lady." He kissed her hand in goodbye.

"Tomorrow then? You'll come to the house?"

"All right," he said.

"You can tell me all about it, hm?"

Good lord. He left the inn still chuckling, until the cold wrapped around him, reminding him of the task ahead. He most definitely wasn't going to the masquerade to indulge in such frivolous things as sex. And certainly not, as Sophia had suggested, *sex with men*. His thoughts and desires on the matter were complicated.

Daylight was fast fading, stretching long shadows across the street. There was no use in stalling. He knew where Charon was, where half the townsfolk would soon be, and he knew what had to be done.

The invite thrummed alongside Charon's note inside his jacket's inner pocket, over his heart.

Perhaps the masquerade was a mere few hours of frivolous fun and Mother's warnings were flights of fancy. But if that were the case, Mother would be alive, Charon would be studying art in Massalia, and well... Brice would likely be married to Sophia and carrying on the family name, Father's watchful eye like a lead weight on his back. Still, at least Charon would have been free. Brice's fate as heir had been sealed at birth.

He walked his horse on the narrow winding track out of town, following a path of flaming torches. The forest quickly closed in, spindly branches arching over the people walking arm in arm. They laughed and chatted, their voices full of childish glee—sweet music to the fae. Lace hems and smooth silks were hidden under overcoats and cloaks, to be thrown off once inside the masquerade.

Six years ago, the solstice had changed the course of his life forever. Would this night change him again? There was nothing left to lose, save his brother. He'd be damned if he let the fae take Charon from him like they'd taken Mother in her madness.

He just had to get in, find Charon, and get out again.

The flaming torches ended, making way for a path lined with flickering candles. Brice dismounted and tied his horse to a tree. People trod the leaf-strewn path, their masks in their hands or already upon their faces. Gems shimmered in the shifting candlelight. There were feathers, lace, and silk of all colors. But it felt wrong, like a rainbow at night. He shook off the rising sense of unease and joined the stream of people. The forest outside the candlelit path had grown dark and cold and seemed hungry, as though the moment the candles were snuffed out, it would rush in and swallow them all whole.

He placed one foot in front of the other, kept his head up, and wished he didn't believe in fairy tales.

The candles were in the trees now and everywhere, throwing their shifting light into the forest where the trees had bent over and laced together, forming an archway. A masked man and woman stood either side of the archway checking the invites. The pair seemed normal at first glance, but therein lay the danger. She wore a gown of midnight black, as though she'd been dressed in night itself, while his slim-fitting suit was all white. He was dressed in frost from head to toe, complete with buckled white knee-high boots and a tailed jacket. Black hair licked down his back in a long braided tail.

The colors of the pair's masks were their opposites, his black, hers white. They were designed to arch over their perfect noses and cover the top half of their faces, revealing only their eyes.

They were fae. Even masked, they couldn't be anything else. Perhaps it was the elegance of their hands, with no gesture wasted, or just some innate warning within Brice himself, but he knew what they were despite never having met one before.

His heart thumped in his throat.

Charon would already have passed through them, having entered with Brice's invite. Would they spot a second invite addressed to the same person? Would they care?

As the line shortened and Brice shuffled closer to the

sentinel pair, he watched their quick hands take and examine the invites. Long delicate fingers traced the name on each invite, perhaps reading some hidden authenticity woven between the layers of the thick paper. The line shuffled forward again and now Brice was just two pairs of guests away from meeting a fae.

The male sentinel snatched the wrist of a man trying to enter and yanked him out of the line. He kicked the man's leg out and shoved him to the ground. A quick grin revealed a flash of the sentinel's small sharp canine teeth. "Only a fool thinks to trick a trickster," the sentinel declared with a luscious, mocking chuckle. The crowd tittered nervously along with him.

The man's cheeks flushed red. "I assure you, sir," he blustered. "It's real!" He clambered to his feet and brushed leaves from his trousers.

The sentinel cast a long look at his rapt and slightly fearful audience, his half smile a crooked question. When his gaze skimmed over Brice, a chill trickled down his spine, but the gaze skipped away.

Turning toward the ejected guest, the sentinel held out his hand, fingers unfurling like flower petals. "And only fools think to lie to liars. Surrender your mask, sir."

The guests looked at the mask hanging from the man's fingers and back at the sentinel. "What for?"

A long sigh spoke of all the times the sentinel had been in this position, asking the same of all the others who'd thought to lie their way inside the masquerade. He struck so fast Brice hardly saw him move—he grabbed the man by the collar and whispered into his ear. He shoved the man away, and off the poor fellow went, mutely stumbling into the forest. Brice knew these woods. They went on for mile upon mile. He hopefully wouldn't wander too far.

The sentinel tossed the mask onto the small pile at his feet and held out his hand for the next guest's invite.

The line shuffled forward.

Brice removed his gloves and took his invite from his pocket.

Brice.

The masquerade awaits.

His name was written in golden ink, the *B* so elaborate that its swirls and loops covered half the paper. He'd never taken the time to admire the writing or the way the nib had impressed upon the paper in places, clearly written by hand rather than printed by machine. A glimpse at the invites being handed over revealed equally elaborate designs but none penned in gold.

He discreetly brought the paper to his nose. It smelled a little musty from its time in the trunk, but there was an unmistakably sweet floral scent, too, with a slight woody musk. Jasmine, just as Charon had immediately recognized on the invite he'd stolen.

The couple ahead of him stepped through the arch, leaving Brice suddenly at the front of the line. The archway made of intertwining branches stretched some distance. He could make out moving figures at its end and hear the tinkle of music and laughter beyond. Around the archway, the darkness pressed in, but there seemed to be some form to the masquerade, perhaps a vast tent of some kind?

The male sentinel offered his hand. His fingernails were

slightly pointed, a quirk Brice hadn't noticed until now. Brice looked up, straight into the man's eyes—no, not a man. The shifting, iridescent color of his irises—purples and blues—made his race perfectly clear even if the rest of him hadn't already. Pink glossy lips parted in silent query and tilted sideways, perhaps in amusement at Brice's sudden attack of nerves. This male was absolutely fae. Brice swallowed and handed over the invite. As with all the others, the sentinel skimmed his fingertips around the design of Brice's name, his gaze tipped downward. Behind his mask, his featherlight lashes fluttered.

Heat thrummed through Brice. Not just warming his face but the rest of him, too, thawing the cold as though the fae were an open fire, one Brice would gladly lean against and soak up. The thought startled him from his reverie. The fae's gaze lifted, catching Brice's stare again, and some measure of knowing constricted the fae's pupils as though he knew Brice's thoughts. But that wasn't possible. The fae couldn't read minds, could they?

"Your name is Brice LeChoix?" the sentinel enquired, raven-dark eyebrow raised, peeking over the top of his midnight mask. Now that Brice was close, he saw the mask wasn't all black but had the finest detailing of silver, like frost at its edges, touched by moonlight.

Brice began to reply, but his voice caught. A small cough cleared it. "Yes."

Seconds stretched into what felt like hours and Brice waited for the sentinel to grab him and toss him from the line, sending him off into the night like he'd done with the other man because there could not be two Brice LeChoixes at the masquerade.

"A problem?" his female counterpart asked.

Brice blinked, pulling his thoughts back into the moment and away from the fae's spellbinding gaze. Clearing his throat, he stepped back and straightened his jacket, anchoring himself in reality and away from wherever his thoughts had just dallied off to. This did not bode well. He hadn't gotten inside yet and he was already distracted by the first pretty hurdle.

"No problem here," the sentinel replied, still half smiling. When he held the invite out, pinched between his finger and thumb, Brice tried to pull it free, but the fae didn't let go.

"You look so very much like your father," the sentinel added.

Brice yanked the invite from the fae's fingers and lifted his chin. He'd known his father had attended the masquerade, but hearing proof of it reminded him exactly why he was here, and it wasn't to fawn over the first fae he'd officially met, thereby failing the first test. "The man you just turned away, he'll get lost in the dark—"

Something devilish glittered in the fae's eyes. "He'll find his way to where he's supposed to be. We all do eventually."

Unease had Brice hesitating. He might have gone after the unfortunate fellow, but Charon was his responsibility. The man had surely known the risk of presenting a fake invite to the fae. Brice could do nothing for him but hope he found his way home. "Then may I enter?"

The sentinel dipped his chin and swept an overly dramatic gesture toward the archway. "Be my guest." Brice made it several steps inside the arch before his name on the fae's lips brought him to a halt. "Brice." The sentinel's smile grew a little more. He flicked his fingers toward his own face. "Your mask."

Like a fool, Brice had almost forgotten the most important thing. He hastily put his father's mask on, sighing once it was finally in place. Masks were designed to hide behind, and now his was on, anonymity relieved his rattling nerves and lent him the strength he would surely need to see the night through.

"Remember, never remove your mask." The sentinel smiled, but his thin tone held a hint of some double meaning, like the thin line of silver thread running through his black mask.

The sentinel turned his attention to the next arrival and Brice hastily strode toward the warm, throbbing light in the masquerade.

Chapter Five

COLOR.

It was as though spring had arrived in the depths of winter. Brice had braced himself to guard against the fae and their ways, but the moment he stepped from the archway into an enormous foyer draped with colored strings and glistening chandeliers, he was glad for the mask hiding his wonderment. People drifted here and there, their costumes splashes of color against ivory walls and marble floors. Someone offered to take his cloak and gloves. He should probably have paid more heed to whom, but he could no more look away from the opulence and fantasy of the ball than stop his own heart.

Piano keys tinkled out of sight. The sweet music drifted through the chatter, dancing around the people to find its way to Brice. He couldn't be sure if the music was even real. He'd stepped from the dark of winter into a brightly lit dream.

His feet moved, carrying him forward. The chandelier above was the size of the carriage he'd sold. A sweeping staircase spilled its steps from a wraparound landing, splitting in half to climb to a galleried floor. Above, people leaned against the balustrades, crystal glasses in their hands, masks hiding half their faces. There would surely be fae among them, but surrounded by so much lavish beauty, the fae were camouflaged, able to move among the townsfolk without revealing themselves. He hadn't expected it to be so difficult to see them and thus guard against them.

A man bumped his shoulder and apologized with the flash of a smile, his face hidden behind a colorful half mask. He might have been a friend, someone from the town, but everyone here was out context, everyone a stranger. There was danger in that unknowing but also a thrill that quickened Brice's heart and warmed his blood again. In a town where everyone knew his name, his family, and his tragedy, he was suddenly anonymous. He could do as he pleased, talk to whomever he wished without them enquiring after the house, his brother, his marriage prospects. He was nobody. Everyone was nobody.

He swallowed, moistening his dry throat, and as though reading his wants, a female server appeared dressed in a gown of blue silk that flowed from her shoulders and swished about her sparkling shoes. Her mask of blue satin dripped pearls like tears against her pink cheeks. She raised a platter, wordlessly offering a glass of wine. Her smile was such an innocent thing, he found himself taking the glass to please her. The moment she turned to leave, a hint of pointed ears gave her away. He set the glass down on a dainty side table and folded his fingers into his palm, thawing their sudden chill. He could not accept gifts. To eat or drink anything here would surely pull him deeper into the fantasy. He had to find Charon and leave before the masquerade got its claws into him.

The piano music quickened, accompanied now by a full band. Some of the crowd flowed through a vast doorway toward its source. Glimpses above their heads hinted at a similarly lavish room but one far larger, probably the main ballroom. Charon had always sought the light. He'd be at the center of it all.

The crowd swept Brice forward, toward the ballroom. He was almost through when the sensation of being watched lifted the fine hairs on the back of his neck. A glance back, only lasting for a few seconds before the crowd swept him on, revealed a man on the staircase, hand resting against the banister and dressed in a tailored black suit similar to Brice's own. His mask was all black silk with golden embellishment. There was some air of difference about him unlike anyone else he'd seen, and it wasn't until the doors closed, sealing off the foyer, that Brice realized the difference was the missing smile, and without it, the brief sweep of the fae's gaze chilled Brice to the bone.

He peeled off from the crowd toward the perimeter of the enormous room. Knowing what Charon was wearing would have helped, but with so many men present—easily half the town's male population—finding his brother was not going to be as simple as he'd hoped. Most wore more understated attire compared to those of their female counterparts, but some opted for the more elaborate. Charon would have been one of those, but he might also be deliberately keeping out of sight.

Another server appeared offering her platter of wines. The *same* server girl, he realized. Petite, with an oval face and pert lips, she appeared almost girl-like, but her eyes were old. "You're very persistent," he said.

She smiled shyly and fluttered blue-glittered lashes. "Take a drink, Brice."

It unsettled him some to hear his name on her lips. "And if I don't?" He was already reaching, so the question was moot, but he was curious as to its answer.

"Then you risk insulting our host," she said sweetly.

He pinched a glass stem between his fingers and plucked it from her tray. "The infamous host. Well then, I had better oblige." He took a sip to appease her and in the hope that she might be more forthcoming with answers. The wine's bubbly sweetness sizzled on the tip of his tongue and slid down his throat with cool ease. One sip surely wouldn't hurt. "Do you know the name of every guest here?"

"I do."

"Then perhaps you can help me find my brother?"

"His name?"

"Ah, well, that's where it gets... complicated." Her polite smile altered slightly with growing interest. "Can you keep a secret?"

Her eyes sparkled. "I like secrets."

"I thought you might." Secrets were currency to the fae, or so Mother had said. "My brother has my invite. So you see, there are two here of the same name."

Her smile twitched. "The other is a lie?"

Given the sentinel's reaction to the fake invite at the entrance, any hint of a lie was better avoided. "A ruse. Not entirely untrue. I *gave* him my invite from another year." If he told her Charon had stolen it, she might be less inclined to help or more inclined to report him to the *host*. If Brice's actions had Charon thrown out of the masquerade, he'd never forgive him. Better to quietly retire.

"An untruth then." She stepped closer, so close her tricolored eyes dazzled. "The host will be most intrigued."

Catching the host's eye seemed like the worst possible outcome. He had to find Charon before their presence raised too many eyebrows. "Perhaps it could be our secret now? Will you take me to my brother?"

"Hm," she purred. "Wait here, *Brice*."

She began to turn, but given how the crowd had swelled in size, it could take Brice hours to find her again. "Your name?" he called. At least if he had that, he could ask after her.

"Chantel." She beamed over her shoulder just as the crowd swallowed her from view.

Brice regarded the glass in his hand, now half-full. He'd been so focused on Chantel, he didn't recall drinking more than a sip. He quickly placed the glass down and stepped away from its temptation.

Chantel's help would come with a price. But if the price were small, he'd gladly pay it to get Charon away from this place and its cloying magic, some of which was surely affecting his will.

A spread of miniature morsels of food caught his eye. Dainty little cakes and tiny pies, all designed to be consumed in a single bite. He glowered at the bounty and at the people heartily filling their china plates, so willing to take what was freely given. His stomach rumbled. When was the last time he'd gorged on such a meal? These days, he never seemed to have enough to fill a plate.

With any luck, Chantel would take Brice to Charon, they'd be gone within the hour, and whatever the true purpose of this pantomime was would happen without them. Charon would despise him for taking him away, but what was a little more hatred when there was already so much?

"You look as though you're attending a funeral."

The man who'd spoken picked up one of the tiny morsel cakes and popped it into his mouth. His silver and black mask covered the top half of his face but left the mouth free to express a smile. It was tied with a long ribbon that trailed through his equally long ink-black hair. Without a jacket, he was dressed more casually than the other guests, but his shirt of dark silk shimmered beneath the sparkling candlelight.

The man leaned a hip against the banquet table and folded his arms, smirking. "Does the display not meet your high standards, milord?" He still smiled, and his tone was light, but he carried a similar stillness to that of the sentinel—likely making him fae. Or was this man the very same fae from the entrance? The tips of his ears were hidden beneath his silken hair. But human ears were not a guarantee he wasn't fae. They could glamour their telltale tapered ears away, should they wish to appear human for the night. Rumors spoke of the fae being able to change their entire appearance, even their gender. They wore more than one mask.

"It's beautiful," Brice said, wondering where Chantel was and if she was planning on returning at all.

The man in the silvery mask snorted. "Said with all the passion of someone with no desire of his own." He plucked a second fancy cake from the spread, seemingly at random, and stole a single step toward Brice, putting him uncomfortably close. "May I?"

What was he asking? Brice held his gaze. Purple eyes held flecks of gold, and the more he looked, the more colors appeared and the more dazzling they became. The heat in Brice's veins had warmth spreading through his chest. This was the same fae from the entrance—the sentinel. Just in different clothes. He was sure of it.

"Hm..." The sentinel's eyes narrowed behind his mask. "There it is," he cryptically said, then dipped his chin and took a bite of the cake between his fingers. His tongue swept across his lips, collecting a bit of cream. Then the last bite disappeared between the stranger's lips and he sucked jam from his finger. His gaze had hold of Brice's and wasn't letting go. Or perhaps Brice had no wish to look away. He was trapped between wanting and not wanting, between desire and disgust that he could be so easily seduced.

That thought snapped whatever hold the sentinel had on him. With a laugh, the sentinel pushed away from the table and was gone, disappearing among the swirling crowd. Brice was left to catch hold of his runaway breaths and slow his heart. He swallowed hard and adjusted his cuffs, his fingers teasing around his father's cufflinks. *You are no son of mine.* Father's voice was in his head again, as loud as though he were standing beside him now. Hearing it in this place of fantasy suitably chilled the heat in his veins, grounding him in reality.

Brice turned his back on the crowd and braced his hands against the table, ignoring the ridiculous food, the seductive music, and laughter. All of this was absurd. These people were fools.

"Brice?"

He jerked his head up and found Chantel half smiling at him.

She offered her hand. "I've found the other Brice."

Straightening, he brushed his fingers through his hair, sweeping it back from his masked face. Using the gesture to settle his nerves, he took her hand in his, surprised at how small and delicate it was. She wove through the crowd, Brice towed behind her. Some glanced his way, but few stares lingered. He was just another body in a sea of them.

Charon's laughter sailed toward Brice, and as the crowd finally parted, there he was, leaning against the arm of a chair with three people hanging on his every word. He wore a pale gray suit with silver buttons and lace as shimmering accents. His mask was one of pure white dove feathers. With his blond locks and typical LeChoix body—not too heavy, not too light—he was as handsome as any man could be.

Brice opened his mouth to call to him, but one of the women, her dress sunshine yellow, took his hand and led him among the dancers. The crowd had parted, making way for the entertainment. Brice should march to Charon's side and demand they leave, but the arrangement of dancers had already begun to move as one to the music. Their colors swirled and mixed, and among them Charon moved with the grace and poise of a gentleman. He stepped and turned and guided his partner in her gown of sunshine yellow about the floor, matching the steps of the twenty or so pairs around him.

Mother had taught them both to dance and of course Charon had excelled at it. He'd been the finest dancer in the balls of their youth, and he clearly still was. The people lining the edges of the dance floor admired him, just as Brice did. Pride made his heart swell. Charon deserved to be seen. He thrived when observed and drew people to him like moths to a flame.

He should have been the heir. He did not sully the ancient LeChoix name, he did not disappoint with every step, and he did not hide in the dark.

Brice looked for Chantel at his side, but she'd slipped away without his seeing. He was alone, standing among the beautiful like a thundercloud on a summer's day.

The dance ended and a swell of applause filled the ballroom. Charon bowed to his partner. She curtsied and took his hand to rise. Together they laughed. Brice knew her laugh and knew the woman his brother now smiled at as though she were the only woman there. Sophia.

Seeing them together and how well they perfectly *fit*, Brice's past slid sideways. They'd played together as children, always Brice, Charon, and Sophia. Charon's glee and Sophia's lighthearted joy. Always together at the many balls they'd been dragged to. Together at the lavish dinners Father had hosted to discuss wedding proposals between Brice and Sophia. Together tomorrow, once all this nonsense was over.

Charon and Sophia were clearly in love.

Brice stepped back from the edge of the crowd.

If he took this night from Charon, he'd lose his brother forever. Charon was a man in his own right. He could make his own decisions and protect himself, as the incident with the wolf had shown. Charon didn't need him and probably never had. Charon had been... protecting him? He raised his gaze to his brother and watched him pull Sophia close, his head bowed and lips moving.

Father had been right. Brice really was a failure.

The music began again, drifting above the chatter to weave its spell. The dancers took their places like marionettes poised on the ends of strings. Piano keys danced and so did the people, swirling and drifting in perfect synchronicity, but a dark thread wove among the dazzling lights and seductive music like a musical note suddenly playing off-key. The man in black from the staircase, with his mask of gold, walked alongside the crowd's edge, his pace slow and deliberate. He scanned the pretty people dancing for him, his lips devoid of any smile, his face hidden. Half the crowd didn't notice him, their attention all on the dancers, but the rest did. Were they the fae? Their gazes were all trained on the powerful figure holding their attention.

The host. He had to be.

No one else could command a roomful of guests by merely walking into it.

The host stopped his slow parade and faced the dancers, almost directly opposite Brice. And between them, Charon and Sophia danced, a blur of bright yellow and stalwart gray. The host's gaze lifted, speared through the dancers, and clutched hold of Brice's heart, wrenching it from his chest. Or so it felt. Brice had only felt true fear once in his life, but he felt it again now.

Fingers laced with his. Chantel must be back. The touch startled him, and he broke away from the host's gaze.

He looked at their hands entwined—pointed nails, slim male fingers—and then up into the gaze of the sentinel standing beside him, his silver mask and long black hair now so familiar. "You."

"Come away," he whispered, turning and drawing Brice from the dancers, and somehow his words cut like glass through the music, the clip of heels, the laughter, and the swish of skirts.

"Who is that?"

"You already know." The sentinel's pace quickened and Brice stumbled along behind him, hands still entwined.

"My brother?"

"Will be fine." He danced through the guests, his steps so fast and light that Brice struggled to keep up. He should pull away and demand what on earth they were doing but didn't. Perhaps it was the mask Brice wore or the realization his brother didn't need him at all, because he suddenly, recklessly had no wish to stop whatever this was. He could pretend, couldn't he? Just a little? Like everyone else here. Take a moment to forget how he'd truly amounted to nothing. Where was the harm in that? The sentinel's firm hand led him through the ballroom and out through an open doorway into a high-ceilinged hall. On one side it was lined with columns, through which Brice saw a night garden filled with purple lilies glistening under moonlight.

The sentinel turned, skipped backward, and set Brice's hand free with a light laugh. "Better?"

He did feel better, somewhat breathless but more in command of his senses now they were outside. Enough to offer this intriguing sentinel a tentative smile. The sentinel saw, and after flashing a grin in return, he jogged up a set of steps into the garden. Other guests were there, loitering among the enormous plants and columns or lounging on the benches beneath rose arches. Their proximity seemed... intimate and Brice was careful not to gaze too long. One couple—both men—was rather heatedly embracing, partially hidden among the columns. The man who had his back to Brice hitched a leg up, trapping his partner against a wall. His paramour's hand gripped his belt, shoving it down and exposing his lower back and the peachy rise of his ass.

Brice tore his gaze away.

The air smelled of sweet jasmine, triggering the memory of the scent on Brice's invite. Had the sentinel been the one to send it? He strode ahead along neatly manicured pathways, running his hand playfully over the lily heads and sending puffs of glittery pollen up in the air.

He moved with hypnotic grace, his hips and ass made for dancing. It was a shame he hadn't been among the dancers. Brice might have been more inclined to join them, had he been.

"Your name?" Brice asked, woefully trailing along behind, occasionally jogging to keep up.

The sentinel glanced behind him, making his dark hair flow over his shoulder like spilled ink. "What are you so afraid of?" At a fork in the pathway, he veered left without looking, clearly knowing the twisting pathways so well he could probably walk them with his eyes closed.

Everything. Brice slowed as the pathway came to an end. The sentinel turned in front of a covered wooden bench and draped all of his elegant self onto it, stretching an arm over its back. He looked like sin in human form, like Brice had dreamed him up. Lean but strong with it—his grip had told Brice that much. Elegant but dangerous. He'd make a good swordsman.

Brice glanced over his shoulder, back the way they'd come. They were alone, in some shadowy corner of a garden far larger than it had first appeared. Anyone might stumble upon them. But what was there to stumble upon? They were just two men having a conversation. Nothing untoward in that.

Brice faced the fae again and found his unblinking gaze once again firmly locked on him. It wasn't unnerving so much as intriguing. "What can I call you?" Brice asked.

"Anything you like." He flicked his hand along the back of the bench and crossed his legs at the knee. His grace allured, reminding Brice of the time he'd found a snake by a stream as a boy and how he'd watched it slither effortlessly through the grass and into the water, leaving no trace behind.

"But you know my name. So it's only fair—"

"Fair?" His lips quirked around the word. "When are the fae ever fair?"

He had a point. But hearing him say the obvious brought this moment of fantasy into stark reality. Brice was alone with *one of them.* He wasn't sure whether he should run or ask the questions that had plagued him ever since Mother had first spoken of the fae as real, living, breathing creatures and not some fairy tale told to keep the young ones from wandering too deep into the forest.

"What do you want?" Brice sounded brave. Though perhaps he was. He had room enough to escape this creature, should he need it. But he was also curious.

"I would have thought that obvious?" He tilted his face up. Pale moonlight licked across his mask.

A question as an answer. That was becoming a theme with him. Or a game.

The fae leaned forward, his gaze at Brice's waist. Then his gaze dropped to Brice's crotch, beautiful lashes fluttering, only to deliberately roam higher, sliding over Brice's buttoned fastenings and up his chest to his face. A flutter of breathlessness caught in Brice's throat. He wore a mask. His fears wouldn't show. It didn't matter here. Nothing mattered. He was nobody—a nobody whose body was on fire.

"To begin with, I'd like your cock in my mouth. We can discover the rest as we—"

Brice turned on his heel. If he walked any faster, he'd be running. He shouldn't have followed this fae into the garden. It was his own fault. He knew better than to go where they led. Was it so obvious how he wanted what he shouldn't, that within a few glances, this fae had offered him what he could not have?

He'd made it halfway back down the path when light fingers encircled his wrist and gently urged him to slow. "My name is Raoul," the fae said.

Brice stopped.

"But names do not matter here." Raoul circled around in front of him, blocking his escape. His finger hooked Brice's chin and tilted his head up. The silver accents in his mask gleamed.

"Then what does matter?" Brice heard himself ask. His body felt detached from his mind and heart, each piece of him demanding different things.

Raoul stepped against him, his chest hard where it pressed against Brice's. The fae bowed his head. "Masks take your pain away. Let yourself go."

Laughter drew Brice's gaze to the others in the garden. He'd forgotten they weren't alone. Shadows danced in torchlight, shifting the figures around, making them blur together as they kissed. And more. The male pair from earlier... One was pressed against the wall, his hands spread either side of him. His partner stood behind him, hands clutched at his hips, thrusting in a slow, easy rhythm. In the soft, shifting light, it took a moment for Brice to understand what he was seeing, but the moment the lovers coupling came into focus, the sight of it punched Brice in the chest and stole his breath. Heat flushed through his veins, his arousal so vicious he staggered.

It had been years since he'd *indulged*... and in the past, it had gone so wrong.

Raoul's fingertips touched Brice's cheek, shocking him back into meeting his gaze. Silver touched Raoul's eyes, too, or was that moonlight? It was difficult to tell in the dark. "Surrender to the masquerade." His soft lips brushed Brice's, coaxing heady desire from the deepest, darkest hole he'd hidden it in. "Surrender to me, Brice LeChoix."

This meant nothing. It was just fantasy. A dream he'd wake from tomorrow with the masquerade gone. He'd failed in everything else, so what was one more mistake? His yearning was a second heartbeat now, a thing alive in his veins. Raoul offered everything Brice could never have. A touch he so craved.

Raoul's lips were the softest of teases, a brush, a whisper, luring him deeper so that all Brice could think of was having this creature of temptation exactly how he'd suggested, on his knees, those sweet pink lips around his pleasure. His desire manifested in his cock's aching weight, so ready for Raoul's promised offering.

Raoul slipped from the kiss and pulled Brice along behind him toward their secret bench. They passed the lilies again, their sweet scent so thick it laced his tongue. Brice blinked. A vast swirl of color wafted from the huge flower heads and from others in the garden, scenting the air. He dug his heels in, jolting Raoul to a halt, breaking his hold on Brice's hand.

They will offer you that which you most desire, but it will come with a heavy price.

The spell or whatever it was snapped, lashing back at Brice like a cruel slap in the face.

The pollen.

It was everywhere, including all over Raoul's hand from when he'd earlier brushed the flowers. His smile faded under Brice's withering gaze.

"It's a trick," Brice said.

The pollen was poison.

Brice wiped his lips on his sleeve, smearing it with glittery pollen. The entire garden was saturated with it. The guests already caught in its rapturous throes were its victims. And Brice had almost been among them.

Brice laughed, but the sound was hollow. "You almost had me, fae."

Raoul's smile twisted. All of his casual grace hardened, turning icy, and his soft smile fractured. "You'd never agree without it."

"No. I wouldn't have."

This entire fantasy was a poisonous lie. To what end, Brice wasn't sure, but it couldn't be good. Shaking off the horrible, residual urge to fuck the pretty fae, he ran from the garden, back down the corridor, and into the ballroom. The dancers still twirled, color still flooded every corner, but it had turned lurid and sour. Did nobody else see the truth of this rotten lie? Even as he thought it, the chandeliers dulled, wilting, turning back into draping ivy strewn among towering oaks, the columns into gnarled bark. It was all a lie.

Brice spotted Charon and Sophia among the dancers and fought through the bodies. He burst onto the dance floor, staggering into a startled couple and earning himself a few vicious curses as he shoved others out of his way.

Charon's eyes first widened, then narrowed in recognition. He held out a hand, probably to fend Brice off, but Brice grabbed his wrist. "We're leaving."

"No." Charon pulled himself free.

"If not for me, then leave for her." He avoided the use of Sophia's name, if only to save her the gossip that would surely spread like wildfire in the town tomorrow. "This place is a lie, all of it. The color, the finery, it's all fake."

The flash of hatred in Charon's gaze stalled Brice's conviction. "Don't take this from me," his brother said, seething. "Don't you dare." He straightened, standing eye to eye. They were matched in height, but Brice had years on him and muscle from working the land after the staff had been dismissed.

"I'm trying to help you," he said through his teeth.

Charon's shove was unexpected. He had never laid his hands on Brice, but he'd seen Father try it. He shoved Brice again. Sophia reached for him, but Charon shook her off.

"You don't get to take this from me like you've taken everything else!"

The third shove was too much. Brice felt the sting in his fist and saw his brother recoil before he knew what he'd done. At the punch, Charon's mask flew free and clattered to the ground.

The dancing ceased, and so did the music. They had an audience now. They were the entertainment for the fae and their games. Sure enough, many of them were smirking, enjoying the spectacle at Brice's expense. Raoul was among them, hip cocked, arms folded, watching. Their masks made them look cold.

"You're all fools." He swept a hand at the wilted ivy, the cold oaks and their naked branches, and the chilling winter forest that had moments ago been dressed in lies. Lies they all danced among. Puppets for the fae.

"Go home, brother," Charon snapped. His brother scooped up his mask, and his face, usually so full of sunshine, held only a hard sneer.

"Charon," Sophia whispered, eyes downcast behind her mask.

"You're leaving with me, both of you. This charade ends now, before someone gets hurt."

A click between finger and thumb, and the dispelled illusion suddenly snapped back into place. Light flooded the room, and shimmering marble floors swept beneath their feet. Luxury and splendor dazzled once more, making Brice's head spin. Charon said something. The words sounded vicious but their meaning was lost in his throbbing head. And then the person whose fingers had flicked to re-magic the place back into existence walked through the parting guests.

He radiated menace like the sun radiates heat but not in the flamboyant way of most of the fae here. His power came from the inside, not from a lie but from the heart of him. And his heart was dark. Brice knew it like he knew he'd made a terrible mistake.

The host stopped in front of them, and all around the guests watched in silence. "Brice LeChoix?" His voice resonated through the room and everyone here, touching not just their ears but their souls too.

"Yes," Charon said over Brice's reply. He lifted his unmasked face and met the host's gaze.

The host tilted his head. Light skimmed down his golden mask and touched his lips. Still no smile. The others of his kind seemed so quick to wear their smiles. The absence of his seemed significant. And terrifying.

The host held out his hand. "Your invites?"

Brice blinked, forgetting briefly why he'd been so furious only to recall it again in the next breath. "Put your mask on," he told Charon. "We're leaving."

The host's dangerous gaze flicked to Brice, rooting him to the floor. "You'll leave at my behest."

"My brother means no disrespect," Charon offered, replacing his mask and tying it off. He handed over his invite.

The host examined it by tracing it with his fingers. The crowd began to filter away, losing interest.

When the host held out his hand for Brice's invite, his gaze lingered like a weight on Brice's soul. He would not look away. This fae, this creature, would be gone tomorrow and everything would return to normal. It would all be over soon. He just had to get through these next few moments. Brice handed over his invite.

"These invites belong to one man, not two," the host declared, handing Brice's back. He glanced between them. "Which of you deserves to be here?"

Charon wet his lips. Sophia's hand tightened on his, even as she glanced at Brice, a plea in her eyes. To go or to stay?

Charon stepped forward. "I do. He only came to ruin everything."

Brice sighed. "Charon—"

The host lifted a hand. "My hospitality ends here, Lord LeChoix. It is time for you to leave. Perhaps we will meet again next year?" The host moved away, but not before Brice caught the smallest of twitches hinting at a smile that never quite made it to the host's lips.

Charon scooped Sophia against his side and the pair walked away, leaving Brice standing alone. The crowd swept back in like water around a stone.

Brice found Raoul among the crowd but ignored him and frowned after his brother. All would be well tomorrow. Charon would have this fantasy, this freedom, for one night, and then he would return home where he belonged.

"Some advice?" Raoul enquired, loping alongside Brice's quick retreat into the echoing foyer.

"I don't want anything from you."

"Such a sweet lie. We both know you want one thing especially."

His gloves and cloak waited on a table beside the long archway opening that would take him back out into cold reality. After putting both on, he faced Raoul, intent on giving him another piece of his mind, but Raoul's pretty eyes stared back from behind the mask. Dark lashes as soft as down feathers around eyes the color of precious gems—nothing true or real was that pretty.

"You accomplished something tonight," Raoul said.

With the exit so close and the cold night looming, Brice worked his fingers deeper into his gloves, hesitating. "And what was that?"

"I've never been denied before." He rubbed at his chest. "It's quite the unpleasant sensation."

Brice didn't believe it for a second. Raoul didn't feel a damn thing. "Unpleasant is having one's desires manipulated." He tugged again at his gloves, anger rising. If he hadn't realized the pollen was muddying his thoughts, he'd have fallen into Raoul's trap just like the others in that forbidden garden. And without free will, whatever might have transpired between them would have been wholly wrong. "The truly tragic part is"—he looked up—"had you not tried to seduce me with lies, you may have gotten your wish and had my cock in your mouth. Now you'll never know that pleasure." The words were out in a rush, leaving him panting, and it felt good to speak of such things. Perhaps the masquerade had given him that small gift if nothing else. Once he left, there would be no more talk of fucking men, because Lord Brice LeChoix, heir to Latchly Hall and the LeChoix debts, could not be seen to engage in such debauchery.

With a soft, luscious chuckle, Raoul straightened. He pressed a finger to his own lips and brought it away with a flourish. "I'll always have our kiss." Bowing theatrically, he backed away, careful to make sure Brice was watching before he turned and strode toward the staircase, long black hair swishing down his back.

The archway led Brice out into the wintery darkness. Unable to face the long ride home, he rented the attic room at the inn and sat at the small window, watching the moon's slow crawl across the sky, waiting for Charon to return.

Chapter Six

THE TOWNSFOLK STUMBLED into town at dawn, cheeks flushed, speech slurred, and drunk on wine and revelry. Brice had slept little, staying awake in the hope Charon would come to his senses and wander up the street sometime in the night. He hadn't. Now Brice waited on his horse by the town's frozen fountain, scanning the steady flow of people for Sophia's sunshine dress or his brother's assured gait, listening for his easy laugh. The flow of people slowed to a trickle, and after a while, sunrise stopped it altogether. Perhaps Charon had taken another path to town or retired to Sophia's, which was closer than the inn and certainly closer than their home.

Brice knocked at the Brodeur's grand town house door, flanked by impressive columns. Not as impressive as those at the masquerade, but reality could hardly compare to fantasy. Louis, the master housekeeper, answered, his wrinkled face lighting up at the sight of Brice on the step.

"Master Brice? It's early, but I can brew some tea—"

"No, thank you."

"Come out of the cold, sir." He ushered Brice inside and closed the door. Like most townsfolk, Louis had known Brice since he was a boy. He'd foiled many a childhood scheme between Brice, Charon, and Sophia.

"Louis, is Charon here?"

"Charon? No, sir. Should he be?" Concern lifted his voice.

"Well, no. I suppose not. But... what of Sophia?"

"Lady Sophia will be home shortly." He smiled, happy he could answer that at least.

But the masquerade was long over. Charon returning late was one thing. Sophia's absence was more worrisome.

"Is there something wrong, Master Brice?" Louis asked. "Shall I wake the rest of the staff?"

"It's probably nothing but... yes, I think, wake them. Just in case."

The staff were woken, wrapped in winter gear, and sent into the town and surrounding lands to search for the couple. They'd be found soon enough. Perhaps they'd accepted an invite to stay at another household. It was true—Brice and Charon had argued, as he later explained to the town constable, but Charon would not risk Sophia's safety, especially considering their apparent *relationship.* A relationship Sophia's staff were clearly aware of. Charon often rode to town to visit, Brice was told, mostly during times when Brice was distracted by managing the land and house and bills. Charon had visited the afternoon of the wolf attack, and there was his real reason for being in town. Most everyone knew, it seemed, and clearly assumed Brice did too. But as the hours wore on and the couple wasn't found,

Brice's anger at his brother's subterfuge weakened like the winter sun.

Brice galloped his horse home to check there and later returned to the inn and the grim frost-nipped faces. *Night was closing in. No more could be done,* the constable told him, and the townsfolk drifted away, returning to their warm, safe homes. Only Louis remained, standing at the inn window and wringing his hands. He gathered his hat and coat. "Patrice may still be in the post office. I'll send a telegram to Master Brodeur." *Sophia's father.* He'd be furious. As perhaps he should be. After opening the door, Louis glanced at Brice. "What shall I tell him?"

Brice fastened his cloak. "That she will be found. He has my word." He feared he knew exactly where the couple was. The one place he hadn't personally looked.

Leaving Louis at the post office, Brice galloped his horse out of town, down the same track he'd walked the night before. Burned torches lined the narrowing path. Darkness closed in, night arriving early in the thick forest. "Yah!" The horse's hooves churned up fallen leaves and pine needles, the path already well trodden by countless velvet slippers and polished leather boots. The rows of snuffed torches ended, but the pathway continued snaking deeper among the trees.

Spindly branches clawed out of the darkness, reaching for him like old hags' fingers. The archway loomed ahead. Branches interlaced to form the entrance to the masquerade, but the path ended abruptly on its other side.

Brice pulled his snorting horse to a halt and quickly dismounted. The archway stood out among the trees for being handmade, but otherwise, there was nothing but trees all around. And the arch itself was only a few meters deep. Brice walked through it, emerging on the other side on more trodden ground but no masquerade, no huge tent, no grand marble floors or enormous staircase. Old oaks loomed, their gnarled roots rising out of the earth. Ice dripped from ancient boughs, but as for any magic or music or fae, there was no evidence they'd ever existed.

He turned, cloak fanning, and kicked over the leaf litter, searching for evidence. Anything to know it hadn't all been a dream. "I know you're here!" His voice barreled into the dark. The forest's heavy, airless silence swallowed it. "You have my brother!" he hollered. "Sophia? Charon!" The oppressive night greedily snatched their names away. "Raoul, you fiend!"

His horse whinnied softly. A swift breeze whispered through the trees, as light as the fae's empty laughter.

The masquerade was gone, and so was Charon. Brice stilled and with the sounds of his own breathless panting filling his ears, he closed his eyes and listened to the hungry silence.

He should never have left him. He should have dragged Charon home kicking and screaming like Father had done to Brice every time he'd strayed with the stable boy. Charon would have hated him, but at least he'd be safe at home. Instead of... with them.

He turned, and the toe of his boot unearthed something glittering in the leaves. Brice knelt and brushed them aside. A hollow mask peered back at him. Black, laced with fine silver thread. Raoul's mask.

His heart stuttered. With gloved fingers, he scooped up the mask and cradled it in his hand. Its silk ribbons trailed between his fingers. A coincidence that it had been left behind or something more?

Brice stood and regarded the old groaning trees anew. He clutched the mask in his right hand but his left folded into a fist. The invites had both belonged to Brice. Charon's fate should have been his. He'd failed, just like Father had expected. Well, damn him and damn the fae. Brice wasn't about to walk away without a fight. He wasn't his parents. The fae would rue the day they had crossed him.

Damn them all. "I'm coming for you!" he yelled. The silence took his vow and squirreled it away for safekeeping.

The townsfolk stopped searching a week later. Brice did not stop. Every day he rode through the woods, searching for some scrap of the masquerade to cling to and finding nothing. Sophia's father came knocking at the house, accusations flying. Brice weathered the storm, as he always had, until the man's anger deflated into sobs. His work soon demanded he return to Massalia City. As the days grew longer, the nights warmer, and the snows began to melt, swelling the rivers, life in Chamonet continued. Nobody mentioned the masquerade. The candles that had been lit in windows to guide the lost lovers home stayed cold. Nobody dared speak ill of the fae, for the winters were already wretched without angering those known to control the storms. By the summer, the mood in the village had changed: Charon and Sophia must have done something to anger the host. Rumors whirled of Charon losing his mask, and the blame fell at Brice's feet. Someone had seen him strike his brother.

Once again, he was isolated, but not by deep snow or winter storms. By guilt. He'd been the one to knock Charon's mask free. What if that was the reason the host had taken him? There was only one rule at the masquerade —never remove your mask.

It didn't matter. Winter would come around again and so would the solstice. And with those dark days and long nights, the masquerade would return. Brice would get an invite. He always did. He'd find Charon and Sophia and bring them home.

Midsummer baked the forest clearing. Pines leaked their sap. Brice raised his axe and brought it down with a hefty *thwomp*, splitting the log in two.

Even in the shadows of the trees, humid air drenched him. He tugged off his sodden shirt, flung it over a sapling, and stacked the split logs on his cart. Hitched to the cart, his horse chewed on grass and flicked her tail to ward off flies. Little bothered Brice out here. He liked the quiet, only broken by the *thwunk* of his axe, the rattle of the horse's tack, or an occasional chitter from a squirrel. It was a living quiet, unlike the house. That quiet was the quiet of a grave.

The sound of a twig snapping stalled his next strike. With the axe raised, he glanced toward the tree line and stilled. The wolf—it could only be the same one from that fateful night—stood in the shadows beneath the trees. Its white coat shimmered like snow even now.

The beast lowered its head and flattened its ears. Its lips unleashed a snarl.

Brice swallowed and slowly lowered the axe, holding its handle across him, should he need to swing it. The wolf's eyes gleamed, full and frozen. It had no fear, this one. If it wanted Brice's horse, it would have to fight him for it. The horse was vital and his only companionship. Without the horse, life at Latchly would be considerably more difficult.

Don't, he silently warned the beast, hoping his body language conveyed his threat.

The wolf's snarls turned to growls.

Brice glanced about the clearing. If one wolf turned to more, he didn't stand a chance. He'd have to surrender the horse to save himself.

Sweat trickled down his back. Grasshoppers chirped. The horse snorted and pawed the ground. If he caught the wolf's scent, he might bolt, taking the cart and the wood with him. And wouldn't that be just Brice's damned luck.

"Don't," he warned the wolf, adding his own growl.

The beast glared back. Perhaps it was rabid, in which case an axe to its neck would be a kinder ending than the madness awaiting it. The beast's growls ceased. Its ears pricked.

The wind had shifted, swirling around the clearing, sweeping the scent of horse and Brice toward it instead of away. The beast sniffed the air. It huffed, slunk backward, then turned and vanished into the trees.

Brice let out a breath and relaxed his grip on the axe. The wolf was likely the reason for his chicken flock having been decimated. He'd seen its enormous prints in the mud near the yard. If it got into the paddock, it would take his horse. It needed to be dealt with.

He finished stacking the logs on the cart, keeping an eye on the tree line, and guided the horse back along the forest track to the yard. After unhitching the cart and safely stowing the horse back in the stables, Brice stripped from his sweat-sodden clothes, washed up, dressed in hunting gear, and collected his father's hunting rifle. He blew dust from its barrel, oiled the mechanism, and tried not to recall the time he'd stared down the barrel of the gun from the wrong end with his father's finger on the trigger. The old ghosts of the past could not hurt him now—or so he told himself. He closed Latchly Hall's door and prepared to track the wolf. It shouldn't be too hard to find. A beast that large would have a sizable den.

The sound of hooves clopping on dirt and the rattle of a carriage pulled him up short on the front steps. A carriage usually meant one thing, and sure enough, as it rounded the steep curve and approached the house, Brodeur's blue and yellows gleamed in the fading light.

The driver reined the two horses to a halt and tipped his hat to Brice. Brice nodded his reply but hung back. If Jonathon Brodeur was here to unleash a new tirade of blame at Brice for losing his daughter, he'd find the door slammed in his face.

He hadn't seen Brodeur since the man had broken down on these same steps in the depths of winter. Today he looked leaner in the face, helped by a neatly trimmed beard. He'd always been clean-shaven before. And as always, he was dressed impeccably. Appearances were everything to him.

Climbing down from the carriage, he straightened and cleared his throat. "Lord LeChoix—Brice."

"Jonathon."

The man's gaze skimmed over the rifle and Brice, taking in his frayed clothing and bristled chin. Not so much a beard as a shadow he'd forgotten to shave off for a few mornings. There had been a time Brodeur had greeted Brice like the son he did not have. Those days seemed as though they belonged to someone else's life. "I wasn't expecting guests."

"I can see that." Brodeur fiddled with his cuffs. "I must apologize for my unannounced arrival, but I have a delicate matter requiring your opinion."

"Oh?"

"Please, accompany me into town? We'll talk more in the carriage."

"Sir, as you can see, I'm dressed for hunting and have an urgent matter of my own to attend. If it can wait—"

"It cannot." He wrung his hands, then caught himself and forced his arms behind his back. A glance at the driver revealed the man looking away. Whatever Brodeur wanted to say must be a private matter, indeed, for him to be so concerned his driver might overhear.

"It's Sophia," Brodeur whispered.

Brice's heart leaped. Sophia had returned? "Then Charon has—"

Brodeur shook his head, abruptly severing Brice's hopes. "No, she's alone."

"But... Then she must know where he is?"

"Brice." He leaned closer and clasped Brice's shoulder in his trembling grip. Unshed tears swam in the man's glassy, fearful eyes. "Our dear Sophia is not who she was."

Chapter Seven

Boyhood memories crowded every corner of Brodeur's town house. All the times he'd hidden beneath the sweeping staircase with Charon and Sophia, taking turns to hide from Louis or to spring from the cupboard to startle the poor man. He recalled sneaking down those same stairs, Sophia on tiptoes, avoiding the creaking steps for midnight kitchen raids. The hat stand where the three of them would dress in Sophia's parents' coats and pretend to be haughty aristocrats. Charon would tip his hat and spin an impression of Sophia's father and have her in fits of laughter. They'd been in love even then. Charon and Sophia. Too young to know physical love but smitten all the same. Brice hadn't seen it, too concerned with his own responsibilities and marriage negotiations. In another life, he'd have gone on to marry Sophia, and Charon would have despised him even more. But not as much as he'd have hated himself and the lie he would have trapped her in.

Louis had already taken Brice's hunting coat. Brice had

left the rifle propped inside the coal store at home. No use in bringing it to town and certainly not in such circumstances. Brodeur had said little else regarding Sophia's state and had spent much of the carriage ride muttering about how he would have come to Latchly Hall sooner, but he'd been away. The setting sun had painted his face in an ominous scarlet hue and all he'd told Brice was how he did not know who else to call on for help with Sophia's care. He hurried ahead now, muttering about preparing her.

"Sir?" Louis approached him as he set foot on the bottom stair. "She's not in her room."

Jonathon's face turned ashen. "By God, you let her leave? Where is she?"

"The dining room, sir. We... couldn't stop her."

He swept through the doorway and the inner hall in the direction of the dining room.

Louis's wrinkled face betrayed concern in all its folds. Brice tried to muster a smile, but the housekeeper shook his head and muttered, "Terrible, just terrible, Brice. Rest her soul." He jerked his chin to follow Brodeur. "You should go to her now. I fear her affliction will only get worse."

Brice frowned down the inner hallway. Sophia had returned, but the staff and her father treated her return as though it were terrible news. What could have stricken her in such a way to have them so afraid?

Louis caught his arm. "It is a curse upon this town."

"What is?"

"*They* are."

"They?"

Louis shook his head. "Go, be with her, milord. She'd want you there."

With heavy trepidation, he left Louis and ventured down the inner hall, footfalls muffled by thick carpet. A few strides in and a sweet and melodic humming reached his ears. The tune flowed and dipped and dallied. It plucked on his memories. He'd heard it before, sometime far away. His pace quickened. The humming was accompanied by the swish of cloth and the sigh of slippers across a floor. Sophia was there, just through the doorway ahead in the candlelit dining room, and she was well. She was *singing*. And if she was well, then so was Charon. There was still hope.

Brice swept into the room, then stumbled to a halt. All the furniture had been haphazardly pushed against the wall to leave room for the girl to dance. She dipped and stepped, twirled and spun, humming the tune. Her hair whipped, matted as it was. Lipstick had smeared from her lips, staining her chin as though it were blood. And her eyes, always so bright and clear, had clouded, smudged with kohl. Tears had stained her cheeks.

He didn't recognize her. Not at first.

Brodeur threw a harried look toward Brice, caught between shame at seeing his daughter so afflicted but fear, too, because he could do nothing. "Sophia? Darling? Brice is here."

She didn't hear, just danced. Her slippers swished across the floor. Her lips twitched, and she arched her arms as though embracing an invisible partner.

"Sophia..." Brice stepped forward. Good heavens. The dark circles of her nipples showed through her nightgown, erect and prominent. She resembled a dancing girl from a music box, a marionette so alone and trapped, dancing to a single song for all of time. She was... beautiful but so fragile, like she might shatter if he dared touch her.

This wasn't his Sophia. His Sophia was strong, carefree, and brilliant. She was a golden light in the darkness of the LeChoix life. This woman was... someone else. Struck by a fierce need to have her back, he strode across the space, caught her arms, and whipped her around.

"Oh, Brice!" She pulled her arms free of his loose grip and flung them over his shoulders, then plastered herself close. Her cheek brushed his. She smelled of too-sweet perfume, of rotting flowers and dug-over earth. "You must dance with me!" Her light fingers skimmed down his arms, and catching his hands, she tugged, trying to pull him along.

"Stop."

She tugged harder, but as he dug his heels in, her eyes turned dark. "Everyone must dance! He'll be angry if you don't."

He yanked his hands free and her tear-streaked face fell. A moment gripped her, a flicker of reality. She saw him; he was sure of it. She saw the dining room and her father. Fear sharpened her breaths. She clutched at her chest and retreated a step, then another. "No... no... I cannot leave. I mustn't leave. I cannot be here. He will be furious."

She bolted for the door.

Her father stepped into her path.

Sophia screamed and spun, hair and gown spiraling around her. Panic wrought her face. The window—the drapes fluttered. She surged, running like a colt for freedom. Brice slammed into her, locked her in his embrace.

"No!" She screamed and kicked and bucked, a wild thing in his arms.

He tightened his hold, crushing her closer. "Stop. You're safe—"

Her screams ran nails down his spine. She writhed, shook her head back and forth. Her fingernails whipped down his cheek. So strong. He didn't want to hurt her, but she would hurt herself like this. He had no choice. Gripping her shoulders, he slammed her against the wall. She wailed, like her soul was being wrenched from her body. Great, harrowing, blood-curling screams. The sound was so terrible, it ate at Brice's own sanity. He slapped her, cutting off the noise.

She gasped under his hands. Her ragged hair curtained her face, but he saw how her lip trembled.

His hand burned like the guilt in his gut. "Sophia."

Her body fell from his grip as she dropped to her knees. Brice dropped with her. He bundled her close, pulling her against his chest. Sobbing gasps tumbled from her lips. She trembled like a small, frightened animal. This Sophia was not the same woman who had danced at the masquerade. They had done something to her. "You're safe," he whispered, stroking her hair. "Safe now. They can't reach you here. You're home. You're safe." Over and over, he whispered the words until her trembling ceased and her panting breaths settled.

Brice tipped her chin up. Her eyes were open but unseeing. Dark pupils swallowed all the color of her irises. Her head lolled as though she were drunk. With the slash of scarlet lipstick and smudged shadows staining her eyes, he looked upon a warped and twisted reflection of the Sophia he knew and loved.

Scooping her into his arms, he carried her from the

room and up the stairs to her chamber, then gently laid her on the bed. "Rest. Everything will be better in the morning." Maybe she heard—he couldn't tell. She stared into the wall, seeing things nobody could see.

He tucked her sheets around her, swept her hair back, and kissed her lightly on her cheek.

She blinked. "He made me come back."

"Who did, Sophia? Who did this to you?"

Her eyelids drooped. She sighed and sleep gathered her up in its folds. Brice sat with her until her breaths deepened, then left the room, quietly closing the door behind him.

"Here." Brodeur handed him a key.

He hesitated a moment, then slipped the key into the lock and turned it over. It was cruel but necessary until help could be found for her.

Brice followed Brodeur down the stairs and into the drawing room. A fire roared behind its grate and candlelight fought off the dark. Brodeur poured two drinks from a crystal decanter and handed one to Brice. His hand trembled.

"Doctor Jemers will be able to help." Brice raised the glass and drank the hot, woody bourbon deep. "I've read there are new techniques of the mind from—"

"Jemers can do nothing for her." Brodeur sighed as he lowered himself into the wingback chair beside the fireplace. "He's already tried."

What could one man do in a day? Unless... The taste of the drink soured on his tongue. "When did she return?"

Brodeur lifted tired eyes. "A month ago."

A month.

Sophia had been back a month, and nobody had cared to tell him? His fingers tightened around the glass. Brice had been summoned here out of desperation, not as a courtesy. "A month."

"She was found." Brodeur lowered his glass to the arm of the chair and swirled its contents. "Wandering the outskirts, not far from the... from the forest. A farmhand brought her to Doctor Jemers, who recognized her and promptly called Louis. I was away." He clenched his jaw and looked into the fire.

There was guilt there, and maybe there should be. He'd left for the city when he should have been searching for his daughter. He should have been here for them, for Sophia.

"She hasn't been wandering the forest for eight months," Brice said.

"No." His jaw twitched. "She was found in the same clothing she went to the ball in." Brodeur met Brice's gaze. "Besides her scuffed shoes, it was as though she had returned from the masquerade that very night. Or so Louis tells it. He has a fanciful manner sometimes, but there's... well... I'll show you." He rose from the chair and Brice followed him through the house to the back pantry. And there hung Sophia's yellow dress. The same dress he'd seen her wearing at the ball. Besides a few dried leaves caught in its frills, it was as pristine as it had been that night.

"Has it been cleaned?"

"No."

That did not make any sense. If she had wandered the forest for any length of time, the dress would show the scuffs and marks of such an ordeal.

He rubbed the fabric between his fingers. It was as

clean as the night it had been removed from its box. "Has she said anything regarding her whereabouts?"

"Fragments, most of it madness. We had hoped she would recover once she was home and safe. But every day she worsens." He finished his drink and pressed the cold glass to his cheek. "I thought I had lost her, but to have her back like this? It is almost worse."

The sunshine dress mocked their misery, like a joke at a funeral. It belonged to the past, to another time, to the Sophia who had danced at the ball with Charon, not to the poor woman who had returned without knowing her own mind. And to make matters worse, Brice knew the madness. He'd seen it before. The singing, the mindlessness... Mother had gone the same way.

He feared the answer to his next question. "What of Charon?"

"She spoke of him once. Said... he lost his mask. She laughed, but it was not a laugh of joy, Brice. There is no joy left in this house." Brodeur turned away. "I'll be in the drawing room."

With Brodeur gone, Brice pinched the dress between his fingers and thumb again and brought the fabric to his nose. The same sickly sweet odor he'd smelled on Sophia clouded the dress. Spoiled fruit, wet decay.

The fae had done this to Sophia. They had taken her, and for some unknown reason, spat her back out. Brice had dislodged Charon's mask, but that did not explain Sophia's punishment. She should have been able to leave once the masquerade ball was over. Why hadn't she? And why had they let her go now? As a message, a sign? A warning?

They still had Charon.

Louis was right. The masquerade was a curse. *They* had done this.

Autumn would soon be upon the town. As the nights grew colder and longer, the fae would be closer and the solstice would not be far behind. He'd accept this year's invite and face them. This had to end.

Chapter Eight

"I've had Louis make you up a room for the night," Brodeur said once Brice returned to the drawing room. "Perhaps you might see if you can speak with Sophia tomorrow morning? She seems to be better in the mornings."

Brodeur fell into a melancholy after that, more inclined toward the drink than Brice's company.

Brice retired to the room for the night, but as he lay in the unfamiliar bed, Sophia's earlier screams haunted the edge of his thoughts. He could not forget the way she had trembled in his arms. So broken. Sophia was not faint-hearted. She was a strong woman who knew her own mind and heart. How could they do that to her? And why?

Brice could no more sleep than he could get to the fae to punish them. He dressed and paced his chamber. Louis had kindly left a razor and soap, probably after noticing Brice's unkempt state, so he took the opportunity to wash and shave off the ragged whiskers.

If he could speak with Sophia when she wasn't so lost,

he might be able to get some sense out of her, even if it was just in snatches. If she was here, then Charon might be close too. Charon might wander from the forest just as she did. Brice would give almost anything to have him back, although the irony was, of course, without Charon, he had nothing left to give.

He toweled his face dry and regarded his expression. Dark eyes, that some might call soft. Dark hair, thick, with a wave, just long enough to tie back if he cared.

You look so very like your father.

He'd done his best to block out Raoul's deep, syrupy voice but sometimes, in the dead of night when his mind drifted, it crept back to him and slithered its way inside.

I'll always have our kiss.

He could see the fae as clearly as though it were happening again. How he had stood, hip cocked, fingers to his lips, tasting Brice there, delight dancing in his eyes while the rest of his face was masked. Brice's body had responded even as his mind recoiled. His member had heated, growing heavy with want. He turned his face away from his own reflection and willed the desire away. There had been times he'd lain in bed at home, taken himself in hand, and surrendered to the dreams. In those dreams, he'd willed Raoul to his knees, clutched at his braided black hair, and relished the feel of the male's lips around his cock. He'd pumped until he'd spilled all over himself. Those times, the memories had gripped him like their own kind of madness, coming over him like a fever.

He had not thought of Raoul in weeks. He had hoped he might have forgotten him. But the memories were back, brighter and harder and hotter than ever, like the fae's poison was somehow still inside him, coiled in the grass, waiting to strike.

A sudden shattering scream burst from outside. Doors slammed along the street. Frantic voices bubbled up through his window.

Brice pulled the drapes back from the opening.

His breath caught. His heart stopped.

A woman lay sprawled facedown on the street below, motionless. Her naked legs and arms shone pale against the dark cobbles. Blood glistened under flickering lamplight, spreading through her thin gown.

Someone howled. It might have been Jonathon Brodeur.

Brice slowly, inexorably, turned his head. Drapes fluttered from the window next to his. The open window Sophia had fallen from.

They'd locked the door but not the window.

Sophia, the brightest light in his life, was gone.

Chapter Nine

Flames licked around his father's suit jacket, making shadows dance up the front of Latchly House. The bonfire crackled and hissed. It seemed fitting.

He had worn that jacket for the last time today at Sophia's funeral. The garment had choked him with every breath. He'd stood beside her grave watching the pall-bearers lower her coffin into the ground and heard her father bid her farewell. Most of the town had been there, their gazes on Brice, blaming him. Sophia was dead because the LeChoix name was cursed. That was what they whispered. Everyone knew he and Sophia had been close. Everyone knew they were to be married. Now she was in the ground, like Brice's parents, perhaps like Charon.

So Brice had burned the suit when he'd returned. Set it ablaze right on the front lawn. He'd thought he'd feel something, but the emptiness inside just grew bigger, feeding, threatening to swallow him.

Standing in the flood of firelight, watching the shadows dance, he considered burning the house too. Just put a torch to it and be done with it. The damned place was so cold and wet, the flames probably wouldn't catch.

From his back pocket, he removed the mask he'd found on the forest floor all those months ago. Black, laced with silver. Beautiful but sinister. Brice glanced at the flames. He should burn the mask too. He wasn't sure why he hadn't already tossed it out. Instead, he'd buried it in the trunk beneath his father's belongings. And that was where it had stayed for eight months. If only the memory of Raoul's kiss would stay buried with it, but Brice still couldn't get the feel of it out of his head or the taste of the fae off his lips.

Stumbling back, he fell over a rock onto his ass in the grass. Laughter burst free. Was he losing his mind too? Was this what insanity felt like? Mother would know, but she wasn't here to ask. Nobody was here. He was alone. And lost. And so damned tired. Maybe a little drunk. He laughed at himself, at the world, and in a fit of madness, raised the mask to his face. It still smelled of jasmine, even now. He breathed in—breathed deep, taking the scent into him—and opened his eyes behind the mask.

It was his drunken state that summoned the wolf in front of him. Because if it was real, then Brice was surely, finally, done for.

The beast lurked at the edge of the front lawn where the grass met the trees, and from Brice's angle on the ground, it was larger than ever. Orange flames painted its white coat the color of a sunset and fire flickered in its otherwise icy eyes.

Brice laughed some more and lowered the mask. "Fine, wolf. Have me. Though you'll find me tasteless and bitter," he muttered.

The wolf's growl chilled his blood, freezing some of the alcohol in his system. He shivered, perhaps more afraid than he'd realized. He wasn't ready to die. Charon was still out there. The fae had taken everything, everyone, but not Brice. Not yet.

He staggered to his feet. "You, wolf! You cannot have me." He stumbled toward the beast. "I am not done, you hear? Desperate, perhaps." He laughed. "But not done, not yet. Go hunt weaker prey." He lunged. "Yah! Go!"

The wolf snarled, ducked its head, and slunk back through the ferns into darkness.

Chuckling, Brice lifted his face to the star-scattered sky. Winter's bite was in the air, nipping at his skin. The invite would soon slip under his door, and the cycle would begin again. One long, terrible night... But this time, he had a plan. He was getting Charon back. The next masquerade would be their last.

Chapter Ten

The invite did not come.

For years, they'd arrived like clockwork, mocking him. But not this year.

He waited every day and night, listening for its soft slip beneath the door. Tomorrow was the solstice. No messenger had ventured to the house, no letter in disguise was waiting at the post office. Because the fae knew he would hurt them. How they knew, he couldn't be sure, but they had their ways. They watched from starlight and listened on the wind. Perhaps they were still in the woods, like the old tales said, and they watched him through Latchly Hall's dark windows.

It did not matter. Brice would steal an invite.

People were always flashing them at the inn, paper glittering as the celebratory drinks flowed. Really, taking an invite could save someone's life. He'd be doing a good thing.

He had no choice.

He had to get in.

He gathered up what remained of the family silver and

bought himself a wonderful, perfectly tailored new suit made of the finest fabric, stitched with silver thread to match Raoul's mask. He had to wear the mask. What else was it for if not to return to the masquerade? Besides, the mask alone might get him in if all else failed.

The buzz about town on the day of the solstice was as before. *Come to the masquerade!* colorful flyers proclaimed. *Invite only!* Multicolored bunting flapped in the wind, strewn from streetlamp to streetlamp. Traders sold the last of their masks at inflated prices and tailors worked tirelessly, making final adjustments to the medley of dresses and gentlemen's attire. No lessons had been learned from Sophia's death. It wasn't the fae's fault. If anyone was to blame, it was Lord LeChoix's curse. The Brodeur girl had killed herself, preferring death to a lifetime trapped in the cursed house high up in the wooded hills. Brice heard the rumors as he walked among the people, keeping his collar up and his head down. A missing younger son, a reclusive heir, dead parents, the decline of a once wealthy and admirable estate, a crumbling house perpetually shrouded in shadows. Like the masquerade, his story had become legend, intertwined with the fae. His name had become part of the fantasy, part of the thrill of the masquerade and its magic. People talked. He would not have to listen for long. After tonight, it would all be over, one way or another.

But first, he had to get his hands on an invite or his plans would be for nothing.

The Laughing Crow's huge fireplace drew him to it. People filled the bar area. Dresses bloomed like flowers among the darker, suit-clad men. Colored feathers sprouted from hats. Jewels shimmered.

Brice's suit was covered by his coat, not that anyone would notice him. He was far too dull compared to the finery here. As he listened to the titters and guffaws, the weight of a small flintlock pistol pressed into the small of his back. Mother's pistol. It held a single iron shot. Brice's gift for the host. Iron, she'd said, could wound them.

Brice glanced at the inn's fogged-up windows. The sun had yet to set. Once it did, it would be time to leave for the path into the forest. He had a while to find and steal an invite. Almost every person here would have one on them. However, few would leave such a treasure unguarded.

Brice hung back, keeping to the fringes of the room. He skimmed his gaze over the townsfolk, searching for that glittery hint of unique handcrafted paper, perhaps poking out of a pocket or a handbag. For years, he'd burned the damned things and wished they would stop tormenting him. And now he coveted just one. Was this how most people felt each year, desperate for a glimpse of magic? So desperate for a night of fantasy and debauchery that they ignored all the warnings.

This time he was better prepared to guard against the masquerade's allure.

This time he knew exactly what to expect.

Some of the townsfolk already wore their masks. One young man sat alone at the bar. He'd had his drink refilled a few times, probably to settle any nerves. Nobody appeared to be accompanying him. His mask was a multicolored work of art, encrusted with what appeared to be precious gems. Worth a year's wage packet to most folks. Had he saved for it, or was this just a frivolous night out for him? His one chance at fantasy? His blue brocade suit was a delight and would not have been out of place at the most lavish gatherings in Massalia. Perhaps that was where he was from? He certainly didn't seem to be local.

Brice might have felt guilty about what he was about to do if he didn't already know the stranger was better off never meeting a fae. He was saving him the torment, really.

Brice pried Raoul's mask from inside his coat. His fingers hesitated, stroking the silk seemingly of their own accord. Firelight licked along the silver trim. Before he could lose his nerve, he put the mask to his face and tied the silk behind his head. He already knew he looked dashing from a glimpse in the mirror at home. *Just like Father.*

Brice leaned against the bar beside the stranger. "May I buy you a drink?"

"Oh." The young man startled. Quick to smile, he was definitely nervous. Blond hair fell in ringlets to his shoulders. He really was quite lovely. "Thank you, sir. I appreciate it." He offered his hand. "I'm Frances and I'm somewhat... out of sorts here."

He shook the man's hand and a stab of guilt tried to knock Brice off his stride before he'd begun. "Brice," he said quickly, hoping nobody heard. Speaking with strangers had never been a problem. He had excelled at social gatherings, taught to be the height of gentlemanly prowess to carry the LeChoix name. And as the heir to a perceived fortune, he had never wanted for company. It was behind the etiquette, in more intimate areas, where his behavior had gotten him in trouble.

He hailed the bartender, thankfully not a face he recognized, and ordered drinks for them both. He could use some liquid courage himself. They talked about the town, about the weather, about the price of corn, and once the man had relaxed some, they talked about the masquerade.

"Your mask is lovely, sir," Frances said. "Understated but elegant. Did you have it made?"

"Ah, no. I... borrowed it."

"They must be a true friend indeed to loan such a beautiful work of art."

"Not quite a friend," Brice said coyly. *More an enemy.* "Tell me, how did your invite arrive? By post or by some other means? I've heard of some being delivered by ravens, although I wonder how true those tales are."

He laughed and absently touched his jacket's pocket. "Not ravens, no. Just by messenger." A slim corner of card poked from inside, its edges dipped in silver. Yes, there was his prize.

"Well', I do not know about you, Frances, but I must admit to being nervous."

The young man puffed out a breath and tittered a laugh. He stroked his tankard of ale and slid his gaze to Brice, his smile slipping sideways. "I have heard the stories, of course. But as I have not been back to Chamonet for many years, I assumed the magic was not for me. To receive an invite while so far away... I never dreamed I'd be chosen."

How were the guests chosen? Was it by chance or some grand design by an architect somewhere, pulling all their strings? Wealth appeared to have nothing to do with it. Nor did social standing. The invites seemed random, but Brice didn't believe it. There would be a reason. A purpose behind it all.

Frances's hand rested over Brice's on the bar. "I hear almost anything goes at the masquerade."

Ah. Brice's responding smile wasn't all pretend. Frances was somewhat young and naïve for his tastes, but the young man was beautiful. His golden locks would surely attract the attention of the fae, as Charon's had. Perhaps that was how they chose their victims: by appearance. Or by some deep-seated desire the guests could not sate elsewhere, like this young man's suggestive glance and how his fingers tightened over Brice's. Charon had sought freedom, and he'd believed the masquerade would give it to him. Brice had sought, well... men. And Raoul had certainly been determined to answer that call.

Brice skimmed his free hand over Frances's shoulder and traced a delicate line up the curve of the man's neck. The touch was so blatant, and so unlike Brice, it ignited a thrilling flame of desire low in his belly. Behind the mask, nobody noticed, nobody cared how Brice LeChoix touched another man in a way that would be deemed scandalous on any other night. The responding fire in his blood revealed how he yearned for this. He'd forgotten just how much until now, with Frances leaning into him, his blue eyes wide and riveted on Brice's masked face. There was no doubt in his mind that if he took Frances's hand and led him behind the stables, they'd begin the night in the throes of passion, full of panted breaths and grasping fingers.

Brice bowed his head intimately close. Behind their masks, they could be anyone, just like the masquerade promised. Frances's lips parted. He tilted his head up, seeking more. The gems decorating his mask shone.

I'll always have our kiss.

Brice eased his hand into the man's pocket and lifted the invite free as his lips skimmed Frances's—not quite a kiss, but as close to one as was proper in public. "Perhaps you can find me at the masquerade?"

"I'd like that."

With a smile, he slipped away from Frances, leaving the man gazing after him.

Outside, the sun had bled its final rays behind the mountains. The townsfolk were stirring from their homes, making their way toward the torchlit pathway. Brice hurried into step and wove his way through their number, just short of running. He tucked the stolen invite inside his jacket. By the time Frances discovered it missing, Brice hoped to already be inside the masquerade.

"I'm coming, Charon." He adjusted the pistol at his back, touching it as though to summon some of Mother's luck. In this small way, she was with him too. She would want this. For Brice to finish what was begun all those years ago.

Now all that stood between Brice and the masquerade were the sentinels at the archway. And for the first time in a year, he hoped to see Raoul again.

Chapter Eleven

Brice was early. Only a few townsfolk waited in line ahead of him. Nerves tightened his insides and had him teasing his shirt cuffs and straightening his jacket. He caught himself fidgeting and made a conscious effort to calm himself. Candles danced and flickered among the naked boughs. Dusk's hues of red painted the forest in golden light.

Raoul wasn't at the arch.

But the female was. She was dressed in a black suit, her mask all white and encrusted with diamonds and soft downy feathers. It wasn't unheard of for a woman to wear pants. Apparently, it was common in the cities but not in Chamonet. She wore men's clothing rather well, Brice thought. Sophia would have adored such a thing, breaking down gender expectations. She would have delighted in taunting her father. She'd once dressed as a boy, tucked all her hair under a cap, and visited the market to prove she could. Brice had been sure she'd be caught, but none had suspected. They'd laughed together on her return.

He'd never laugh with her again.

The female sentinel took the guests' invites and ran her slim fingers over the names.

What was it Raoul had said before? *Only a fool thinks to trick a trickster*. He'd said something about lies too. Brice was about to do both. The invite in his hand wasn't his. The mask wasn't his either. Didn't matter. He just had to believe he belonged here and be convincing.

The line shuffled forward.

The pistol felt heavier. They hadn't searched the guests for weapons before and didn't appear to be concerned by such things this time either.

Once inside, Brice would find the serving fae, Chantel, and like before, she'd help him find Charon. He'd get his brother to safety and give the host his *gift* on the way out, ending this dangerous fantasy forever.

The man ahead was ushered inside and the female fae lifted her gaze to Brice, meeting his eyes through their masks. Her eyes were beautiful, tricolored, like so many of the fae—the color of sunset, golds and browns and reds—but menacing too. In the way that autumn's colors signaled decay and the end of things, hers spoke of a wisdom belied by her youthful appearance.

"Your invite."

He handed it over.

This was the moment.

His heart thumped in his throat.

She skimmed her fingertips over the name. "Frances?"

"Yes."

Others had arrived, waiting in line behind him to begin their evening of fantasy and lust and debauchery. They watched politely, hungrily, secretly wishing he'd move along so they could get inside.

The fae crooked her finger.

Brice stole a step closer.

The dark pupils of her eyes widened, made darker by the startling white of her snow-white mask.

He wished Raoul were here. Something he'd never thought he'd want.

"This is not your invite."

Brice breathed in. "It was given to me."

She blinked. Her glossy lips twitched up at their edge.

He sounded like the man who had tried to enter last year and been sent off into the woods. *Only a fool thinks to trick a trickster.* "I know Raoul." The name sounded strange on his lips, as though it was wrong to speak it. But it was all he had left to get him inside.

"That is not your mask." She ripped the mask from his face, yanking it so hard she jerked him forward. He stumbled into her. She caught his shoulders. Her hands were so cold, like ice. Her touch burned through his coat fabric.

Her lips brushed his ear and her whispers spilled into his soul. *"Wander away, mortal thing. Follow where your lies lead."*

Brice blinked again and again. He couldn't clear his vision. Smudges and blurs floated around him, forms and shapes that made no sense. "No..." He stumbled, lifting his hands to reach for something to hold, to orient himself. He'd come here for a reason, hadn't he? But where was he? His mind had closed like a fist with the secrets inside. He needed to get to it. He was here for something. But the reason had slipped far away. If he could just reach it... He stumbled over a root or a dip in the path and fell against gnarled tree bark.

Charon would be waiting for him at home. He had to get home. Yes, that was the way. If he could just find the path. Pushing from the tree, he groped the air in front of him, seeking obstacles, and gingerly shuffled his way across the forest floor. The air smelled of wet leaves. *Go home.* He had to go home. *Follow where your lies lead.*

Only a fool thinks to trick a trickster.

He saw him then, in his mind. The fae with the long black braid and the sideways smile, his eyes so bright behind his silver mask. He lounged on the bench, legs crossed at the knee. Black boots climbed his calves. His doublet glinted with gold. But it was the mask that drew Brice's gaze back in his mind's eye. The mask he'd found here. Brice reached for his face, but the mask was gone. He'd lost it… somehow. Panic gripped his heart. He couldn't lose the mask. He needed it.

Why was he here?

Nothing made sense.

He'd come for a reason.

He didn't want to be here. He *had* to be.

For *Charon.*

He stumbled. His heel caught some upright obstacle and he fell, tumbling to his hands and knees. He couldn't see! Why could he not see?

And then, so startling, so sudden, it all came crashing back—everything at once. Charon was missing, Sophia dead. And he'd come to end the masquerade.

He looked at the pattern of leaves around his fingers, studied each leaf and the intricacies of its decaying veins, then crushed them between his fingers. Everything was startling in its clarity. He'd failed the test. They'd seen through his lies and locked him out. But he wasn't done. It wasn't over. No mask, no invite. Well then, he'd just have to get both back.

Standing, he turned and spotted the distant glow from the pathway torches. The night was still young. There was time to get inside. He'd be damned if he was going to give up now.

Straightening his coat, he brushed leaves from his knees and ran a hand through his hair, smoothing everything back into place just so.

If the fae thought he could be so easily turned around, they were severely mistaken. He was getting Charon back this night no matter the cost, or the obstacles, or their threats. They could not hurt him because he had nothing left to hurt. "There are few things more dangerous in this world than a desperate man," he sneered.

Following the light, he made his way back toward the line of guests and hung back among the brush. He crouched, peering through a mass of prickly briars. The sentinel was still there, still ushering the townsfolk inside. And at her feet lay Raoul's mask alongside a small pile of confiscated invites. If he could get his hands on those and slip inside, nobody within need know he wasn't invited.

All he had to do was distract her.

Chapter Twelve

Night had descended in earnest, thickening the pockets of shadows between the trees. Brice slung his coat from a few branches, then placed the few candles he'd stolen behind it, creating an awkward-looking silhouette of a figure. Up close, it wasn't menacing, but at a distance, it would be disconcerting. At least, he hoped so.

Careful to make himself presentable, he fell into step alongside the few guests that had come late to the masquerade. Satisfied nobody had seen him emerge from the trees, he searched for the figure he'd made among the gloom and found it suitably lurking some distance away. In the shifting candlelight, the figure appeared to *move*. Perfect.

A glance ahead revealed the sentinel's attention was firmly on a guest.

"Goodness, what is that?" Brice put some drama into it. He wasn't Charon, who could swoon like the best of the traveling players that sometimes came to entertain the town, but once they caught sight of the scarecrow he'd made, he hoped the people would take matters into their own hands.

"What, sir?" the guest in front of him enquired.

"There, you see it?" He pointed toward the lurking, glowing man. "Someone is out there."

Whispers carried down the line. Someone gasped. A few startled women squawked their alarm, and sure enough, the sentinel looked up. Brice stepped back, discreetly concealing himself behind the curious guests.

"There!" someone said in alarm. "Someone is out there!"

The sentinel peered into the dark. Did she think she was being watched? Did the fae have enemies out here? He hoped so.

The sentinel stepped away from her position. "Wait here."

Brice slipped along the back of the line, keeping outside the reach of candlelight. Everyone watched the sentinel stride through the forest toward the lit figure. It appeared the candles might have licked at Brice's coat rather too closely. Flames crawled up the unfortunate scarecrow's body. The figure was now ablaze.

With no time to mourn the loss of his best coat, he ducked in, grabbed the mask and invite, then hurried through the archway toward the bright lights and sounds of tinkling laughter.

"Hey! You there! LeChoix!"

He bolted and burst into the stunning entrance foyer with its sweeping staircase and sparkling chandeliers. All at once, color and heat and the noise of hundreds of gathered people washed over him, stealing a breath and a heartbeat. He'd forgotten how it dazzled. Forgotten the echoing sounds of so many voices, the clicks of heels, and the undercurrent of murmured desires. It all came back now in a heady rush.

A few people glanced his way.

The mask!

Hastily donning the mask, he strode into the throngs of people, carving a path away from the main entrance and exit. The crowd eagerly swallowed him up. His heart raced, thumping hot blood through his veins and body.

He was in.

He was back.

The masquerade.

He was closer now to his brother than he'd been in twelve long, terrible, lonely, wretched months. Charon would be here. There was nowhere else he could be. He was close. Brice knew it. Now to find him...

He roamed from room to room, scanning the masks, the faces—what he could see of them. The main ballroom, where he'd struck Charon, throbbed with dancers. The fae mingled with glittering townsfolk. Even Brice could see how the people tried too hard to be perfect. Their makeup smudged, sweat glistened, and their grace was stunted and lacking. But the fae, they moved like liquid. They shone like perfect stars. Not a hair out of place, not a frayed thread in sight. The more Brice looked, the more he saw their polished brilliance and how cold it all seemed. The prettiest of things could hide the rottenest cores. Their spell no longer worked on him. He saw them all for the terrible, hollow creatures they were.

At every glance, the fae laughed their silver laughter and smiled their razor smiles.

And they danced like petals on the wind drifting across the vast, shining ballroom floor with their partners in hand.

The music... its sweet melody. Brice recognized it. Sophia had hummed the same tune over and over as she'd danced in her slippers. Danced like they all danced now.

Brice stopped at the edge of the watching crowd. The colored dresses blurred and swirled, all bright paints mixed in a pot. The men, too, shone like wonders. Nobody put a step wrong. Nobody talked. They all smiled and danced as though they were wooden dolls made to dance to the never-ending music. The masquerade had ahold of them all.

The crowd stared in wonder, but Brice did not. The music's sweetness turned sour. The dancers' smiles turned sharp and wooden, cracking at the edges. This was wrong. These people weren't dancing because they wanted to, they danced because they had to.

Blond locks swept by on a handsome figure Brice would recognize anywhere. Charon! He stepped forward but stopped himself from rushing to him. The last time he'd been here, he'd caused a scene that had begun all of this madness. There had to be a better way to get to him.

Charon danced with a fae. His white mask, his soft gray suit, it was all the same. Nothing had changed. Just like Sophia's dress. Had Charon been here this whole time, trapped to dance forever?

"Wine, sir?"

He blinked at the young woman in a blue dress beside him. Fae—her piercing eyes of multiple blues and greens confirmed as much. Her mask was the color of the ocean. Pearls dripped from its edges. Oh, but he knew her. "Yes."

He plucked a glass from her tray. She moved off. "Wait, Chantel?"

Her glittering lashes fluttered. "That mask... How familiar it seems."

He absently touched the mask. He'd forgotten he was even wearing it. "You must help me."

"Do I know you?" She cocked her head, tilting it birdlike.

"My brother... He dances—"

"Oh! It is you! How did you get inside?" She grabbed his wrist. Wine sloshed from his glass over his fingers. "He will be furious. You cannot be here." She pulled him away from the dancers, away from Charon.

"Wait. Stop." He yanked from her grasp. Chantel teetered. Her tray toppled from her hand and struck the floor, ringing like a bell. Glass shattered, wine splashing over the shoes of those nearby. People lurched away, protecting their fine silks. Brice snarled at them all. The idiots. He swung his glare back to Chantel. "My brother—how do I get to him?"

She looked up and narrowed her eyes. "You cannot. This is not the place for you."

Brice caught her wrist. "My brother is right there—" He pointed into the dancers, some of whom had begun to slow. "I'm not leaving here without him, so tell me now or I will cause more of a scene."

Her brows knitted together and while he couldn't see much of her face, he didn't need to. Anger radiated off her. She squared up to him, not an easy thing to do given that she was a foot smaller. But she stood on her toes and peered into his eyes. "Blundering fool."

"Is there a problem?"

The male voice sent ripples of fear and needles of pleasure dancing down Brice's back, urging him to flee while at the same time demanding he turn and face the creature. He reached inside his jacket, curled his fingers around Mother's pistol, and whirled, extending his arm to aim between the host's dark eyes.

The music stopped.

The dancers stopped too.

The host smirked behind his gold inlaid mask. "Brice LeChoix." Power thrummed around him, beating in waves. Or perhaps that was Brice's heart pounding in his ears.

Pull the trigger.

Pull it and end this nightmare.

The words were loud in his head, but he couldn't be sure they were his own. The words were correct, though. He just had to pull the trigger and the iron shot would pierce the fae's skull. Ageless or not, he wouldn't get up from that.

Brice's aim wavered, his arm trembling.

The dark fae's eyes stared through him, unblinking.

Why hadn't he pulled the trigger? His finger twitched, but the final command wasn't getting through.

"My brother?" Brice said. "Charon!" The shout echoed above the heads of everyone here, fading into silence. Charon did not reply.

The pistol rattled in his grip.

Slowly, calmly, the host raised his hand. Brice saw it happening. Saw how the host laid his fingers over the pistol and pointed the weapon downward. And Brice did nothing. A part of him screamed inside, but the sound was so far away, just a tiny voice now. What was this hold the fae had over him? He had to break it before...

"Brice." The sound of his name on the host's lips did strange, incomprehensible things to his body, flushed him with sensitivity and heat and *lust*. Firm fingers interlaced with his. The host raised his free hand and swept a lock of hair from Brice's forehead. The delicate touch sent a bolt of lightning through Brice's body. "Dance with me."

He screamed silent refusals, rattled the mental cage his thoughts were trapped in, but the words never made it past his lips. He'd become a prisoner in his own flesh at the mercy of the host's next move.

The pistol was gone, slipped from his hand. He was falling but standing still. Lost, but right there in the moment.

The host stepped back, leading Brice to the dance floor. The firm hand raised Brice's while the other rested on his hip, burning where it touched, spilling some unknown power beneath Brice's skin, filling him with want and the desire to obey. He looked the host in the eyes, raged at him, hurled insults, and spat accusations, but none of it made it past his gritted teeth.

Brice's lips pulled into a wooden smile.

The music began. The rhythm wrapped around him, poured into his mind and flooded his thoughts, and together with the host, he *danced*.

Chapter Thirteen

UNABLE TO VOICE a single noise or stop his body from stepping in perfect unison with the host, the only thing Brice could do was examine the host's face. His mask was mostly gold traced with fine filigree of black. The design was intricate but subtle and only visible now he stood close to the fae.

But the host himself, he was something worth remembering, if only so Brice might recall his expression when Brice ended this nightmare. A fine, smooth jaw. Soft lips, currently parted in a suggestive tilt. He appeared to be no older than Brice, but considering how the masquerade had been a yearly event since Brice's youth and the host had always been its central feature, his youthful appearance was clearly another mask. He could be twenty-five or five hundred.

His mask hid the upper half of his face, leaving just his eyes uncovered. Brice avoided peering too long into them, fearing whatever hold the host had on his body might take hold of his mind too. But he wanted to see, to study, to know the creature that had caught him in its web.

With every step and every beat of his heart, a warm, powerful throb of heat washed over him. He'd been without desire for so long that its allure was almost irresistible.

They stepped and twirled and dipped while Brice studied the host's terrible beauty. Eyes made of gold-ringed black pupils—gold and black, so dark, unlike the other fae here who adored color and light.

He wanted to yell at the fae. Wanted to hurt him. But he could do none of those things while the music played and they swirled. The touch of the fae's heavy hand burned its way through Brice's clothing into his skin, demanding attention. Brice focused on his fingers and tried to channel his strength into making them move to no avail. The fae's hold on his body was complete.

He couldn't see the crowd, couldn't see the other dancers, could only see the host, could only feel the movement and the music.

If Charon was trapped like this and had been for over a year, Brice feared for his brother's sanity. The reason for Sophia's madness became very clear and viciously real. There was no doubt she had endlessly danced for the host, and it had killed her.

Brice had vowed to bring her home. He'd failed.

But he would save Charon. This was still a victory. He was here. So close he could almost touch his brother. There would be a way to reach him. But to reach him, he had to stop the dance.

I'm here, Charon. You're not alone. I will end this nightmare.

Only a fool thinks to trick a trickster.

But a fool might succeed if the trickster underestimated them.

The fae fed on dreams. They offered the guests the one thing they truly desired for a single night. What did the host want? Why was he doing this? If he could discover what drove the fae, what all this was for, he might be able to bargain with him.

The dance went on and Brice's thoughts swirled. He became dizzy in his own mind, despite his vision of the host being startlingly clear. He was the marionette in a music box, just like Sophia. He should have danced with her, just one last time.

"You never need leave," the host said, although Brice didn't see his lips move. It had been so long he was no longer sure if he was dreaming. Or if any of this was real.

"The masquerade will satisfy your every desire."

The ballroom blurred behind the host, swirling and shining, its sparkles sharp like jagged briars reaching for him.

"What is it you want?" Brice asked the host inside his own mind.

Violins screeched, strings twanged. The dancers, the music, the host—they stopped. Everything stopped. The host's touch vanished. Brice gasped, thrown back into his own body.

He reeled and staggered, almost falling into another masked dancer. The world spun, his head dizzy and limbs heavy. All of the guests stared at him, their glares burning through their masks, under his clothes and skin, trying to unpick him, make him come undone. He wouldn't. He was still himself, still in control. He knew why he'd come, and he knew what had to be done.

"Charon?" he croaked. He was here; he had to be here. He whirled, searching the masked faces for one he knew. Charon's golden locks and his bow-like lips, his cherub's smile. He searched for those things. "Charon?" He pushed through the silent dancers. His brother had to be here. He *had* been here.

"Ladies, gentleman, fae." The host raised his voice, sending it out far above the heads of everyone here. Brice didn't look. He didn't care. He had to find Charon before the ungodly dance began again. "This evening is all yours." A resonate cheer went up and the crowd burst into motion, swallowing the host, vanishing him among them. The music played, different this time. People milled and chatted, some danced, but it wasn't wooden and fake like before.

Brice stumbled among them like a ship tossed about a stormy ocean, hating them all. Why did nobody aid him? Could they not see his distress? Or how all of this fantasy was poison?

"Charon? Call out! I'm here. I've come to take you home." The crowd mostly avoided him now, eager to step out of his way. They looked down their noses at him like he was mad, but he wasn't mad—they were for willingly stepping into this trap.

There! A man in a gray coat, his mask of white. Golden locks bounced as he laughed. Charon! Brice grabbed his arm and whirled him around. But the jaw was all wrong, the shoulders too heavy.

"M-my mistake." Brice backed away. The man glowered. His fae partner smirked.

They were the couple he'd seen on the dance floor. Not Charon. But his brother had been here. Brice was so sure.

He'd seen him.

He had to get away from the music and the laughter to clear his head. He shoved through a doorway, strode down a hall, and jogged down a flight of steps, entering gardens draped in moonlight and fireflies. There were others here but just a few, walking and talking among the enormous flowers. Nothing insidious. So far.

Stumbling, he propped his trembling body against a low wall and bent double, clutching his thighs. *Breathe.* His heart beat so loudly, surely all in the garden could hear it. He had not been prepared for *that*—for the host's absolute power over his body. Nobody could prepare for such a thing, to have one's will torn out and replaced by another's. The host could have had him do *anything* and he would have been powerless to stop him.

The host had made him weak. But there was something worse hidden in that sense of helplessness. A guilty realization that, briefly, the host's words had tempted him. Much about the fae had tempted him. What was there in his life worth going back to?

"You wear Raoul's mask."

Brice started.

Chantel leaned against the wall alongside him, holding a wineglass lightly between her fingers. Her blue dress gleamed. So did her eyes. He wanted to remove his damn mask and throw it at her, but that would not be the gentlemanly thing to do, and while the host had taken his wits, Brice had his control back for now.

Clearing his throat, he swallowed, smoothing his voice. "I found it."

"Hm." She sipped her drink, painting her lips red. "I believe *it* found you."

Well, that wasn't likely, seeing as Brice had been the one to discover it half-buried in leaves a year ago. "Where is Raoul? I must speak with him." Raoul had tried to seduce him, but the fae had at least been approachable. He might help Brice for a price. And if that price was something intimate, well then, so be it. Brice had lost Mother's pistol and almost lost more than that. He couldn't face the host again without help. He was running out of options.

Chantel's smile wasn't friendly. "He hasn't been seen in quite some time. Not since that night."

"What night?"

"The *last* night."

Wait... "The night a year ago?"

Chantel's left eyebrow arched. "A year for you, perhaps. It seems Raoul *lost* his mask."

Brice touched the mask in question. To lose one's mask was the greatest of crimes here. "Is he"—he almost couldn't bring himself to say the words—"being punished?"

"Oh yes, I expect so."

Well, that wasn't Brice's fault. But perhaps he could make it better and thus have the fae indebted to him? "What if I were to bring his mask back to him?"

"That would leave *you* without a mask, Brice LeChoix." She sipped her drink but kept her eyes on Brice, as though waiting for him to catch up.

"But he'd be grateful?" Grateful enough to help Brice find Charon?

Her eyes sparkled and her smile danced. "The unmasked are not welcome at the masquerade. You know this."

"Why? What's the point to all this?"

"The masquerade is a beautiful lie upon a lie. Nobody wants to be faced with the ugly truth of their insignificant lives."

Insignificant to the fae, perhaps. "Will you help me find my brother?"

"I cannot." She straightened and faced him. "I'm merely a tiny cog in this vast machine of the host's making. Your brother is likely deep within its gears."

"Can Raoul find him?" Brice was aware he sounded desperate, but he was rather beyond pretending not to be.

She cocked her head. "Perhaps."

"Then help me find Raoul and return his mask."

She studied him closely, her eyes cold. "It has been a very long time since a guest such as you has entertained me. I cannot determine whether you are foolish or mad. But I am curious to see where this ends, Brice LeChoix. I will help you, providing you do one thing for me."

"I'm not dancing."

"No." She laughed and offered the crook of her arm. "Come. I believe you will find my offer rather... stimulating."

He could not trust her, the same as he couldn't trust the very air he breathed, but so long as he remained alert and in control of his own will, he'd make it through this. He had to. Chantel was surely some kind of seductress in disguise. He knew that, so he wasn't blind. She'd offered him a deal to help find his brother, and that was exactly why he was here. What choice did he have but to take her offer?

At his hesitation she smiled and said, "I promise I will offer you only that which you desire."

"All right." He looped his arm in hers.

She downed the remainder of her wine and left the glass on the wall. "A tour of the garden, milord? After all, you have all the time in the world in just one night." Sharp teeth glinted behind wine-wet lips. "So let's begin to enjoy it."

Chapter Fourteen

THE GARDENS BLOOMED with impossible flowers, some larger than a man, others shaped like horns or huge tubes. Purple dominated, the color of autumn nights, but pinks and whites sprouted here and there. The air hung still. There was no wind here, no breeze to whisper. It made for an eerie quiet. But Brice would take that over the sound of the ballroom music any day or night.

The ghost of the host's hand at his hip still haunted him. As did the throb of desire the fae had summoned in his blood.

This entire event would haunt him, but nothing lasted forever. This night would pass. He'd survive, and he'd save Charon. He clung to that mission, locked it in his mind. He was ready to deal with the fae.

The path they walked down meandered through flower beds and took a small arched bridge over a trickling stream. Chantel led him along the water's edge to a pond hidden among reeds and weeping willows. Fireflies dallied in the air. At least, he thought them fireflies. He was tempted to reach out to catch one but feared the little creatures might bite.

"Here," Chantel said. "Look."

The pond had once been formal, but nature had crawled back in and blurred its edges—or whatever passed for nature in this place. An island at its center had probably once been a fountain. Latchly Hall had a pond just like it, all overgrown now too.

"What am I looking for?"

"Look into the water, Lord LeChoix."

The water's edge lapped at his scuffed shoes. His masked reflection looked back, but where his eyes should shine, only darkness loomed, as though his mask were empty. "I don't..." The water rippled and his reflection melted. A walking figure swept across the undulating surface. His arm stretched outward to receive his dance partner. The man was familiar, but as Brice tried to see his face, the reflection rippled and warped, obscuring his features. He pulled a woman into his arms, skimmed his touch over her shoulder and through her hair. She laughed and whispered against his cheek. Their love was a bright thing even in this dark place. They danced and whispered, stealing touches and kisses. The curve of her mouth, the sweep of her chin, so familiar...

With a gasp, he stumbled from the water's edge.

"Their love was a thing of true beauty," Chantel said softly. Unshed tears glistened in her eyes.

"No." He stepped to the edge again, and there they danced, the beautiful pair. So thoroughly in love that nothing could touch them. But tragedy had touched them. The fae had touched them and ruined their lives and his forever. "No!" Brice dropped to a knee and splashed the image away. No... the fae could not ruin his memory of them too.

"You look so like your father."

He stood and glared at her. "What is the point of this?"

"Only to show you how the masquerade does not revolve around you, little lord. Mortal lives have come before yours and will come after you. The dance never ends."

"It will end." He grabbed her wrist. "With me." *Enough games.* "Where is Raoul?"

Chantel tipped her head back. A cruel smile danced on her lips. "Didn't your mother ever tell you not to threaten the fae?"

The way she spoke, as though she knew so much more. "What do you know of my mother?"

Her smile widened. "Oh, Brice, your pistol and your hopeless honor cannot save you here. You run, but you are already caught." She pulled her wrist free.

The pond's surface rippled and bubbled. Shadows swayed and danced. Fireflies twirled from the brush. Brice backed up. There were others here. Things beneath the water. Things in the shadows. He had walked out here into the fringes of nowhere alone, with no weapon and no way out.

"You said you'd take me to Raoul," he snapped. "What is this?"

She laughed and the sound tinkled like china bells. "You didn't think it would be easy, did you?"

Something snagged his foot. He tripped but caught himself and whirled. The pathway *moved*, as though the pond water had flooded his only way out. To get back to the noise and light of the masquerade, he had to pass through it. It could only be a few inches deep. Just water… Why then did fear squeeze his heart?

Chantel's laughter bubbled around him. He glanced over his shoulder. Her dress rippled and flowed. Her mask shimmered, like water molded to her face. She had tricked him. She was some kind of water sprite, and he'd stupidly walked into her trap. Was everything here always a lie?

He stepped into the water.

The ripples flowed and faded. He didn't fall. Nothing happened.

Another step.

Another.

He ran. Something snagged his ankle, yanking his leg back. Brice fell forward. He hit the water, landing with his hands just a few inches beneath its surface. Roots looped around his fingers, tying themselves in knots around him. He fought to pull free, only to have them constrict. The roots climbed his arms, tugging him down. They crawled over his legs and looped around his thighs, thick and strong. "No…" Water splashed at his chin, rising higher. He tried to lever himself above its surface, but it lapped at his neck, his chin, his lips. It would drown him. He'd die here, vanishing like all the other forgotten people, and nothing would change. Nobody would care. "No! Stop!"

Chantel stepped around him. He arched his head back, barely able to keep his mouth and nose above the water. Her dress was the water now, the roots its threads. She controlled it all; she was drowning him.

She knelt and smiled. "Do not worry, milord. Death has no power here. But I do. Relax. I promise you'll like it."

Water bubbled through his lips and up his nose. He dared not breathe. His chest burned. His lungs screamed for air. Roots tangled around his waist, crushing him in their embrace, pulling him under.

Chantel stroked her fingers down his face. "Surrender and everything will be easier."

He closed his eyes. Water squeezed between his lashes. How had this happened? How had it come to this?

Heat thumped against the inside of his skull. His chest blazed. He had no choice. He had to *breathe*. He had to surrender. He opened his mouth—gasped. Suddenly weightless, he fell, tumbling through darkness. Once, long ago, he'd been in a carriage when its wheel had broken free. The carriage had rolled to the sound of screaming horses and shattering wood. There were no screaming horses here, just the sound of his own heart, but he felt the same tumbling weightlessness.

A sudden halt stunned him back to himself. He blinked, desperately trying to piece together his surroundings. He lay on a four-poster bed. Roots tied his limbs to each corner. Some unseen breeze rippled the sheer blue drapes. Shadows moved outside of them. Figures.

He panted hard, shivering, and flexed his fingers. The roots gave him little slack to move. He was caught, unable to free himself. But who had caught him? The host? Chantel?

Fingers slipped between the folds in the drapes, gently

easing them apart. A blond-haired man emerged, naked but for the golden mask hiding half his face. Brice swallowed and tugged at the roots holding his wrists. He wet his lips, about to demand the man free him, but it soon became clear this male was no mortal. Golden ink played across his bronze skin. It swirled in some places and in others it lay still. Brice blinked again, trying to put things right in his head. Tattoos did not move. But these did. The male's shoulders glistened wet, his hairless chest, too, and down over his abs where water gathered and dripped in tantalizing rivulets. He'd been one of the forms to rise from the pool. Then he was part of Chantel's offer?

This was... Brice swallowed hard. "Let me go."

The masked fae rested a knee on the edge of the bed.

Brice could not fail to notice the fae's erect member. He tore his gaze away. He should despise this, should be thinking of escape. He twisted his wrists, trying to fight. But his veins were hot with lust, his body already sizzling inside his clothes.

A second male parted the drapes to his right. This one was made of earthy skin with golden shimmering ink and tight black curls close to his scalp... and other places. His golden mask gleamed. He licked his lips. Brice blinked. The fae's tongue was split, like a snake's.

No, not real.

Oh, by heavens...

Brice squeezed his eyes closed. This was not real. It wasn't happening. He was drowning and dreaming, probably dying. This was some kind of lucid nightmare.

A firm hand touched his ankle.

He snapped open his eyes and looked down at the

blond. He was closer now and had risen up on his knees between Brice's spread legs. Honeyed eyes roamed seductively over Brice's body. His lips parted, and his tongue stroked over them—split, like the dark one's.

"W-wait..." Brice croaked.

Another male emerged through the drapes to his left, this one with hair of fiery orange and a body as pale as milk. His shifting ink was golden too, his face all sharp angles with prominent cheekbones, striking more than handsome.

Brice closed his eyes and shook his head. Perhaps when he opened his eyes, they'd be gone. *Wake up,* he told himself. *This isn't real. Wake up.*

I promise I will offer you only what you desire.

The blond's hands traveled up Brice's calves, bunching the trouser fabric. Brice kept his eyes squeezed closed. "Don't." His heart thumped in his throat, trying to choke him. His body burned, his blood heavy. The blond's touch stroked over his thighs, fingers kneading—and stopped.

A small whimper slipped unbidden from Brice's lips. It should have been a whimper of fear. But the real fear came from how much he wanted those hands to continue their path so they might meet where his cock already betrayed the truth behind his denials. They would surely see how his body wanted and would know every word he spoke to be a lie.

He hadn't come for this.

He knew it happened. He knew what went on here. But he didn't want it. This wasn't why—

The hands lifted off his legs and tackled Brice's trouser fastenings. Knuckles brushed his heated need. Brice bit into his lip. The fasteners were open. The fae's hand slipped in.

Fingers wrapped around his length, startling a gasp from his lips.

He snapped open his eyes. "Stop!" He fixed his glare on the blond. *Don't stop,* the truth in his head begged.

The fae smirked and brought his wet mouth down, sealing his lips over his member's leaking crown. Pleasure spilled down Brice's spine. His will to deny them failed. He arched toward the fae, filling his luscious mouth.

Brice tugged at the roots but not to writhe free—to get his hands on the males, for good or for bad, to touch. He ached for it. The want overcame him, emptied out his mind and filled his soul.

The fiery one licked at the corner of Brice's mouth. He didn't think, just turned his head and opened, letting the fae slide his forked tongue inside. Brice was falling again, only this time he welcomed it. *Surrender*, Chantel had said, and he was so tired of fighting for others, for a name he'd never wanted, for a house that buried him, for a brother who didn't care. What was freedom worth if he was cursed to spend a lifetime of it alone?

The earthy-skinned fae tore open Brice's shirt and sucked Brice's exposed nipple between his teeth. They were everywhere suddenly, lips and tongues and fingers, sucking, stroking, touching. There was no stopping it now. And Brice didn't want it to end. They knew his desires, knew it all, and finally, for the first time in forever, he willingly surrendered.

Chapter Fifteen

Brice still wore Raoul's mask, detaching him from who he was—from Brice LeChoix—making him faceless and nameless, removing all responsibility and guilt. If he was nobody, then none of this mattered. He could take it and relish it.

The earthy fae mouthed and kissed his neck. The fiery one kissed him like he fucked with his tongue. And the golden one used his remarkable forked tongue to stroke Brice's swollen, starved cock, lavishing attention where only snatches of pleasure had been given in the past. Brice had so little experience to draw from: a desperate adventure with the stable hand, a carriage driver one Christmas, and a paid-for encounter behind the Laughing Crow. Mostly Brice had only his imaginings and his own hand to relieve his urges—at least since Father had put a stop to Brice meeting his desires. But there was nothing to stop him now. He had them. Three of them. Sucking and fucking, and he was utterly at their mercy, tied and spread, surrendered for their taking.

Gold pulled his mouth from Brice's cock and prowled up his body. The other two wordlessly moved aside. Gold's body shimmered with glittery wetness. Brice ached to lick him, kiss him, grab him. Did he taste as sweet as he looked? All that muscle and slick skin, his member so proud a thing. Brice writhed on the bed and panted hard.

Gold reached down between them and did something with his hand, pulling on Brice's cock. Breathless, with his vision a blur, Brice peered down between their bodies. He was still clothed for the most part, although his garments had been pushed aside, whereas Gold was resplendent in his nakedness, his tattoos like brandings on his amber skin. Gold aligned Brice's cock with his own and somehow worked them both together, sheathing the two members as one, head to head. The gloriously wet sucking sensation came—not from Gold's mouth, but from his own glistening member *sucking* on Brice's. Gold smirked and rocked his hips. His cock teased Brice's, as Brice's must surely have been teasing his. Brice watched, bespelled by such a thing. He hadn't known it was possible. But was any of this real? Did Gold relish this as he did? Did he *want* this? Brice was the one tied down. Should he fear them? Perhaps he did, and perhaps he wanted that too.

Earth rubbed his member against an exposed strip of Brice's hip, leaving droplets of pearly precum. Brice flexed his hands, needing to hold, to touch, but the roots held fast. "Untie me," he growled out, but before any of them could reply, a shadow moved outside the drapes.

He turned his head to see who was there but was met with the stunning design of Fire's abdominal muscles and his delicious *V*, interrupted by the male's jutting cock. Fire dropped his hand. Green eyes behind a moss-colored mask locked on Brice. He knelt closer on the bed and stroked his cock over Brice's shoulder. Muscle rippled and glistened. The fae arched his back and rolled his hips in some rhythmic tease that had Brice transfixed. *Yes, come. Spill over me.*

Gold quickened his wicked trick with their conjoined cocks, pushing Brice's pleasure higher and higher. His heavy balls ached and his spine sizzled, tight with ecstasy. Earth slipped his thick finger beneath Brice's balls and entered. It was all and everything at once, too much and not enough. The figure still moved outside the drapes, a ghost, listening to the wet sounds of fucking and Brice's moans.

Fire bucked, stuttering a groan. Streams of come dashed Brice's chest. The fae's green eyes blazed through his mask, tugging on the last strings of Brice's pleasure. Brice tore his gaze away to keep from spilling, only to find the deep molten pools of Gold's glare. Gold laughed, and the sensory overload crested to an impossible high, crashing over Brice's restraints. He cried out, spine arched, and came as hard as he ever had, his cock spilling against Gold's. Gold slumped over him, gasping in Brice's ear. His slit tongue flicked over Brice's cheek, seeking a kiss.

The sweet, boneless ecstasy faded too soon. Guilt and shame and wrongness crept over him and burned where the fae had touched. Three men—not men, three *beings*. By heavens, what had he done?

Brice turned his face away. Earth smirked. Brice squeezed his eyes closed. This wasn't right. He hadn't come for this. He didn't want this, damn them!

The fae peeled off, one by one, and slunk away, back

through the wispy curtains. The quiet returned. No music, no chattering voices. He was finally alone with just his racing heart, his cooling body, and a horrible sense of shame urging him to crawl into himself and hide.

The roots at his wrists unraveled, setting him free, but he stayed on his back staring up at the bed's canopy. The evidence of Fire's climax cooled on his chest as well as the other places where they had spent over him. He swallowed, unsure what happened next. If he moved, did that make it all real? Shouldn't he be waking now, in the gloom of his chamber at home? If he wasn't waking, then what did that mean?

He carefully propped himself on his elbows. His clothes were askew, buttons missing. A strange, squirming sensation ate at his insides. It wasn't guilt. He knew guilt well. No, this was something else... It felt unclean. *He* felt unclean. Like a tool to be used and discarded, its purpose spent. Come dribbled down his chest.

He shoved from the bed and pushed through the drapes. Spotting the door, he hurried over and tried the handle. It rattled but didn't open. Locked.

A note pinned to the door caught his eye, written by the same swirling hand that had penned his name for years on the invites.

Brice,

You have my mask.

Meet at the bench, at your leisure.

Truthfully yours, Raoul

Raoul had been here? He'd witnessed *that*?

Fury burned away the horrible, wretched sickness. It mattered that Raoul had seen, although Brice didn't linger on why. The trio of fae had spoiled him, opened him up and exposed him, and left him used. He'd fallen into their trap and *liked it.* He could smell them and taste them again and his cock warmed, seeking more. Raoul would know everything, and he'd laugh. That thought stoked Brice's anger hotter. He scanned the room, searching for something, not knowing what. A weapon, a way out. No windows, of course. This was some hideous dungeon Chantel had dragged him to after somehow poisoning him, making him see things, stealing his will. A dresser, washbasin, and the bed—he tore his gaze from the bed.

The door lock clunked.

He tried the handle again and this time the door opened. Throwing it all the way open, he stepped out into a candlelit hallway expecting to see whoever had unlocked it, but he stood alone.

Stepping back inside, he tore the note from the door and thrust it into his pocket, then frowned at his disheveled shirt. He reeked of sex, of sweetness and sin. Anyone just had to glimpse him to know what he'd done.

He washed off at the basin as best he could and straightened his clothes, rebuilding the illusion of being in control even as his hands trembled. There was nothing to be done for the missing buttons or the unseen stain of shame. He had to live with those until he could leave this wretched place. Dampening down his hair, he straightened his shoulders and lifted his chin. Lord Brice LeChoix. Heir to nothing. Come to take his brother home.

He would not fail in this.

"I'm not afraid of the fae," he told the empty room.

Somewhere far away, someone laughed. Someone who sounded very much like Raoul.

Chapter Sixteen

He wandered the elegant hallways searching for a way out. Raoul's note had failed to mention how to find the night garden again. A few masked people glanced over as he passed. The ones who smiled like hungry cats were fae. He passed closed doors and ignored the sounds of gasps and slapping skin coming from within. He wasn't the only one being seduced.

His skin tingled where the trio had touched him—kissed him, laid their hands on him. There was no time to dwell on it. If he allowed himself to think, he feared his guilt might overwhelm him. If Father were alive to find out, Brice would face the barrel of his rifle again. Even after his death, Brice feared disappointing the man.

Spotting a curved staircase, he quickened his pace and began to climb. He'd assumed the room he'd been... molested in, was underground. He recalled falling *into* it. Therefore, going up the stairs made logical sense. But as the staircase spiraled around, corkscrewing higher, it seemed as though logic had fled this place. There had to be an end, didn't there? Stairs could not climb forever.

A fae jogged down the steps toward him.

"Sir, excuse me, the way to the ballroom?" Brice asked.

The fae looked him over from head to toe, laughed, and continued down. Leaning over the banister, Brice watched the fae's hand run along the spiraling rail—around and around, water down a drain.

This place was playing tricks on his mind. Nothing made sense here.

He climbed and climbed. A door slammed somewhere high above. Stopping to catch his breath, he grasped the banister and peered up through the void. A man stood several flights above wearing black and gold. The host. His black-and-gold mask made him unmistakable.

Brice quickly stepped back out of sight. Minutes passed, and when he looked again, the host was gone.

After climbing a few more flights, he came upon a rose-lined archway through which the sounds of people and laughter bubbled. Finally. Straightening his clothes and hair, he lifted his chin again, centered his thoughts, calmed his heart, and ventured through the arch and into an icy courtyard. Countless candles were scattered about the tables, illuminating an otherwise dark, walled-in garden. A fae juggled for her rapt crowd, performing impossible tricks. Applause fluttered through the air. Brice skirted their revelry, in no mood to blend in among them.

The people were like children, led along by the hand, lulled into believing they were safe.

The masquerade had layers. Brice feared he'd only touched the surface. He had no wish to dive any deeper.

Coming upon the main building, he found the ballroom, kept his head down, and quickly passed through the crowds, heading back outside. The night garden was as he'd remembered. The same flowers turned their heads toward starlit skies, their pollen misting the air. He steered away from them, keeping to the middle of the gravel path. There were others here, standing intimately close. He forced his gaze ahead. He would not be led astray again.

The path took a left turn toward the covered bench. And sure enough, Raoul was there. He rested one booted leg on the seat, peering out at some part of the garden Brice didn't care to see. It had been a year since he'd last seen the fae in the flesh and not in his dreams, but it felt like yesterday. Raoul wore a perfectly fitted black tailcoat frosted with silver lace that accentuated his slim figure. His black braid lay over one shoulder and would reach down his back had it been left to swing free. His purple mask with a lower veil of sheer fabric clashed with his outfit—obviously not his.

Brice's heart quickened. Raoul was the only one here who might help him. For a price.

Clearing his throat drew the fae's eye.

Raoul lowered his boot, straightening. His lips twitched into a smile, although it could also have been a sneer. In the shadows, it was difficult to tell. The veil section of the mask hid his expression. His eyes, though, were clear. Purple and blue, with full dark pupils and long black lashes. So delicate. They were likely the only delicate things about this creature.

"About what you saw..." Brice began, keeping his voice low. Although their corner was hidden from the rest of the garden, noise traveled far.

Raoul's smile cracked. "You think I care who you fuck? Fuck a tree if you wish, although I do not recommend it." He strode closer and met Brice on the path, stopping a little too close. Brice held the male's gaze, keeping his chin up. Raoul had seen Brice in the throes of passion, being serviced by three of his kind. Brice had lost the moral high ground and felt the heat in his face to prove it. The smirk on the fae's lips seemed to be a permanent fixture. Or had it grown some?

Raoul held out his right hand. "Return my mask." With his left, he reached for the mask he wore. "I've brought a replacement. The exchange must be quick so it goes unnoticed."

Raoul's mask was the only chance Brice might have at bargaining but now he faced him, he wasn't entirely sure what to say. He'd expected the smooth-talking, sultry fae from before. Raoul wasn't interested in anything but the mask. Once their transaction was over, he'd leave and Brice would be stranded.

"No."

Raoul's hand stalled near his mask. "What?"

"I want your word first."

"What word?" he sneered, teeth flashing behind the veil.

Brice's heart thumped. "Help me free Charon."

Raoul's sudden sharp laugh echoed about the garden. "Your brother is beyond help."

No. No, that couldn't be. Charon was alive. He was sure of that. And so he could be found, he could be saved, and no trickster fae was going to deter him. Brice folded his arms. "Then I shall keep your mask."

Raoul's pretty kohl-lined eyes narrowed. "Fine." He tossed a hand and lifted his chin. "I don't need it."

Well, that had to be a lie. Chantel had said Raoul was being punished for losing his mask. "But you do. Or you would not be here. Also, the one you're wearing truly does not suit you."

Raoul paced a few short strides across the path and back again. His heeled boots crunched on gravel. "You do not know what it is you ask."

"I'm not asking. I'm bargaining. This is a transaction. Help me and I'll hand over the mask."

"Help you how?" Raoul snapped. "Be specific. Vagueness leaves room for misunderstandings, and trust me, *milord*, we do not want any misunderstandings." He mocked with his tone while his eyes flashed their warnings.

"Help me find Charon and get him free of this place."

The hardness in Raoul's gaze and his body began to thaw and the smooth, sweet-talking fae from their first meeting returned. "You assume he wants to be free?"

"He certainly doesn't want to be trapped here at the mercy of your kind for the rest of his life."

"No?" He lifted a shoulder and tilted his head. "You seemed to be enjoying yourself."

Heat flushed Brice's face, making him grateful for the mask and the shadows they stood in. "That wasn't—What you saw... it wasn't voluntary. I did not want that. I made a bargain for a fae to bring me to you and that's—" His voice cracked. He cleared it. "What you saw was the result. I was tricked," he said stiffly.

"Well, she did deliver you to me." Raoul stepped close again, too close. Almost touching. He met Brice's gaze eye to eye through their masks. He seemed to be searching for something. But whatever that thing was, it eluded him. "A bargain fulfilled, no?"

"I didn't ask for..."

"You certainly agreed. Your name, LeChoix—means choice, does it not?" the fae asked, so close now that to others their discussion might appear more intimate.

"It does." Brice fought with himself not to step back.

Raoul's gaze lingered, peering deep. All the colors in his eyes sparkled. "Very well. I will help you find and free Charon from this place, Brice LeChoix. Now hand over my mask."

Finally, an ally. And a step closer to saving Charon.

"Hurry, before we are observed." Raoul placed his fingers on the front of his mask, dislodging it. As the mask came away, Brice saw the whole design of Raoul's face for the first time. His eyes burned with emotive intensity. His cheekbones cut a profile the finest artists in all of Massalia would struggle to capture. A fine nose swept to soft lips, making him not just beautiful but breathtaking. He was surely made so pretty to seduce. Was his face another mask designed to lure people in?

His gaze slid catlike to Brice and his lips curved into a sly smile. "My mask, Lord LeChoix?"

Brice blinked and quickly pulled Raoul's mask free. "I'm sorry about the... it broke," he stammered, fussing over the torn silk tie.

Raoul took the mask, shoved the purple one into Brice's hands, and with a twirl of his fingers, the silk ties danced together, mending themselves. Raoul affixed the mask to his face in one smooth motion. He sucked in air through his teeth, filling his lungs, and his smile grew. Some of the mischievous glint in his eyes returned. It was that glint that had been missing before, when he'd been without his original mask.

"Wear your mask, Brice. Lest the host see your face and I have two hapless LeChoix lords to save."

"Yes, of course." Like a fool, he'd been staring. Raoul was impossibly even more alluring now his mask had been returned. The mask didn't just change his face; it had changed how he moved. His choppy, anxious steps from earlier were gone, replaced by slow, deliberately seductive movements, more like those of a dancer who knew where and how to place his every step.

Rather clumsily, Brice tried to put the mismatched mask on. It didn't quite fit and felt heavy on his nose. The veil fluttered over his lips. He hated it. But he had no choice.

"Hm, allow me?" Raoul swooped in, took the mask's ties, and adjusted it on Brice's face. The fae was suddenly intimately close. Close enough to kiss, although Brice would never do such a thing. He'd had his fill of lust for one night—maybe forever. Still, the male's proximity made his skin tingle as though Gold and Earth and Fire were here with him, sweeping their tongues across his skin. He'd been starved of intimacy for so long, and now it appeared to be everywhere, thrown carelessly at him, unbalancing him.

Raoul's light fingers briefly skimmed his cheek and jaw as he fitted the mask—the accidental touch stole a beat from Brice's heart. The thrill of it came from this place, these people. They had a hold over the senses. But he was aware of it now. He could fight it. Mostly. What had happened *below* the masquerade wouldn't happen again.

Raoul didn't appear to notice Brice's internal wrangling. If he had, he'd have probably made some crude remark. He seemed the sort.

"Hm." Raoul stepped back and frowned. "No. This really will not do." He cast a glance into the garden, then flipped Brice's new mask off. "Wait here."

Unmasked, Brice opened his mouth to tell him to stop, but Raoul had already vanished down the path. He could do nothing but wait and backed up to the bench. The creeping sensation of being watched grew. To be unmasked at the ball was to incite the host's ire. Everyone knew the rule. Maybe this was Raoul's plan, to steal his mask and leave Brice stranded?

No, he'd made a deal. Mother had told him the fae did everything they could to wriggle out of commitment, but their word was their bond. Their code dictated they could not break a bargain.

"Ah." Raoul returned with a grin and waved a new mask in his hand, this one mostly gold with black accents. It reminded Brice a little too much of the forked-tongued Gold, who had so thoroughly fucked him not so long ago, but admittedly it was better than the purple veiled mask. And it matched his outfit.

"Whose is that? Won't they miss it?"

"Never mind that." Raoul stood close again, tying the mask on with deft fingers. His breath fluttered over Brice's lips. Before Brice's mind could wander again, Raoul stepped back. "There." His appreciative gaze lingered. "Hm," he purred. "Delightful." Raoul's grin sobered. "However, you are ill-equipped for the task at hand. Perhaps with some luck you might survive what is it come. Are you a lucky man, my lord?"

Luck was not something Brice had much faith in. He preferred to make his own. "I've come this far."

"Indeed. Well, at least you've done one right thing."

"Which is?"

"Meeting me, of course." He bowed with flair and straightened, flashing his dazzling grin. "Your guide for the evening. At your service."

Brice had to fight to keep himself from smiling. The fae carried a joy about him that might almost be infectious. "And is meeting you a stroke of good luck or bad?"

Raoul offered his hand and fluttered his lashes. "Darling, we're about to find out."

Chapter Seventeen

"Some food, I think." Raoul swept by the long banquet table, scooped up a tiny morsel of food, popped it in his mouth, and swallowed it in one. He quickly continued. "And wine. Much wine." He collected two glasses and turned to present one to Brice. "You're going to need it."

They were back in the ballroom, surrounded by guests, color, light, and music. Brice watched Raoul upend a glass and swallow its entire contents in a single gulp.

Brice was thirsty. Not hungry so much, too many butterflies, but he needed water—not wine. "No, thank you. I've had my fill of poison."

He grinned and set the empty glass down. "You believe Chantel poisoned you?"

"I know she did." He didn't want to discuss it and scanned the dancers instead, looking for Charon.

"Easier to blame it on poison than choice?" Raoul leaned against the banquet table and folded his arms.

"I didn't choose to be tied down and *have that happen*,"

Brice whispered. "It doesn't matter. What matters is finding my brother."

Raoul cast him a sideways glance that seemed to say a great deal without him having to say a word. "Let us begin at the beginning then." He downed the second glass of wine in a single go and bowed low with a rolling hand flourish. "Dance with me, Lord Brice LeChoix." His long black braid flopped over his shoulder. Laced inside the plait, a lock of silver shone. Brice hadn't noticed it before, but having seen it now, he couldn't look away. Silver and black, just like his mask, like his clothes. So perfect, not a frayed thread or strand of hair out of place. His perfection could not be real. Nothing in nature was without imperfection. So what was this fae's real face like? Who was he behind the mask?

Raoul lifted his head, keeping his hand extended for the taking, and winked. "Now or never, hm?"

A circle of guests watched on, intrigued by the flamboyant fae and whether Brice would refuse him. Brice's smile felt wooden. "I'd prefer not to." He had no wish to dance again, especially if it meant catching the host's eye.

Raoul straightened, caught Brice's hand, and took a single sweeping step toward him, applying his hand to Brice's waist just as the host had done. And now they stood together in the dancing pose, poised to begin. "You made a deal," Raoul whispered against Brice's ear. "And this is how we do it. Trust me."

"Trust you?" He laughed around the heavy thud of his heart in his throat. "I am not mad. Not yet."

"What is madness?" Raoul stepped back, and with little choice, Brice stepped with him. Raoul backed up again, drawing Brice along. Suddenly, they were among the dancers and *moving*. Raoul led to the beat of the music, sweeping Brice with him. The dance was one Brice knew well, although Raoul had him in the woman's position. "Madness might be one thing to some, and something else to another," Raoul added.

"Madness is this nightmare." The rhythm had caught him. Raoul *made* it easy. Made it enjoyable. A good dancer could carry a bad one. He'd suspected Raoul could dance, and Brice hadn't been wrong. Raoul moved as though he were made of music, as though its beat was his own.

"Madness is clinging to a legacy while it drowns you." Raoul's eyes flashed their sly delight.

Did he speak of Brice's life? No, surely not. He couldn't know anything of what was outside the masquerade. "Madness is trusting anything I see here is real, including you."

Raoul chuckled. "Well, if this is madness, isn't it time we had a little fun with it?"

The music quickened. The dance sped up. The beat lived within Brice, in Raoul's warm hands, in the sway of his hips. It was curiously intimate, but after the stifling dance from before, dancing with Raoul felt liberating. There was no force, no coercion. He could stop this at any time. And therein lay its pleasure. Brice caught himself smiling.

"Ah, there it is." Raoul's voice rumbled, not quite a whisper but close. "A real smile."

The dancers around them laughed and spun. Some took a misstep and giggled at their mistakes. It appeared to be harmless enjoyment, but Brice couldn't forget the host's hold over him. "The masquerade is the host's music box," Brice whispered, "and you are all its dancers."

"*We* are its dancers. You're among us now."

A touch of fear almost tripped his stride.

"Or"—Raoul brightened—"think of the masquerade like a cake. What you see here is its elaborate icing. The smooth finishing touches hiding its imperfections beneath." Raoul's hand slipped from Brice's hip, around his waist, and drew him close. They swayed, groin to groin, and Brice found himself forgetting the steps or barely hearing the music. The dance had become an afterthought. Raoul consumed his consciousness. The feel of him pressed close, the sweet jasmine smell of him, the shimmer of that silver streak, and the colors of his beautiful eyes. He had to remind himself how Raoul wasn't real—at least, this Raoul wasn't. But so long as Brice didn't forget that, where was the harm in enjoying just one dance?

"To reach your brother, we first must find him." Raoul spoke close to Brice's cheek, brushing the words against his skin. Brice's heart thumped. This was intimate but not in a sexual way.

"The cake has layers. Dreams within dreams." Raoul spoke low, his voice just above a whisper. They were hiding here, among the dancers.

"Layers made of razors and thorns?" Brice wondered aloud.

Raoul turned his head, bringing his masked face close. "You know more than you let on."

"My mother knew the way of the fae."

"Did she?" His lashes fluttered. The music rippled, and the dancers danced. Around and around. "Look at me, Brice, not them."

He did and swallowed. The dizziness passed, but now he was trapped staring into Raoul's gaze. His smile had vanished and when that happened, Raoul turned into someone else. Someone cold. The coldness wasn't aimed at Brice, though. For the first time, some glimmer of truth showed through. How long had Raoul been a dancer for the host? How long had he been trapped in these layers?

"First, we find your brother. Then we pry him from the host's grip. Neither of those tasks will be easy."

Nothing had come easy to Brice. Not in reality, so why would this fantasy be any different?

"Brice?"

Dizziness wobbled Brice's focus. Perhaps it was all catching up with him or perhaps there was more poison at work. Whatever the reason, he had to leave the floor before he fell. "I... please, stop?"

Annoyance pinched Raoul's brow, but he wordlessly led Brice from the floor. Finding a chair, Brice clutched its back and bowed his head, focusing on breathing. What was wrong with him? His limbs felt leaden. Shivers chilled him. "What is this?"

"Exhaustion, I suspect." Raoul propped his ass on the arm of the chair. "I did offer you food."

"But I've only been here a few hours."

Raoul breathed in through his nose and cast his gaze out, into the crowd. "You are mortal. Beautiful only for a short time. You wilt, like a flower, if not fed and watered." A server passed by them. Raoul plucked a glass from her tray. "Drink. Or you'll be of no use to your brother."

Brice eyed the glass and its sparkling golden contents. "How do I know it's not poison?"

With a long-suffering sigh, Raoul took a sip himself and offered the glass again. "Perfectly adequate."

Thirst strangled him. As did fighting the inevitable.

"Darling." Raoul sighed. "If I were to poison you, it would be with more imagination than a glass of wine."

That wasn't exactly comforting. "Like the pollen in the garden?" Brice took the glass.

Raoul grinned. "Exactly."

Brice raised the wine to his lips and tasted it. If it were poisoned, would he even taste its wrongness? Mother had always said to never accept gifts from the fae, never to eat or drink anything they offered. But like everything else here, what choice did he have? He swallowed. His body took over, demanding he sate his thirst. He emptied the glass in a few breathless seconds and slumped against the wall. He just needed a moment to gather his wits.

Pressing the cool glass to his cheek below his mask, he focused on his breathing, aware of how Raoul had taken up his perch against the arm of the chair and watched him with those keen colorful eyes of his. His mask suited him more than it had Brice. It belonged on his face. Silver and black.

"How did you lose your mask?" Brice asked.

"A mistake. I make them sometimes." He stroked a piece of fluff from his thigh. "Rarely, you understand."

"I found it outside last year, after the masquerade had ended."

Raoul lifted his head and looked away. The muscle in his cheek fluttered. "Let us focus on your brother—"

"Can you ever leave?"

Raoul's stare cut back to Brice. "Does the ballerina ever leave her music box?"

He was trapped here too? Did that mean they were all trapped here—pretty fae with their seductive touches and alluring glances, with their promises and games—they were all the masquerade's prisoners? The townsfolk used the masquerade as an escape, used the fae... If they were trapped, that perspective changed things.

"Why?" Brice whispered. "Why is all this happening? Why is the masquerade here? Why does it ruin lives?"

"It began with love," Raoul said softly. "But it did not end with it."

Love? What part could love play in any of this madness?

A ripple passed through the dancers. Their colors flared brighter. The chandeliers grew sharper, candlelight guttering under a gust of restless wind.

The host carved his way through the crowd. The music still played, but an off-key note tripped through its rhythm. Dancers twirled, colors blurring.

Raoul caught Brice's hand. "Come," he whispered, guiding Brice along the wall toward the night garden's doors. "Before we are seen."

"We have an uninvited guest among us." The host's voice rose like a wave over the music until it cut it off. Silence plunged in.

Raoul shoved at Brice. "Go!" The doorway was just a few steps away, blocked by staring guests.

"Raoul?"

The name on the host's lips jerked Raoul to a stop like a dog on a leash. He dropped Brice's hand. His eyes flared a warning for Brice to leave. Everyone turned, the swish of fabric so loud it sounded like thunder.

Raoul took a step back, then another. Fear flickered behind his mask. Then with a forced smile, he spun on his heel and marched toward the dance floor, drawing the crowd's collective gaze with him.

Brice swallowed, staying back. For now, everyone appeared to be more interested in Raoul than him.

"I do not recall inviting you." The host stood in the center of the floor, his mask on as before. The same heavy throb of power accompanied him. Much like the pollen in the garden, his presence tainted the air, making it bitter on Brice's tongue. The host stood taller than Raoul, but they appeared similar in their dark clothing, the host's accented with gold against Raoul's silver.

Raoul dropped to a knee and bowed his head. When he looked up, his lips didn't hold his smile. "My mask has been returned. Everything is restored. I thought—"

"That decision to release you from punishment is mine, not yours."

"Of course." He bowed his head again. "Forgive me."

The host plunged his hand into Raoul's hair and jerked the fae off his feet, bending him backward, exposing the arch of Raoul's throat. Raoul's hand went to his hair, holding where the host grasped him. His teeth gritted, his pain clear.

Brice lurched forward but stalled. He could not stand against the host.

Some knowing passed between the two fae. Of course they *knew* each other, but it was more than familiarity. Raoul's glare burned with hatred. And the host returned its fervor in kind.

Brice could not get involved. None of this was his concern. Only one thing mattered—

The host tore Raoul's mask from his face and tossed it to

the floor. Countless gasps echoed in the now-silent ballroom. "Clearly, the punishment was not sufficient."

Raoul's unmasked face twisted with fury, turning his beauty sharp. "I welcome it."

Why provoke him so?

Brice recalled his wits. The crowd watched the host, fae and mortal alike. *Everyone* watched the host and the scene unfolding. Brice could slip away unnoticed, but he still did not know where or how to find Charon. His dance with Raoul had told him nothing. He was no closer to saving his brother now than he had been when he'd first arrived. But he had made a bargain. Only Raoul could help him. If the host punished Raoul, hid him away down in those rooms, Brice's only chance at saving his brother might be lost for another year. Charon might not last another year. Brice certainly wouldn't, not alone in Latchly Hall.

There was only one thing to do.

Brice straightened his shirt cuffs and forced his way through the crowd. "I took Raoul's mask. So—" He swallowed, acutely aware of how everyone now observed him. The host's glare skewered him to the spot, like a butterfly to a board. "His punishment should be mine."

Chapter Eighteen

All the fae leered, grossly pleased with this new entertainment. All but the host. He frowned through his mask and threw Raoul to his feet. Raoul grabbed the mask, hastily put it back on, and fixed Brice under his own disapproving gaze. "That man is a fool," Raoul declared. "He does not know the meaning of his offer."

"All men are fools," the host replied.

Brice lifted his chin. He was no fool, but he was desperate. Chantel had said death did not belong here. The fae did not kill their guests; they allowed the real world to do that for them. So, what possible punishment could the host administer? More dancing? He'd take it. He'd already been spread and fucked and shamed. What else could the host take?

The host stepped around Raoul kneeling on the ground. Raoul bowed his head. Brice didn't see the rest. The host was now in front of him, filling his vision. Filling his whole world.

"I knew a man like you, brimming with pride and

honor. A foolish man who did not understand the perils he toyed with. A child playing with a wolf, unaware of its bite."

Brice looked into the same cold eyes he'd had when they'd danced. And like with Raoul, there was old knowledge there. An understanding that passed Brice by. Something was happening here, some shift in dynamics, more layers he was unaware of. More razors and thorns.

But he needed Raoul. He needed this all to be over.

The host's small leisurely smile grew from the corner of his mouth. He held out a hand to someone in the crowd, and one of the serving fae brought her tray over. On top lay a cat-o'-nine-tails. A leather whip with multiple ends—nine lashes in one. Brice only knew its name after reading about the archaic punishment at school. "This gives me no pleasure."

A whipping? Good lord. He'd thought them civilized.

Brice straightened even as his heartbeat tried to deafen him and his hands shook. "None of this brings you pleasure, does it?" That was what was missing from the host whenever Brice had laid eyes on him. The host stood apart from the others, a cloud on a summer's day, because their laughter and joy and delight didn't touch him. Brice knew that feeling well.

"What happened to you?" he asked.

Love, Raoul had said. *It began with love. But it did not end that way.*

The host swept the whip from the tray and nodded. Two male fae pushed from the crowd. Thick fingers sank in as they grabbed Brice's arms.

Their roughness rattled his resolve. He was about to be whipped like an animal. It would hurt, probably more than anything Brice had endured. But he'd take it. Deserved it, even.

"Wait." Raoul—back on his feet—stepped forward. "He is mortal. Fragile. Their kind cannot withstand—"

The host whirled and raised the whip as though to bring it down on Raoul. Raoul winced, expecting a blow. Gasps peppered the crowd.

"I know who and what Brice LeChoix is," the host growled. His body trembled, too, but not from fear. Terrible, choking power boiled around him. "Perhaps you should have thought of that, Raoul, before leaving your mask for him to find?" The host raised the whip, cracking it in the air, and brought its tails down on Raoul's shoulder with thunderous force. Raoul dropped to his knees. The whip came down again. He buckled under it.

"Stop—" Brice tore from the pair of fae holding him and grabbed at the host's raised arm. The host shoved him away as though he were nothing and brought the tails down on Raoul again, barely missing a beat. Raoul—on his hands and knees—buried under the blows. His fine black-and-silver clothing darkened with blood. Another lash landed. His hair spilled from its braid, the silver line a defiant slash in the darkness.

Brice readied to plunge in again when the host turned his face toward him. "If you wish to ever see your brother again, do not interfere."

The words hit him as sharply as a lash of that whip. He stumbled, rocked backward by their verbal blow. Charon was alive? He was here?

The host waited for Brice's reply and his next move.

Blood dripped from the whip's tails. Raoul's breaths sawed out of him.

This wasn't Brice's fight.

Besides, he had no weapon to fight the host with.

He grimaced at the host and backed away. The crowd closed in, filling the void he'd left behind, blocking his view. But the horrid sounds of the lashing went on, turning wet as each new blow rained blood.

Brice's feet carried him away, out of the ballroom, into the night garden. He had to get out of here, get Charon away, go home, where none of this madness could reach either of them. With Charon's help, they'd fix the house together, make it right again. Make their lives right again. Far, far away from this madness.

He staggered down the path. Snowflakes fluttered through the air, silently landing on the flowers. He reached out to catch one. It landed on his palm and stayed there, unmelting, so intricate and delicate in its beauty. One landed on his finger. It was a snowflake for sure, like the others dancing around him, but this one was blood red. Another pirouetted from above, dancing with its white companions. More fell until most of the falling snow was red, not white. It settled on the path, his clothes, the grass, turning the world red.

Blood snow. His shoes crunched through it. Could it be real? He was losing his mind. The masquerade was turning him inside out, working its way under his skin. Every breath invited more of it inside, every second stole another piece of his mind. He feared he might never escape if he lingered too long.

"Quickly, this way." Chantel waved from behind a crumbling stone archway.

He frowned at the temptress. Like before, she looked sweet and helpful, but that was how she'd caught him. "Not after the last time."

"Oh, Brice." Her laughter tinkled. "You got what you asked for, did you not?"

"I didn't ask to be used like a piece of meat!"

"Did I not take you to Raoul, as was our bargain?"

He sneered. "I should throttle every one of you and be done with it."

"I do not think that would end well for you."

"Do you know what's happening back there? Do you know what's being done to him? It's wrong. You're all monsters."

"Come away now." She gestured through the arch. It appeared to lead into a narrow tunnel, but there was no way of knowing where that tunnel led. To another torture room where more fae would fuck him hollow?

"I'd be a fool to go with you."

"I'd argue you're already one. So what do you have to lose?"

He huffed. "No."

"Consider your options. Come with me, and you'll be a step closer to those things you seek, or stay here and wander the gardens, each step taking you farther from the truth."

He swallowed and glanced behind him. The gardens were muffled by the thick blanket of red snow. It was a hellscape, surely. He was the only one out there. Alone. He wasn't even sure he knew the way back. "I should wait for Raoul," he said quietly.

"Raoul will be indisposed for some time." She emerged from the undergrowth in her fine blue gown and offered her hand, peering through blue-tinged lashes. The pearls along the edges of her mask rippled. "What is it you fear, Brice? Nothing here can hurt you if you do not wish it."

Was there any going back? He had come too far to turn around.

He could not leave, so really, forward was the only way.

He took Chantel's hand and followed her into the tunnel.

Chapter Nineteen

The tunnel began as a steep descent. Brice slipped a few times on the loose gravel, but the floor soon evened out and opened into a candlelit chamber, one that wasn't man-made. The stream that flowed along the back wall had carved the space over hundreds of years. Glass jars had been strung from alcove to alcove high above their heads. Trapped fireflies danced inside, illumining the domed ceiling, making its natural salts sparkle. It was equal parts magical and... sad. This did not feel like part of the masquerade. It felt like a hole in the ground someone had adopted for their home. Stacks of books made impromptu tables for a collection of empty bottles. This was somewhere hidden away from the lies and the pomp and fantasy of the masquerade. Somewhere... *real*.

"Come. Sit," Chantel said. "Wait for Raoul."

He wasn't sure what to make of the place. A new trick, or some honesty for once? He sat at the bench beside the simple timber table. Chantel pushed a bowl of fruit toward him and nodded. "Go on. Mortals must eat."

He wasn't sure he could bring himself to after seeing what he had inside the ballroom, but he gave her his thanks all the same.

"It is better for you to hide for a little while until the furor dies down. You'll be safe here, unmolested. You can sleep if you wish."

"Sleep?"

"You must be tired."

He couldn't sleep here or anywhere at the masquerade. "I'm fine. Thank you."

She plucked a grape from the bowl and popped it into her mouth, watching him closely. From her lascivious smile, she clearly had something on her mind. Whatever it was, he preferred she keep it to herself. She had been the one to instigate the bedchamber incident with the trio. Did she know the details of what had transpired? She smiled like she did.

Brice rubbed at his arms and cast his gaze about the chamber. His chill had more to do with shock, he suspected. His hand brushed a slip of paper in his pocket. He pulled it free.

Raoul's note, pinned to the door after he'd witnessed Brice at the mercy of the trio. Unfolding it, he read the words again.

Truthfully yours.

It seemed like days ago, not hours. What was it Chantel had said? The masquerade was like a machine? Everyone had their own analogy to explain it. But one thing was certain: the more Brice tried to grasp the workings of the place, the more it turned to sand and slipped through his fingers. Had it been hours or days?

"Raoul said it began with love." He met Chantel's gaze and saw her glance down.

"It did. A celebration of love. Rumor is only true love can end it. Do you know love, Brice?"

His frown gave her his answer before any reply could. He wasn't sure he was destined for love, at least not the traditional kind between a woman and a man. He didn't think he was broken. His lusts ran differently to most, but they had never felt wrong. Others thought him wrong. Some would have called him foul, had Father not gone to great lengths to buy off any witnesses or participants in Brice's *incidents*. There was no room for love as the LeChoix heir.

"A fae's love is a fierce thing," Chantel said. "Everlasting. Consuming. It outshines stars and outlives mountains."

Brice plucked a grape from the rest, chewed, and swallowed. It tasted normal, like a grape should taste. If it was going to poison him, so be it. He was too exhausted to jump at shadows.

"So when love goes wrong, it can darken those stars and level those mountains." She kicked her boots up on the table and teetered her chair on its back legs.

"Or create a masquerade where all its guests are trapped and made to dance forever for a monster?"

"Not all. Most get to go home and live their lives, dreaming of the exotic. Just those who wrong the host never leave."

She made it sound perfectly reasonable. Did she not see the wreckage it created or just not care? "What did my brother do to wrong the host? What did Sophia do? She's dead. Threw herself out a window trying to get back to this wretched place. What did she do that was so wrong the masquerade had to shatter her heart and soul?"

Her playful smile twitched and died. "I'm sorry for your friend."

"If it began with love, how did it go so wrong as to create all this?"

"She left him—the host's mate. Or he banished her for some terrible indiscretion. I'm not sure anyone remembers. We were all there, enjoying the freedom of the ball. But when she left, banished or abandoned, she cursed the host to live in misery forever. Never to taste joy again."

That didn't sound like the love Brice had seen in others or read about in books. It sounded like obsession. But he was no expert in matters of the heart. He just knew he had one, and that it ached when alone. "A mate is...?"

Chantel sighed. "Mortals," she said mockingly. "A mate is... our other half, our missing piece." She paused and studied Brice's face. "No, you wouldn't know. Not yet."

"Then tell me."

"A connection between two people, on all levels, soul"—she curled her fist over her sternum— "heart"—over her chest—"and mind," and touched her forehead.

"Then it's love?"

"More than love." She tutted. "The mortal mind cannot

comprehend. When a mate bond is broken, it shatters the individual, devastating those around them. Thus began the masquerade." Chantel leaned forward. "*Come to the masquerade. Spend a night in revelry and laughter and lust,*" she said mockingly. "It ends for your kind. You come, you wear the masks, and you leave, but for us this night never ends. We cannot leave, Lord LeChoix, and we cannot choose, and we cannot remember. We are all cursed."

The scatter of gravel and scuff of boots signaled someone's approach down the tunnel entrance. Brice stood, expecting some horrible trick or perhaps one of the trio he'd been so thoroughly acquainted with, but Raoul stumbled into the room. He reached for the wall to steady himself, leaving a smear of blood behind. He still wore his mask, but his jacket was in tatters and blood dripped from its sodden edges. His fluttering gaze slid from Chantel to Brice. His sneer twitched.

Chantel didn't move to help him, just looked up as though he'd walked in for a glass of wine. He clearly needed aid. Brice tensed to help. Raoul staggered forward and waved him back. "Don't." He peeled off the sodden tailcoat, made his way toward the stream, and let it slop to the floor.

The shirt was in shreds, and when Raoul finally lifted it off, the skin beneath was a pulp of flesh and blood.

Brice squeezed his eyes closed and turned his face away. When he looked back, Raoul knelt by the stream. He'd removed his mask and was splashing his face.

Chantel took an apple from the bowl and crunched noisily into it.

Brice glared. Didn't she care that he was hurting, at all? "Raoul, is there anything I can do?"

"Yes. Stay there."

Chantel arched an eyebrow. "Brice wants to find his brother."

"I am aware. That is what got me into this mess."

She stared at Brice, head tilted, eyebrows raised above her mask. "I was under the impression, Raoul, losing your mask got you into this mess."

"That too."

It was Brice's fault. He had taken the mask. And then, when he'd offered to take Raoul's punishment, Raoul had known the whipping would have crippled Brice. Raoul had saved him from that.

"I, er..." Brice cleared his throat. "Thank you."

"I have half a mind to throw you out," Raoul grumbled.

Panic gripped his heart. "You can't."

"Can't I?" Grabbing a cloth from a pile nearby, he wet it in the pool and began wringing it against his shoulders. Water poured down his back through the crosshatched slices taken from his skin, washing them clean.

"We made a deal. The fae can't lie."

"And isn't that our biggest lie of all?" Raoul chuckled.

Chantel smirked and took another chunk from her apple. Was she enjoying this?

"Do not concern yourself, Brice. I may bend a deal, but I will not break one. This"—he gestured at his back—"for all its mangled ugliness, will heal." He wrung more water over his shoulders. "It always does."

Brice could stand the guilt no longer and crossed the room. Collecting a fresh cloth, he dipped it in the stream, wet it through, and perched on the rocky edge, his knee close to Raoul's. Raoul—unmasked—glowered and Brice found himself needing to break the gaze before he fell into studying Raoul's face. "It will heal quicker with two hands tending, no?"

"Did I not suggest you stay over there?"

"Did you hear me agree?"

Raoul's smile sprung open and bloomed like a flower. "You like to disagree."

"I can be stubborn, yes. My mother's trait."

"Ah yes, she taught you about our ways. And taught you well."

"She did."

"What happened to her?"

"She... died." *Lost her mind.*

Chantel planted her boots loudly on the floor and made for the door. "I squirreled your man away, Raoul. You owe me a favor."

"I think you'll find we're even," he called after her. Her light chuckle faded until there was just the quiet burble of the stream in the chamber.

Brice raised the damp cloth and Raoul obliged by shifting his shoulder downward. The flesh had already healed some, and as Brice focused on dabbing away the spilled blood, the wounds no longer wept.

"Don't trust her," Raoul said. "She'll trick the stars from night itself."

"I don't intend to." *Nor do I trust you.*

Raoul propped himself on an arm and bowed his head, stretching his shoulder, giving Brice better access to his back. He twitched as Brice worked but he stayed quiet. Brice's thoughts turned to how Chantel *had* taken him to Raoul. Raoul had been down there in one of those rooms, apparently being punished? What did that look like? Not the whip, that had been for the purposes of display and entertainment. "I am sorry you had to endure such a terrible thing."

Raoul swallowed and said nothing.

Things were more complicated below the prettiness of the masquerade than Brice could have imagined.

He shouldn't think on it. He could only save his brother and himself. The fae's business was their own.

"You have a gentle touch," Raoul said softly, keeping his head bowed. His hair had slipped forward over his shoulder, hiding his marvelous face. Brice resisted the urge to sweep it back and tuck it behind Raoul's slightly tapered ear so he might see Raoul's unmasked face again. He might be tempted to do more—everything about Raoul was temptation, reminding Brice of the times he'd summoned the fae's body to mind and pleasured himself to the memory.

I'll always have our kiss.

No, he could not think on that, at all. One out-of-control sexual indiscretion rousing his desires was more than enough. Never mind it had been with three partners. He still wasn't sure it had been real.

Brice steered his thoughts back to where they needed to be, and as he worked, he considered all the times he'd tried to protect Charon. As a boy, Charon had been unafraid. He'd plowed into most things with abandon. Brice had often envied him that freedom. What must it feel like to be so free you did anything you pleased?

Raoul lifted his head and tucked his hair back behind his ear, just as Brice had imagined. "You're thinking of your brother." He straightened and rolled his shoulder.

"I, er... your back is almost healed. Remarkable, really. How you're so... er..."—Raoul turned to face him, shirtless and wet, with his hair loose and his face unmasked—"so resilient." Resilient? Was that the right word for what Raoul was? Words were proving difficult, as was resisting the urge to stare at the partially naked male in front of him.

Brice quickly took himself halfway across the chamber. Desire hadn't crept up on him—it had slapped him across the face. Was it the fruit? No, he'd only eaten a single grape. And there was no pollen here to cloud his judgment. Good lord, he needed to control himself.

He had been touching Raoul's back, feeling his warmth through the cloth. There was something about Raoul that radiated comfort and made Brice want to lean closer to him —a dangerous thought. And clearly not his own. The masquerade was working its magic. But he recognized it, so he could control it. And himself.

"Are you well?" Raoul enquired.

"Fine. You should, er... you should put on your mask?"

Raoul rose to his feet and after briefly rummaging through a stack of folded clothes, found a shirt and shrugged it on. There were more clothes, Brice noticed. A journal of sorts. A desk area with quill and ink and golden-edged paper, no words yet written on the blank leaves. *Does he live here, in this... cave?*

"Does my face bother you so?"

Brice spluttered a laugh. "What? No. I just... I'm eager to find my brother."

Raoul's dark eyebrows lifted in suspicious query.

"We do not want to give the host any reason to punish you again," Brice hastily continued.

Raoul sighed and collected his mask, putting it on once more. "No, we do not want that." He gathered his hair together and expertly braided it until the long silver-touched tail swept down his back and only his missing tail-coat hinted that anything untoward had transpired.

What would it be like to kiss him? Brice already knew to some extent. They *had* kissed. And its memory had warmed many a lonely night. But what of a kiss that wasn't coerced? A true kiss?

He shook his head free of the frivolous thoughts. These fantasies weren't getting him anywhere and would lead only to trouble. He had to focus on Charon and not Raoul. "Our dance... before the, er... before the host arrived. *Begin at the beginning,* you said. Did it help?"

Raoul brightened, sliding effortlessly from his truer self to the one who teased. "Did you enjoy it?"

"That's not the point."

He chuckled softly, clearly enjoying Brice's discomfort. "It helped. Insomuch as I needed to get a closer look at the dancers to be sure Charon was not among them. He is, I suspect, at the heart of the masquerade where the host keeps his most precious possessions."

"How do we reach him?"

"What lies ahead is not for the faint of heart or mind. Each layer is more devious than the last and we will likely have to descend through many to find Charon."

"All right." He'd do it. To have Charon back, he'd do anything.

"Brice." Raoul's eyes narrowed. "When we find him, he may not wish to leave."

"He will. He'll want to go home." And he didn't get a

bloody choice in it. Charon's poor choices had brought them here, and now Sophia was dead and Brice was surely losing fragments of his sanity with every passing hour. No, Charon was returning with him. Only a madman would want to stay at the masquerade.

Chapter Twenty

"THE MASQUERADE KNOWS your weaknesses and wants. It will answer those desires and feed your every wish." Raoul jogged down the spiral staircase ahead of Brice, the same circling staircase he had climbed earlier.

His explanation of how the masquerade worked sounded simple, as though nothing could go wrong, but as Brice followed Raoul's confident steps downward, he suspected the devil was in the details. The fae were not benevolent. They were selfish, greedy, self-serving, and could be cruel.

"But it also knows no limits," Raoul went on. "It will devour you if you allow it."

"What do you get out of our gluttony?" Brice asked.

Raoul threw a grin over his shoulder. "Sport."

He swept down the hallway, shirt billowing and long braid swishing. His dark colors touched by silver made him stand out in the all-white corridor. His heeled boots clipped the polished floor. He'd recovered well from the lashes, almost to a point where Brice would say he was back to the same wily, mischievous fae he'd met a year ago. But it was clearer now how Raoul's mask brought his flamboyant character out, a character who wasn't truly Raoul. Part of him, yes. The rest was hidden in the impatient Raoul who had snapped at Brice prior to having his mask returned and the selfless Raoul who had stopped Brice from making a mistake, taking the lashings for himself. No doubt there were many facets to the fae striding ahead of him, and to survive this, Brice would likely have to meet them all.

Sport.

Raoul would try and get his sport from Brice too. This was all probably a game to him.

Brice had to keep his wits about him.

They breezed by closed doors, with Raoul's long-legged pace just short of running. He apparently did not want to linger, and Brice couldn't say he wished to linger either—knowing, as he did, what went on behind these doors.

Some doors weren't closed.

Brice stared ahead when passing those. But he couldn't close his ears, and his imagination found the sounds quite stimulating. The muffled grunts, wet slapping, heavy panting. He couldn't help but wonder if he'd sounded like that. "You, er… you were down here before I arrived?"

"I was." Raoul's voice lifted. He arched an eyebrow as Brice hurried to walk alongside him. "My punishment for wandering."

"Wandering?"

"Being where I should not be. I have a knack for such things, and…" He trailed off as a couple spilled from the room ahead. Two female fae, utterly naked—but for the masks—intimately locked together, grinding and groping breasts and nipples. Raoul and Brice didn't exist as they maneuvered around them. Raoul's soft smile was all that showed beneath his mask. If he desired what he saw, he hid it well.

Raoul caught Brice's glance, likely seeking his reaction. Determined not to give the fae any more personal insight than he already had, Brice measured his expression, keeping it neutral.

"Very good." Raoul chuckled. "Though had they been two males, I'd be peeling your tongue off the floor, no?"

Heat flushed his face, quickly betraying him. "Am I so obvious?"

Raoul's smile turned sympathetic. "Fae do not feel shame. The concept is uniquely mortal. You made your own rod to beat yourselves with. It's rather fascinating."

"You really don't feel shame?"

"We want, we act. Why would we be ashamed of that? There are no regrets."

"How very honest for a race so enamored with lies."

Raoul chuckled lightly. "You have much to learn, Brice LeChoix."

There was no doubt of that, but he didn't plan on learning anything more than was necessary to get him through this. After tonight, he wouldn't need it because he would never set foot inside the masquerade again, the fae be damned.

"Raoul," a deep male voice purred from the hallway behind them.

The voice held enough of an edge to stop Raoul in his stride and turn him on his heel. Brice turned and was met with a vision of a male, one who had so thoroughly seduced him. Gold mask, golden glittering muscles. At least he wore low-slung pants, although they did little to hide his generous manhood.

Brice immediately closed his eyes and turned his face away. Shame came boiling back to his face. He'd hoped it was a dream. Apparently, Gold was very real.

"We aren't finished," he said. His voice was heavy, deep, like it rumbled all the way though him before making it to his lips. He hadn't spoken with Brice. None of them had.

"Ah yes, well, Vine, I have been released from that punishment and been sent another. I'm sure you heard how the host took a cat-o'-nine to my back. And now I have this mortal to entertain, so as you can see, I'm occupied elsewhere. Now, if you'll excuse us—"

"You eluded us before we completed," Vine said.

Raoul spread his hands. "I may have left a little early, but I fully intend to return once I have—"

Vine lifted his right hand and flicked his fingers. Torchlight flared and the walls vanished, puffed into smoke. All at once, the contents of every single room were displayed for all to see. Brice swallowed. This was where the guests came to satisfy their lust when a quick fuck in the night garden wasn't enough. Exposed skin simmered and writhed. Men and women alike, fae and mortal. Forked tongues, glistening breasts, trembling thighs, and other intriguing appendages. Sex. On every surface, in every bed, against every wall. Men on men, women on women, genderless and androgenous. Wine and blood, come and cream. Every desire, every wish, spread out like a banquet for the taking.

"You." Vine stopped in front of Brice, eye to eye, mask

to mask. Molten eyes peeled all Brice's layers off. The masquerade knew his needs, better than he knew them himself. He could not hide from this. "I see more want in your eyes." His forked tongue slipped between his lips. "Allow me the pleasure of laying my tongue on you again."

"No."

Brice had opened his mouth to say exactly that, but the word came from Raoul's lips, not his own.

Raoul stepped forward. Now both of them were too close. Raoul's darkness against Vine's golden radiance. Vine was heavier, more muscular. But Raoul carried with him a wiry intensity that suggested he'd be quicker should they come to blows.

Vine's companions emerged from whatever corner they'd been engaged in and stood behind him, bolstering Vine's threat. They were naked, erect, and glistening wet from fluids Brice would prefer not to name.

Brice attempted to hold his head high, to hold on to some measure of pride, but how could he?

But he still wore his mask. It had become so familiar a weight that he'd forgotten it. The mask, thankfully, gave him some power. The power of anonymity. The people all around them, they were nothing but ghosts. They didn't know or care who Brice was. They weren't even people, just objects. Each and every one, just skin and want, cock and tongue, cunt and ass. Meat for the taking. Just so long as their masks remained.

"You may have me," Brice said. He thought he saw Raoul blink at him but dared not look, fearing he'd lose his nerve. He held Vine's gaze instead. "Later. Once my task is over. I... want this. Again. With you. Instead of Raoul finishing his commitment to you."

Vine's gaze slid to Raoul, then back to Brice. He stepped back and dipped his chin. Brice suspected that, should he look down, he'd find the fae as aroused as his companions. He swallowed, turned, and made for the curtain covering what he believed was originally the end of the corridor before Vine had vanished the walls.

Sweeping it aside, he hauled open the thick oak door and plunged through. Raoul followed silently on his heels and clunked the door closed behind them. Away from that thick sweat- and sex-heavy air, Brice braced against the wall of another corridor.

"If you believe you can escape the deal you've just made, you are mistaken," Raoul said, each word clipped by barely restrained anger. "Vine, Laurel, and Claude will not forfeit a bargain."

Now he had all their names, the reality of what he'd offered began to sink into his bones. "It doesn't matter."

"Why did you do that? Why offer yourself for me?"

"Because you've already suffered. Like I said, it doesn't matter."

"Doesn't it? What you had before, that was a sample of what they can do." Raoul stood back, arms crossed, lips thin. "The host was right. You are a child playing with a wolf. When the wolf tires of you, it will rip you apart."

Raoul's eerie clarity and lack of smile drove home the threat.

"Only Charon matters. The rest... I don't care. None of this is real."

He barked a laugh. "I hope your brother is worth it

because they will fuck you out of your mind. See how real that is."

Anger heated Brice's veins. Anger at all of this, at having to be here at all, at having his whole life dictated, his future mapped out. Marriage, children, and the ruined LeChoix name. "Perhaps I want to be fucked out of my mind?"

Raoul's hand was suddenly at his throat and his back was hard against the wall. He gasped and was met with Raoul's mask an inch from his, his eyes like storms. "You do not know what you want, and they will tear you apart because of it."

Brice shoved at him, trying to pry him off, but Raoul twisted and Brice's hands slipped off. "I know my desires!"

Raoul's grip tightened. Viciousness made his eyes darken, the pupils swelling to consume all their colors. "Rarely has there been a guest so lost as you." His grip eased. He slipped his fingers down Brice's neck. "It's a beacon to them... to me."

Brice grabbed Raoul's chin and kissed him hard, nudging his mouth open and forcing his tongue in. Raoul responded like fire to kindling, plastering himself close, body and tongue thrusting into the kiss. The kiss burned. It was messy and harsh, vicious and sharp. Full of want and rage.

Raoul tore himself away and staggered halfway across the corridor, the shock behind his mask very real.

"God, I... I'm sorry." He was a cad to force a kiss upon Raoul as he had. Fae or not, there was such a thing as consent. "That was wrong of me."

Raoul wiped the back of his hand across his lips, indignation blazing in his eyes, and straightened. "Wrong?" He looked as though he might lash out, or scream, or curse Brice to dance in the masquerade forever. All of those things Brice might have understood, but instead, Raoul suddenly huffed a laugh. "Whoever hurt you? Whoever made you believe you're not worthy? They're what's wrong. Not you." He pivoted on his heel and strode off.

Brice wiped his mouth and bent double, catching his breath and his runaway thoughts. That had been... exhilarating, terrifying, wonderful.

Did he want the trio to fuck him? Did he want to be a part of that debauched display behind that door? Maybe he did. Maybe he wanted a whole lot of things. He certainly wanted Raoul. He'd wanted him since they'd met. Since he'd kissed him in the night garden and Raoul had offered to suck his cock. He'd lied to himself, told himself it was just forbidden desire, just dreams. Maybe it was, but Brice wanted Raoul, yearned for him, and that was real.

And when he found Charon, these exhilarating new discoveries about himself would end. The breathless rush of another man's touch, the heady weightlessness after his kiss. He couldn't have that *outside*. He'd have to take off the mask and be Lord LeChoix again.

He didn't want to.

What if he could stay in the masquerade and have three gorgeous fae fuck him forever? That wasn't what good men wanted. It wasn't what Lord Brice LeChoix wanted.

But it could be.

Maybe he was done pretending to be someone he was not.

Madness is clinging to a legacy as it drowns you.

"Brice!" Raoul called. "Hurry, before our jaunt is noticed."

Find Charon.

That hadn't changed.

Although perhaps Brice had and was only now realizing he could.

Chapter Twenty-One

A FROSTED glass door barred the way. Raoul pushed through and stepped into a starlit meadow. A full moon hung low in the ink-black sky. Brice's steps slowed, if only so he could absorb what his eyes showed him. Hills stretched to the horizon with not a single interruption—no housing, no sign of civilization, just miles upon miles of swaying flowers. Of course, it could not be real. There was nothing like this land within a hundred miles of home. He breathed in. The air smelled of summer grasses after the rain.

Raoul strode through the waist-high grass, stroking his hands over the grass seed heads, bending them as he passed. Moonlight glinted in his silver streak and the silver stitched throughout his clothing. He was perhaps the only thing here more worthy of admiration than the midnight meadow.

Raoul glanced over his shoulder.

Brice blinked away but not before seeing Raoul's coy smile.

"What is this place?" Brice asked.

"One of my favorites. Another layer, another gift, from the masquerade to you."

Brice glanced behind him, searching for the doorway they'd walked through, but saw only more rolling hills. Impossible. And curiously wonderful. He nearly laughed, skimming his hands across the grass and letting the fronds tickle his palms. It felt so real.

"You'll find the masquerade far more enjoyable once you stop fighting," Raoul assured. He turned and walked backward through the grass while watching Brice. "Allow yourself some guiltless pleasure. Nobody here will begrudge you some joy."

Joy.

He couldn't remember the last time he'd felt it.

He breathed in, filling his lungs, and scanned the meadow's gentle slopes. Miles of freedom. His pace quickened, one foot in front of the other. The grasses swayed, rippling like an ocean's surface. Quicker, he jogged, then ran, zigzagging in the grass because nobody could stop him. He was a boy again, running through the forest at home with a wooden sword, chasing after Charon's laughter. There had been flowers in the forest back then but not anymore.

A tiny voice told him to stop being a fool, to act like a man, not a boy. The voice sounded so very like his father's. He pushed it aside, lifted his arms, and spun in a circle. Because why shouldn't he? Behind the mask, in this place of myth and magic, he could be whomever he wanted to be.

The soft breeze stole his laughter and toyed with it above the fields. He hadn't realized how much he'd craved this. He laughed some more and twirled in the grass, dancing to his own tune. Was it madness? It would have been at home. The times Father had brought Mother in from the forest where she'd been dancing and singing with the shadows, everyone had called her mad. But what if she had been the sane one?

He stumbled, catching himself before he fell on his ass. Raoul's little laugh drew Brice's gaze to the fae, standing hip cocked and arms crossed a few strides away. His sideways smirk held a hint of satisfaction and something else, too, some softer touch. A hint of sadness?

Whatever did he have to be sad about?

An insane urge came over Brice to ask the fae to dance with him, here, in this endless field under the starlight. Yes, this was definitely madness. He laughed and twirled. He was mad. Finally. Mother had had it right all along. She had laughed at them all in the end.

He stumbled, dizzy and perhaps a little sick. But it was good. And he wasn't ashamed, did not regret his foolishness. Nobody here judged him. But more importantly, he did not judge himself. Raoul was right, so right about so many things.

"Raoul... I..."

The fae walked down the hill toward a house nestled at the valley's bosom. Its windows shone and its towers poked like spears at the sky. He knew it instantly, of course. Latchly Hall. Only it was different to how he'd left it. The grand house glowed from within. Every window blazed with candlelight. Figures moved inside.

His feet carried him closer, carving through the grass until he was almost upon the entrance, with its featured fountain and manicured gardens. Raoul tilted his head up to admire the house's facade. Candlelight from within illuminated his masked face. "What a wonderful home."

Brice frowned. That was not how he would describe Latchly Hall. Since his parents' deaths, it had become a carcass left to rot. It did not glow and sparkle like this version. Laughter did not spill around closed doors.

"Shall we go inside?" Raoul asked.

Fear held him rooted to the ground. There were people inside, guests at a party like the large events the LeChoix family had hosted when he was a boy. He remembered chasing Charon through a sea of ladies' gowns, which had gotten Brice in trouble with Father. A young gentleman of the house did not frolic among ladies' skirts. Of course, Charon was an adorable rascal, not an errant young lord. Things would only get worse from then.

Raoul offered his hand. "Won't you show me?"

Obliging, Brice took Raoul's warm hand and escorted him up the steps. Father's footman opened the door. The reedy man was a vague memory. He looked through them, unseeing. Nobody greeted Brice or acknowledged him at all because they weren't really present. To test his theory, he reached for a passing guest. His fingers sailed through the man's arm. They were ghosts from the past. Memories. Or dreams. For all its wonder, this moment in time wasn't real.

Brice tried to place the era from the faces he vaguely recognized. Lords and ladies from wealthy families throughout the land. Glasses chinked together—toasts made to the future, to wealth and fortune.

The man at the heart of all this glamour stood tall and proud. A striking gentleman, a man of poise and grace. Leon LeChoix. He was young, no sign of weary lines around his eyes nor gray in his hair. This was some twenty years ago, before tragedy enveloped Latchly Hall. Which meant... *Mother is here.*

Brice abandoned Raoul's hand and made for the stairs. He took two steps at a time and tore down the hallway. Mother's door hung ajar. He almost knocked, almost turned around and left too. What good would resurrecting her do? But he wanted to see her, to change the last horrible memory he had of her. The mother he'd almost forgotten but for snippets of her laughter and the occasional whispered fairy tale as she tucked his hair behind his ear and kissed him on the cheek.

A golden-haired boy dressed in a suit of blue velvet dashed by Brice's legs and burst through the door. "Mother!"

She was as beautiful as he recalled. Hair of golden waves and a gown of blue silk and white lace. She scooped the boy into her arms and twirled with him, laughing. "Charon! My little prince, where have you been?"

"I won!" Charon beamed. "Brice did not find me, so I won!"

"Ah, well then, your reign as the king of hide-and-go-seek continues. What reward would you like?"

"The box! The box!"

"Very well." She sat him down on the dresser's stool. He dangled his legs and beamed, rosy cheeked.

Brice drifted into the room, pulled by the force of the past and the love of a mother who had been taken too soon. Here she was radiant. Lady Anette LeChoix, Mistress of Latchly Hall. Wife and mother, but so much more.

She opened the dresser drawer and from inside took a

small box wrapped in blue silk. Placing it down on the dresser top, she carefully untied the silk, letting it slip free to pool around the box. It was beautiful in its simplicity, crafted from oak and painstakingly painted with delicate flowers and swirls.

Charon clapped his hands and grabbed the hand crank on the box's side. He turned the handle, then leaned back and blinked up at Mother. She smiled, flicked open the latch, and lifted the lid.

Music tinkled and inside, on her own platform, a tiny blue ballerina danced. Charon stilled, enraptured.

Brice ventured closer, not wanting to insert himself within the intimate moment. This wasn't his memory. What was this then? A fantasy? A dream? Charon's memory? Letters sparkled inside the box's lid: A & S. Initials? But whose?

The music slowed, bleeding its last note, and the dancer came to a jolting, wooden halt. So like Sophia, her arms held out, embracing an invisible partner.

"Again!" Charon said.

Mother laughed and closed the lid. "Just the once or the magic will fade. This is our little secret, Charon." She knelt and ruffled his mop of golden locks. "Your father and Brice must never know."

Charon nodded eagerly. "But one more? Just one more?"

Mother's eyes glistened with joy and tears. She pulled Charon close, almost feverishly clutching him to her chest. Her stare found Brice and plunged right through him, reaching into his chest to squeeze his heart.

"Anything for you, Charon. My secret, sweet boy."

Chapter Twenty-Two

Her words wrapped ice around his heart. What had he just witnessed? Mother wound the box again. The dancer danced and twirled, forever at the mercy of the music. Charon giggled and Mother laughed. Jealousy soured Brice's tongue. This wasn't right. It was lies. This room, this house, these people. Lies.

Brice stumbled from the room.

My secret, sweet boy.

No. He could not allow the lies purchase. They would burrow inside and eat his mind.

There was nothing secret about Charon. He was Charon, Brice's younger brother. A joy and a frustration, but his brother all the same, and Brice loved him with all his heart, as brothers did. But the music box... its letters A & S... it meant something. The masquerade had shown him a secret.

He almost fell at the stairs' first step and grasped the banister.

Father climbed the stairs, coming closer. His shoes

clipped the wooden steps. Brice blinked, fooled for a moment into believing he watched himself come closer. *You look so very like your father.*

He froze, afraid even now of failing him. Disappointing him.

"Anette, you must speak with Brice," Leon bellowed. "The boy is testing my patience."

"Father." Charon burst from the room and leaped into Leon's arms, knocking him back a step. Father laughed and lifted the boy into the air, then dropped him into his arms. Charon yelped with glee.

Mother swept from the room. "Leave Brice be. He merely wishes to play."

The family embraced, Brice excluded.

Brice was the boy to be spoken to. Told to mind his manners, told to oblige and obey. To stand tall, to follow the rules, to be seen and not heard, the pillar of sophistication. The heir.

Father nuzzled Mother's neck. "Would the boy be more like you and less like his real mother, we would all be better off."

Silence rushed in, muffling the sounds of the house and its guests—suffocating all but the sound of Brice's heart.

"Hush now," Mother scolded. "Tonight is a celebration. Leave the past in the past, my dear."

Brice refused to hear any more, could not witness these lies. He pounded down the stairs and bolted from the house, stumbling on the front path. Trees loomed all around. The meadows and the moon were gone. Trees stood between him and freedom, like bars over a window.

He whirled, afraid to go into the forest, afraid to go back.

The house was dark, its windows black and silent. Ivy had grown over much of its once-grand facade, crawling through windows and doors, slowly choking the life out of it.

A pistol shot rang out inside the house. Brice jerked.

He closed his eyes and swallowed the sharp knot in his throat.

The shot wasn't for him. It was the shot that would draw him to his mother's room, the shot that signaled the end of his old life and the beginning of the nightmare. He didn't need to go back inside to know what awaited him.

He'd been the one to find her sprawled on the bedchamber floor with her pistol beside her and blood creeping across the floor.

He had found her, and it was all his fault.

He turned and stumbled into Raoul. The fae gripped his arms. His fingers tightened. "Brice... remember what I said? It will swallow you whole if you allow it. It doesn't know your trauma, just that you want to torture yourself with it over and over."

He stared into the fae's eyes. Did it mean he was doomed if the only thing he could trust in this wretched place was a fae who surely had his own motives for all of this? "Is it true?"

"Is what true?"

"The things it showed me. My mother... she's not..." He couldn't say it. Father's words hammered into him. *More like you and less like his real mother*. "Are they true or is it all lies?"

"Only you can answer that."

He shook him off and marched toward the trees, then stopped. This place, these fae. He'd had enough. "I want my brother back!" The forest gobbled up his yell. "Show me Charon!" When only silence replied, he picked up a rock and threw it into the trees. The forest took that too. "Damn you!" He spun on Raoul. "Take me deeper, Raoul. As deep as we can go. I'll not be stopped by lies and stories."

Raoul licked his lips and swallowed. "Are you sure?"

Sure? No. He wasn't sure about anything anymore. Was his mother—his mother at all? Was Charon a secret kept from him? What other lies were hidden in his past? It didn't matter, because despite the things he'd been shown, nothing had changed. "He's all I have and this place is taking him from me. I have to get him back."

"Very well." Raoul took the overgrown track leading from the house. Brice followed. The forest watched their passing, its oppressive weight pushing down.

"What happened to her? Your mother?" Raoul asked.

Brice's memory supplied the sound of that single deadly shot again. "A madness overcame her in the final years until she took her own life. Her death destroyed my father. He turned to drink, neglected the estate and my brother and me, accrued debts, and one night he walked into the snow and never returned. He was found a week later by a game hunter stalking the edges of our land. Leon LeChoix was discovered half-naked, propped against a tree, frozen to death." He recited it as though it had happened to some other poor family, not his. Because it had never felt like it belonged to his story. Maybe it was Brice who did not belong?

He loved his mother. Her madness had not taken that from him, and the masquerade wouldn't take his memory of her either.

The masquerade *had* taken Charon, but he was getting him back.

"Your life is touched by tragedy," Raoul remarked.

"What of your life?"

"Mine?"

"You don't age, no? You must have had many lives."

"I age differently, that's true. But as for my life? The memories are faded. The masquerade takes them." He flicked his fingers toward his head. "There is just dancing and revelry over and over, until all of it loses meaning."

"You don't remember anything from before?"

"Sometimes flashes, scents, a glance here and there. It means little. So much means so little. The sweetest of pleasures quickly sours without meaning. Allow me to tell you a secret, Brice?"

"Go on."

"When the host threatened to whip me, I wanted it. Ached for it, even." His smile belied the haunted look in his eyes.

"Why?"

"Because the sting of a whip can be a relief in a world devoid of feeling."

Brice had accused the host of being joyless, but it seemed the masquerade had sucked the joy out of others too. "None of you can leave?"

Raoul tipped his head to the sky and smiled. "I doubt there is much out there I would want to leave for."

"But you don't know? You don't remember?"

"Perhaps that is the masquerade's gift? Not knowing what we should miss, freeing us of its grief. Wouldn't it be worse to know the things you cannot return to?"

The masquerade appeared to be a beautiful thing from the outside when in fact it was an endless torture for all the fae within it. A torture they'd forgotten they were trapped in. Good lord, the horror of the place grew thicker and deeper with every new revelation.

Brice pitied them. He never would have believed he'd think such a thing. But there it was.

"Do not fret for me, Brice. I have ways of getting what I want. Eventually."

Brice chuckled despite Raoul's nefarious undertone. If anyone could wriggle free of the masquerade's curse, it was surely Raoul. "I believe it."

A closed door stood abruptly in the roadway, out of place and surreal. Roses bloomed around its frame. Cleary, this was the way to the next layer.

"How many more doorways?" he asked.

"Two. Or two hundred. There's really no knowing." Raoul gestured for Brice to take the lead. "Go ahead."

Brice opened the door and stepped into... the same forest, or at least it looked the same. The same trees, the same track. The door was just a door in the roadway. That couldn't be right. Something must have changed. He ventured deeper down the road. The sky burned orange, dawn's light creeping in. Something scuttled in the roadside grass. A fox barked from far away. A snowflake twirled and dallied in the sky, joined by others. Some of it began to plink against the ground, heavier than snow. But not rain. He reached out and captured a few flakes.

Ash.

He smelled it then. Woodsmoke. But if ash was raining down, then the orange glow bleeding across the sky was not the dawn but light from a wildfire.

"What is this now?"

Raoul strode past him. "This layer is not your desire but mine."

"Fire?"

"Yes." He fluttered a hand but kept his grin. "Somewhat dramatic, I know." His grin made lies of his words. "The masquerade occasionally brings me here. Perhaps it is a memory I am unaware of, but I like to think of it as an escape." As he spoke, fire surged from tree to tree, cutting off the road ahead, flooding the night in smoke and roaring light.

Raoul stopped in the road and watched the wall of flame rise up like some hungry beast and devour the trees. Heat prickled Brice's arms and face. Raoul just… watched.

"What desire is this?" Brice cautiously asked.

Raoul's throat moved. He gazed at the fire and when he faced Brice, embers reflected in his eyes. "To burn it all down."

Hot ash singed Brice's hand. He hissed and shook it off. Nearby trees burned and snapped and hissed as fire danced from branch to branch. Heat beat in waves. Dry air cracked his lips.

"Shouldn't we run?"

"Yes." Raoul's hand caught his. "Not away or this will never end. We must run toward it."

"What? Are you mad?" Steam rose from the wet earth and spiraled in the air. Blazing embers rained down.

"Trust me," Raoul said. Brice might have been more inclined to trust him if the fae's eyes didn't sparkle as though he thrived on this chaos. He tightened his grip on Brice's hand and bolted toward the wall of flame, pulling Brice with him.

Waves of heat and light grew so intense, Brice had to turn his face away. At the last second, when the heat became almost too much, he brought his arm up. Panic turned his veins to ice. Smoke burned his eyes, his tongue, his lungs.

He gasped. Raoul plowed into his side, sending him tumbling through the fire and out onto cold, wet grass. Brice spun and patted his clothes, sure he was ablaze. But there was no fire, no ash, no smoke. Just a grassy bank, a starlit sky, and a stone wall wrapped in roses. Raoul flung himself onto his back on the bank and grinned at the stars. "That never gets old."

Brice scoffed a spluttered laugh. That confirmed it; the fae was quite mad. He frowned down at him, stretched so casually on the grass. With a knee drawn up and an arm behind his head, he didn't have a care in the world. Did none of this matter to him?

"We just... we just ran through fire."

"Yes, we did." Raoul arched an eyebrow. "Thrilling, isn't it?"

"Thrilling?" Brice brushed absently at his shirt, sure it must be burned. It wasn't, of course. The whole thing had been an illusion, just like Latchly Hall. "Thrilling is not the word I'd use."

"And what word would you use, my lord?"

"Insane, perhaps. Careless. Even dangerous."

Raoul huffed. "Nothing here can hurt you, Brice, unless you allow it."

Yes, well, he was learning that. Convinced he wasn't about to combust, he took a look around them. The stone wall stretched both left and right as far as the eye could see. But behind Raoul there was a pair of closed gates as tall as a man and impossible to see over without a ladder. On closer inspection, the gates had been carved with an elaborate rose design. Beautiful, really, although much of it was hidden beneath real roses.

"We're here," Raoul said, climbing to his feet. He flicked his hair over his shoulder and faced the gates.

A sprig of grass jutted from Raoul's hair, upsetting the perfect portrait. Brice plucked it free and tossed it away, only to find Raoul's glare fixed on him. "There was a..." Raoul's eyes had narrowed and his permanent playful smile had vanished. This wasn't impatient Raoul, nor was it sympathetic Raoul. It certainly wasn't playful Raoul. This was some other facet Brice had not yet met. The intensity of the fae's glare made Brice's skin prickle. His heart thumped again, readying his body for fight or flight.

"Are you ready to see your brother?"

"He's inside?"

Raoul blinked and tugged his shirt down, realigning it. "Come along then, my lord." He faced the gate and the roses recoiled, curling in on themselves to clear the handles. "Should the host discover us, our lives will not be worth living."

Grasping the gate's handles in both hands, Raoul heaved them open and said, "Welcome to the rose garden."

Chapter Twenty-Three

Small stone buildings had crumbled, but some had clung to their form enough to still hold up partial slate roofs. People huddled in groups. At first, Brice thought them beggars or vagrants, but on closer inspection, their stained and dirty clothes were ballgowns and formal attire. Elaborate hair designs had fallen free of their curls and pins and lay in rats' tails about their faces. They didn't speak, not really, just mumbled and shuffled—strange husks, ghosts almost. They didn't seem human.

"Are they..." Brice whispered, following Raoul's soft-footed steps.

"Real? Yes."

They were unmasked. Captured. This wasn't a garden but a prison.

Brice glanced over at Raoul, if only to try and read his expression, but the mask hid too much, making his face blank. Still, there was some glimmer of pain in his eyes. A sympathy he could not hide.

There had to be fifty people here tucked away in shadow, hidden from the light.

"Avoid the roses," Raoul whispered. "They're poisonous and hungry."

Was anything within the masquerade benign? Brice gave a rose bush a wide berth. "What is this place?"

"A gift, from the host to his mate. It was said to be the most beautiful of gardens. But like their love, it soured, turned vicious."

A squat, wide-spreading tree loomed ahead. Its leaves had long ago fallen away. Roses had climbed its trunk, choking each branch. Their flowers hung from above. And below, huddled among the tree's roots, hunched a man. He'd wrapped a blanket around his shoulders and stared at the ground between his dusty shoes. His shock of curly blond hair was the brightest thing in this empty place.

"Charon..." Brice knelt in front of him. He didn't reply, just stared at the dirt. "Charon?" Brice captured his face in his hands and forced him to look up, to see. Clean tracks marked the passing of old tears down his filthy face. His blue eyes, always so bright and laughing, had dulled to a soulless gray. "Charon. Look at me." He smudged the dirt from Charon's cheek, trying to clean it. "It's Brice, your brother." Golden lashes fluttered.

"Why are the roses dying?" Charon croaked, voice broken.

This place, it had sucked all the life out of him, just like it had the others roaming aimlessly around the roses. His eyes were empty. The masquerade had taken him!

Brice tore off his own mask and made him look. "See? You know me? Your brother. Brice."

Charon blinked and stared into Brice's eyes.

Raoul knelt and flicked his fingers in front of Charon's face. Charon twitched. "There is some sense in him yet. He will recover." He looked up at the canopy above them, then around the courtyard. "We must get him away from the roses."

Were the flowers doing this to him? Keeping him like this? Brice slipped an arm around his brother's shoulders and hauled him to his feet. "Come, Charon. We're going home."

"Home?" He looked up, finally focusing, and his eyes widened. "Brice?"

"Yes, brother. I've come for you. We're leaving."

Charon dug his heels in and mumbled a string of words Brice struggled to make sense of. "Cannot leave."

"Yes, you can."

"Cannot leave." He weakly shoved at Brice.

Brice wrapped him tighter. He smelled of sweet, rotting earth and trembled in Brice's arms. "Yes, you can, brother. It's all right. It will be over soon. We'll go home, away from this place." Emotion clogged his throat. His bright, laughing, carefree brother... This place had hollowed him out. He had to get him out, get them both out.

"No. Sophia—Sophia is here." He shoved again at Brice, putting more strength into it.

Brice's gaze caught Raoul's. Why he should look at the fae in that moment, he didn't know. Raoul swallowed and looked away, knowing the truth. "Hurry." He stiffened. "The host is coming."

Back at the gate, the roses were wilting, curling up like dead spiders and turning to dust, but those above them, tangled in the tree, bloomed larger, swelling, raining their mind-numbing pollen into the air. Brice felt it creeping into his head, dulling the edges of his thoughts.

"Sophia?" Charon fought free. "Sophia!" he called.

"Charon, stop." Brice grabbed his arm and pulled him back. "She's not here." He tried to pull Charon toward the gate. Charon fought, his calls growing more and more agitated.

"Brice," Raoul warned. "We must go."

More roses by the gate wilted while others came alive. Opening flowers tasted the air and began to slither their tendrils across the ground.

If the host found them, it would be over.

Charon bucked. Brice grabbed Charon's arms and rattled him, trying to shake some sense into him. "Stop. Listen! Sophia's not here. She made it out!" The lie burst free. "She's at home." His heart twisted in his chest. "She's outside, waiting for us. I'll take you to her, but you must come with me now." Let Charon hate him. He already did, so what was one little lie worth if it saved his brother's life?

Charon grabbed at him and his face lit up. "Truly? She's free? She got out?"

"Yes." The lie almost choked him.

"Brice! Hurry!" Raoul's shout snapped him around. The roses swept in, bubbling in a liquid wave, tumbling and rolling toward them. Raoul suddenly lunged, grabbed at the heaving mass of thorns, and shoved them back. More boiled in around him, threatening to swallow him whole. Sharp thorns whipped at his clothes and face. "Go!" Raoul yelled. He hissed, gritted his teeth, and shoved, driving the writhing thorned barrier back.

Brice ran, dragging Charon into a sprint alongside him. Roses whipped and lashed across their path. One caught Brice's neck, zipping open tiny cuts. Another snagged his wrist. He tore free, spinning. Another grabbed Charon, wrapping around him. He cried out and thrust a hand toward Brice, his eyes pleading. He'd done this before, those eyes said—he'd tried to run. The roses had caught him every time.

Not this time.

Raoul swept in, got his hands around Charon, and hauled him out of the knotted briars. The roses had stolen Charon's blanket. They lifted it into the air like a flag and ripped the thing into a hundred pieces.

They ran, Raoul ahead, Charon between them, Brice at the rear. At the gateway, roses knotted and twisted in on themselves, wilting and crumbling, making way...

The host was here.

Raoul spat a word that sounded like a curse, then veered left toward an old stone shack. The weight of the shifting roses had dislodged some of the roof. The timber frame leaned against the outer wall, providing a ladder. Brice needed no instruction. He bolted for the roof, shoving Charon ahead of him, and followed him up. Slate tiles slipped under their feet. It would not hold for long.

Charon dropped over the wall out of sight. Brice clambered higher and tumbled over the top, landing hard in the grass on the other side. He backed up, waiting for Raoul to appear. Roses slithered and hissed, flooding along the wall, interlacing—reaching to block the gap.

"Raoul!"

Brice's heart thumped in his throat. Raoul had to get

out. He'd come this far with him. If the host caught him, the whip might be the least of his punishment.

Raoul jumped from the wall and landed, crouched in the grass. Breathing fast, his mask and clothes torn, he took a moment to steady himself, then looked up and flashed a grin. "Riveting."

A horrible wail rose up from inside the walled garden. A howl of rage that rolled over the silent land like thunder.

Raoul dashed for the long grass, keeping low, and waved for Brice to follow. Charon followed behind them.

Staying low and quiet, they eventually left the walled garden and its hungry roses far behind. The grass turned to thick brush, then damp wetlands. Trudging through the cold and the wet, nobody spoke. Raoul kept on moving, and Brice followed that silver streak in his hair like a beacon in the dark, Charon's hand firmly locked in his. Charon stumbled a few times, then went down to his knees. Brice gathered him into his arms. "It's all right, Charon." His brother trembled, teeth chattering. "How much farther?" he asked Raoul.

"Rest a while," Raoul said, crouching. "He cannot find us here."

Charon shivered against Brice's chest and mumbled his nonsense. He said Sophia's name over and over, and each time it felt like a nail being driven into Brice's heart. The lie might have cost Brice his brother's love, but it would be worth it. "Thank you," he told Raoul.

The fae's dark gaze burned through his scratched mask. "This is far from over."

Chapter Twenty-Four

The sun did not rise. The moon did not travel through the sky. The landscape never changed. On and on they walked. Occasionally Brice thought he heard snatches of laughter and music, but the wind would tease the sounds away before he could be sure. He began to understand how Raoul could tire of monotony, because in his tiredness, the relentless, unending night began to gnaw away at his mind. But he had Charon. He'd made it this far. All they had to do now was get back to the top layer. Escaping the masquerade would be only a ballroom away.

The grounds around them changed from formless grass to gardens with manicured borders and gravel-laid pathways. They had to be close now. Brice managed to cling to Charon, keeping him upright and moving, but his own limbs burned with effort. Exhaustion was winning. Raoul didn't seem to suffer from tiredness at all. He walked ahead, alert and stealthy. Several times Brice had blinked and the fae had vanished like a ghost in front of him, only to reappear at the next blink. Sometimes he heard laughter that sounded like his own. Other times he heard Mother's music box. *My secret, sweet boy.* Charon's golden locks, his bow-like lips, and his lust for life—so like Mother. Brice had none of that. Perhaps because the masquerade was right, and she hadn't been his mother at all.

Didn't matter.

Nothing mattered.

Just saving Charon and getting him home.

But then the laughter turned to cries. A pistol shot jerked him awake, and for a brief moment, he had no idea who or where he was.

Raoul peered down at him. "You fell asleep. We're almost there." His hand on Brice's shoulder gave a squeeze.

Brice reached for his head. His thoughts split apart, leaping from one random thing to the next. The dazzling feasts of yuletide, glistening snowflakes on his fingers, a lover's breathless gasp. Around and around the images spun.

"It's the roses." Raoul was suddenly in front of him, holding him up it seemed. "You breathed in their pollen. I have an antidote, but you'll need to retain your wits long enough for us to get to safety."

Retain his wits. He might have lost those some time ago. He laughed and Raoul's face behind his mask frowned. He could tell by the narrowing of his eyes. That was amusing too. He rather liked to see the fae annoyed or angry or frustrated. It made him more real and less of a dream he'd summoned into his own head for pleasure. Brice reached out to touch this Dream Raoul's lips, but Raoul grabbed his wrist, holding him off. He was angry now. Hm, he already knew what Raoul's angry kisses tasted like. He'd like to sample them again. He stepped close, heating with desire for the forbidden fae.

Raoul's slap came from nowhere, flooding Brice's face with pain and heat and staggering him on the spot. He rocked, gasping, face on fire. "Ow."

"Well, there is no antidote for foolishness."

Oh God, he'd tried to kiss him. Again. In the midst of all this? What on earth was wrong with him? "I... My apologies. My head, I—I'm not in control—"

"Oh, do stop." Raoul arched an eyebrow. "You're exhausted, intoxicated, and, given the circumstances, proving to be remarkably resilient. I dare say I'm impressed. But that does not change the fact we have the hardest part yet to come. I need you focused. Charon needs you focused."

Brice rubbed his cheek and glanced down at the dozing Charon. "What hardest part?"

"Getting you both back through the masquerade without being seen."

Yes, that might be a problem. Brice's clothes were creased, bloodstained from the roses, and torn in places. He'd lost buttons too. Charon, in his current state, would never pass as a guest and with his mind so fragile, there was no knowing what the brightly lit ballroom with its medley of memories might do to him. Sneaking through several hundred guests without raising suspicion was going to be a challenge.

Raoul gathered his braid over his shoulder. It had lost

some of its tightly woven form. Some tufts of dark hair sprang free. He tried to finger them back into place but failed and frowned, then noticed Brice watching. With a smile he said, "Do not fret, my dear. I have a plan."

He had a plan for most things. Wily and slippery, the fae clearly knew how to play the masquerade to his advantage. Brice had probably only seen a small amount of what Raoul was capable of. He did regret that he would not see more, once he'd gotten Charon to safety. If they succeeded, he would, in fact, never see Raoul again.

Charon stirred awake. Brice helped him to his feet and they continued down the track. More snatches of laughter sailed on the breeze. They were close now. Raoul walked ahead, somewhat frayed at the edges. His shirt had come untucked at his back where he hadn't noticed. Brice stared at it. That one little imperfection made him so much more real. Brice had been wrong about the masquerade. There was true beauty here, hidden behind its mask. It began with love, Raoul had said. Its heart had once been true. Its beauty, real. Brice saw it still, hidden in the smallest of snowflakes, in Raoul's sly glances, the freedom of the midnight meadow. The beauty was there but twisted and made ugly by the host.

Raoul approached what appeared to be a small quarry. A waterfall poured over its top into a deep pool below. Lilies floated on the mirrored surface. Raoul waded into the water up to waist height and peeled back a canopy of ivy, revealing a small opening in the rock face. Without a word, he vanished inside.

Brice drew Charon into the water, wincing at his renewed shivers. The opening brought them into the back of the cave Raoul used as his sanctuary. Lit candles filled the cavern with warm light. Raoul gestured toward the pile of blankets on the floor in one corner. "Help yourselves to dry clothes, food, water. It's not the extravagant offerings of the masquerade, but it is safe."

Brice hurried toward the bed area and sat Charon down. He'd stopped mumbling but his gaze was unfocused again.

"Here." Raoul produced a small bottle of liquid with no label, just a cork stopper. "Two drops on the tongue. It will help."

Brice recognized the small bottle from his visit before. It had sat beside the bed as though in regular use.

"What is it?"

"A way to forget for a while."

As Brice took the bottle, his fingers brushed Raoul's. A tingling traveled through the touch, or perhaps that was Brice's tired, starved brain seeking comfort.

"And this." Raoul produced a second bottle, larger than the first. "To negate the roses." After handing it over, he moved away toward the tunnel opening. "I won't be gone long."

"You're leaving?"

"My absence will have been noticed. I must be seen to avoid suspicion."

He had to go out there and mingle, and smile, and charm, and be the wooden dancer in the box for the townsfolk who had no idea he was trapped here. A pitiful ache throbbed through Brice's chest. Foolish, perhaps, to pity them. But he could not help his feelings.

Raoul hesitated at the entrance, his hand on the wall

next to the dried bloody handprint. "I do believe I will miss your company, Brice, when you're gone." And with that, he left without looking back.

Chapter Twenty-Five

Brice administered the potions to himself and Charon, then, with his brother pliant, stripped him, washed him as best he could, and dressed him again in Raoul's spare clothes. Charon and Raoul were of a similar build, so the clothes would help him pass for a drunken guest but not for long.

With his brother dozing, Brice turned his attention to his own care. He drank from the stream, ate the bread and fruit left out, and washed the sickly smell of rose pollen off, but curiously, when he looked at his reflection in the stream, he didn't need to shave. His body's aches and strains knew hours had gone by, days even, but his usual shadowy stubble hadn't grown. Time was strange here, not like it should be. Charon probably wasn't aware a year had passed since the last masquerade. Perhaps that was for the best.

Feeling somewhat refreshed and more normal than he had since arriving, he drifted about Raoul's sanctuary, curious as to what the little clues could tell him of the real Raoul. The things he liked: Reading, clearly. Some sketching, too. The drawings were of flowers, mostly, all in various states of wilted decay.

With his brother sound asleep, Brice investigated the desk area. The quill and inkpot were there as before, as were the stacks of glittery paper. He picked up a sheet. Candlelight caught the beautiful edging dipped in gold. He knew its weight. He lifted it to his nose, knew its scent: jasmine.

The unassuming stack of paper was unwritten invites. Each sheet waited for Raoul's pen to scribe a name and perhaps change a life.

A sketch peeked out from under the stack. A man, wearing a mask he knew well. His father's mask. His father, Leon LeChoix? Brice pulled the sketch free. The quill strokes were quick but almost perfect, but the subject was not Brice's father. The eyes weren't as hard and the body not as lean. The sketch was of Brice.

"I wrote you many an invite," Raoul said.

Brice startled and dropped the drawing. "Good heavens, you're quiet."

"Hm." He approached. While gone, Raoul had straightened his hair and clothing so as to blend in with the others. He'd found his long tailcoat, too, with its silver edges. He looked divine at first glance, but as Brice looked deeper, a slightly frayed aura still clung to him. His smile barely lifted his lips. He was... tired.

The drawing, the invites. Brice didn't know what to say. Nothing seemed adequate. Did Raoul choose the guests? Why had he drawn Brice? Had he thought of Brice when he'd been alone, as Brice had thought of Raoul—and perhaps dreamed of him too?

Raoul leaned against the desk, folded his arms, and looked down at the drawing. "Every year. I'd wait to see if your invite was accepted. I'd run my fingers over all the names at the entrance, but the invite never came. *You* never came."

Was he... sad? His mask hid most of his face but not the tightness around his lips. Brice had never wanted to tear that mask off more, just to read the truth.

Raoul's tone lightened. "I'm sure you can imagine my surprise when I finally held your invite in my hand, but it was not Brice LeChoix looking at me from behind a mask but a man I could only assume to be his brother."

Anger sparked alive in Brice's chest. "You could have turned him away."

"Why should I? You denied me over and over, but here was someone who had answered my summons. Slipping an invite of my own onto the host's list is one of the few pleasures I have. My invite brought him here, so I allowed him entry."

This was all Raoul's fault? The endless invites taunting him every solstice? Charon's coming here? He glanced at his sleeping brother, checking he still slumbered, and leaned closer to Raoul. "Had you denied him entry, none of this would have happened! Sophia would still be alive!"

"By that logic, had *you* answered my invites, your brother would not have come at all, so—"

Brice grabbed the fae by the shirt and hauled him close. Raoul's eyes widened, but his smirk stayed firmly on his lips. He wanted to strike him, to punch that smirk off his face. He might have, had Raoul not suddenly leaned in and pressed a kiss to Brice's lips. Anger became a roaring fire in his chest, burning through his veins. He shoved at the fae with one hand while the other gripped him tighter.

Raoul wrestled Brice against the desk. His fevered mouth scorched Brice's lips. The shock of it demanded Brice push him away, but instead he grabbed Raoul by the arm and his firm ass and dragged him into his arms, kissing him back, feeding the fire with heat of his own. Violence wove through their passion, fueled by anger and need. Raoul's wired strength held Brice pinned. Brice still shoved at him, trying to push him off while at the same time clinging to him, needing him.

Raoul's hands held him down, pushing against Brice's struggles but yielding too. They fought and kissed, and when both their struggles ceased, Raoul's dark laugh poured lust down Brice's spine, painfully arousing him. Raoul leaned back and tore his own mask off. He tossed it carelessly aside, shook his head to loosen his hair, and bit at his bottom lip like the impossible temptation he was.

Brice had nowhere to go, no escape. He hated this creature, what he'd done, what he was, but by God, he wanted to hold him down and taste him, feel him gasp and hear him moan. He wanted to spread him and bury himself in him in a way that was far from gentlemanly.

Raoul took Brice's mask in hand and tore it free, then grabbed Brice's chin, holding him still to get a good look. Raoul roamed his gaze over Brice's unmasked face, drinking him in, absorbing him. A touch of desperation sharpened his gaze and tightened his lips, but before Brice could think what that meant, Raoul skimmed his lips over Brice's in a kiss that promised more. The achingly soft touch summoned a moan from deep within Brice. He should not want this, want *him*, but he did. He wanted it more than he'd wanted anything in his whole life, like some foolish boy besotted by a dream. Brice kissed Raoul back like he might break if he pushed too hard. Kissed him softly, teasing his lips and tongue. He poured more feeling into that kiss than any other he cared to recall. He was hard for the fae, desperate with lust, but this gentle kiss demanded more than lust. It demanded to be remembered—would never be forgotten.

Raoul's fingers slipped from his chin, freeing him. Plastered entirely against Brice, he rested his forehead against Brice's and peered deep into his eyes. The colors around his dilated pupils glittered with intent and lust and maybe a touch of joy too. "Where can this go?" he whispered.

Brice touched Raoul's face like he'd wanted to since first seeing him unmasked. There were no masks now. Just the two of them, exposed and raw. "What do you mean?"

"You and I?" Raoul turned his face away, then peered sideways through his lashes. "Is it lust? Or more? Or nothing at all?"

The ache around Brice's heart was real, like grief for the horrible parting that had yet to happen. He took Raoul's hand and twined their fingers.

Raoul looked down at their hands, then lifted his gaze. "I am a trickster, a dancer, a player behind the scenes. This isn't my story. It's yours."

"It could be ours?" What was he saying? It was madness. But it did not feel insane. It felt like the only true thing in this place. What if he stole Raoul from this place like the host had stolen Charon? Would that be so terrible a thing?

Sadness softened all the sharp lines on Raoul's face. "I can never leave, Brice."

Brice delicately touched Raoul's chin and turned his head back to face him. The real Raoul was lost and alone. Brice knew those feelings. He'd felt them most of his life. And as the fae's eyes glittered with emotion, Brice understood he'd only now just met the real Raoul. Scared, tired. A fae who wanted to watch it all burn just so he could feel something again.

"Leave with me," Brice blurted out.

Raoul's sad smile cracked a line through Brice's heart. He slowly withdrew, taking his body from Brice's and with it his warmth. "It doesn't work like that."

"Why not? You're outside when you examine the invites. Just walk away with me."

"Brice—"

Brice stepped toward him, but Charon stirred, rousing. "Raoul..." He lowered his voice, trying to buy more time. "You want to escape. How could you not? The punishments, this cave you live in? This isn't a life. You deserve more."

Raoul shook his head and bent to pick up his mask. "You do not know what I deserve."

"Live with me," Brice said. "At the house." It didn't seem such a terrible idea. In that moment, it made perfect sense. Latchly Hall was far too large for just him and Charon anyway. Raoul could glamour his tipped ears away. Nobody need know.

"Brice, stop!" Raoul snapped. "Do you think if I could so easily walk away, I would not have done so? There is no escape!

I've tried! I've tried over and over. With my every breath, I try. I write his invites and set them free where I cannot go. The guests come, they feast and make merry and leave again. I smell the forest on them. I smell decay and age. I smell time on them, and I yearn for that change, for the passage of seasons, to see leaves fall and flowers bloom. I yearn for winter nights in front of blazing fires and summer days in baked meadows." He hastily put his mask on. "You remind me of all the things I cannot have. I think that is why—" He abruptly cut himself off.

"Why?"

"That is why—" Taking a breath, he plowed on. "—I feel the way I do about you."

"You... do?" Then this wasn't all some lie, some fantasy between them to pass the time? There was some truth in their kiss? Some meaning to it that went deeper.

Raoul winced and squeezed his eyes closed, then rubbed at his forehead. "You are right, though. It doesn't matter. Nothing here matters, certainly not me. You must leave."

Brice sighed, releasing a tight breath. He wanted to go to him, to cross the floor and kiss him again, but a void had opened between them—one he didn't know how to fill. "But I can save you." Even as he said the words, he heard their lie.

Raoul heard it too and, shaking his head, strode for the exit. "Make your brother ready. You will both leave when I return."

"Raoul, wait—"

"Brice?" Charon mumbled. "God, where am I?" He pressed a hand to his head. "My mask... I have it here somewhere… I must find it. Brice—my mask, I can't lose it. If I lose it and he sees…"

Raoul vanished out the tunnel with a flick of his silvery coat. Brice closed his eyes and fought back the trembling urge to yell or scream or sweep all the invites from the desk and rip them to shreds. This wasn't right, but nothing had been right since he'd stepped inside this forsaken place. This was not his world. He was powerless to change things here. Powerless to save Raoul. But he could save Charon. He could save one soul. He had to do that.

"Who was he?" Charon asked.

Brice pinched his lips around their quiver and swallowed the horrible, bitter taste of failure. "Just another fae."

Chapter Twenty-Six

Raoul returned a short time later with a spare mask and handed it without comment to Charon. He skipped his gaze over Brice, and when Charon took the mask, Raoul backed up, keeping his distance. He was shutting down, locking Brice out, and perhaps that was for the best. To dream of more would only prolong the pain of its ending.

"Keep behind me, both of you," Raoul said. "With any luck, our passing will go unnoticed."

Charon paled. His eyes were bright, alert, but brittle. Brice took his hand and squeezed. "I've got you. It's just the garden and the ballroom. A few steps and we'll be free." He couldn't look at Raoul, knowing he had to leave him behind.

"What if he comes?" Charon whispered, casting jittery glances between Brice and Raoul.

"Then you run," Raoul said.

"We'll deal with it," Brice added more softly. "It's not far now. Soon we'll leave this place and its... people behind us." He couldn't look. Would Raoul sketch more pictures of

Brice? Images without their masks? Would he draw them together?

Charon nodded. Brice filled his lungs and calmed his racing heart. It was almost over. Just one last push.

Raoul led the way from the tunnel. Brice followed close with Charon trailing behind, his hand as cold and hard as ice. They left the sanctuary and passed through the poison gardens. The air hung wet and heavy with the scent of heady pollen, dampness, and sex. Brice's shoes crunched on gravel. Not too fast, not too slow.

Raoul kept his head up, kept his smile, as though nothing were amiss. He played his part well. Of course he would—he'd been playing it for years. So Brice tried the same, keeping his chin up, his strides true, and his smile warm beneath his mask. Charon's hand tightened on his. He squeezed back. Everything was going to be fine. Raoul had gotten them this far. He'd see them to the end. Brice was confident of that, if little else. They'd made a deal. And he might bend them, but he never broke them.

They came upon two lovers embraced on a bench. Their clothes hung askew. The woman's breast had escaped her corset and swayed with the rhythm of their lovemaking, her nipple erect. There were others, too, spread about the garden, lost to the pollen and the masquerade's careless way in which it answered every desire. Brice understood it now. He'd been here before, scared and aroused by what he'd witnessed, and perhaps he still was, but he knew what drove them—he knew why the masquerade was the way it was. This was their escape as much as it was the townsfolk's. Perhaps more so, as they had nowhere else to go and no memory to remind them who they were.

Laughter teased from inside the masquerade's ballroom. The brilliant chandeliers shone brighter than ever, luring everyone in. There was nowhere to hide under a thousand candles except in the middle of it all.

They stepped inside. Nothing had changed. The banquet table still overflowed with plates and bowls of fruits and pastries and cakes and meats, all the things anyone could imagine. The wine still flowed. The fantasy went on. Brice had the inexplicable urge to smash a glass or shove over a tower of tiny cakes, just to upset the painfully exquisite perfection so that *something* might change.

Burn it all.

Raoul glanced over his shoulder and for a moment candlelight caught in his dark eyes, setting them ablaze. He would burn it all if he could.

The exit was close now. Brice could almost feel the forest air sweeping over him. They just had to pass through the ballroom, into the hallway where the stairs rose to the galleried landing, and out through the archway. A few more breaths of sickly-sweet air, a few more steps through the dream, and they'd be free.

"Wait." Raoul stopped suddenly and faced the banquet table. He scooped up three glasses and smiled. *"Smile like you want to be here,"* he said through his teeth.

Brice pulled on a grin, sure it was wooden. He took a glass and handed it to his brother. Charon's hand trembled so much the contents spilled over his fingers. "I can't..." He leaned into Brice. "I can't do this, Brice. The music... it's the music. It's in my head. I might scream."

"Raoul!"

Raoul's eyes widened with a touch of panic. *Stay*, he

mouthed, then whirled and stepped into the path of the approaching fae. Scooping an arm around her shoulder, he turned her around. "A delight, as always—" The pair vanished inside the throng of bodies.

Brice dropped his head and pretended to examine an elaborately carved fruit of some kind that covered his fingers in gold leaf. The fae Raoul had neatly diverted away had been the sentinel he'd slipped around to get inside the masquerade. She would have undoubtedly recognized him had she looked over.

"Brice." Charon's teeth chattered. "He's coming. I feel it. He's close. We have to go."

Brice slipped his arm around his brother. It was just the two of them now. If the host saw them, Brice had nothing to defend Charon with. He'd lost Mother's pistol.

"We have to go." Charon panted, eyes shot and skin glistening. "We have to go now." He looked around. "He's coming, Brice."

Brice clamped down on his hand. "Be still."

Guests were looking over. Whispers hissed.

The music still played and the dancers still danced, but the atmosphere prickled, the air thinning.

Brice felt it then too.

A shudder rippled through the gathered dancers.

The host was here.

Charon muttered the same fears. He pulled at Brice's grip. "No, I have to go back. He'll find me. I have to go back —I can't leave." He tugged harder. "I can't do this. He'll make me cold again. I don't want to be empty. Brice, please. Please, brother. *Let me go*," he begged.

"Stop." Brice tried to keep him still. He fought to hold

him, to quiet him, but the more he tightened his grip, the more Charon fought. Where was Raoul?

Run, a panicked voice in his head said.

Run from him.

It might be their only chance.

Charon bucked and twisted, slipping from Brice's grip. He shoved through the crowd, knocking them aside. Gasps rose up. A glass smashed, wine and jagged fragments scattered between silk shoes. Brice ran too, close on Charon's heels.

Run.

They just had to make it through the foyer.

Run.

Just a few more steps.

Charon burst out the ballroom doors, spilling into the foyer, and skidded to a frozen stop. Brice stumbled into him, then staggered back a step.

Raoul stood in the center of the grand foyer, the lost pistol in his hand, its barrel aimed at Charon's head.

"Raoul, what—" Brice sealed his lips.

Raoul's sneer revealed sharp teeth. His mask hid the rest of his expression, but his eyes burned with the same fire Brice had seen before. Another facet, this one darker than the rest. Angrier. More desperate.

"What is this, Raoul?" The host's voice boomed from the gallery above.

Charon whimpered.

Brice couldn't look. Looking to the host would change nothing. He stared only at Raoul. "Raoul... lower the gun. *Please.*"

The exit was there, behind Raoul. Freedom, so close.

"End this now," Raoul said, skipping his gaze toward the stairs and the host's slow descent.

"What has come over you to threaten a mortal so?" said the host, sounding so reasonable.

Raoul's lips twitched and tightened, but his aim stayed true. The gun's aim never wavered. "This one..." Raoul began. He glanced at Brice, and his mouth twisted. He quickly faced Charon again. "This one is your mate's son. I saw it. I saw the music box you gave her. Your name and hers inside. Anette and Sinclair. The masquerade showed *him*. I invited Brice here—the LeChoix heir—the one name you told me never to pen, the one name that *never* came, until he did. I invited him so I might remember how it began, so the masquerade might show me something true in his memories, some reason for all this. And it did."

"Raoul," the host purred. "Lower the weapon. The boy is of no consequence." The host's tone hadn't changed, but his power throbbed hotter and heavier than before.

"Charon LeChoix is your mate's son! Half-fae! Half *her*." Raoul bared his teeth and tightened his grip on the trigger. "End this nightmare or the last piece of your love dies with him."

No... Raoul had played him all this time? He'd wanted the memories, the truth, facts Brice hadn't even known. He'd wanted Charon. Brice raised his hands and inched closer. "Raoul, don't do this. Whatever was done, Charon is innocent."

Raoul's aim wavered. His gaze flicked to Brice, then back down the pistol sight. "Your life is fleeting, Brice. For you there is an end. But I must live on—*we* must live on, forever dancing for *him*! It never ends. *I can make him end it*." Raoul's aim trembled, as did the rest of him. "She cursed us all the night she cursed you. End the masquerade, Sinclair, or your love's precious boy dies."

His words cut Brice to the bone. They were real, as real as Raoul's torture.

Raoul turned his head and looked up at the host, now standing on the last step. "You knew."

The host said nothing, just stared back from behind his black-and-gold mask.

"You knew who he was. All this time."

"Please..." Brice stepped closer still. "Don't do this. He's all I have left."

Raoul's breath sawed through gritted teeth. "I have to." His finger tightened. "End the masquerade or Anette's son dies and his blood will forever be part of the fabric of this nightmare."

It could not end like this. Whatever the past, whatever had truly happened between the host and his mother, Charon did not deserve this.

Another step. Brice reached for the pistol and fixed his gaze on Raoul. "It began with love, remember?"

"Love?" Raoul spat a harsh, bitter laugh.

"It should not end in blood."

Raoul's lips turned down. He shook his head and flexed his fingers on the pistol. "No, Brice. Don't take this from me. It must be like this. There's no other way. It has to end."

"Not like this. This isn't you. I've seen you. I know you. You helped me find my brother—"

"A deal, nothing more."

"Your smile, your laughter. You light up any room. Your kiss... Raoul, you're not a killer." Brice settled his hand on the pistol. Raoul barely fought, and as Brice pushed down, Raoul lowered the gun. Brice stood in front of him, watched him break apart, and wished he could take him away too.

Raoul's mouth trembled. "You don't know who I am." He lifted his chin and swallowed. "Run," he snapped. Then he lifted the pistol and swung his aim toward the host. "*Run, Brice!*"

Brice grabbed Charon's hand and ran.

He ran through the standing fae, ran through the aghast guests, ran from the foyer and through the archway. He ran by the sentinel, out into the forest and into the night. He ran until his lungs burned and his legs threatened to fall and his heartbeat sounded like drums in his ears. He ran with Charon down the track, out of the trees, into the town. He might have gone farther but at the town's fountain, he fell, pulling Charon into his arms. Another step might kill him.

They slumped together against the fountain's edge. The night was alive with sounds and smells—the fountain's tinkling water, a drunken man yelling outside the inn, a clattering carriage, the smell of horse dung and straw and woodsmoke. The smell of dirt and sweat and Chamonet. Home.

People emerged from nearby houses, lamps in hand, lifting them in the dark to better see. "Can it be? Lord LeChoix?" they said, whispering the name as though it were a myth. They asked if it were truly them, where they had been for so long, if they needed help.

Brice sobbed with his brother. They were out. They were free. He closed his eyes and breathed. Finally, he was free. And finally, Charon was safe. The nightmare was truly over.

All he had to do now was forget the fae, forget the people in the rose garden, shuffling from foot to foot, their hearts empty. Forget the trickster still trapped inside.

He had to forget. Because Brice could never, ever go back.

Chapter Twenty-Seven

People fussed over them, bringing water and blankets. Brice struggled to focus on their words or their faces. Patrice's booming voice took command when Brice failed to, and they were bundled into the inn. It was early, the sun just rising. Kris offered a room and Brice muttered his thanks. Charon said nothing, just trembled and swayed on his feet, as pale as a sheet.

A moment came when the familiar faces peered at Brice as though waiting. He gazed at them, unsure if any of this were real.

"Your mask, Master Brice?" Patrice enquired.

He blinked at her, unsure what she was asking.

"You still wear it."

He touched his face—the mask. He'd forgotten it. "Yes, of course." He fumbled the ties and removed it. Sprigs of grass clung to it, glittering pollen, too, from the endless fields. A few scratches marred its design from where roses had snatched at him. He half expected the mask to crumble to dust in his hands, but it was just cardboard and silk, nothing magical.

Charon handed Brice his own mask and slumped at an empty table near the fireplace.

"What happened?" Patrice softly asked. The concern in her voice threatened to pull Brice apart. He was barely holding himself together as it was. Kris looked on, worry tightening his face. They cared, and it was kind to see, but Brice couldn't stomach it. It was all too much. The horrors he'd been keeping inside—the touch and taste of the fae, the loss of control, their sweet whispers and maddening lust. It all scratched around the edges of his mind, trying to escape, and he feared he might let it, right there. He might fall to his knees and howl and sob.

Two strides took him across the room, and before he could stop himself, he tossed the masks into the fireplace. Fire warped and twisted the silk, spat and buckled the cardboard. And then they were gone.

Charon's blue eyes shimmered, swimming with tears.

"Our room?" Brice enquired.

Kris led them up the stairs and unlocked the door. The room was bland, simple, but a small fire sizzled in the grate. The air was smoky and warm. "Thank you," Brice said, shutting the door on Kris. He made it to the dresser, spread his hands on its top, and braced himself.

His heart tried to choke him. Pain attacked from within. Bruises, cuts, scuffs. On their own, they were minor, but his body remembered all the hurt at once. And inside... that was where it hurt the most. He closed his eyes, but the aches grew heavier.

"Brice?" Charon slipped an arm around his shoulders. "Is it over? Is this real?"

"Yes."

His brother fell into sobs. Brice clutched him close and silently cried with him.

Brice woke some hours later, still sore but somewhat grounded in his own skin again.

Charon was already awake and focused on stoking the fire back to life. "Good morning."

"Morning."

He seemed almost like Charon again. Brice could imagine the masquerade had never happened, but the real damage was inside both of them, and that would take longer to heal. He'd take him home today. They'd fix up the house. And someday soon the masquerade and its twisted games would fade like a bad dream.

Charon glanced over and smiled. The smile was tight and thin, nothing like his typical broad grins, but it was good to see nonetheless. It was all worth it, just to see that smile and to see his brother safe.

Brice swung his legs over the edge of the bed and rubbed sleep from his face. "After we've eaten, we'll head home. Perhaps Kris will lend us a horse—"

Charon straightened. "Before we leave, I must see Sophia."

Brice quickly looked away, out the window. He'd forgotten his lie.

Sickness roiled in his gut. He must look Charon in the eye and tell him Sophia was dead. He wished it weren't so. He wished Charon had been here. Perhaps he would have been able to save her. But wishing changed nothing. "Charon..."

"It's late afternoon. If we go now, we can return to the house by nightfall. I need to see her. I must know she's—"

"She's dead." Brice bowed his head and stared at his cupped hands in his lap.

Silence. He couldn't look up, wasn't brave enough to face him.

"No... no, you said—" Charon crossed the room and stood in front of him. Brice slowly lifted his gaze. Charon's eyes sparkled, too hard and sharp, and his lips pulled into a sneer. "You said she got out." His grip on the poker tightened.

"She did. But her mind was gone—"

"No." He snarled. "You said she got out!" He brandished the poker. Brice winced. He deserved it.

"You said she was out!" Charon threw the poker down and bolted from the room.

"Charon, wait!"

Charon sprinted down the stairs and fled the inn. Brice chased him, close behind. The townsfolk stopped to gawk. Charon plowed through several, knocking them aside. He ran down the streets toward the Brodeur house.

"Charon, don't!"

Charon hammered on their door. "Sophia!"

"Stop." Brice grabbed his arm. Charon whirled. His fist struck Brice in the jaw, whipping his head to the side. He staggered down the steps. Fury twisted Charon's face. Both his hands scrunched into fists. This was Brice's fault, his stare said. And Brice had no reply. Raoul was right. Had Brice answered the invites and gone to the masquerade himself, none of this would have happened. "I couldn't tell you."

The door swung open. Jonathon Brodeur loomed in the doorway, as commanding and austere as always.

Charon's shoulders stiffened. "I-I need to see her."

Brodeur peered at Charon, then at Brice. "The LeChoix are not welcome here. Kindly vacate my doorstep." He stepped back and attempted to slam the door. Charon shoved it open again.

"Where is she? Let me see her!"

"She's dead, you wretched boy!" Brodeur shoved Charon backward. He stumbled down the steps, falling against Brice. The door slammed. Its boom echoed down the street. The people who had left their houses to watch the unfolding spectacle gawked.

Just a few strides away, where the cobbles gleamed from a recent rain shower, Sophia had lain dead.

Brice squeezed his eyes closed. "Come away."

Charon shook his head and muttered words Brice didn't catch. "You!" He pointed at Brice. "You killed Mother and now Sophia! What good have you ever done? It should be you who is dead!"

The words ripped Brice's heart from his chest. He gasped and rocked on his heels as though hit a second time. He knew the words were true, of course, but it had never been said. He'd hated himself, still did, but the past was over. Rage boiled seemingly from the depths of his soul, suddenly rushing through him like Raoul's wildfire. Raoul's words came back to him, about how he wasn't wrong, how clinging to a legacy was madness, and the rage boiled over. "How dare you! Had you not damn well stolen my invite none of this would have happened! It's your foolish selfishness that brought this upon us and killed Sophia. She died right behind you, on those cobbles, after leaping from that very window above your head—because *you* just wanted a bit of fun with the fae. Was it worth it, Charon? *Your* actions killed her, not mine. I only tried to save you both!"

Charon stumbled in horror and stared at the shining cobbles. "No, no... I didn't. I didn't."

People stared and whispered, just like at the masquerade. For all Brice knew, they could be the same people here as there, just without their glittering finery and masks.

"No, no, no." Charon clutched at his hair.

Guilt swept the rage away, leaving Brice wretched. "Charon, I'm sorry. Please. Let's just go home."

Charon lifted his head. Tears skipped down his cheeks. "You killed my mother, because she wasn't yours. Father told me before he left us. He told me! And you killed Sophia for the same reason. I loved them. They were both mine. And you took them from me!"

"Enough!" Brice lunged for him. Charon skipped away and bolted again. He disappeared around a corner in the direction of the forest. A part of Brice wanted to let him go. What use was there in trying to save him over and over if he was just going to hate Brice in return?

Because Charon was his brother. He was family. And despite everything, he loved him.

He trudged after Charon while the townsfolk stared, whispering among themselves. He heard them mutter the cursed LeChoix name. *All mad. All doomed.* Brice growled at them. "Go get your entertainment elsewhere!" he snapped, and they scurried back inside their homes or continued on their way, scoffing their displeasure.

He followed Charon's path out of the town, knowing exactly where he'd be. The breeze whispered though the forest's leaves. Some daffodils sprouted here and there. Wasn't it winter still? Why were daffodils sprouting so early? He'd entered the masquerade just days ago on the solstice. But the forest hinted at spring. How could that be? His thoughts idly tumbled as he followed the path back.

Charon sat on the leaves ahead, knees drawn up and head bowed. His shoulders bobbed and the soft sounds of sobbing drifted through the quiet air.

The wicker archway led to nowhere, just like it had the last time Brice had left the masquerade. It had gone and taken its dreams—and Raoul—with it.

Only reality remained, and it was a painful, ugly place. For all the masquerade's glittering falsehoods and pretty, shallow pictures, it had offered a sense of joy and a hint of freedom. He'd run through the midnight meadow, tasted lust without disgust, and kissed a trickster. There had been wonderment at the masquerade, and now Brice feared the grim reality of his life was pale and harsh in comparison.

"It's time to come home, Charon." Brice heard the words, and they were right, but his heart was hollow.

Chapter Twenty-Eight

A NEW SECTION of Latchly Hall's roof had fallen in while they'd been away. Rats had taken up residence in the old dining room. Ivy choked every window. Brice barely knew where to begin. But it was easier to fix the house than his relationship with his brother.

Weeks had passed since their return, and Charon hadn't spoken but for a few words here and there.

Brice learned from the townsfolk how his one night at the masquerade had lasted over four months. He'd entered in December and emerged in April. It didn't make any sense. Four months in a night? It was impossible. But so was the masquerade.

Patrice had sent a hunter to check on Brice when he hadn't returned from the masquerade with the others. The hunter had found Latchly Hall empty and cold, with no master in sight. After a while, people had assumed Brice had taken himself into the woods, like his father, and sat down to die. They'd dismissed the LeChoixs as the tragic, doomed family who lived in the big house on the hill among the trees and wiped their hands of it all.

Until Brice had suddenly reappeared at the fountain with Charon. The new rumors didn't reach Brice's ears, but he could imagine the people of Chamonet had much to gossip over.

He set to repairing the house while the days were long and warm. He fixed the roof and replaced old pipes while Charon cleared the land and gardens. He even planted some hardy crops that would grow at higher altitudes. But his brother did not speak.

So this was their life now.

A grind to maintain a house he did not want, a name weighing him down like a shackle at his ankle. *Madness is clinging to a legacy as it drowns you.*

He thought of Raoul, mostly at night when his only company was wine and memories. He dreamed of the wily fae sprawled on the bench, smiling up at him. Dreamed of their kiss after he'd removed his mask, his melodic laugh and his tantalizing touch.

He'd known it a trap and still fallen into it.

Raoul had lured him there, seduced him to discover the truth about Leon and Anette LeChoix—Charon's mother. A fae.

Brice sipped his drink, already swimmingly intoxicated. His thoughts drifted, wandering to the sound of the crackling fire.

His mother, the woman he'd loved and cherished, wasn't his mother at all.

Leon LeChoix had conceived a child with another woman. There was no first marriage. Brice was a child outside of wedlock, technically not the heir at all. Whatever had happened to his real mother, Brice might never know. Was she someone in Chamonet? A maid or a woman of social standing?

The truth changed everything and nothing.

Charon was the legitimate lord. But society frowned upon bastard children and Leon had had the problem of what to do with his bastard first son. So Brice had simply belonged to Anette. Brice was the firstborn, and nothing else had been said. Then Charon arrived. The sunny-haired, brilliant boy, so loved and cherished. The son they'd wanted, not the one they didn't. *My secret, sweet boy.*

A fae's love is a fierce thing. Everlasting. Consuming. It outshines stars and outlives mountains. So when love goes wrong, it darkens those stars and levels those mountains.

Brice had many a drunken evening to turn over the truth the masquerade had shown him. And every time he turned it over, he wondered about his place in it and if he fit this life at all.

Hot summer days soon waned. Cold nights drew back in.

He tried not to think of Raoul trapped in an endless parade of brittle laughter, cloying desire, and tortuous dance, tried not to think of the forgotten people left behind in the rose garden, and he tried not to think of his place in it all. The solstice would approach, like the irrevocable passage of the seasons Raoul so pined over. He'd always anticipated the arrival of an invite with a sense of frustration and fear. This year he did not anticipate its arrival at all. Raoul wrote the invites. Raoul was a creature of pleasure, not torture. He would never invite Brice again.

Chapter Twenty-Nine

THE SOLSTICE WAS three days away. No invite had arrived. The nights were long again, the days fleeting, spent mostly collecting logs to heat the vast house and keep the chill at bay. Brice lit the candles and fires every night, ensuring the house glowed from within. He and Charon had performed a miracle. Latchly Hall was almost as it had been before. To celebrate, Charon had suggested a gathering to mend their sullied reputation. They invited the townsfolk for dinner, provided they bring their own food—Brice swallowed his pride for that and was surprised to find people still wanted to come.

Most likely they just wanted to satisfy their curiosity, but on the night of the gathering, when the carriages arrived and the people stepped into Latchly's brilliantly lit reception hall, he found himself smiling for the first time in months. Of course, Charon shone, and having seen the fae at the masquerade, Brice saw in his brother the same liquid ease and mesmerizing charm they possessed. Brice had always paled next to him. At least now he knew why.

The house filled with voices and laughter again. Brice finally greeted the baker and his wife, Jeremiah and Esme, after years of promising to host them. They beamed and *oohed* and *aahed*, complimenting him and Charon on the work it must have taken to smarten up the place. Charon's idea of the colored strings and sprigs of holly really did make a difference. Each new guest brought kind words, and Brice swelled a little with pride. Perhaps they weren't as alone as he'd believed.

Patrice brought stewed apples in cinnamon and took herself off to the kitchen to help with preparations. Brice hadn't considered how to manage such a feast without staff, but Patrice had it in hand.

When the clatter of the Brodeur carriage sounded outside, Brice's throat dried. Charon had suggested the invite. Brice hadn't been sure he would come, yet here he was. Hopefully to mend bridges, not burn them.

"Lord LeChoix." Jonathon greeted him at the doorstep in his top hat and tails, more gentlemanly than Brice.

Brice took his gloves, scarf, and hat. "Please, just Brice." He hadn't the stomach to tell him he was no more a lord than Jonathon was. "Welcome." He cleared the creak from his voice. "And thank you for coming."

Brodeur nodded stiffly and stepped inside. Thankfully, another guest recognized him, drawing him away. Alone in the hall for a moment, Brice paused to breathe. The evocative smell of cinnamon came from the kitchens. The lounge fire crackled, and Charon's laughter bubbled up. It was almost like before, like the dream the masquerade had shown him. There would be no chasing Charon through the ladies' skirts or Brice annoying Father with some wrong-footed foolishness, but it felt familiar and safe. It felt like a home again. It felt like the past was far away, and they just might be able to make something of their future.

A cold puff of air blew an envelope under the front door.

Brice looked down and froze, trapped between one breath and the next.

Whatever barriers he'd erected in his head to keep out the past began to quiver and crumble, the weak foundations failing. The envelope wasn't real. It wasn't here. He'd dreamed it up.

"Oh!" Patrice swooped in. For a large woman, she moved remarkably fast. "Best not leave that there—someone might stand on it!"

Brice snatched it out of her hand so fast she gasped. "My apologies, Patrice. I'll just... set this aside." He tucked it behind a framed family photograph.

Patrice's face fell briefly before she noticed the photograph. "Oh, what a lovely moment."

The framed picture was a stiff black-and-white image taken years ago when a photographer had ventured to town. A layer of dust covered its glass. Brice wiped it clean with a thumb. "Yes... from better times."

Some part of the image he hadn't seen before caught his eye. Behind the four of them, behind the mirror on the dresser, almost completely hidden, Brice saw the carved corner of a music box.

The masquerade's illusions tumbled forth.

The silk-wrapped music box Mother had played for Charon.

It was real.

It existed.

"Are you all right, Brice?"

"Yes," he snapped. "Fine." Patrice broadened, filling out as she straightened. Good lord, he hadn't meant to offend. "Forgive me. The image is rather... poignant."

She immediately softened and sighed. "Aye, you were all so beautiful. Was terrible, what happened. But they'd be proud of you, Brice. We're proud of you. The town, I mean. In many ways, we think of you as our lord. We care, you see?" Warmth touched her eyes. "Come, have a drink with us?"

"I will, yes. In just a moment?"

"Of course. My pie will be ready soon, you know." She chuckled. "I expect you to eat it. Need to put some meat on those LeChoix bones!"

She took herself into the lounge, where the sounds of chatter and chinking glasses rose and fell. Brice turned and looked again at the photograph. He wiped dust from its glass. The box was definitely as the masquerade had shown him. He took the stairs to the second floor and pushed into Mother's room. Unlit and cold, its chill immediately slunk under his clothes, reaching his skin and raising goose bumps. He blinked. His long shadow grew from the doorway, stretching across the floor and over her dresser. He could see her there in his memory. Charon seated on the stool, swinging his little legs in anticipation of his reward. Laughter sailed up the stairs, just like it had in the masquerade's waking dream.

Dust covered the old dresser, fogging the mirror's glass. It had been left in place, untouched, since her death.

He grabbed its edge and yanked. Cobwebs stretched

from the wall behind. Dead spiders hung suspended in the gap. But no music box.

Father had sorted through her things after her death. Would he have found it and thrown it out? A gift from the host to his beloved mate. A & S. Anette and Sinclair. If Leon had known what it was, if he'd seen their initials, he would have surely burned the thing.

Perhaps it was gone like his father was gone, like his childhood was gone, and the lies with it.

She was still his mother. She had still raised him. He still loved her.

He closed his eyes.

"I'm sorry," he whispered into the dark.

A cupboard slammed downstairs in the lounge, but Brice heard it like a pistol shot, like he had that night. It had been here, in this room, where he'd found her. Here, at his feet, where his mother had lain dead, her eyes open, her blood seeping between the floorboards. Killed by a single pistol shot.

He'd tried to wake her. And when that hadn't worked, he'd sat with her, numb and mute from shock.

Brice dropped to his knees on the creaking floorboards. She'd hated the fae, or so he'd thought. She'd warned him, sometimes lucid, sometimes ranting. She would curse them, and oftentimes it had sounded as though she'd hated herself too. Others had called it madness. Now he knew why. She had left her mate, her love, had cursed him as her parting gift. A curse that had begun the masquerade.

For the first time since she'd taken her own life, he finally understood why.

Tears wet his face. He slumped forward and touched

the board where her head had lain, her golden hair spilled around her like liquid sunshine. "I forgive you," he whispered. His tears fell onto dust-coated floorboards.

Something glinted in a gap between the boards.

The board had warped over time, just enough for Brice to dig his fingernails beneath and lift. It came away with a groan, and nestled beneath sat a silk-wrapped music box. The silk had slipped, exposing the glint of the turning handle. It was real. Hidden among all the lies, the masquerade had shown him a truth. Brice reverently reached for the box, fearing it might turn to mist and vanish the second he touched it.

Carefully, he lifted it out, separating it from its silk wrap. After setting it down on the dresser, he sat on the same stool as Younger Charon and took a moment to admire the carvings that looped and curled. Clasping the hand crank, he turned it over. Once. Twice. And opened the lid.

The little blue ballerina twirled on her small stage.

Tinkling music flowed. It danced around him, filling the room with its fantasy. Shadows fled, candles flickered, light poured in. Mother hummed from behind him, but he dared not look. She had hummed the same tune when he was a boy, the same tune as the box played now, the same music the masquerade dancers forever danced to, the same lullaby she'd hummed to him at night when she'd kissed him on the cheek. A kiss before bed to guard against the fae, she'd tell him. Then she'd tucked him in and bid him a goodnight, until the night she didn't come.

Their initials shimmered in the lid. A & S.

The music began to die, and the dancer's motions slowed.

Frantically, he wound the handle, and it began again.

Brice ran his fingers over the box's design, along its edges, to its corner, snagging a hidden seam. A slight push against the seam dislodged a tiny drawer. Inside lay a note rolled into a small scroll. He had to look. He had to know. Unrolling the slip of paper revealed two little words, the ink faded, almost lost.

Forgive me.

Emotion crested over Brice, washing away what was left of his barriers.

Forgive me. He touched it, ran his fingers over it. A note for him. A note for his father, for Charon, for them all, perhaps.

Forgive me.

He already had.

The music died, the light faded, and the humming stopped. This time he let the dancer rest and closed the lid. He slipped the note into his pocket, set the box down on the dresser, and dried his face.

He would go downstairs. He would face the people. He'd smile and laugh and be Lord LeChoix of Latchly Hall as was expected of him. And when they were content, and fed, and satisfied, he'd see them off. Then, and only then, he would tell Charon about the box. And the note. And perhaps his brother would finally forgive him too?

Chapter Thirty

Charon had fallen asleep on Mother's chamber floor with the box cradled in his arms. Brice laid a blanket over him, left the door ajar so the hallway light lay over his brother, and trudged downstairs. After the last guests had gone and the celebration was over, Brice had told Charon about the box and the note. His brother had reacted much the same way he had.

He wanted to believe it was over, that the box was the last piece. But as he descended the last step, the framed family photograph caught his eye, drawing him to a halt.

The invite's presence behind it plucked on his nerves.

Not yet.

The fire in the lounge burned low. He should stoke it and add logs to keep the flames burning, but instead, he filled two glasses with wine and left one next to the chair beside the fireplace as he always did the days before the solstice. "For you, Mother."

He downed his glass, swayed a little on his feet, then refilled it. Getting blind drunk was a family tradition. That was how Leon had handled things. But Brice could no longer bring himself to be angry at the man. Leon had fallen in love with the forbidden. A mortal and a fae—that story was never going to end well. Hadn't Brice almost done the same with Raoul? Not love but certainly infatuation. He still wasn't sure how much of what he'd felt was real and how much was induced by the fae and their ways. He'd been intoxicated, not fully in control. It had been a mistake. One he had moved on from.

He stumbled into the hallway and glared at the photograph—or rather, what rested behind it. An invite. It couldn't be anything else. Bills didn't come in gilded envelopes.

Shoving the photograph frame aside revealed the envelope behind it, mocking him. Like it always had. *I do not like to be denied.* He'd thought the summons were over. He'd thought Raoul wouldn't be so foolish as to try and invite him back. It *had* to be over. Brice snatched up the envelope. Better to get it over with, like ripping off a gauze. His name glittered in messy writing. He tore it open and a waft of jasmine slapped all the memories in his face. Raoul laughing, Raoul sneering, Raoul teasing and taunting, Raoul dancing, his breath in Brice's ear, Raoul's hand in his.

He shook his head free of Raoul and pulled the invite out.

save me

Brice read it again. ... *save me*... The words were sweeping, hurried, barely touching the paper and slightly slanted, like they'd been scrawled in a feverish rush.

save me

Despite its rush, the writing was indisputably Raoul's penmanship. He'd had no time to scribe a name. The invite was a desperate plea.

Brice slumped against the sideboard. The last eight months and his efforts to rebuild a life crumbled and turned to dust.

save me

He had to go back.

Charon groaned on arriving in the kitchen. He plodded across the flagstone floors and grabbed the steaming kettle from the stove.

"Good morning," Brice greeted.

Charon ran a hand through his curly hair and mustered a smile as he fixed himself some tea. "I fear I partook in too much wine. Have you been awake long?"

All night. Brice cradled the mug in his hand. His tea had long ago gone cold.

Charon bustled about, making comforting noises. "It was good to see everyone. Esme says the little lad two doors down from her tried to steal a loaf of bread, and instead of punishing him, they put him to work in the bakery. He seems to like it. They did something similar with me, I recall. Three a.m. starts to ready the ovens. I shall not forget." He chuckled fondly as he pulled a chair from the table to sit opposite Brice and sipped his tea. Blue eyes lifted and Charon's smile warmed. "Thank you for last night." He sighed. "I know you don't enjoy entertaining, but I think I might have gone mad without some company."

"It's fine, really." Typical that Charon would warm to him exactly at the moment he was about to deliver dire news.

"And thank you—for the box." His gaze danced away. "I thought it lost."

Brice reached into his pocket and stroked the invite, reconsidering just for a few seconds if this was the right course of action. But how much choice was there, really? ... *save me...* He withdrew it and placed it neatly on the table between them.

Charon didn't leap away, but he tensed like he might. All the warmth drained out of him, turning him to ice. "When did *that* come?"

"Last night."

"And you opened it? *Are you mad?*" Charon reached for it, as though he might throw it into the stove. Brice flicked it under his own palm, shielding it from his brother. It hadn't been so long ago that Brice had been the one trying to throw an invite in the flames to keep it from Charon's hands. How things had changed.

"You can't be considering it?" Charon fell back into his seat.

"I *have* considered it. I'm going."

"God, why?"

He didn't know how to explain his need to return without it sounding like the fae had bewitched him. One fae in particular. So he removed the invite from its envelope and showed Charon the words.

... save me ...

His brother's golden eyebrows pinched together. "It's a trick."

"It could be," he said.

"You were right about them. Their ways are wicked. We barely escaped." Charon reached across the table and captured Brice's hand in the first show of caring toward Brice since they'd returned. Perhaps since long before that. Charon squeezed his hand. "Brother, we're only now setting things right. Why would you leave?" He searched Brice's face for the answer.

Brice looked down at the hastily scrawled cry for help.

Charon's hand vanished from his. "It's the fae, isn't it? The one you were yelling at. The one who held Mother's pistol to my head. I saw the way you looked at him."

There was no way Brice could win this discussion, but he had to try. "Raoul is complicated."

"Yes, he is. He tricked you to get you there, to get *us* there, and he's tricking you again to make you go back. It's all a lie. You can't go."

"I must."

"You think you feel for him? A fae? Do you hear yourself? This is exactly what Mother warned us about."

Did he not remember Raoul's words? Or was his ignorance just wishful thinking? Brice slammed a fist against the tabletop, rattling their mugs. Charon would damn well listen now. "*Mother was a fae!*"

Charon startled. "What?"

"Do you truly not see or do you not want to?" Brice

sneered. "The note I showed you. The words: *forgive me.* It wasn't *for us.* Mother wrote that for everyone she left behind at the masquerade. It came *from* the music box, a box given to her by her *mate—Sinclair,* the host. She left the host for our father. She cursed them all, and she never forgave herself. She was fae, Charon. You know it inside, the same as I do."

"That's... That's not true," he said. "She didn't even look fae."

Brice snorted. "She told us how they change their appearance. She even said how they make themselves look like us. She was telling us the truth our whole lives and we dismissed her as mad. You've seen them. You know how they can make themselves look... *different.*" Images of Vine's forked tongue slithered through Brice's head. He winced them away.

"If she was fae, then how did she take her own life? Are they not immortal?"

The memory of the single shot and finding her body surged to the front of Brice's thoughts. Not even a fae could withstand a single iron shot to the head. "Iron. It was the iron shot."

Charon's shoulders slumped. "Sometimes it feels as though we're the ones who are cursed. Not them."

"They're trapped. We escaped, they cannot. They've been trapped in that godforsaken place since before you were born and they will be trapped there until long after we're gone. Whatever the host did to deserve Mother's ire, the rest of them had no part in it, and they're hurting. The guests use them for pleasure and leave again. Raoul is... he was desperate. He held the pistol to your head because he saw no other way out."

Charon frowned. "Or because they love theatrics."

Raoul did enjoy the dramatic; Brice couldn't deny it. But he *knew* Raoul. Four months he'd spent with him, although it had felt like far less. "He wasn't lying. Not then. Yes, he lured me there to discover what really happened to Anette, and he used you to force the host's hand. He planned to end it, to... kill you—that is true—"

"And you side with him?"

"He couldn't do it. Don't you see? He turned the pistol on the host so *we* might escape. He saved us, Charon. We would not be here without him. And now he's asking for help. I owe him."

Charon rubbed his hands down his face. "If you go back there, the masquerade will kill you, Brice. Not directly, that's not what they do. They twist everything, real and unreal, and they make you witless. Then they let you go... like they did with Sophia." He swallowed loudly. "And you're all I have left."

Suddenly, Charon was a boy again, looking up at him with big blue eyes, asking where Mother had gone. It broke Brice's heart. "You're a brilliant, capable young man. You survived horrors that would break most people. You're brave, Charon. You can do anything you put your mind and heart into. I was wrong to keep you here. You were right. It was selfish to keep you from everything you loved, including Sophia. And I'm sorry for it all. You are a free man. You are more the lord of this place than I am. I don't belong. I never did—"

"That's not true." Charon caught Brice's hand and

clasped it between both of his. "You're my brother and I love you. I've said terrible things, but that is not all I feel for you. You saved me whenever I was lost. Even before Mother was gone, you were my world. I can't lose you to *them* too. Please, don't go. Don't leave me. Their world is not ours."

"I'll come back." Brice tried to smile, in the hope it might make the words true, but they both knew he could not promise such a thing.

"I'll come with you."

Brice swallowed a *no*. "If you wish, but there is only one invite, and the host wants you more than me. You are his mate's son. If you go back there, I do not know his plans for you, but I doubt they are benevolent. At the very least, he will keep you locked in the rose garden until your mind is gone—just like the others."

Charon bowed his head and squeezed his eyes closed. "I am a coward," he said. "I cannot go back there."

"It is not cowardly to protect yourself. It's brave. Stay here. Keep the fireplaces lit and the house alive. I will do everything in my power to return."

Charon released his hand and sighed. "Is he worth it? This Raoul? Is he worth perhaps losing everything for?"

"I'm not going for him."

"Then for who?"

"I'm going to save them all for Mother. To end what she began. It's what she'd want."

Chapter Thirty-One

Saving them all was a grand idea. But as he stood in line for the masquerade, dressed in his repaired suit, a new mask back on his face, he wasn't sure he knew how. He'd find Raoul first—save him, probably from punishment. After that, the wily fae would know what to do. Unless the invite was a trap. In which case, he might never leave. And would that be so terrible a thing? There was only one way of knowing.

He clutched the invite in both hands and shuffled forward. Strange, dainty fireflies dallied about the lit pathway. Strange, seeing them in winter. Whispers rustled through the waiting townsfolk. History seemed to be repeating itself.

Ahead, the female sentinel dressed all in black with a white mask skimmed her hands over the invites. Raoul wasn't opposite her. Had he been whipped again for holding a pistol to the host? Or sent to the pleasure rooms? Or worse. There would be worse. There was no use in speculation about his absence. Better to focus on facts.

Of course, one fact was how his invite wasn't technically an invite. It didn't have Brice's name on it, though he knew without any doubt it was for him. The sentinel knew Raoul. She'd hopefully read its words and its meaning and let Brice through. If she denied him entry, it was unlikely she'd fall for the burning scarecrow a second time.

When it was his turn to greet her, he stepped up and met her keen gaze through her mask.

"Hello again," she said without looking at the invite. "You are a glutton for punishment and pleasure, young lord."

The familiarity of her words had those behind him in the line discreetly leaning closer to overhear.

Brice shifted his position, blocking their view. "I apologize for my previous indiscretion. It really was very unseemly."

"Hm." She took the invite and skimmed her fingers over the words. A small gasp escaped her lips. She looked down and traced the desperate words a second time with her fingertips, and when she looked up again, her eyes shone a little brighter. Suddenly clutching the back of his neck, she pulled him close, and for a moment he feared she might be about to kiss him. But she turned her head and whispered in his ear, "Thank you." Straightening, she fixed her stare on his. Her eyes hinted at fear and gratitude.

She gave him an encouraging shove in the shoulder toward the wicker arch. His feet briefly stuck in place. Fear tripped his heart and thoughts. Half of him knew he shouldn't follow the laughter and light, but the rest understood it was inevitable. There was no going back. He'd made his decision. He inhaled and stepped into the dazzling light and hauntingly beautiful music that instantly entwined with his soul.

As soon as he stepped into the foyer, it became clear something fundamental had changed. Not in a good way, such as the passage of the seasons Raoul so craved, but in a more subtle way. The chandeliers still sparkled like captured constellations and the guests all dazzled and shone. The music played—the same music from the music box, only with the depth and heart of a full band. It was all here, but... too much. The laughter had become tighter. The smiles sharper. And some stray note in the music made the whole number sinister. The fae were still here, mingling because they had no choice. Smiling and dancing and entertaining, the perfect marionettes, their strings held by the host.

A host Brice had to avoid if he was going to survive this third foray into the masquerade.

Find Raoul. If he could do that, he was sure they'd succeed together. Raoul had the energy, the wit, the guile. Brice had... well, Brice had the will to see it through.

It didn't take long to slip through the crowd and out into the night garden. He ignored the others, tucked away in illicit corners, and made straight for the hidden entrance to Raoul's abode.

He didn't expect to find him inside, but it was a safe place to start his search. He emerged from the tunnel and slowed. Smashed, jagged glass crunched under his shoes and sparkled across the floor. The bed area had been tossed about. Raoul's drawings lay strewn all over, their corners curled and rippling in the breeze. Even his clothes had been scattered. Nothing had survived the wrath of whoever had done this.

Brice stepped around the broken bottles to the desk area. The invites were gone. The inkpot had been knocked over, its ink spilled across Raoul's marvelous drawings. Then the ink had dried and buckled the paper, twisting the images. One such image was a new sketch of Brice. Although the quill strokes had been light and fast, he recognized the midnight meadow and how he'd raised his arms to the stars. Raoul had captured Brice's quick smile with his light strokes, drawing him glancing over his shoulder. The sketch was so perfect Brice could almost smell the cool grass.

Spilled ink had stained the page, almost as though someone had tried to erase the beautiful picture. Or *destroy* it. Had Raoul done that? Was he furious with Brice for leaving?

He didn't believe so. Raoul had been the one to tell him to go.

There was one other person who would destroy this place and Raoul's beautiful pictures. The host.

The destruction took on a more sinister feel. If the host had flown through the chamber in a rage, what had he done to Raoul?

He folded the sketch together and tucked it inside his coat. With no clues as to Raoul's whereabouts, just chaos, there was only one other person he could rely on to help. For a price.

Chantel.

Raoul had said not to trust her, but she and Raoul were

close. She would know where he was. She'd be in the ballroom at the heart of the masquerade. But so would the host.

Steeling himself, he gathered his bravado and his wits and left the cavern.

All would be well, just so long as he stayed focused. He knew what to expect now. This place had nothing left to throw at him.

A boom rumbled through the night. Light flooded the night garden from above, then quickly died again. A whistle screeched. Brice looked up in time to see a rocket explode into dazzling stars. Fireworks. He'd seen them before just once when the traveling carnival came to Chamonet.

Another rocket joined that one. Color and light lit up the sky while below, in the gardens, shadows danced and swayed.

People still rutted and swooned and teased one another. In the shifting light, their couplings became twisted, almost hideous. Teeth flashed, skin glistened. The fireworks boomed and color rained.

Brice hurried toward the ballroom, but the crowd spilling into the garden blocked his path.

Guests and fae alike headed down the garden paths, their masked faces tilted toward the skies. He'd have to find another way. But wandering about these gardens was dangerous. Chantel had tricked him here. The pollen alone could render him witless without his knowing. He had to think. Keeping his head ducked, he hurried back down the path, passing the large purple blooms Raoul had stirred to loosen Brice's inhibitions, and there, ahead, he saw the covered bench where Raoul had thought to seduce him.

A figure was on the bench, and Brice's heart skipped. Raoul was there! He was all right!

Another step and the figure looked up, gold glinting through his mask's design. A slanted smile revealed sharp fae teeth. Distant fireworks spilled their noise and light, lighting him up, only for the shadows to rush in once more, leaving just the host's shining eyes glowing in the dark.

"Welcome back, Lord LeChoix."

Chapter Thirty-Two

The host rose to his feet with predatory elegance. Shadows flocked to him like things alive.

Brice stayed rooted to the path. A childish voice inside told him to run, but where? The crowds blocked the way out of the gardens. If he ran to the cavern, he might be able to make it back out through the gap where the stream ran in behind the waterfall. But where to go from there?

The fae approached. Taller than Brice, he lowered his head to speak. "Love is a terrible mistress, is it not, LeChoix?"

"I wouldn't know." His voice sounded steady, unlike the furor in his head.

The host laughed softly, then caught Brice's arm and drew him closer. So close now it was almost intimate. "He surrendered the last of his freedom so that you might escape." The host stepped around him, circling. Their suits skimmed together like a soft sigh. "And here you are, drawn back to the masquerade. A hopeless moth falling into the flame even as it kills you." The host's breath touched his ear and the hand stroked around Brice's hip in a slow dance. "Thus his sacrifice has been for nothing."

"You speak of Raoul?" There was no hiding the quiver in his voice. "Where is he?"

"Many a mortal has fallen in love with the trickster." The host's fingers skimmed down Brice's neck and a defiant lick of lust slipped down his spine. "Did you think yourself unique?"

He didn't *love* Raoul, but clearly the host believed it. Or perhaps he saw love everywhere since he'd been denied it. It was hard to believe Mother could love a creature like this. But she had, once. And she'd been sorry to let him go. *Forgive me.* Perhaps the host, like Raoul, had many faces behind his mask. The host had to be more than the monster they all feared. He'd been hurt, of that Brice was certain. *It began with love.* Perhaps if he could understand the host, he might better know how to stop him. Stop all this.

He did have something that might get through to him. Something he hoped might help change things.

Brice reached inside his jacket.

The host circled back around to face him, his masked gaze dropping to where Brice's hand had vanished inside his jacket. The host caught his arm, holding it rigid, then slipped his free hand inside Brice's jacket to find whatever Brice reached for. Their gazes locked. His knuckles brushed Brice's chest through his shirt fabric. Then the host pried Mother's note from between Brice's fingers and withdrew it.

Raoul's sketch of Brice slipped free and fell to the path.

It lay there, Brice's carefree moment in the midnight meadow revealed, his face full of unmistakable joy. Raoul had captured that perfectly.

The host's lips twitched. He dropped the forgotten note and gripped Brice's wrists, yanking him close. "*You will never be free again.*" He hauled Brice into motion, dragging him along the path.

"Wait!" Brice twisted, tore an arm free, and tried to find the note. A gust of wind fluttered the sketch across the path, and with it went Mother's note. *Forgive me.* The sketch and the note rolled and skittered and were gone, vanished in the dark. "*No. Damn you!*"

The host stilled. A few nearby guests looked over.

Brice struggled in the host's grip, trying to pry his iron-like fingers off. More guests arrived, drawn from the fireworks to the host.

"Damn me?"

He barely saw the host move, just felt the rush of air. Pain jolted down his back. The host held him pinned to a wall.

The host clamped his grip around Brice's neck and lifted. Fingers squeezed his throat, choking off air. His feet dangled. The host laughed. "Fool. We are already damned! Now so are you. You should never have returned." The swirl of gold in the host's eyes pulled Brice's glare into their depths.

The fae in the crowd laughed too. The shrill sound of it cut through Brice's mind. Lack of air darkened his vision. The host wouldn't kill him... would he? Sound throbbed and melted, turning all he could hear and see into a mangled soup of nonsense and then finally into silence.

Chapter Thirty-Three

Coming around felt as though he waded through syrup. His body was lead and his head full of wool. He rolled onto his side and peered into tufts of dry grass. Grass? That didn't seem right. Where had he been before this? Where was he now? He raised a hand to his head, hoping to clear the fog. Where the sky should be, enormous roses bloomed. Swollen and vibrant red petals hung over him, the only color in this gray place.

A memory niggled. Something about the roses... but as he tried to grasp its meaning, it slipped away.

Groaning, he propped himself on an elbow and frowned at a dark courtyard. High walls cut off any distant views. Old stone huts had crumbled, leaving just shells behind. A fountain lay dry and desolate. Roses spiraled around its base. So many roses...

God, what was it about the roses? Why couldn't he think?

He pulled the mask from his face and frowned at it. He had no recollection of putting it on or why.

Climbing to his feet, he tightened his jacket, trying to fix the odd sense of detachment, and stumbled forward. He should know this place and its people, but all of it felt distant, as though this were a dream. A dream within a dream...

It's the roses.

He turned, expecting to see the man who had spoken, but there was nobody behind him, just people moving like wraiths through shadows. The voice was a memory then?

The roses... The reason for his being here lurked at the edges of his mind, but his thoughts couldn't catch it. It was important, though, that reason. He knew that much. Important enough to rattle his nerves.

He drifted, looking for something or someone, not knowing what or who. Cold seeped beneath his clothes and skin, into his bones. His teeth chattered until even the cold faded to nothing. Strange, he didn't feel much of anything anymore.

He was here for a reason.

Something important.

It slipped away like sand through his fingers.

Roses barred a gate. He walked by, unconcerned. Roses had climbed walls and smothered old dwellings. They were everywhere, the air full of their sweetness. He liked them. Without their color and scent, the garden would be a desolate place. Perhaps he'd come here for the roses, to tend the garden.

No, no... that's not it.

"Think..." he muttered. It was in there. Inside his head. Important. Slippery. If he could just remember...

Around and around, he walked—searching for something—until his legs ached and his feet throbbed from sores. He kicked his shoes off and kept on walking, searching for the reason...

Sometimes he rested, sometimes he slept under a canopy of roses, but most times he walked. His feet bled, but that didn't seem important.

When the golden-haired male fae appeared, he seemed to be a dream, just like the other people in the garden. His hair spilled over his bare shoulders and was tied in a loose tail behind him. Tattoos marked his chest and shoulder, crawling over him like vines. Vine... Hm. Forgotten instincts twitched, as though perhaps he should listen, but the fae held a cut rose in his hand and brought it to his nose, and that simple motion held Brice enraptured. Golden eyes locked on Brice. The stirrings of desire warmed his veins, thawing the numbness, filling him up, making him real again.

The golden-haired fae sauntered closer. His loose trousers clung to his hips, fixed there by some impossible fastenings. Once the fae was close, Brice lifted his chin and held his gaze. He exuded sex, this one. Had Brice dreamed him up? Was he real? Brice reached out to touch his face and found his jawline firm and warm under his fingertips. His lips, too, were soft, almost delicate, like rose petals.

But Brice wasn't here for *him*.

He turned his face away.

There was something else... some other reason eluding him.

The fae's fingers caught his chin and tilted his head. *Vine...* a fluttering memory supplied. Brice had met him before, somewhere. He knew his voice was deep and smooth, knew how he tasted, too, sweet on the tongue.

Vine handed him the cut rose. Brice brought it to his nose. His thoughts clouded. The garden and its roses spun, then firm arms closed around him, holding him on steadier ground. "Come with me. He will never know," Vine's deep voice rumbled. He radiated hard and warm masculinity, drawing Brice closer. It had been so long since he'd been held, touched. He'd been so cold, but the fae's embrace thawed all the ice from his blood and body, made his heart beat again. He buried his face against Vine's shoulder, closed his eyes and breathed in.

"You're safe," Vine said. Brice dug his fingers in, falling while standing still. He squeezed his eyes harder, suddenly inexplicably afraid, like a boy again, facing his father's gun.

"Open your eyes and look."

The fae's grip loosened and Brice reluctantly eased back to see. The gray garden with its vibrant roses was gone. He stood in a bedchamber lit by countless candles adorning every surface. There were roses here, too, cut and arranged in vases placed among the candles. Another dream, then.

It's the roses...

Brice sucked in a breath. The urge to flee made his heart race, but he couldn't place why. Nothing in this room was dangerous. It was just a room... and the fae, smiling, as though they were friends. Perhaps they were. Brice's body burned under the fae's sultry gaze.

Vine moved away, found a pitcher of wine, and poured two glasses.

There was no threat here, no pain. So why did Brice's heart race so? He swallowed hard. If he could just put the pieces of his broken thoughts together again to make the full forgotten picture, he'd know how to proceed. He was here for a reason. Was that reason Vine? The buzz in his veins seemed to suggest so.

Vine offered the glass. "Drink, you must be parched."

Brice stared at the shining glass and its blood-red contents. The thirst came on fast. He couldn't recall when he'd last eaten. Suddenly, he craved it. Food. Wine. And the fae with golden eyes. Craved *him*. Savage desire tore through him, demanding to be satisfied. But it wasn't his desire, it couldn't be. He was not supposed to openly desire men. The LeChoix heir did not partake in such things. He remembered *that*.

"I, er..." His voice cracked and creaked, hoarse from lack of use. His thoughts fogged some more, swirling and drifting. His body thrummed, want welling up in him, making him hard. He couldn't reason like this but couldn't think to clear his head.

Brice turned away. Where was the door? There had to be one. Just walls and drapes and candles and roses... and the bed. His fingers fluttered to his forehead. He had to get home, didn't he? No... he had to *find* someone.

"Here." Vine slipped his arm around Brice's waist from behind. His warm, firm body pressed close against Brice's back, holding Brice upright. The rod of the male's arousal dug against Brice's ass, stealing a gasp from his lips.

The fae brought Brice's mask around and sealed it over his face. Suddenly, the fog of fear and uncertainty vanished. Gone, like mist burned away by the heat of the sun—the heat of desire. Vine's fingers trailed down Brice's neck, so light and soft. Such a tease. He leaned his head away, exposing his neck. Soft lips brushed his skin, raising goose-flesh. The fae's breath fluttered, coming fast, and with every inhale, his cock dug harder against Brice's rear.

It had been so long since he'd been taken by a man. If he could think beyond this room, perhaps he could remember when, but his thoughts were all lost, and now he wore the mask, nothing mattered anyway. He was nobody again. Free to do as he pleased. And he very much wanted to be pleased by Vine.

Vine brought the wineglass around and tipped it against Brice's lips. "Drink and let us finish what was begun, hm?" the fae purred.

Without hesitation, Brice drank the contents down. Vine suckled his neck, his cock ground against his ass, and his breaths came fast. When the glass slipped from Brice's fingers, it didn't matter. When it smashed into a thousand pieces, it didn't matter. Nothing mattered because nothing was real.

"You want this?" the fae whispered in his ear. "You want me."

"Yes." He wanted it so badly he was hard and aching, desperate for Vine's intimate touch.

"Hm," Vine purred. "In good time."

Now, his body demanded. He wanted to be fucked in the rawest and most animal way. He wanted the fae inside him. Begging words came to his lips, but he wasn't sure if he spoke them. The room spun. His body blazed. Only Vine's firm hands kept him steady.

Vine circled around, peered into Brice's eyes behind the mask, and dropped to his knees. This had to be a dream because this didn't happen. Not to Brice. Starved so long of the pleasures he craved, to have them offered now left him reeling. The fae's expert fingers untied his trousers and dove inside, seeking his cock. Sparks lit up his spine the second the fae's fingers found it. Then Vine drew his length between his soft lips, and the whole world narrowed to the sensation of the male's strong, wet tongue sucking hard. Brice was falling. He knew somewhere distantly that this wasn't right, but he didn't care. He needed it like he'd needed the wine, like he'd needed the mask, like he needed to live and breathe and fuck. Brice sank his fingers into the fae's gold hair, loosely holding him as he sucked and teased. The fire within simmered hotter and higher, rising up until there was nothing but wave upon wave of pleasure, each one building on the last until the pleasure threatened to spill over.

Vine suddenly pulled free and stood. His fingers pinched the tip of Brice's cock and crackling pain instantly dampened the cresting orgasm. Brice gasped and Vine's smile twitched. "Not yet." He yanked, pulling Brice forward, then stepped around him and shoved him between the shoulders.

Brice stumbled against the end of the bed, reeling, desperate, flushed with lust.

"Get on."

The fae's tone was no longer friendly. His smile had turned sharp too.

Brice's cock jumped, leaking silvery streams onto silk sheets.

Vine shimmered behind him like some dream made real. The body of Adonis, the beauty of a god—Brice would do anything for him. He climbed onto the end of the soft bed. Vine lunged in, grabbed his trousers, and yanked them down, exposing his buttocks and thighs. Warm hands spread Brice's ass and kneaded his flesh, dancing the line between lust and pain.

Vine pressed against him—still trousered—but his heavy cock pushed in as he leaned over Brice's back and gathered him in his arms. He hauled Brice upright, took his jacket and tore it free. The underlying thread of rage had Brice snatching his breaths, caught between devastating arousal and fear. Vine's manhandling was rough, his body strong. Brice wasn't weak, but in the fae's arms, he felt lesser, and that, too, had him whimpering for more.

Vine hauled Brice's shirt over his head and now he was almost naked with only his trousers caught around his knees. And his mask. His cock jutted, exposed in the cool air. A stutter of shame tried to have him cover up, but Vine swooped in and kissed Brice's shoulder. His hand came around, confidently taking Brice's cock, and suddenly Brice was surrounded by the male, his cock in the fae's hand, his back against the fae's chest. Kisses trailed his shoulder and neck. The fae's fingers pumped slowly, gathering Brice's own wetness to slick his grip. The fae's free hand skimmed his hip, then his fingers found a pert nipple and pinched. Teeth sank into Brice's shoulder. He had never been touched with such confidence, such desire.

Brice grunted and breathed and throbbed. His heart raced and Vine's hand pumped and he was going to spill all over these silk sheets at any moment.

A second pinch at the tip of his cock threw cold water on his rampant lust. "Please." He moaned and writhed, his cock caught in the fae's fingers.

Vine's laugh stirred all the madness in Brice's head. "Not yet."

Oh God, was this the fae's game, to bring him near to climax and cut him off? So cruel a notion. But Brice wanted it. "More, then." He growled. "Give me more."

"My pleasure." Vine's chuckles turned to laughter. He pushed Brice forward, shoving him onto his hands and knees. Taking Brice's ass in both hands, he ground his fabric-trapped erection in the valley, massaging himself between Brice's buttocks.

Then the fae's trouser fabric was suddenly gone and his slick cock slid between the tight valley, making Brice gasp. His cock skimmed Brice's hole, threatening to sink in with every new stroke. Brice wanted it, might beg for it, certainly already whimpered for it. What would it feel like to come with the fae's thick cock inside him?

A hand reached below him, cupping his balls. The touch startled him, not least because he could account for both of Vine's hands on his ass. This touch was new. Someone else's.

Brice peered down between his braced arms and found the flame-red hair of Laurel between his knees. Fear tried to rob him of pleasure, but Vine still stroked his cock between Brice's ass, and Laurel tilted his head back, smirked, then reached around Brice's thigh to clasp his cock in his fingers and lower it to his mouth.

Brice could watch no more.

He lifted his head and squeezed his eyes closed as Laurel—on his back between Brice's legs—took Brice's straining member between his own lips. Pressure pushed at Brice's ass, and the weight of Vine's cock stretched him wide and sank in, widening and stroking the part that made ecstasy sing through his veins, making him want to come a thousand times harder and faster. Vine withdrew, then sank in, and slowly found a delicious rhythm. That same rocking motion had Brice fucking Laurel's accommodating mouth. Vine thrust, Brice rocked, a cock buried in his ass while his cock drove down Laurel's throat. It had to be some bewitchment because he'd never felt anything as exquisite as being fucked while fucking another.

Vine's pace quickened. "Yes!" the fae's deep voice growled. He pumped into Brice, and Brice fucked Laurel's mouth, intensity building. Ecstasy danced down his spine, pulling his mind out of the moment until there was nothing left but the hot feel of skin on skin, the tightness of wet lips, the pressure of weight inside him, and then the moment of sweet crescendo was upon him.

The pair suddenly disengaged together—Laurel freed Brice's cock and Vine withdrew, leaving Brice moaning their loss on his hands and knees, breathing hard. If he could just take his cock in hand, he'd come in two strokes. He might come just thinking it. Oh God, they were cruel, but he wanted more.

Claude—the dark-skinned beauty—crawled on all fours onto the bed in front of Brice. He tipped Brice's chin up. This third fae's skin glistened like night. His cock stood proud, and Brice needed no encouragement to suck it between his lips.

Claude's cock filled Brice's mouth as Vine's filled him from behind and his filled Laurel's mouth. He could no longer track who touched whom or where. Hands and tongues, teeth and nails, thrusting and grunting. He gagged on Claude's member and didn't care. He was present but not. Pleasure set him ablaze, turned his body into a vessel for need and sex, with no thought, just desires to be satisfied.

Whatever he had come to this place for didn't matter. There was nothing else in his world, just the trio of fae fucking him into oblivion.

Pleasure crested. He was so close to spilling down Laurel's throat. He'd never wanted anything more.

The trio withdrew as one, suddenly denying Brice his climax. He growled, cursed them between breaths, sobbed a little too. Wetness dripped down his balls and thighs. He ached to finish. "Let me come, damn you!" He reached down to grasp himself, but Vine caught his wrist, held him rigid, and spoke in his ear. "All in good time... After all, you're ours now. Forever."

Claude drew Brice up onto his knees and kissed him hard on the lips. His forked tongue slipped around Brice's. It should have repulsed Brice, but he was beyond caring. He'd become a creature of need, thinking only of where he could stick his cock next and when he might be allowed to come to completion.

Vine pressed against his back, and at this angle, Vine's cock penetrated just enough to stroke over Brice's prostate. Brice ground his cock against Claude's, and Claude dropped his hand, gripping both members in his fingers.

Brice kissed him harder, faster, as though Claude was the air he needed to breathe. Vine fucked Brice, grunting in his ear. Claude pumped their cocks together, Brice so close to coming that a single word might be enough to tip him over the edge. But the fae knew when he had climbed to the edge and was ready to spill, they knew when he was about to fall, and every time they pulled back, leaving him gasping and desperate. He begged them to let him come, his cock leaking for it. He dripped with sweat and the fae's own sticky sweetness, but still they held him back, walking him to the edge but not letting him go over. They fucked and licked and bit and drove their cocks into every hole, over and over. Brice fucked their pretty mouths and tight asses, too, so close to coming that his body crackled and sparked with unspent need, and still they curbed him. Every time they stopped, and every time Brice begged. Just one more suck, one more pump, he'd do it himself, take his cock and fuck his own hand to completion, but they were everywhere, holding him off, holding him down, making him crazy.

He didn't know when or how, but the dream turned into a nightmare he couldn't escape from. A nightmare of pleasure and pain, of frustration and agony. But still, he begged for more. One more thrust, just one more kiss, because that might tip him over the edge, might have him spill and scream and fall and have it finally be over.

But they didn't relent.

They didn't finish him.

And it didn't end.

Chapter Thirty-Four

"Well," a familiar voice said, dripping with irony. "You were supposed to save me. Now look at us both."

Hm. Brice blinked at the new fae leaning over the bed. This one had black hair with a silver streak, braided in a long tail down his back, and he spoke as though he knew Brice. He wore a black silk tailcoat edged in silver lace. The coat was long enough to cover his hips and thighs. Beneath it, he wore a waistcoat and stockings, of all things, tucked into knee-high leather boots. And a mask, too, of course, silver and black.

The fae frowned—at least, he seemed to. Dark eyebrows dove in behind his pretty mask. "You don't recognize me at all, do you? They've had their fun then, I see."

Brice rolled onto his back and spread his legs. He was hard. He was *always* hard. Where had the trio gone?

A bundled-up shirt struck Brice in the chest, then a pair of trousers followed.

"Put those on. Hurry. They'll return soon."

Brice looked at the trousers, trying to fathom what this fae was asking. "I can't leave."

The fae definitely frowned this time. "I don't suppose if I asked you to trust me, you'd listen?"

"I don't know you."

He rolled his eyes, stepped back, bowed with a sweeping flourish, and rose wearing a scowl that not even the mask could hide. "My name is Raoul. You *do* know me, but Vine and his companions have seduced you out of your mind, as I warned you would happen. Clearly, like most mortals, you hear but you do not listen. Now come—"

"I don't want to go."

Raoul touched his forehead, exasperated, but how Brice could have offended him, he couldn't imagine. The fae paced and his boots struck the floor. He was really quite a handsome male, especially in the silk-and-lace outfit. Perhaps he could be persuaded to join Brice in bed?

"Tell me your name," Raoul said. "Prove to me you still have your wits, that you're here of your own choice, and I will leave."

Although he did seem rather prickly.

"My name?" Brice laughed. "Absurd." Of course he knew his own name. It was... right on the tip of his tongue. Right there... somewhere.

Raoul folded his arms and cocked his head. "Well?"

He had a name, didn't he? There was Vine and Claude and Laurel and... him.

Raoul knelt on the bed and caught Brice's chin, forcing him to look. "You have a life outside this room, even though you do not recall it. You're here for a reason and it is not to be their plaything. Trust me, Brice LeChoix."

Brice. Yes. That was his name. And he *was* here for a reason. A reason he'd forgotten. And that reason was... Raoul?

He knew this fae.

He'd seen him before, in dashing silver-and-black attire, seen him laughing, danced with him, saw him hold a pistol to Charon's head.

Brice threw the clothes back. They struck Raoul in the chest and fell to the floor. "You betrayed me."

"Of all things, you remember *that*?"

"Do you deny it?"

"No."

"Then why should I go with you?"

Raoul snarled and lunged, grabbing Brice's wrist. He tried to haul him off the bed, but Brice dug into the sheets, gripping hard. A waft of sweet-smelling rose scent dizzied him.

Raoul smelled it too. Disgust pulled his lips down. "They've intoxicated you. This is not consensual. If you stay here, you will lose your mind forever. The masquerade will consume you, like it has everything else in my life. It cannot take you, Brice. I won't allow it. I won't let *him*. You may not know me or even believe me, but I am trying to save you so that you might save me. Surely *that* you can believe?"

"What is this?" Vine's deep voice filled the chamber. All the candles fluttered.

Raoul instantly let go of Brice's arm and backed away from the bed. "Vine, a pleasure, as always. Did you lose your shirt again? You do have such unfortunate luck holding onto clothing."

Vine sneered. "At least I do not prance around in female attire."

Raoul cocked a hip and fluttered his lashes. "You say that like it doesn't arouse you." His gaze dropped to the male's generous anatomy, clearly limp inside his thin trousers. "Ah well, perhaps not."

Vine's eyes narrowed behind his mask. "Why are you here? You know this was our bargain with him."

"Well, I'm... just passing through, clearly."

Vine slid his gaze to Brice. Anticipation of what Vine would give him had Brice's chest heaving and his body wanting. But Raoul had brought a thread of doubt into the room, one that wrapped around everything Brice had believed. And began to unravel it all.

He was Brice LeChoix. He'd come here for a reason, and that reason was not this room with the trio. He wasn't yet sure of anything else. Just that Raoul was a trickster. But even so, Brice inexplicably trusted him. His memories were a muddle, mixed up with dreams and fantasy, but Raoul felt like a friend.

"I recall you are acquainted with this mortal?" Vine asked Raoul.

"Barely." Raoul shrugged. "They all look so much alike."

"No, he made a deal, and it included you."

Raoul stilled. "You are mistaken. I was not included."

"Mistaken? Me? Never. He vowed to return to us, to let us have our way with you both, and here you are." Vine's smiling mouth turned sly. Lust sparkled in his eyes. "Perhaps we have room for a fourth. Our mortal is very accommodating."

Brice was the mortal. He had to remind himself of that. And they were speaking of adding Raoul to their couplings. An agreeable thought. The fae was pretty in a way that the others weren't. A way that appealed to Brice. He had kissed Raoul and remembered it well now. Raoul was both sharp and soft, angry and kind. He was a puzzle, one Brice wanted to riddle out. He very much wanted to taste his naked skin and feel him writhe beneath him, or over him, or in him. Any way, really.

Raoul, however, did not appear to be pleased by the notion. He glanced at Brice, reading his readiness in his panting breaths and hard cock. "Vine, you tread a dangerous line. The host himself put Brice in the rose garden. Should he discover him missing, his punishment will come down on you—"

Vine moved so fast Brice saw it only in its outcome. Raoul danced away, and Vine's companions rushed in. Three on one was hardly fair. Raoul spun, landing a punch that knocked Claude backward, but Laurel tackled him, and then Vine had him, too, and the pair pinned the snarling Raoul to the wall.

"I know you're fond of restraints."

As Vine spoke, roots sprang from the walls and looped around Raoul's wrists, tying him up. In seconds, he was bound, arms spread, the toes of his boots scuffing the floor.

Raoul bucked and snarled. "Don't—"

"Don't what?"

"Don't do this to Brice."

Vine patted Raoul's cheek. "Jealous?" He slid his hand down Raoul's chest and spread it over his crotch. "Isn't it time you got to watch? So many watch you, after all. Besides, it's just a little fun, Raoul."

"For you." Raoul slumped, the fight quickly draining out of him. "But not for him. You'll break him. Please... don't."

Vine stepped back and admired his catch in Raoul, then glanced at Brice. "You like him? Care for him, even. Hm... how interesting. The trickster is caught. But he made the deal."

"He never believed he'd have to settle it."

"That is the price of unkept promises." Vine fluttered a hand and his two companions moved in, climbing onto the bed. Wickedness gleamed in their eyes, behind their masks. Brice welcomed them, but having Raoul trapped and watching made unease squirm in his gut.

"Don't do this," Raoul begged.

"It's all right," Brice said. "I want it."

Raoul's mouth tightened. "You really don't and if you were yourself, you'd fight."

"I am myself. It's really all right."

"Take off your mask then," Raoul said. "Remove it and test your truth in this moment. Test if what you want is real."

Vine clicked his fingers and Laurel straightened to attention. "Silence him."

Raoul renewed his efforts to break the restraints as Laurel collected a slip of silk from a shelf and closed in on Raoul.

Raoul kicked out, forcing Laurel back. "Gag me, and I swear I will find you days from now and geld you, Laurel. See how you like to fuck mortals without your balls."

Laurel hesitated, the slip of silk tight between his fingers. "Vine?"

"Empty threats." Vine crawled onto the bed. Brice couldn't resist falling into his gaze. Distant sounds of Raoul's struggles were lost in the way Vine's delicious body moved up the length of Brice's. He could already feel Vine's searing touch, could already taste his spicy sweetness on his tongue. His naked body bloomed under the fae's gaze like a flower opening especially for him.

But what if it wasn't real?

What if Raoul was right, and Brice's mind was not his own?

Removing his mask would reveal his true feelings. He'd know then, wouldn't he?

He reached up.

Vine caught his wrist and pinned it to the bed, golden eyes flaring.

"Wait, I—"

Brice reached for the mask with his free hand, but Claude caught it, holding him down.

"I want to know—"

Vine knelt, poised over him now. His heavy silken cock trailed over Brice's hip, spilling glittery precum. "You really don't."

Raoul's distant, frantic mumblings pulled at the edges of Brice's thoughts.

This did not feel right. "Stop," Brice said.

"You should not have told him." Brice caught the words from Laurel meant for Raoul. "Ignorance is bliss, Raoul. Now he is aware."

Raoul bucked. His muffled voice turned angry.

Brice turned his head away to keep from falling any further into Vine's allure. He didn't know what this was, but it wasn't right. He saw Raoul's face then, saw the fear behind his mask. Raoul thrashed his head and heaved against the roots holding him to the wall. His muscles trembled, taut behind black lace. He stared at Brice, willed him to *know*.

God, what was Brice doing here, in this bed, beneath this fae? Why had he let them hold him down just because his cock demanded it? He was more than want and desire. More than a lustful animal. He was a man, and he had a voice, he had pride, he had a choice. And he *did not want this*.

He brought his knee up, crashing into Vine's hanging balls. The fae let out a strangled bark and sat up, letting go of Brice. With an arm now free, he flung a fist at Vine's face, cracking his knuckles across the fae's jaw. Pain lashed down his arm.

Vine rocked aside, but now Claude moved in. His thick fingers locked around Brice's throat and slammed him down. Claude bared sharp fae teeth in a snarl.

Brice shoved at Claude's chest, twisted under him, slammed an elbow back and caught something fragile that gave under the impact. Hands grabbed him by the hips and dragged him down the bed. Brice kicked out, striking Laurel. Vine loomed—his eyes furious and teeth bared. They were everywhere, just like they'd been during their coupling, but now they were vicious. He couldn't fight three. Couldn't fight one. But he was damn well going to try and if they fucked him now, he'd bite their wretched cocks off. "Let go!"

Glass sparkled above Vine. Brice blinked, saw the vase and Raoul holding it, then quickly turned his face away as Raoul slammed it down over Vine's head. Broken glass rained. Brice gasped, struck by cold water. Vine whirled and was met by Raoul's right hook. The blow knocked the fae to the floor.

Flames licked up all the flowing drapes, set free by toppled candles. Or perhaps Raoul had deliberately kicked them over. He looked like some raging fiend, backlit by fire, with the heat of vengeance in his purple, tempestuous eyes. Roots hung from his bruised wrists—he'd torn himself free.

He snatched up a second vase and swung it bat-like at Claude. Claude turned, and the vase struck his face and shattered just like the first had, exploding roses and glass and water in all directions.

Raoul grabbed Brice's hand, hauling him to his feet. Brice scooped up his fallen clothes, and they tore through the doorway out into the hall. Brice glanced back and saw only fire and smoke and Laurel, standing in the doorway watching—letting them go.

Brice had no idea where Raoul was taking him, but he ran, naked, down snaking corridors until they found an empty side room. Raoul pulled him inside. "Quickly, dress. They will give chase."

He did with fumbling fingers. He couldn't think about what had been done, because if he stopped to think, he feared his thoughts might shatter like one of those vases and everything he was keeping inside would spill over.

The moment he was dressed, Raoul suddenly caught Brice's face in his hands and peered into his eyes. "Are you all right, Brice?"

"No."

"Do you know me?"

Brice nodded. "Y-yes. I think so." His teeth chattered, the cold seeping in again.

"They hid you well. I could not find you... in time." He swallowed hard. "It's the roses, Brice. Don't worry. I can help you remember."

Brice wanted to tell him he was fine, that it didn't matter, that he felt nothing, but all of those things would have been a lie, and Raoul likely knew it.

"Follow me. Stay close. Do not stop for anything. I'll get you somewhere safe."

His eyes seemed to silently say *trust me*, although the words never left his lips.

He nodded and hurried behind Raoul—the only thing Brice did trust in this madness.

Chapter Thirty-Five

They stumbled along old crumbling pathways through abandoned buildings and out into a never-ending forest—all layers of the masquerade. Brice fell over gnarled roots and slipped on wet leaves, but Raoul was there, scooping him up and pulling him back into step. The forest thickened, closing in around them. Shadows moved in the dark, things not quite there or real. Things that turned to dust when Brice tried to focus on them. He didn't like this place or the way his heart pounded against his ribs and his legs burned. He wasn't even sure what he was doing here, running through the woods after Raoul. It all seemed so terribly wrong.

He fell again and this time landed on his hands and knees. Roots shifted around his fingers, rising up out of the dirt like fingers of their own, trying to grab him and pull him into the ground. He scrambled backward, almost knocking Raoul over in his haste.

"Brice." Raoul caught his face in his hands like he'd done before, and even with their masks between them,

Raoul's eyes betrayed fear and anger and confusion and frustration and many, many things that proved this fae knew him. And that he *cared.* "Don't think on it now. There will be time afterward. We must get out of these woods."

Something large rustled in the dark behind them.

"Hurry, Brice." Raoul pulled him back to his feet and they ran again. Somehow Brice kept up, and then the forest spat them out next to a small waterfall pool. Moonlight made the surface sparkly like molten silver. Raoul splashed through it and dragged Brice with him through the curtain of falling water, into the space behind, then up and over rocks and into the back of a rock cavern.

Raoul's fingers slipped from Brice's. He strode into the cavern, then turned and swept his gaze over the spilled books, ruined sketches, and smashed bottles.

Brice sank to his knees, lost to the tremors racking him. He wrapped his arms around himself, but wading through the pool had taken the last of his strength. He feared he might fall in a heap and never wake again. "God... what did I do?"

"Here." Raoul snatched the blankets off the floor and nestled them together in a corner to make a bed. "Brice?"

Brice blinked. Had the candles been alight when they'd arrived? They must have been, but he didn't remember it. A small fledgling fire crackled in a stone circle. That definitely hadn't been there before. Had he fallen asleep?

Raoul stopped in front of him, clasped him by the upper arms, and maneuvered him across the chamber to the bed of blankets. "Remove your wet clothes," he said tersely. "And dry off."

"Yes, of course." Brice fumbled with his shirt. His

buttons didn't match up with the correct holes. He fought with the little buttons, trying to get them back through their holes with numb fingers. Why were they so vexing?

"Allow me." Raoul made quick work of the buttons, avoiding Brice's gaze, and carefully slipped the shirt off Brice's shoulders. His dark lashes came down as he looked away.

Raoul unfastened Brice's trousers clinically and stepped away, letting Brice finish. "Rest," he said. "While I fix this mess." He picked up some broken glass, cradling the jagged pieces in his hand and placing them on the desk area. Raoul looked over the ruined artwork and with a sigh, he removed his mask, setting it down alongside the torn sketches and spilled ink.

When he finally looked over, his concern and wariness showed. His gaze dropped, roaming Brice. "Curse them," he muttered, looking away. "Sit, Brice, and cover yourself."

It seemed easier to obey than to think, so Brice sat and arranged the blankets over his knees, tucking himself in. Removing the wet clothes had helped warm him, and now, bathed in candlelight and warmed through, sleep tried to drag him under.

Raoul set about searching for something. "You will hate this once you remember," he muttered. And then so softly Brice almost didn't hear, "Perhaps you'll hate me."

Brice drew his knees up and rested his chin on them. He watched the fae mutter and tut as he moved about the chamber tidying and searching until he came upon a tiny bottle and brought it over.

Raoul crouched and offered the bottle to Brice. "This is the antidote for the roses. You don't recall, but you gave it to your brother to help him recover." He hesitated, then caught Brice's hand and pressed the bottle into his palm. "Take three drops. But Brice, the events you recall will hurt you."

He looked down at the small bottle in his hand. Just a tiny thing. But it held all his memories.

"There's the option, of course, not to take it. To never remember. I'll not deny that for some, it is the better route. Ignorance truly is bliss at the masquerade."

Take it and hurt, or don't take it and don't hurt. He struggled to understand why he'd take it.

Raoul lifted his gaze. "The Brice I know would take it, no matter the pain. He'd want to expose the truth. However ugly."

He moved to straighten, but Brice caught his wrist, holding him still. "What if I don't like the truth?"

"Unfortunately, that does not change it." Raoul smiled sadly. "Whatever your choice, I'll be here. I owe you that, at least."

He moved away, weighted down by a sadness Brice didn't yet understand, but if he drank the potion, he surely would. "Raoul... are we... Is there something more between us?"

The fae hesitated a step, and keeping his back to Brice, said, "No."

"It's just—You came for me. You *know* me."

Raoul busied himself by clearing a broken bowl from the floor. "Yes, well. It's my fault you're here. Again."

Whatever Raoul was to him, the fae had brought him to this place, a place of safety and calm in a storm of dreams. He watched him awhile, admiring how the candlelight moved over his lace-clad body and how the orange light played in his raven-black hair. He watched him so long that he might have fallen asleep in the warmth and safety of the chamber corner.

He woke to the tinkling of the nearby stream and to Raoul sleeping softly in a chair, slumped over a table. He'd changed his clothes into a more casual cotton shirt with billowing sleeves and loose dark trousers. His braid had sprung tufts in all directions. Brice wanted to touch it, to see if his hair was as silky as it appeared. He wanted to touch Raoul too.

Quietly climbing to his bare feet, he approached the table and spotted a drawing under his arm. This one wasn't stained or torn like the others. Raoul had just drawn it. Brice recognized his own face immediately, although the lines around his eyes were somewhat harsh. But it wasn't his likeness that startled him. It was the fact that Raoul had clearly seen him without his mask and for long enough to capture the smallest of details. And that he had bothered to draw him at all.

Brice pulled his mask free now and set it down on the table. He sighed and made his decision. He could not live a lie, especially when he knew it to be an illusion. Not knowing what he'd forgotten had to be worse than the truth, right? Removing the bottle stopper, he upended the bottle, let three drops land on his tongue, and swallowed.

Whatever awaited him on the other side, Raoul had promised he'd be there too. Brice knew one thing—he wasn't alone.

Chapter Thirty-Six

MEMORIES EXPLODED in his mind like fireworks. One triggered the next, then the next, until they were all he could see and hear. There seemed to be no order to them. Charon falling in the pond, Father reading, Vine's poison kiss, pain from a twisted ankle, Mother's song and her tears, a hand in his, Sophia dead on the street, Raoul's laughter. On and on in a reel of unconnected events, each one a new assault.

Raoul had said there'd be pain, but Brice had prepared for physical pain, not this need to crack open his own skull and empty out the noise.

He heard Raoul somewhere in all of it, but whatever he said was lost in the memory of when he'd found the pistol on the floor next to Mother's hand, lost in the feel of three pairs of fae hands on him, their mouths so hot their kisses branded his soul. He wanted to wash them off, wash it all off. He recalled trying to get to the water, but Raoul had been there, standing in his way like the sentinel he was when they'd met. *Be my guest.*

The memories became so much that all he could do was sit and let them roll over him in waves. Eventually, the clamoring faded, leaving him cold, shivering, aching, and like he might vomit. The masquerade and all its sharp beauty waited outside. He'd come to end it, to save Raoul and the others, but he'd lost the note. The host had caught him, taken him to the rose garden, and from there... Vine had...

Brice had failed, like he'd failed at everything.

He shot to his feet and dashed for the ivy curtain hiding the doorway and the tunnel beyond.

Raoul—who'd been busy by the stream—darted in front of him and thrust out a hand, holding Brice back. "You cannot leave."

"Let me go, Raoul."

"If you go out there like you are, the host will be on you in seconds—"

"Good!" Brice pushed against the hand at his chest.

"No." Raoul gave a little shove. "I'll not have the cycle start again. Hate me if you wish, but you cannot leave. Not yet."

"Hate you?" The anger rose in him. It had always been there, simmering below the onslaught of memories, unable to get through, but it was waking now. "I do hate you. Every part of this began with you and those invites and your failed plan to use my brother for your own escape!"

Raoul frowned but kept his head high and his arm out. "I am much to blame, that is true. But it did not begin with me. Look closer to home for the source of all this. Your mother cursed us. This is *your* legacy. And perhaps if you were the man you claim to be, you'd help fix it."

"I tried!" He curled his hands into fists.

"Not hard enough!" Raoul lowered his hand. "Strike me if it will help—"

He swung, catching Raoul in the jaw. Heat washed through his knuckles as the fae stumbled back. The quietly furious look Raoul threw Brice made Brice want to curl in on himself in shame.

"Oh God." He took a step toward him. "You told me to," Brice snapped.

Raoul rubbed his jaw and moved away from the curtain of ivy toward the table, where he poured himself some wine from a pitcher. "I didn't think you would."

"You'll heal," Brice said pathetically.

"And that makes it all right?"

Raoul kept his back to Brice. Which was all Brice deserved, he supposed. He was a wretched man. The memories proved it. The things he had done with those fae, the things that had been done to him... He'd come to save Raoul from this, gotten lost in some debauched den of lust, and now he'd lashed out like a child.

He slumped back down onto the nest of blankets in his corner and rubbed his sore knuckles. "God, I'm so sorry."

Raoul sighed, poured a second glass, and brought it to Brice. "I know you are. You're also tired, confused, and in pain." He crouched and handed over the glass.

"Forgive me."

The fae smiled softly. "It is forgiven."

Brice leaned back against the cavern wall. The broken bottles and chaos had all been cleared away. This little cavern of calm with its trickling water and flickering candles did go some way to calming Brice's heart. But it would be some time before he felt anything like himself again.

"What if he comes here?" he whispered.

"The host?" Raoul sipped his drink. "He doesn't know about this place."

"But everything was wrecked. I assumed that was him?"

"Ah, no." Raoul pulled a chair from the table, flipped it around, and straddled it. "That was me. Not my finest act, I confess."

He lowered his gaze to his glass, and Brice recalled his words about the fae not feeling shame. They did not regret. But Raoul's face was full of it. "What happened... after I left?"

"I could have ended it. But obviously, I did not." He smiled bitterly. "You and Charon were safe. All I had to do was fire the pistol. Not even Sinclair could survive a shot between the eyes."

"Why didn't you?"

"I have asked myself that very question time and time again since you left." Tilting his head back, he blinked at the chamber ceiling. "You were right. I couldn't do it. I had the pistol. I could have ended it, but evidently, I am not a killer. Damnable time to discover that pertinent fact."

"I assume the host did not react well?"

He drew in a deep breath, held it for a few seconds, and sighed hard. "Public lashings at first. Until the skin fell from my back. Then I was to serve the guests in any way they wished." Lowering his gaze, he folded his arms on the back of the chair and rested his chin on them. "And they wished it in multiple ways." He smiled, and even his dark eyes glinted, but his careless tone and wry smile were all masks to cover his pain. "It's fine, really. It is the way of things here."

He did not deserve that treatment and the fact he was accustomed to it made the horror a hundred times worse. "I'm sorry, Raoul."

"You got out." He flicked a hand. "And for a while, that was enough. But somewhere in all of it, I began to hate you for that. In all the years I've danced and played the trickster, I've resisted hate, but not after you left. At least I felt something. I hated the guests. Hated their hands on me even as I smiled and laughed and fucked any who wanted it. When I closed my eyes, I saw you running like a fool through the meadow under the stars. And I hated that too. I'd enjoyed our time together. I'd forgotten what joy was. And when you left—when I told you to go—you took that rediscovered joy with you."

"I should have stayed."

"No, you did the right thing. Understand, I am not blaming you. I do not begrudge anyone their escape."

He wanted to tell him he would have returned eventually, but that seemed like the wrong thing to say, as though it would ease Brice's own guilt more than Raoul's pain. "You escaped the host's punishment?"

"I did my time, came back here, sketched you over and over. I'm not even sure why—to try and find that joy again, I suppose—and when I failed... well, the result was the carnage you saw. I'd have burned this place down if it weren't made of rock."

"If you hate me so, why ask me to save you?" he quietly asked.

"Because in my rage, I scrawled two words on an invite

and sent it into the wind." *Save me.* "I wanted you to know I hadn't forgotten. I wanted you to remember me. And I wanted you to feel like I felt," he said quietly, eyes downcast.

"I did not forget, Raoul. I thought of you—I could not stop thinking of you. I wanted to. Because I knew I should never come back." He laughed at his own naïve defiance.

"Did it hurt? Remembering me?"

"Yes."

"Then I suppose we are even."

Hardly. Brice hadn't been tortured since fleeing the masquerade. He hadn't been made to pleasure an endless stream of guests for their entertainment. He hadn't wished for hatred, desperate to feel *something*.

"I heard Vine had a new infatuation and snuck to the pleasure rooms to take a look," Raoul went on. "You took some finding. I am not often surprised, but seeing you sprawled and spent on his bed... I wondered if I'd dreamed you up—if the masquerade had brought you back to me only to take you away again." Raoul swallowed and looked away. "I regret I considered leaving you there."

Then he truly did hate Brice. "I'm glad you didn't," he replied in a small voice.

Raoul didn't look like he hated him, though. His soft lips lifted into a small, crooked smile. "You have a tendency to make me feel things I haven't felt in as long as I can remember—which perhaps isn't saying much, considering I only remember the masquerade. Around you, I make mistakes. You make me regret those mistakes. You show me joy in the simplest of things and honor in doing what's right.

I dare say, Brice LeChoix, I am a better, more complete person with you."

"I, er..." Brice cleared his throat. Nobody had ever said such kind things to him. He wasn't sure what to do with it. "I'm sure you've always been that person, but the masquerade took it from you."

"Perhaps." He didn't believe it, but Brice saw the truth. Raoul *was* a good person. He tried to be.

"Vine and the others will be searching for us," Raoul said. "But they won't tell the host they took you, so we have some time."

"Time for what?"

"For you to recover. For us to think of a way we might end this. If you're willing to help?"

"That is what I returned for." He mustered a smile.

"Then we shall drink to that." Raoul raised his glass, then threw his head back and swallowed its contents in one gulp.

Brice sipped his drink, fearing he might vomit it back up if he consumed too much.

He did not feel like celebrating. Everything was too raw, as though he'd been cut open and exposed. He'd hoped, perhaps ridiculously, that Raoul would be pleased to see him. But things were more complicated than that. He had suffered, and that felt like Brice's fault. He should have done more. Guilt and shame knotted inside him. He felt like dirt on the chamber floor, like he'd been trodden on and kicked over. His capture at the hands of the trio and what had been done between them sickened him. He'd wanted it, he'd begged for it, but he couldn't shake the feeling he'd been used by the fae as the guests had used Raoul.

"How long?" Brice asked once his glass was empty and his thoughts soft around their edges.

"What?" Raoul had moved his chair back to the desk area and had been busy tidying his work. He twisted and peered over his shoulder.

"How long did they keep me for... in mortal time?"

Raoul sighed and refilled his glass, his back to Brice, perhaps to hide his face. "Will knowing help?"

"Maybe not... but... it feels like a long time."

"Could be two days or two months."

Brice sucked in a breath through his teeth.

"Considering the compliant condition I found you in," Raoul continued, "it is likely to be somewhere between the two." He faced his desk again and shuffled his papers.

"Oh." A month or more? He'd been gone so long Charon would think him lost.

Perhaps that was for the best. Charon would be the master of the house. He'd make a better lord. A better son. The rightful heir. He was bright and brilliant, better off without him.

Was there any place he belonged?

Raoul spoke of being joyless, but the last time Brice had felt joy was while running through that meadow at night. He'd felt joy there, with Raoul, under the stars in a world that wasn't real.

He wished he'd left the memories buried.

Chapter Thirty-Seven

Brice woke alone in the chamber. Raoul had left fruit and bread on the table and a fresh washbasin nearby, so he took that to mean he could wash up and eat as he pleased. Despite the chamber's hard rock walls, the space was safe and solid, and with its array of candles and a tiny stove, it was curiously homey.

The familiarity of menial tasks kept the bad memories at bay, so much so he felt almost like his normal self again.

His mask and Raoul's sat together on the table. One of gold accents, one of silver. They made a handsome pair. Brice was in no hurry to wear his again. The time would come when he'd have to put it back on and face the host and probably the trio, too, but not yet. He couldn't stomach it.

Dressed, clean, and fed, he wandered the cavern, soaking up its solid ambiance, then caught sight of the opening where the stream entered. A veil of water blocked the view into the moonlit pool beyond, but as he watched, the water occasionally split, revealing a tantalizing glimpse of the pool. And Raoul.

Brice almost turned away, fairly certain peeping on someone as they bathed was not a gentlemanly thing to do, but the glimpses were so fleeting, flashes really, as though he were barely there at all. Raoul's dark, wet hair glistened down his back to his waist like spilled ink over his skin. He raised his arm and washed over his bicep and shoulder. Brice followed his hand's path and absorbed how Raoul gathered his hair in his fingers and swept it over his other shoulder, exposing his pale back. He didn't look real. Moonlight shimmered on the water around him and painted his black hair silver. His face in profile made Brice wish he could draw just so he could capture its perfection like Raoul had captured him. The waterfall closed again, then split apart, and now Raoul swept his hand over his other arm.

Brice swallowed hard.

Good lord, the male was so beautiful it hurt Brice to think of him in pain. The host had said many a mortal had fallen in love with Raoul. Brice could believe it. But surely such carefree handsomeness was its own kind of curse too. The guests used him. The host whipped him. His life was an endless cycle of pleasuring others while feeling only pain. But he stayed standing, kept his smile, kept his wily humor. He truly was remarkable.

Raoul glanced over his shoulder and Brice ducked out of sight. Raoul probably hadn't seen him through the waterfall, but he didn't want to be caught staring, so he withdrew back inside the cavern and busied himself tidying away the plate he'd used.

Raoul returned a moment later, damp from the pool and absolutely naked. He padded bare-assed across the chamber to collect a towel, then rubbed himself dry. His masculine beauty continued below his waist, over pert buttocks and firm thighs. Brice caught himself staring and suddenly had no idea where else to look.

It wasn't uncommon for men to be so free around other men when intimacy wasn't a consideration. But he'd kissed Raoul. Raoul had desired Brice before he'd begun hating him. Where did they stand now?

In his haste not to look, he fumbled an apple from the bowl. It bounced off the table and rolled toward Raoul, then rocked in a divot near Raoul's bare foot.

Raoul spotted it as he tied his trousers. He bent to pick it up and with a grin, bit into it. Shirtless, he sauntered toward Brice. "May I ask a favor?"

"Y-yes. Of course," Brice blustered.

"Will you braid my hair? It's so much easier with another pair of hands."

He opened his mouth to issue some excuse not to but found he had none.

Raoul stopped at the table with his back to Brice and glanced over his shoulder, waiting.

During long winter nights, Brice had dreamed of running his fingers through Raoul's hair. Was it as silky as it appeared?

He slipped his fingers beneath its smooth, wet expanse and lifted it from where it clung to Raoul's naked back. The beginnings of desire thumped through him. With some effort, he pushed the idea of sex from his head and focused instead on the silken locks between his fingers. He split the smooth, cool layers into three and began to pass them over each other. Once the braid had tightened, Brice's mind unhelpfully supplied the imaginary image of him kissing Raoul's neck and what would happen after when Raoul leaned back against him. It wouldn't be like with Vine. It wouldn't be like with anyone. Raoul was too precious. He needed to be loved, to be shown love, how it was supposed to be, not at the hands of guests who'd be gone the moment they were satisfied.

Brice knew so little of love himself, but he knew Raoul deserved a slow seduction. If he'd even want it. Though clearly not from Brice—someone else, then?

"Did you have someone? A family... a lover? Before the masquerade?" Brice asked, focusing on the rhythmic braiding and not how he wanted to lean in and taste Raoul's smooth shoulder.

"If I did, the masquerade has stolen their memory."

"Do you wish you remembered? If you could take your potion to bring it back, would you?"

"No."

He'd answered quickly. And it hadn't been the answer Brice had expected. "You don't want to know the truth?"

"The masquerade is my truth. Knowing the past will not change how I'm trapped in the present."

"If I'd thought like that, I'd still be the pathetic fool you saved from Vine's bed."

Raoul twisted and peered over his shoulder into Brice's gaze. "What happened to you does not make you weak or pathetic. Never think that. You're stronger than you know."

Brice wasn't sure he believed that, but Raoul clearly did. He nodded and when Raoul faced ahead again, Brice tied the braid off, finishing it with a small leather band.

"Thank you." Raoul flicked the braid over his shoulder. He moved away and threw on a smartly tailored jacket to match his fine trousers: masquerade attire. He was leaving to entertain. Brice's heart fluttered. When Raoul returned to the table to collect his mask, Brice touched his hand, stalling him.

"I have to go out there," Raoul said. "If the host is content, if he doesn't know you're missing, then we'll have more time. I must determine his mood."

"Just... be careful."

Raoul put his mask on and grinned, perfecting the trickster act. "I am always careful, darling."

Not long after Raoul had left, the persistent memories crept back in. Brice paced the cavern but it didn't prevent the sounds of his father's scolding tone, as though he stood in the chamber with him, reprimanding his behavior. He heard his mother humming the masquerade lullaby and tried to squeeze the sound from his head, but the more he fought it off, the more it tangled around his consciousness and tried to choke off all reason.

"Brice?"

He looked up from the pistol in his lap.

Raoul was back. How long had he been gone?

"The pistol?" Raoul removed his mask and held out his hand to take the pistol. "Give it to me."

The pistol.

He didn't recall finding it or why he held it, just that it brought him closer to the answers.

"Brice, look at me."

He looked up again. Raoul's kohl-lined eyes conveyed worry. His emotive mouth thinned in a line.

"The pain you're feeling is old, brought here by your

memories reasserting themselves. Do not allow them purchase."

He was right, of course. Brice set the pistol down on the table, instantly feeling better for having let it go. "Good lord." He touched his forehead. "I'm not sure what I was thinking."

Raoul threw a few sheets of paper over the pistol and slumped against the edge of the desk. "Do you know me? Do you know where you are?"

Brice looked around them at the flickering candles and listened to the tinkling stream. "Yes, of course. I just... For a moment, I was elsewhere."

"It will take some time for your past to settle and the emotions to fade again. You'll get there. Until then, please avoid handling the pistol."

"I'll try."

"Well, there is good news and bad from the masquerade. The host is unaware you're missing from the rose garden. However, my absence has not gone unnoticed. I should return to my place on the dance floor."

"Which involves pleasuring the guests, no?"

"Well, yes."

"No." Unequivocally and absolutely no. Brice would not allow it.

Raoul smiled a little. "Your concern is appreciated but not required."

"It's wrong," Brice added. He wasn't certain of much, but this was a certainty.

"How is lust wrong?" Raoul asked.

Did he genuinely not know? "It's not lust. It's forcing it upon you that's wrong. Tell them no."

Raoul, still smiling, folded his arms and leaned back. "*No* is a slippery word at the masquerade."

Only because the fae let it be. "No is not a negotiation."

"Everything here is negotiation."

"Yet another reason why this must end."

Raoul's smile grew. "What if I told you there are times I've rather enjoyed my punishment. Better some feeling than none at all."

"That is no way to live." Brice got to his feet, struck by the need to prevent the vicious circle of pleasure and pain that was Raoul's life. He took Raoul's hands in his. He was worth so much more than the guests' plaything. If only there were a way to show him how much.

Raoul still had a smile, but its edge had softened. He lifted his gaze to Brice. "What else should I do, Lord LeChoix?"

Brice had an idea. An idea that might be foolish, but it felt powerful, like it had wings and could carry them away from this nightmare. "If we leave this cavern, will we be caught?"

"Do you have somewhere you need to go?"

"Yes. And I think we both need it."

Chapter Thirty-Eight

When Brice had suggested the meadow, Raoul had first laughed, then frowned. *Foolish risk*, he had said, but he hadn't said no. They left the cavern without their masks and snuck through shadows and out through the overgrown briars into distant fields.

Raoul muttered some more about how he should keep Brice safe inside. He mentioned how the masquerade might not show them the meadow, but then beyond a few lawns and through an orchard, the midnight meadow appeared, flooded in moonlight just like before. Its sudden arrival surely meant the masquerade approved. Grass seed heads shimmered like silvery crowns. Flowers of all kinds bobbed their heads. The meadow stretched as far as Brice's eye could see.

"It should not be here at all," Raoul grumbled. He folded his arms. "You've seen it. It's wonderful. Now let's return before—"

Brice strode into the grass. It hadn't changed at all and just like last time, with every step his heart lightened. Something about the vast open space beneath the sparkling stars called to his soul.

"Brice? If we're seen—"

He waved Raoul's concern away. "It's fine. We're alone." With his heart tripping over itself to run, he grinned. "Tell me you don't like it here and we'll leave."

Raoul shrugged. "I've never lingered before." The breeze teased a stray lock of hair across his face. "Your presence here has me seeing it... differently," he said, albeit begrudgingly. He could be stubborn sometimes. They both knew the meadow was magical, but he wasn't going to relent since he'd argued not to come. Brice found his stubbornness endearing. Raoul was so desperate for joy, but when presented with the potential of it, he refused.

"Run with me." Brice offered his hand.

Raoul slowly unfolded his arms. "I do not think that wise."

Brice grabbed his hand and pulled, almost toppling the fae into him. Raoul straightened, and now Brice had him so close he could make out the glitter in his eyes. "Say no, and I'll relent."

Raoul quickly righted himself. "If we're seen without our masks—"

"Didn't you say you do not see the joy in the small moments?" Brice stepped back and would have freed Raoul if he'd wanted, but the fae's hand stayed in his and Raoul stepped with him, even beginning to smile. "This is one of those moments." Brice turned and broke into a jog. Raoul's fingers tightened around his, and together they ran.

It was silly and reckless, exactly as Raoul had said, but the faster Brice ran, the fewer memories caught up with him. He ran and for a little while he lived in the moment, not in what had happened to him and not in the past he'd left outside the masquerade. Raoul's hand slipped from his, but only so the fae could raise his arms and spin.

He shouldn't have been so entrancing, and Brice told himself he wasn't. Brice had stopped to catch his breath, that was all, and not to stare at the fae dancing among the long silver-kissed seed heads. His braid flew out, and with his arms spread, he twirled, tipping his head up and laughing at the sky. The joy on his face was clear. Brice's heart constricted, squeezing a gasp from his lips. He'd thought Raoul beautiful before, but when happy, he truly shone. He deserved this. And it didn't matter if Raoul hated him for leaving. Brice would still find a way to end the masquerade and his torture with it. It was the right thing to do.

Raoul caught Brice's gaze and stopped spinning. His grin turned sly. He staggered toward Brice but missed a step in his dizziness. Brice dodged and was about to bolt into a run when Raoul's light fingers caught his hand and reeled him in as though to dance. Suddenly, they were face-to-face, chest to chest. Raoul adjusted his hold, capturing both of Brice's hands. "Dance with me," he purred.

Brice's heart pounded and, breathless from the run, his chest heaved against Raoul's. "There's no music."

Raoul tilted his head. "Yes, there is. You hear it?"

Brice couldn't hear a damn thing over his thumping heart.

Raoul stepped and Brice stepped with him, and as simple as that they were dancing in a meadow under moonlight. That same moonlight sparkled in Raoul's dark eyes and stroked over his soft lips. A flutter of fear shortened Brice's breath, because as he looked at Raoul's face, at every tiny reveal in the quirk of his lips and the spark in his eyes, he feared he might be falling. Perhaps he'd been falling since he'd met the fae, but he'd only just now realized it. He danced with Raoul under a full moon among a meadow of grass and wildflowers and it felt so right. More right than anything else in his whole life.

Raoul bowed his head and, cheek to cheek, he whispered, "I may have lied to you, Brice LeChoix."

Panic chased the fear around Brice's heart. Whatever the lie, he didn't want him to say it, couldn't stand for this small glorious moment to be ruined by some wretched lie. Leaning back, he pressed a finger to Raoul's lips. "Don't tell me."

Raoul stopped dancing. His eyes widened. Brice still held his finger to his lips, but they couldn't stay like that. Nothing lasted forever, except the masquerade.

"Say it, then." He lifted his finger.

Raoul's gaze fluttered downward but quickly lifted and fixed on Brice's face. His eyes narrowed, and it seemed as though whatever he was about to say might change things. "I tried to hate you. It would have made things easier if I had. But the more I tried to find hate, the more my mind strayed to this place and to you. I would draw you here and study what it was about that moment that had me so bespelled, but the answer eluded me. So I drew you some more and more." His grip tightened on Brice's hand and his gaze skipped away again.

He could be saying many things, but Brice knew the truth. It wasn't in his words but in his glances, in his touch.

Brice looked down at their joined hands and Raoul's slim but strong fingers.

Father had fallen in love with a fae and now it seemed Brice had done the same. And perhaps everything Raoul *wasn't* saying told Brice he loved him in return. *Save me...* It hadn't been written in hatred but in desperation, in fear, and in love.

Raoul had fallen silent.

Brice lifted his gaze from their hands and looked into his eyes. It was there, right in front of them, between them, and all around. Love. And it hurt, because Raoul surely feared loving a mortal the same as Brice feared loving a fae. *Where can this go?* Raoul had once asked.

In the past, a love like theirs had ended in tragedy.

Raoul gently shoved Brice away and let go, then backed away. "I should never have asked you to return. You saved your brother and that was your happy ending." He turned on his heel and marched back through the now-flattened grass.

"Wait." Didn't he see Brice's own feelings? Perhaps he didn't want to or perhaps he couldn't? So Brice would show him. He chased after him, dashed in front, and blocked his path.

Raoul planted his feet and glared. "This cannot go anywhere."

Brice closed the final step between them and for a second time, placed a finger to Raoul's lips. Lifting his finger, he placed a kiss there instead. Just a small delicate thing, as light as a snowflake. "It began with love."

The emotions Raoul could not express with words must have surged through him because he swept Brice against him and kissed him hard. Brice's gentleness shattered under the fae's strength. He grabbed Raoul in his fists and took the fae in a kiss as though he could devour him whole. It was a madness, surely, feverish and chaotic. Raoul gasped from the kiss, then skimmed his tongue and mouth along Brice's jaw to his neck, where sharp fae teeth nipped.

Brice clutched him closer and dug his nails into Raoul's back. Almost a thousand nights he'd dreamed of this and a thousand days he'd denied himself the truth. He loved Raoul. He loved the obnoxiously flamboyant way he demanded everyone watch him, the way he laughed when he shouldn't, the way he sketched Brice with all the feeling and heart he'd denied himself. He was the dancer trapped in the music box, and by God, Brice would burn it all down to set him free.

Raoul laughed now, suddenly, and leaned away, only to laugh some more with moonlight in his eyes.

"Is the thought of us so amusing?" Brice asked, bemused and entranced.

"What else can it be?"

Brice grabbed him by the jaw and kissed the laughter from his lips. Raoul's eyes widened, then narrowed with intent, and he returned Brice's kiss with a savage one of his own, marching Brice backward through the grass. His heel caught a root or a rock. He stumbled, and Raoul swooped in to scoop him off his feet and dump him on his back in a bed of hay.

Brice no longer laughed, and neither did Raoul. The fae straddled Brice's thighs, pinning him down, and with the moon behind him, he looked like every forbidden dream Brice could have imagined. Brice reached up and cupped his face. Raoul leaned into his touch, seeking more, and when he didn't get it, he fell onto braced arms and peered into Brice's eyes. "I wish to ravage you in all ways, so many I hardly know where to begin, but the choice must be yours."

Brice's pulse thumped at his neck, drying his throat. He wanted Raoul too. His body buzzed with need and his cock made his desire clear, but his head... His head was still a muddle. Yes, he wanted to take this fae in the grass, in all the ways he could, but recent events loomed like ghosts at the back of his thoughts. He all too easily recalled Vine and Laurel and Claude holding him down and holding Raoul, almost making him watch. Those memories were raw, like open wounds that had some healing to do.

Raoul smiled and flopped onto his back in the grass next to Brice. They lay like that awhile with the moon watching over them. Raoul's hand found Brice's and they laced together. And for now it was enough. It was perfect.

"You should despise me for bringing you back here."

"Yes," Brice agreed and smiled over at him.

"It was never hate I felt for you." Raoul rubbed absently at his chest over his heart. "That's why it hurt so."

Brice sighed. "I'm going to get us both out of here."

Raoul's soft smile was a lie. He didn't believe it.

"I'm beginning to understand how my father, Leon LeChoix, must have felt as he tried to save his love from the host."

"Yes, and she cursed us all on her leaving and later ended her own life, thus driving your father to madness. The LeChoix history is rather lacking in happy endings."

Brice rolled onto his side and tried to frown, although his smile ruined it. "I am not my father."

"No. You are not." Finally, Raoul smiled and turned his head to meet Brice's gaze. "Half of me wishes you'd stayed away, while the other half never wants to let you go. You deny me, you puzzle me, and you tear me asunder. Yet I'd surrender the last of my immortal moments if I could spend a mortal life with you. I see now why my kin fear love."

Love.

There it was, on his lips.

The little word full of fireworks.

Brice swallowed and brought Raoul's fingers to *his* lips. "We will find a way."

Raoul's smile wavered, still disbelieving. He faced the sky and sighed. "The making of this memory is enough for now," he whispered. "May it outshine all the others."

Chapter Thirty-Nine

Brice slept well in the cavern that night, but when he woke, Raoul—who had dozed beside the bed—had gone.

He lay on his back and watched the candlelight shift over the cavern's undulating ceiling. Raoul would be back. He wanted to ask him about the fae, about their lives and whether a mate could be someone *not* fae. Raoul didn't remember much of his people or his life, but still Brice desperately wanted to know even the smallest of things.

His mind soon wandered, beginning to turn over things best left buried, forcing Brice to his feet. He drifted awhile, admiring Raoul's drawings, absently leafing through the stack until he came upon one of himself lounging on the edge of a pool, exceedingly naked. Good lord. He'd never seen himself posed so seductively, fingers trailing in the water, one leg bent, and, well... his manhood so exposed. At least he wasn't erect. And to think Raoul's pen had made those strokes and had done so with confidence, without error or correction. Brice swallowed hard, then heard a scattering of gravel in the tunnel and quicky tucked the sketch back beneath the others.

By the time Raoul appeared through the curtain of ivy, Brice sat nonchalantly in the chair, hoping the heat on his face didn't translate into color.

Raoul removed his mask and set it down on the table, then arched an eyebrow. "What is it?"

"Nothing. I just wondered where you were."

The corner of Raoul's lips lifted. "Hm, did you not hear me once advise a mortal not to lie to a liar?"

"I do recall that, yes." Brice picked at his sleeve.

Raoul was too astute and Brice too flustered, so of course Raoul deduced the culprit in mere seconds and plucked the sketch free from its hiding place. He studied Brice, who looked away. "You don't like it."

"Lord, no." He laughed. "That's not it at all."

Raoul perched his ass on the edge of the table. "You like it *too* much?"

"Oh, stop," Brice spluttered.

"What then?"

"I just... My life, where I come from, the town, my family... desire between two men is frowned upon."

Raoul grunted a laugh. "It is good then that I am not a man but fae. I can desire whatever or whomever I wish. And so can you." He dropped the sketch onto the table and lowered himself to his knees in front of Brice. His hands hovered, wanting to touch Brice's thighs.

Brice leaned forward. "Will you draw for me?"

"Draw what?" Raoul arched an eyebrow.

"A picture of you. Like that."

"Must it be accurate or am I allowed to embellish some?" His eyebrows lifted.

Brice almost laughed, but Raoul meant it. "You are beautiful as you are. No embellishment required."

"Are you sure?"

"Why would I want embellishment when you're already perfect?"

He dropped back, sitting on his heels and tilting his head. "Do you truly think so?"

Brice barked a laugh—he was jesting, surely. How could he not know he was beautiful on the inside and out? But Raoul had stiffened at the laugh.

"I'm sorry." It was easy to forget Raoul hid behind his confidence. In moments like these, with the fae looking up at him, he clearly had no idea of his worth. Or worse, he thought himself worthless. "I wish I had the words to describe how perfect you are." He kissed him quickly, or had planned to, but under the little peck Raoul's mouth opened, and Brice slipped his tongue in—tasting, seeking, yearning. The more Raoul responded, the more Brice gave, until they rocked together as one.

Brice might have gone further. He was already thinking of how he could pull Raoul to his feet and kiss him while taking the fae's cock in his hand. But Raoul ended the kiss with a heavy sigh and withdrew across the cavern, dousing the heat they'd shared.

Brice shifted uncomfortably. His gaze snagged on the sketch again, and the uncomfortable arousal stiffened more. Raoul was right to stop their passion before it spilled over into more erotic wants, although Raoul appeared to have his own reasons for denying their lust. Reasons that had nothing to do with Brice's choice and everything to do with Raoul's inability to see himself as desirable. Raoul was a paradox. Lustful and sultry with others while sometimes shy and anxious with Brice.

"Vine accosted me," Raoul said. He'd picked up his mask and was idly examining it, letting its ties trail through his fingers. "I was able to shake him off, but our time here is short. He will tell the host once his desire to have you outweighs his fear."

Vine. Just the thought of the trio turned Brice's insides over. "Hasn't he already *had me* enough?" Brice said with a snarl. "Why must he continue?"

"Because I took you from him. Stealing another's plaything is frowned upon."

Brice winced at *plaything*. He did not want to think about Vine or what had happened. He should focus ahead on what could be done to end all this.

He straightened in the chair and looked up. "I brought a note with me from my mother. I believe it was meant for the host. I was reaching for it when he caught me, and it slipped from my fingers. But if we could find it again and show it to him, I think it will help get through to him—"

"You mean talk with him?"

"Yes. Without distractions."

Raoul shook his head. "The time for discussions passed long ago."

"There must be some reason left in him?"

"Why?" Raoul asked.

Brice had no reply to that. Because if the host could not be reasoned with, then what means did they have of stopping him? "I lost the note in the garden. Will you look for it?"

Raoul put his mask on again and headed toward the tunnel exit. "What did it say?"

"Forgive me."

Raoul froze mid-step. Then, with renewed enthusiasm, he swept the ivy curtain aside. "I'll find the note."

Chapter Forty

Raoul returned sometime later, removed his mask, and without a word went straight to the stream at the rear of the chamber. He removed his jacket, loosened his shirt, and splashed water over his face. Perhaps Brice was seeing too much in the fae's silence, but Raoul's quiet did not feel like him. Raoul wasn't the quiet type. Brice didn't want to push. What they had—whatever it was—was new and fragile and different. He feared losing it. Losing Raoul.

When the quiet went on so long it began to suffocate, Brice moved from the table and approached Raoul. "Is everything all right?"

"Hm." Raoul rolled up his sleeves and plunged his hands in the stream, washing them off. He lifted his gaze and tried to smile, but it didn't stick. "Forgive me. I'm not used to having company who will listen." He flicked his hands dry.

"There's nothing to forgive."

"I didn't find the note." His chest swelled as he breathed

deeply. "Vine cornered me. I had to... be seen. If I didn't return with him, he'd have alerted the host."

Something had happened. Something Raoul hadn't wanted. And knowing Vine as Brice did, that something was probably sex.

Raoul saw the direction of Brice's thoughts on his face. "It's nothing I haven't done before."

What was it the host had said? Brice wasn't the first to fall in love with Raoul? Brice shouldn't feel jealousy. He had no real claim to Raoul. But what he should and shouldn't feel didn't matter. He couldn't help hating the thought of Raoul *with* others, especially if one of those others was Vine.

"Although this time was different," Raoul said, watching Brice's face, and as much as Brice tried to hide his feelings, he likely failed. "I had to go with him, you understand?"

"Did you want to?"

"No, but I... always have. It's the way of things."

"Because you let it happen."

Raoul frowned. "Then what should I have done, Brice? What would you have done?"

"I don't know. Tell him no. Fight?"

He laughed like the idea was absurd. "What is there to fight for? Another day in the masquerade?"

Us, Brice wanted to say. But it was too soon. There wasn't an *us*. He wanted there to be. In Raoul's absence, he'd thought of little else. But for there to be an "us," there had to be an "after." And that hope seemed so far away.

"Come with me." He cast his gaze along the stream, through the narrow gap in the rocks, to the waterfall beyond. "I'll show you what there is to fight for." Without stopping to check if Raoul followed, he climbed over the rocks and slipped through the gap to where the waterfall tumbled down the rock face into its moonlit pool. Discarding his shirt, he stepped to the end of the ledge, felt Raoul's gaze warm his naked back, then dove through the falls into the pool. The water was warm, of course. The masquerade made it so.

He rebounded off the pool's gravel bottom and broke the surface, shaking his hair out of his face. The waterfall poured in, but there was no sign of Raoul. He'd been so sure the fae would follow, too curious not to.

There. Raoul's hand parted the falling waters as though parting curtains. He peered from the darkness, eyes glittering. Brice's heart skipped.

Would Raoul stop this now, before it had begun?

Raoul's hand vanished and the water obscured him from view. Perhaps that was it. Brice lifted his gaze to the moon. Bright stars pinpricked the night sky. Maybe Raoul didn't want him after all? He wasn't fae, and perhaps Brice was a fool to think he could offer Raoul anything he hadn't had before, anything he'd want.

The waterfall parted and Raoul dove knifelike into the pool, barely making a splash. He kicked back to the surface, gasped, flashed a grin, and ran his hands over his braided hair. "Very well, LeChoix. You have my attention."

"May I?" Brice reached for the end of his braid and after Raoul nodded, he loosened the tie, then pulled his fingers through the plait, freeing his hair. Black locks fanned across the water. So beautiful.

"You don't have to ask to touch me," Raoul said.

They were close now, treading water together. "Do you prefer I don't ask?"

A slight dip of his chin, and Brice threaded his fingers into Raoul's hair, pulling him into a kiss. Raoul opened, arched, and moaned. Water lapped at Brice's chin. He chuckled, slipped an arm around Raoul's waist, and gathered him close, swimming the few feet toward shallower water where they wouldn't sink. As soon as he set his feet down, Raoul's mouth claimed his. He swept his hands up Brice's back and pressed in so close that his heat became Brice's and his hardness pressed into Brice's hip, tantalizingly close to his own aroused member. Brice shifted his hips, deliberately twisting to rub against him. Their cocks touched through fabric, and Raoul gasped free of the kiss to glare deep into Brice's soul. Brice might have thought his gaze angry, but he knew it was more complicated. Raoul was desperate and starved of joy and love and all the good things in life. Brice knew because he'd felt the same for so long. Hollow, lost, alone.

"Is this worth fighting for?" he asked, voice as rough as his grip on Raoul.

"Yes." Breathless, Raoul's mouth smothered Brice's, then burned lower, down his neck to his collarbone. Raoul's kisses sank lower still until he dropped beneath the waterline and suckled one of Brice's nipples, flicking and teasing with his tongue.

He gasped back to the surface and cupped Brice's cock in a confident hold. Brice staggered on the loose gravel, freed Raoul's hair, and clutched his ass instead.

"I've wanted you in my hands since you first denied me," Raoul growled into Brice's neck. "Wanted to make you come crying my name. Watch your skin flush and your eyes widen and your cock harden again and again. There aren't words for the things I want to do for you."

If there were adequate words for any of this, Brice couldn't find them. He kissed Raoul's neck and kneaded his ass, sinking his fingers in so damned hard it surely hurt.

"Your clothes..." Brice muttered, nipping Raoul's shoulder. "I need you naked in this pool, now."

"Hm," Raoul purred. He stepped back, whipped off his shirt and with a few lithe motions, removed his trousers and flung them toward the bank. Now he was naked under the moonlight. A vision, a dream, one Brice had never imagined would be his.

"Now you." Raoul jerked his chin.

Brice struggled to balance while trying to remove his trousers, almost falling once, which of course had Raoul fighting a smirk. Brice circled around, facing him again once he'd thrown his balled-up, sodden trousers to the bank. And now they were both naked, standing at arm's length, breathing hard. Whatever Raoul saw in Brice, his hungry eyes devoured it. Brice saw a man, firm shoulders perfect for biting, a heaving chest he wanted to run his tongue down and sample, fingers he wanted to suck and kiss. And that was only the things above the water. What lay below was even more tempting for being hidden.

They crashed together, wet skin on wet skin, kisses blurred and messy, cocks grinding. Raoul threw his head back and laughed. It was perfect. *He* was perfect. Brice nipped at his jaw, sucking and teasing, and captured his cock in his palm, sealing his fingers around its silken firmness. A shudder ran through Raoul and when he met Brice's gaze, he dared him to continue. Brice ground his own cock against Raoul's hip as he slowly, firmly, mastered Raoul's hard need. Raoul's shudders intensified, his hips twitched and jerked, occasionally thrusting. His breaths shortened, and Brice worked more quickly, pumping the fae. Hearing him gasp, feeling him arch and knowing Brice was doing this, pleasing him, it made his own cock leak its want and throb with need.

Raoul's nails dug into Brice's shoulder. They rocked together, body to body, Raoul fucking Brice's fist like it was his hole. Raoul's gasps quickened, his body tensed, just his hips and cock locked in a savage rhythm.

"Yes," Brice hissed against his neck. "Raoul, please. Yes, I want to feel you spill in my hand. Hot and pulsing. Please, come for me."

"I can oblige." He grunted, voice strained. "My lord." Raoul arched, let out a silent cry, and heat filled Brice's fingers, pumping in time with Raoul's shuddering jerks. He was even more beautiful like this, thrown open and raw in Brice's arms. No mask, no lies, just the truth of him.

Raoul's glare scorched. He captured Brice's cock in his hand, then dove underwater. His sweet lips encircled Brice's hot member. His tongue pushed up and over. Not deep, just enough to suck him in. It wouldn't take more than a few strokes. He'd been close to coming just watching Raoul's ecstasy. He pulled to mind that image again now, of Raoul arched, head thrown back, eyes open and mouth apart—the mouth now sucking and tongue firmly stroking. Faster, Raoul took him. He came up for air, grinned like a devil, and dove back under, and this time he swallowed Brice so damn deep that it was Brice who cried out. A few devastatingly deep strokes, and he could hold out no longer. His release poured through his restraint and down his back, launching his mind and body high as his cock throbbed and spilled over Raoul's sucking tongue, delivering wave after wave of delicious pulses.

Raoul broke the surface gasping and slammed a kiss on Brice's mouth. He tasted of saltiness, and Brice—maddened by lust—kissed him back so hard it surely hurt. They writhed together, spent and alive—so thoroughly alive.

Brice loved him. He knew it more with every kiss, every gasp, and every time Raoul looked into his eyes and exposed another piece of himself. He loved him no matter what, because love didn't reason. It didn't make deals. It did not wear a mask. It was true. And that was how Brice knew it was real. He could only hope Raoul felt the same.

Chapter Forty-One

Only at the masquerade could he lie on his back on the pool's sandy moonlit bank as naked as the day he was born. Raoul lay next to him, hands laced behind his head. Moonlit, Raoul was devastating, and Brice was helplessly drawn to him, unable to gather his wits enough to force his gaze away. So he stared unashamed while Raoul smiled at the stars.

Was there ever a moment so perfect as this one?

Brice rolled onto his side and propped his head in his hand.

Raoul turned his head at the movement. He arched an eyebrow. "That settles it, my lord. You are a figment of my imagination. A masquerade dream. Because Brice LeChoix told me once that he does not frolic with the fae. He would certainly disapprove of this shamelessly naked display." He swept a hand, encompassing them both.

Brice tried and failed to keep from smiling. "That man had much to learn."

Raoul snorted a laugh. "If this is a dream, let it never end."

"I almost wish it wouldn't."

"Hm... that's how it traps you. Ask yourself, is any of this real?" Moonlight glittered in his eyes and painted his skin silver. Brice had tasted him, felt his fingers grip his thighs, heard him gasp, and those things had sparked in Brice feelings that lifted his heart and soul. They were real, the way his heart soared was real. The masquerade was made of fantasy, but the feelings it summoned were real.

"Does it matter, so long as we're both happy?"

He turned onto his side and propped his head up, mirroring Brice. "Yes. After a while the truth becomes all that matters." His gaze softened, turning sad. He flopped onto his back again. "There is no happiness without truth."

Brice knew the truth. He was looking at it. But Raoul had been trapped here for so long, perhaps he had genuinely lost sight of it.

He likely feared Brice would leave again. He feared everything they'd just done was a dream and, in a blink, it would be taken away. Brice watched the fae's lashes flutter softly against his cheeks. Others had come, other guests. They'd used him, probably told him over and over how beautiful he was, but they always left. The dancer never got to leave his music box. The lid closed. And there was only darkness until the lid opened and it all began again.

"Raoul." He said his name softly. "I'm not going to leave you."

Raoul didn't look over, just stared at the unchanging stars.

"Look at me," Brice said.

He rolled his head and his eyes. "If I hadn't sent the last invite, you'd be Lord of Latchly Hall, married to a dependable man, living a grand life alongside your brother, as is right for mortals."

"Married to a man?" He laughed sourly. "If only such a thing were permitted in fair Chamonet. In Massalia perhaps, but the city is not a place for me. I'd be married, no doubt, as is proper, but without love. And drowning in debt, carrying a name I have no right to."

"Still a life of choice. You vowed to never return."

... save me... If those two words hadn't found him, he couldn't know whether he would have ever returned. He'd vowed not to, that was true. But his heart would have pulled him back eventually. "I cannot say for certain what I'd have done—"

"You should have burned it like you burned your father's suit. Like you burned all the past invites." Raoul rolled away and began to climb to his feet.

Father's suit? What? Brice caught Raoul's arm and pulled him back down to the ground. He threw a leg over him, trapping Raoul's firm, naked body beneath his. Raoul made no move to fight and flopped back again, smiling up as Brice straddled him. "I never told anyone I burned his suit."

"Did you not?" His lashes fluttered. "Perhaps you said it in your sleep? You do mutter, you know. It's rather adorable. You've said my name many a ti—"

Brice caught his wrists and pinned them loosely against the cool sand. "Hold that sweet tongue of yours. I did not mutter such things." Raoul made a pathetic attempt at squirming free—or perhaps he was shifting to make room for his filling arousal warming Brice's inner thigh.

"Hm," he purred. "Keep this up, and my sweet tongue and I will be wrapped around more favorable things than this argument."

A pulse of lust warmed Brice's cock, but he wasn't going to be distracted. "How do you know I burned the suit?"

Raoul's left eyebrow twitched upward as his lips tucked down. "The same way I know you chop wood shirtless in the eastern clearing."

"How?" How had Raoul seen those things? It wasn't possible. Unless... the wolf? Ice blue eyes, its coat so white it glittered silver. It couldn't be... "No? It was you!"

"I really have no idea what you're referring to."

Brice leaned in as though to kiss him but held off, making Raoul lift his chin, trying to capture Brice's lips. Brice pulled back, teasingly out of reach. "Tell me the truth, Raoul. You can change your shape, yes? Become something else?"

"If I tell you yes, will you kiss me?"

This trickster. Brice should be mad, but he felt only laughter. "My horse threw me because of you!" He pushed upright onto his knees, torn between indignation and an increasingly playful desire to ravish the fiend he held pinned under him.

Raoul lay limp and compliant, making no attempt to move. "A mistake, I assure you. You startled me." His gaze skipped downward to where both their desires were becoming more evident.

"But you can't escape this place—"

"It's not escape, more a reprieve. Always fleeting and very temporary." He gripped Brice's thighs and spread his fingers, kneading the flesh. "And the price is high on my return." He looked up. "I age, become vulnerable, and there is little out there for me. Or that's how it used to be. The cost became worth it to see you swing your axe, my lord."

The wolf *was* Raoul! "I thought that beast meant to kill me."

"You were the one brandishing the axe."

"Wait—my chickens!" Brice motioned a playful punch toward him but Raoul grabbed his wrist and in a swift, dizzying movement, had Brice on his back in the sand. Raoul straddled him, tight fingers around Brice's wrists, thighs clutching him close.

"No, not me." The fae chuckled. "But I did see off a scrawny pack of wolves who would have made light work of your flimsy coop. You're welcome."

"I almost hunted you down." Brice squirmed some but failed at playing the victim when his cock twitched, betraying him. Brice recalled the moment he'd taken up his father's rifle. "I would have killed you!"

Instead of making Raoul wary, the words seemed to further arouse him. "Hunt me now." He fell forward onto his hands, then lowered himself chest to chest, skin to skin over Brice, their rodlike arousals pinned between them. "If you wish." Raoul freed Brice's wrists.

Brice clutched at his face and sank his fingers into Raoul's hair, holding him. "You are remarkable."

Raoul's gaze turned hungry. "Your being here, is it real? Do you mean the things you say and do or are you some illusion sent to try me?"

"I mean to end all this madness. I mean to save you. That is as real as I am."

The laughter vanished from Raoul's eyes. Desperation

and need filled the void. Raoul clutched the back of Brice's head and pulled him into a wild kiss. Then, breathless, he tore free. "Promises made under moonlight are forever, LeChoix. Don't break my heart with empty words."

This was real. This was true. This was a moment that would define all others. "Never. You will see the autumn leaves fall and the spring flowers surrender to summer. I promise you this under moonlight and the stars and whatever gods you have forgotten who look down upon us."

Raoul's eyes shone. "I want with all my heart to believe you," he whispered.

"Then believe me." He pressed his forehead to Raoul's and peered deep into his tearful eyes. Those tears didn't fall. Not yet. One day, they would be tears of joy. "Trust me." He caught Raoul's free hand and gripped it hard. "I am not like the other guests. My word is true. And if all else fails, we will burn it down together."

Chapter Forty-Two

They made love again in the pool and later in the blanket nest in Raoul's enchanting cavern, beginning slow and reverent, then turning frantic and desperate, as though Raoul feared their lovemaking would not last. Raoul seemed to sense he was giving too much of himself away, and when he did, he turned sly, grabbing the wine and pouring it over Brice's chest so he could lap it up while fixing Brice under his heavy-lidded gaze. It was while Raoul licked and teased that he discovered Brice had a ticklish spot near his hip. And Brice's torture began. Fits of laughter turned to wine-addled kisses and heavy gasps. Raoul's body became his obsession, like the fae himself. Brice couldn't get enough, couldn't taste him enough or make him laugh enough. But he lived for the moans, the sweet hisses, the gasps at the tip of every thrust.

Raoul's body surrendered in the most remarkable of ways. He arched and shuddered. Candlelight played over his dancer's physique, trickling down his abs and pooling at his hip.

In the throes of their joining, with Brice buried inside, Raoul shifted onto his knees and Brice wrapped his arms around him from behind. The angle made his thrusting shallow but all the more exquisite. "Is this reason enough to fight?" he asked Raoul again, then sucked his earlobe between his teeth and gently bit down. The sound that rumbled through Raoul was part growl, part moan, and all animal, reminding Brice of the wolf.

Raoul pulled Brice's arms tighter around himself. There was no need for words; his body talked for him.

Spent and aching, Brice lay tangled in the sheets with Raoul tucked against him. "Do you ever dream of what comes after?" he mumbled against the back of Raoul's neck.

"A dream within a dream? I used to. The others would tell tales of how it was before and of how it could be again, but over time the stories stopped. We have forgotten what freedom looks like, forgotten who we are and where we come from."

"You don't remember your home?"

"No. A blessing, I think. To know what has been taken would be torturous."

Brice silently vowed again to end this. He vowed it every time Raoul dozed in his arms. The mood had soured, and he hated to see Raoul without his smile. "If you could make yourself a new past, what would it be? Anything at all," he asked him.

Raoul twisted onto his back and laid his head on the pillow with his black hair cushioned around him. "Who do you want me to be?"

Brice chuckled and flicked a curl of hair from Raoul's

cheek, then stroked his knuckles along his jaw. "No, it's not about me. Who do you think you were, before?"

"Perhaps I was a nobody, a nothing, just a side character in someone else's tale."

Brice flicked Raoul's nose. "I don't believe that and neither do you."

Raoul laughed, swatted his hand away, and faced the ceiling. He took a deep breath and fell into thought. "I could have been anyone. A courtier, perhaps. I seem to recall courts for every land, not just yours. Perhaps I am a lost prince?" He arched an eyebrow. "The harrowing tale of the much-loved fae prince, vanished—no, *taken* from his home! His people continue to search for him despite the passing years. They will not rest until their beloved prince is found." He checked Brice was watching and grinned. "Is that backstory romantic enough for you?"

"A prince..." Brice pinched a laugh behind his lips.

"What?"

"I don't... You're not exactly the princely type."

His eyes flared. "Why, sir! You dare insult me so!" he mock-bellowed. "If I wore gloves, I would take one and strike you." He dove in, dug his fingers into the spot near Brice's ribs that they'd both discovered made Brice squirm, and attacked, throwing Brice onto his back in a fit of laughter. Raoul pinned him down, spreading his knees either side of Brice's hips and swooping in for a kiss. Like this, he was so full of passion and life, of joy and humor, Brice really had no choice but to love him. "Perhaps, my lord"—Raoul braced beside Brice's head and stroked his fingers lightly over his chin and down his neck—"I am the villain of some forgotten tale. Wicked and insidious, I lured mortals into my clutches. Is that a more suitable fantasy for you?"

Brice ran his hands up Raoul's warm thighs, eager to soak in more and more of him. "You could never be a villain."

"Hm." Raoul leaned in and slipped his tongue between Brice's lips, seeking a kiss. "Ah." He suddenly straightened and gracefully climbed off Brice to reach for his nearby stack of drawings. Pulling a sketch from underneath, he sat near the edge of their bed and handed it over. "There. A promise made. A likeness, I fear. The nose is too long, the arms quite uneven. The fingers vexed me."

Brice saw none of those imperfections in the picture, just Raoul sprawled in the grass, gloriously naked and utterly unashamed. No smirk. He looked terribly serious. The style was different to that of Raoul's drawings of him. Pencil lines dug deep, and some were angrily drawn over.

"You hate it—I knew you would." Raoul tried to snatch it back but Brice lifted it out of reach. "Brice, tear it up. I'll draw another. Perhaps I'll add a crown?" He reached again, but Brice kissed him and hid the drawing behind his back as Raoul melted against him. "Distracting me with sex, milord?" Raoul mumbled around the kiss. "My weakness," he whispered.

"Sex is your weakness?"

"No, you are."

He couldn't be sure who was distracted more. What had begun as a kiss was quickly turning into more. Brice growled and clutched Raoul closer. "The sketch is beautiful," he said, pulling away just enough to see Raoul's face.

"And it's mine to protect. Nobody else can have it or use it. It's too precious."

Raoul looked away but his little shy smile stayed, and he soon looked back, testing to see if Brice still watched. At moments like these, Raoul's sudden shyness made Brice's heart beat so hard it would surely explode. Brice kissed his doubts away, long and deep and definitely distracting. There was desperation in Brice, too, because this must surely end soon. They'd have to find the note, face the host, and reason with him. That thought terrified Brice because unlike before, he'd found he had a heart to lose.

Raoul had slipped out to look for the note, as he'd taken to doing whenever the urge struck him.

Brice washed, dressed, ate some crackers and sipped wine, and rattled around the cavern, pacing from wall to wall and waiting for the sounds of Raoul's scuffs from within the entrance tunnel. With no clock and no day or night, a minute could last an hour in the cavern, especially when waiting. How long had Raoul been gone? The candles had burned down, hadn't they? A day, at least. Perhaps more. He should have returned by now.

He always returned.

As a distraction, Brice examined Raoul's drawings. There were more of them now. Of Brice and Raoul together. Raoul's drawings of himself were always messy and rushed, but the drawings he made of Brice had a level of detail that stole Brice's breath. The drawings of them entangled were as erotic as they were beautiful. Raoul clearly liked those the most. Brice smiled as he casually browsed the collection. There had been a time when seeing himself so flagrantly exposed would have embarrassed and mortified him, probably enraged him too. Had the masquerade changed him or had Raoul? He thought perhaps a little of both. He didn't hate the masquerade as he had before. He understood. Understood *them*. And that was how he was going to reason with the host.

His mask caught his eye. He'd need to put it on again soon and face the music. A layer of dust dulled its shine.

Scuffs sounded in the tunnel. Finally, he was home. "Raoul, I..."

A fae in blue pants and a finely laced riding coat entered the cavern. Her dark hair was cropped short around her face, and it took Brice a moment to recognize her behind her blue mask.

Chantel didn't need to say a word. Her sad eyes said enough.

"What happened?" he asked.

"Vine has him."

Brice snatched up his mask and put it on as he shoved by her and through the tunnel.

"Brice, wait..." She grabbed for him.

He shook her off. "Are they in the pleasure rooms?"

"No... the garden."

That wretched garden. So close to the cavern. Raoul had been nearby the whole time. Well, damn Vine and his cock. No doubt he'd coerced Raoul into performing something horrid. Raoul would have had no choice but to distract the horrible fae with the only weapon that worked on him and his two companions.

Brice didn't have to walk far from the cavern before seeing the small crowd gathered around a wooden pavilion. There were no roses here, just the carved variety crawling up the pavilion's frame. He caught glimpses of heads and naked shoulders between the crowd and heard snatches of gasps and moans.

"Brice." Chantel hissed his name, finally pulling him around to face her. "Every time you bluster in, you fail. You must be careful, or you'll endanger both yourself and him."

He didn't trust her, but that didn't make her wrong. She appeared to care, even from behind her mask. He saw that much in the frown pulling at her lips.

"You're as bad as they are. Why should I trust you?"

"Raoul is my friend. I've only ever tried to help—"

"By introducing me to Vine?" he said in a hiss. "I don't need your kind of help, Chantel."

"I took you to Raoul, as was our deal. As is the way of the masquerade."

"A lie you all tell yourselves to wash your hands of blame." She staggered as though stunned. "You don't like to hear the truth," Brice added, sensing he'd found a chink in her blue silk armor. "You've spent so long hiding from what's real, you can barely see it when it's right in front of you. I care about Raoul—that's real—and I'll not let the likes of you sabotage what we have."

Her smile slowly appeared. "Such fire in such an unassuming exterior. I see why he likes you. Follow my lead." Her grin turned eerily convincing, and she excused her way through the crowd.

What he saw might have been enchanting if consensual. Laurel and Claude had a woman between them, her dress spilled open and up around her hips as they fucked her from both ends.

Raoul lay sprawled on a bench seat behind them, knees spread around the red-headed woman between him and Vine. She sucked him while Vine took her from behind. The display was as shocking as it was erotic.

Raoul had his eyes closed, his hand twisted in her hair. His mask hid much of his face but not the sneer at his lips. Brice could only stare. Part of him wanted to believe it was consensual, because then Raoul had chosen this. But when Raoul lowered his head and opened his eyes, fixing them on Brice at the front of the crowd, his beautiful eyes were dull and empty and unseeing. He performed what was expected while his mind was elsewhere. It was cruel. And these fools watched with heavy breathing, wet or hard in their undergarments, desperate for their turn.

The urge to yell, to march into the midst of it and haul Raoul out of there, almost overcame him. Anger and hurt stole his reason, locking him still. He wanted nothing more than to go to him and end this now.

Chantel placed a hand on his arm and without looking back, she stepped from the crowd. Shrugging off her coat, she discarded it, then began to unlace her corset. By the time she reached Vine, her bare shoulders gleamed under the moonlight. She slipped her hands up Vine's back, making the fae shudder and glance behind him at the new touch. Chantel turned his head back again and kissed his neck, then his shoulder, then whispered in Vine's ear.

When he next turned his head, his gaze found Brice and a cruel smile lifted his lips. He still fucked the female guest. Her gasps around Raoul's cock had hastened. Raoul hadn't moved at all.

Brice knew how to stop this.

And as the crowd watched, enraptured by the orgy, he stepped from their relative safety. With his fists at his sides, he stared back into Vine's startling glare. "It's me you want."

Vine slid himself from within the woman's folds and turned toward Brice. The guest, denied her pleasure, lifted off Raoul and peered glassy-eyed over her shoulder. Her pupils were blown. She was barely aware of her surroundings. She probably believed she wanted this. Hadn't Brice thought the same when he'd been under their spell? The flowers, the pollen, the allure of it all.

"Go," he told her. "You'll thank me tomorrow."

If the masquerade let her have a tomorrow. Gathering her skirts, she stumbled away.

Raoul had tucked his cock away but still hadn't moved from the bench. He looked up, watching, his masked face artfully blank.

They still had an audience, eager to see if Vine fucked Brice. They had all come for their evening's entertainment.

"You want me and him together?" Brice asked.

Vine glanced behind him, as though having forgotten Raoul was even present or to see if he was still compliant. "I do." As he turned his gaze back again, Brice caught his chin and kissed him hard enough to have him backing up. He thrust his all into that kiss, hating it but needing for it to be believed. His mask helped. He kissed like he remembered Vine liked, with tongue and teeth, rough and vicious. He kissed him like he owned him, backing him up a step with every heartbeat until Vine bumped against the bench.

Brice ran a hand up the fae's chest and wrapped his fingers around his throat, then slammed him down on his ass and held him there. Vine's wicked smile turned vicious as Raoul's keen eyes watched on. "You had me. Our deal is done. You don't touch me or Raoul again. You don't look at him, you don't accost him, you don't fucking say good day to him unless he speaks to you. Do you understand me?"

Vine's golden eyebrow arched. He dug his fingers around Brice's and pried his grip open. "Who are you to command me?"

Brice leaned in and answered. "I'm the man who will set you all free."

Vine's eyes narrowed. Then he laughed, bright and loud. "Free?"

Raoul launched forward and slammed a hand down over Vine's mouth, silencing his laughter. "Hush or we'll all be under his gaze. You stole Brice from the rose garden. The host will punish *you*, Vine. You remember what that's like, don't you?" Raoul's gaze briefly flicked to Brice, then back to Vine. "You remember the feel of the lashes coming down, spilling blood. You remember the reason for inking your skin, for hiding that pain? You remember what it is to hurt so badly you wish for death, only it never comes in this place, so you must suffer endlessly. I know you remember that because it is all any of us remember. Brice is going to end it. *We* are going to end it."

Vine shook his head. "He'll break your minds for this. And maybe I'll tell him your plans, hm?"

Raoul pressed his smiling lips to Vine's cheek and sneered. "The host cannot break what is already broken." He shoved off Vine and took several steps backward.

Remembering their audience, he scanned them all, his thunderous gaze further darkening. "Your entertainment is over!"

The tone of the crowd changed, turning sharp and restless.

Brice stepped away from Vine, leaving him sprawled on the bench with his hard cock out for all to see. Vine smirked as though nothing could touch him because he knew he'd had them both and words were just words here. He'd tell the host.

"Ladies and gentlemen, esteemed guests." Brice raised his voice and turned to regard the crowd. They each gazed back, their eyes full of need and lust and madness. Aroused and hungry, they stood poised on a knife's edge and their masks made them blameless. "This fae"—Brice smiled—"is all yours." He swept a hand toward Vine. "A *gift*, from the masquerade."

Vine smirked and shrugged a shoulder, uncaring. The first masked guest stepped forward, then the second, then the third. Then all at once they surged over him in a single heaving, desperate attack.

Raoul yanked Brice away, but that did not stop the sounds of moans and grunts and the strangled sounds of choking that came from Vine's gold-touched lips.

Vengeance tasted sweet. Vine deserved it.

Chapter Forty-Three

THEY HASTENED DOWN the garden pathway and once out of sight, Raoul caught Brice's shoulders and turned him to face him. "You came for me?"

He swallowed the sickly sourness at the back of his throat. "Of course."

"What you saw—"

"Wasn't consensual. I know. I couldn't let it go on."

"He followed me, demanding I give you up. He knew you were close. I distracted him. It was really nothing—"

Brice touched his face, silencing him. He ran his thumb over Raoul's soft bottom lip. "That wasn't nothing. It hurt you. It hurts you every time, Raoul. Perhaps you don't see it anymore, *can't* see it. But I do."

"Yes, well, I didn't used to care who fucked what part of me. Apparently, now I do." He pulled Brice close. "I suppose I should thank you for that."

Brice tasted his lips slow and easy, kissing him as though they had all the time in the world. He'd have liked nothing more than to draw Raoul into the shadows and perhaps go down onto his knees for him, but as they kissed, Raoul pressed a slip of paper into Brice's hand and the harsh reality of what had to be done broke their spell.

"You found it?" Brice unrolled the small piece of paper. *Forgive me.* He almost sobbed in relief. This was their chance.

"It's special. I feel it. Just like you said." Raoul lifted Brice's hand and the note cradled within it. "It could be the key to ending the masquerade."

"I hope so, for all our sakes."

Raoul folded Brice's fingers closed over the precious slip of paper and met his gaze. His silence spoke more than any words. Fear but also hope shone in his eyes.

"It will be all right," Brice told him.

"What if you hand him his mate's note and everything changes?"

"That's good, isn't it?"

"What if it changes me, changes *us*? What if I remember and I'm not who... whom you love?"

He wanted to tell him everything would be fine, but there was no way of knowing. If—*when* the masquerade fell, everything *would* change. The dominoes would fall and the world Raoul and the others had known for decades would vanish. They'd be free to do as they pleased, go anywhere, be anyone, to have their old lives back, wherever those lives were.

Raoul chewed his bottom lip and laughed darkly. He let go of Brice's hand and stepped back, beginning to shut down. "Here I am, made a fool by feelings when I'd thought I'd forsaken them."

"It's not foolish to be afraid of change."

His quick smile was bitter. "We could stay here, you and me? As we are? My cavern is no Latchly Hall, but it's... well ventilated..." He trailed off with a sigh.

Brice wanted that, too, but it wouldn't last. "'There is no happiness without truth.' You said those words. We can't live a lie."

Raoul huffed. "I used to believe that before I met you." He lifted Brice's hand and skimmed his lips across his knuckles. The touch shivered through Brice. Thunderous eyes lifted and peered from behind his mask. "Would it frighten you to know I've considered trapping you here? As you lie sleeping beside me, I've conjured to mind all the ways I could lie to you, tell you there is no escape, this is our life now. I'd make you believe me. I almost added a dash of forgetful poison to our wine so we might both forget how this has to end."

With every confession, Brice's heart raced faster. He plucked his hand free of Raoul's and slipped the precious note into his pocket. Poison? He'd trusted him. "Why are you telling me this?"

"Because it's the truth." Raoul backed away. "I don't know who I am, but I know what I'm capable of. For so long, I despised our host, yet I've begun to understand him. He lost his love, and when I think of losing you, it sets my soul ablaze. I would keep you here as I suspect the host kept Anette, earning her ire and her curse. You'd hate me, but it would still be worth it. Because you'd be mine. Forever. My mate." Whatever he saw on Brice's face, it was enough to make Raoul grimace. "I've said too much." He winced and carried a new pain on his face. One that spoke of regret and frustration.

"No, it's..." It was a lot to absorb and much of it reminded Brice of all the warnings his mother had given him about the fae and their ways, but also Chantel's words of how a fae's love was a formidable force. "Well, yes, it's a lot. I just—"

Raoul came striding back and paced short steps back and forth, hands clasped behind his back. "I *didn't* poison you. That should count for something, no? I don't know what exactly. I've never done this before. At least, not that I recall. I'm afraid, Brice. What if it ends and so do we?" Brice pulled Raoul against his chest. He instantly softened in his arms. "Do you hate me?" Raoul asked.

Brice fancied he could feel Raoul's heart beating against his own. He smelled of jasmine, and his taut body fit so snugly against him it was as though they were made for each other. He breathed in, drawing the taste and smell and touch of Raoul into him. "I can no more hate you than I could hate the sun for shining or the snow for falling. You are who you are, and I love you for it. That won't ever change." Even when their worlds undoubtedly parted them and reality came crashing in, nothing could take their love. It was a part of them now. Always.

Raoul's grin lit up his face. He clasped Brice's face in his hands, kissed him, and laughed in that way he did that meant he understood no more of this than Brice did. "If it must end, let it end in love." Pulling from Brice's arms, he tugged him along the path. "Come then, Brice LeChoix, let us make ready for our final masquerade."

Raoul was a whirlwind in motion. He took Brice's gold-laced mask and made it glitter with a swirl of his fingers, then tended his suit and shirt, using his talent for illusion to make his clothes appear good as new. Raoul then applied a line of kohl to Brice's eyes and had Brice admire his reflection in the stream. With his mask on, the whole effect lent Brice a sultry, dark-eyed handsomeness he really rather liked, and by the glimmer in Raoul's gaze, he appreciated the new look too.

"Let us hope we survive so I can delight in undressing you later." Raoul gathered his own clothes and spun them into elaborate finery—seams stitched themselves together, creases miraculously fell away, and all beneath a sweep of his fingers. He was bewitching to watch, and Raoul knew it. He delighted in Brice's rapt attention. When it came to dressing, he stripped off his previous attire, leaving himself splendidly naked under the candlelight. It would be too easy to swoop in and take Raoul into his arms, but he didn't want to upset Raoul's work. And besides, Raoul was distracted with dressing. Lust was likely the last thing on his mind.

Brice reveled in watching, free to admire the male form in a way he couldn't do outside the masquerade.

Raoul perched a foot on a rock and glanced over, eyebrow arched. With a devilish smirk, he picked up a flimsy slip of black silk and brought the stocking to his foot, then slowly rolled its length up his leg, over his knee, and to his thigh, where its lace hem rested perfectly against his pale skin. That lace was as delicate and virginal as icing on a wedding cake.

Brice hadn't known seeing a man putting on women's stockings could be so thoroughly arousing. But arouse him it did. Painfully, in fact. He adjusted himself rather awkwardly.

"Something the matter, Brice?"

He barely heard Raoul over the hot blood thudding in his ears.

Raoul's eyebrow remained arched and his lips tilted in a smirk. He reached for the second stocking. This one went on as slowly and seductively as the first. An old voice in Brice's head demanded he look away. But Past Him had no place here. And neither did shame.

Raoul collected a black suspender belt and with deliberate grace, he drew the belt up his firm legs to his hips and clipped on the stockings.

Lust, denied for so long, burned through Brice's body and set him alight.

Raoul straightened, cocking a hip and his head. "Something you like, my lord?"

He could take no more of the teasing and lunged at Raoul, lifting him off his feet. The fae gave a laughing cry and flung an arm around Brice's shoulders. He stopped laughing the moment Brice set his backside down on the desk, legs spread with Brice between them.

Brice peered down at him. Raoul was a feast, the most devious and delicious kind. Brice could never sate himself. But he'd make a start, especially as Raoul's body was fast responding to his rough handling, his cock proudly stiffening as Brice watched.

Raoul propped himself up on his elbows and rested a stocking-clad foot over Brice's shoulder. "Hm," he purred. "I think we found your weakness."

Words were too cumbersome. Brice grasped Raoul's ankle and kissed through the silk. With Raoul's gaze burning, Brice kissed a lazy path up Raoul's leg. When he reached the hem of the stocking, he slipped his tongue under the lace pattern and tasted Raoul. Raoul hissed in through his teeth and spread his thighs apart, opening and inviting Brice to take more. The fae's smile had vanished, but the heat in his eyes burned a hundred times hotter.

Raoul's lips parted. He ran his pink tongue across his bottom lip, then pinched his lip between his teeth. His erect cock twitched against his lower belly, its flushed tip glistening.

He didn't know where to begin. Couldn't think. To take that cock between his lips or bury his own aching need inside Raoul's hole, tantalizingly hidden between the buttocks pressed against the desktop. His need burned him up, making him so damned desperate he wasn't sure he could trust himself not to be too rough.

"Allow me a moment of practicality." Raoul reached across the desk and upended a bottle, spilling clear oil over his fingers, then reached between his legs and stroked his fingers into the valley of his ass, slathering glistening oil where it was needed. "Now do as you wish, milord," he said, voice rough. "You won't break me."

Brice tore open his own trouser buttons, grasped his cock, grabbed Raoul by the hip, and jerked him down the desk, hovering his ass off the edge. Raoul lifted his balls with his fingers—his stare locked on Brice's face—and Brice stroked his cockhead through the smeared oil between Raoul's tight buttocks. Raoul's hole eased under the pressure of the tip of Brice's cock, and then lust and need and hunger and rage at being denied all this his whole life conspired to devour his restraint. He forced himself in, out of his mind as pleasure rippled down his back, into his balls. He moaned, gripped Raoul's thigh to hold him in place, and shuddered, cock sheathed in tight, sublime muscle. Raoul's hips shifted and Brice's body demanded he thrust and fuck, but despite Raoul's words, Brice had to be sure he wasn't hurting him. The fae had been used a thousand times in a thousand different ways. He no longer believed his own pleasure mattered.

"Tell me you want this," Brice growled, sounding more animal than man. "You, not the player."

Raoul's smart mouth was open and gasping, his chest heaving. He'd thrown his head back, but now that Brice had stopped, he lowered his chin and narrowed his eyes. "Take me away, Brice."

The words weren't what he'd expected, but they were everything he needed to hear. He shrugged Raoul's right leg over his shoulder, spread him wide, and after easing out with excruciating slowness, he slammed in, jolting Raoul and the desk. Raoul growled. His flushed erect cock leaked and Brice knew this was right. It was fucking, but it was more too. Raoul wanted him, ached for him, needed him. His body shook for Brice. He *moaned* for Brice.

Brice thrust again, slamming into Raoul with force. Then again. Until he found a delicious rhythm of pounding at the same rate as his heart, perhaps matching Raoul's heart too.

Raoul threw his head back again and rocked, surrendering. Their joining became less about each thrust and more about the motion of their bodies entwined as one. Raoul's groans and snarls drove Brice harder and faster. Raoul gritted his teeth, brow furrowed, and pinned Brice under his stormy-eyed stare. "There... *harder*... oh, by the stars, *yes*."

Exquisite pleasure—its demands lifting him higher—drove every thought from Brice's head. There was just Raoul, moaning, clutching Brice's arm, cock straining. His black hair spilled from its leather band. True color touched his face, not like the rouge he sometimes applied. He was so damned beautiful, caught in the throes of lovemaking. Brice never wanted it to end.

Raoul's spine arched. He threw his head back, and his untouched cock jerked once, twice, and spilled its cream over Raoul's ripple of abdominal muscles.

Raoul's eyes blazed back to Brice's. His body shivered and trembled around Brice's cock even as Brice still pumped harder, faster, chasing that precious moment. He garbled words, said he loved him, loved being *in* him. Then ecstasy racked him, cresting so hard he came with a messy cry, releasing into Raoul's ass in mind-numbing shudders. Every new ragged thrust set him ablaze, the pleasure suddenly so sharp, it threatened to shatter him.

Buried balls deep in Raoul, he finally came back to himself to find Raoul's smirk even more devilish than before. Creamy come dashed his chest and Brice had the sudden startling urge to lick it off and begin again.

He swept his fingers through a pearl-like drop near Raoul's hip, brought it to his lips, and under Raoul's gaze, licked his finger clean.

"You are insatiable." Raoul chuckled. "However did the stable boys survive you?"

"I'm only this scandalous for you." He leaned over but was met with Raoul's hand against his chest, holding him off.

"Darling, you and that suit are perfection. Kiss me, and we'll both be covered in cream."

"I find I'm beyond caring." He pushed against Raoul's hand. Raoul gave way with a laugh, a laugh Brice cut off with a kiss. Still buried inside him, he kissed him gently, relishing the soft touch of his lips and the sweet thrust of his tongue. He committed the firm feel, the sweet taste, and the flowery smell of Raoul to his memory forever, secretly fearing that one day it might be all he had.

Over his stockings, Raoul wore heeled boots with silver buckles running up the sides. Formfitting black trousers went over the stockings, too, but Brice knew they were there. A silver-lined corseted frock coat and a black silk shirt with billowing sleeves completed Raoul's outfit. His nails glinted silver, matching the silver streak in his hair, and with his black-and-silver mask on, he was everything the masquerade promised—more alluring than even the host himself. Brice now knew the fae behind the mask, knew what made him laugh, knew what he feared, and he knew exactly where to kiss him to make him gasp Brice's name.

Raoul bowed. "Does my attire please milord?"

Brice took his hand and lifted him out of his bow, then kissed his fingers as was proper. "You're a wonder.

However, I prefer you naked under moonlight. Mostly naked... Will you wear the women's undergarments again when this is over?"

Raoul fluttered his lashes and flicked his braid from his shoulder. "For you, I'd wear a gown. I daresay I'd enjoy the freedom. That would surely catch the host's eye, no?"

He'd been on board with the fantasy until the mention of the host. His rising lust wilted and reality flooded back in. They could delay no longer. It was time to attend the masquerade.

Raoul pried himself free of Brice's hand, and breathing in, he straightened his shoulders. "Flatter him, as I know you can." He'd already said as much as they'd dressed. He paced as he went over the same ground they'd discussed before. "Treat him with respect and he'll return the same. Your first meeting—and all your meetings thereafter—have not gone well, probably because you represent all he hates and you have a tendency to challenge him at every opportunity. You won't win that way. Not here. Remember, this world is his life. He breathes in, the masquerade breathes out. They are one and the same. The truth is the only weapon you have. Wield it well, Brice." Raoul pressed his hands to Brice's chest and held his gaze. "Leon LeChoix stole Anette from the host's heart and his world. If he felt for her just a fraction of what I feel for you, then her leaving and the subsequent curse destroyed him. We will only know if he's beyond repair when you present him with the note."

Brice nodded. "He will see reason—I'm sure of it. He cannot want a life trapped in misery."

"I wish I had your optimism. If optimism fails, there's

always this." Raoul reached beneath the papers on the desk and handed over the pistol. "I speak from experience when I say he doesn't react well to having a pistol drawn on him. If you do draw it, make sure you're prepared to fire." He pushed the pistol into Brice's hand. "Freshly loaded."

Brice tucked a finger under Raoul's chin and lifted his head. "Will it kill him here?"

"We can only hope."

He didn't sound confident. The pistol was the last resort. If it came down to that, they'd likely already lost. "Whatever happens, we will survive this."

"I will," Raoul replied grimly. "I have no choice in that." He brushed Brice's lips with his own. "You could just walk away," he whispered. "I might hate you, but I wouldn't blame you."

"Never. And you would."

Raoul's smile melted into a kiss. He tasted of fae sweetness, of sweet wine and bitter sadness. He didn't believe anything would change; he didn't believe Brice would succeed. He thought this was goodbye. Brice tasted it all in that soft, waning kiss. When it ended, Brice whispered back, "This isn't goodbye."

"Then perhaps it will be hello?" His lashes fluttered and his eyes darkened, turning stormy.

If the masquerade fell and Raoul remembered his life from before, then they would meet again for the first time. "Perhaps." Brice brushed a thumb over the fae's bottom lip, wanting to kiss him once more, but their time had passed. The masquerade awaited, like bated breath.

Stepping back, Raoul offered the crook of his arm.

"Brice LeChoix, you are hereby invited to the masquerade. Guard your mask and your heart, for the masquerade takes both from fools in love."

He looped his arm with Raoul's. "It cannot take my heart when it already belongs to another."

Chapter Forty-Four

THE MASQUERADE'S sour ambience had turned bitter while Brice had recuperated. Perhaps he'd seen so much of the masquerade's illusions that his mind was deliberately picking holes in it. Candles burned low, their molten wax captured falling from the stands. Lace tablecloths had frayed edges trailing loose threads. And the music dragged its beat like a party winding down under the harsh light of dawn, regrets seeping in. The air tasted rich with damp and decay, pollen and sweat, and all the pretty fae smiles flashed like razor blades. Pearls still shone, gems still winked, gowns and masks and feathers and velvet. It was all here but over-ripe and spoiled.

Raoul and Brice entered the ballroom like a breath of fresh air. More than a few heads turned their way and raked their gazes over Brice. After so long alone with Raoul, the heat of the collective stares burned through his clothing and simmered against his skin.

The note, too, burned a hole in Brice's pocket as though everyone here could see it and its meaning.

Raoul simply led Brice to the dance floor, bowed, and their dance began.

It wasn't like any time before. Brice gathered Raoul's hand, caught his hip, pulled him close, and they *moved*. Raoul mirrored his every step, every turn, every sway, as though they were one, joined by something deeper than touch and music. The other dancers blurred in the corners of Brice's vision. The masquerade became an afterthought. Brice saw only the delight in Raoul's gaze and the quirk of his lips below his mask.

The music played, spiraling around them. Brice had never been so content or so thoroughly at peace with life and himself. In the arms of the man he loved, he'd never felt stronger.

He told Raoul, "You are radiant."

"Not I." Raoul's lips brushed Brice's cheek. "It is you they watch."

"Us then," Brice said.

"Us." Raoul's lips twitched, his real smile showing through.

They danced, and Brice's heart soared. In all of the madness since this had begun, this moment felt like a lighthouse in the storm. The masquerade and the fae and the guests all lived and breathed around them, churning their pleasure and pain, but he and Raoul, they shone in the dark.

"I don't believe I've ever been so afraid," Raoul whispered.

Brice eased his hand from Raoul's hip to his lower back, and they danced as one, hearts and souls entwined. "Not even the magic of the masquerade can take this from us."

The music abruptly curdled, bubbling to a sudden

demise. Silence spilled in. Brice only then noticed the dancers had moved away, leaving the floor open. They'd been dancing alone while the entire masquerade looked on. Brice thought he saw tears glisten like diamonds on the faces of some of the fae. Perhaps they saw love and were envious.

Slow, deliberate clapping punctuated the silence. *Clap, clap, clap.* The crowd peeled apart, and there he was, the host. Black and gold, his mask embossed with golden silk filigree. Black hair tied back with a single golden silk string. Brice instinctively stepped apart from Raoul but kept his hand on his lower back. From the corner of Brice's eye, he saw Raoul straighten. His lips thinned, pressing together, probably to keep any brash words behind them.

"Lord Brice LeChoix." The host's deep voice purred the words. "A glutton for pleasure." The host stopped a stride away. "Raoul makes a fine player. His prowess at delivering my masquerade's promises is second to none. I do hope you've enjoyed the fantasy—because that is all it is. A reflection of love, pretty to look at but shallow and meaningless."

Raoul's top lip curled.

Brice spread his fingers on Raoul's back, hopefully conveying that nothing the host said could hurt them.

"I have a message." Brice reached inside his jacket pocket and removed the scrolled note, then held it out. "She didn't hate you. She came to regret her actions. She was sorry."

The host's eyes narrowed. He looked down at the note, then back to Brice's face, reading what he could see behind the mask. His gaze briefly skimmed the crowd. They observed him in return. Tension crackled.

Brice couldn't make him take the note, couldn't make him read it. He could only hope there was something in the fae, some part of him from before that wasn't full of hate and despair. There had to be.

The host plucked the note from Brice's fingers and unfurled it. He looked down.

Forgive me.

His head stayed bowed.

Candlelight flickered.

Time dragged or stopped altogether. Brice's heart thumped. Raoul stood frozen. The masquerade and its guests held their breath.

Forgive me.

A plea from years ago, from a fae who had walked away and cursed every soul to live an eternity trapped in heartless pleasure. The host's mate, his opposite, the other half of his heart. Brice knew that love; his stood next to him. He knew that if Raoul were to ever curse him so, it would destroy him heart and soul. Love, he had learned, could be vicious. But it could also be full of wonder and joy and give life to every breath, every beat of a heart. Before Raoul, before the masquerade, he'd been empty. Now his heart was full.

The host had loved Anette. And she had loved him once too. Would he remember?

Sinclair could end this never-ending nightmare. He

could save the soul of every fae who danced for him. He had the power to free them all.

All he had to do was forgive her.

The host lifted his head.

Power sparked in the depths of his gaze.

His lips twitched.

His fingers slowly curled around the note, crushing it against his palm. He raised his hand, snapped open his fingers, and dust rained over the marble floor.

Raoul twisted and shoved Brice back. "Run!"

It happened so fast—yet so slow that Brice saw every moment in sharp, jagged clarity. Behind Raoul, the host raised both hands palms up. A blast of icy wind tore through the ballroom. A storm of snowflakes blurred all the color and light. A thousand candles snuffed out. The wind howled, glasses smashed, doors slammed. And the masquerade began to unravel and warp and twist. Walls buckled. Cracks danced through the ceiling.

Raoul suddenly had hold of Brice's hands. His brilliant eyes blazed. "Go, now—go back to your life and never return. Do this for me!"

"No."

The wind howled, whipping Raoul's hair about his face and tugging on their clothes. Snow dashed between them, sharp, like a thousand tiny knives. "There is no escape from this."

Brice pressed his hand to Raoul's cheek. "I'm not leaving."

The wind tried to pry them apart. Sharp-edged snowflakes zipped across Brice's face, drawing blood, turning each tiny flake blood-red. Raoul hauled him close. "You fool. He'll kill us for love."

Brice clutched him tight, his hand in his hair, holding him cheek to cheek.

"I'll live. It doesn't matter," Raoul said into Brice's ear. "I'll heal. But not you."

"It's not the healing that matters—it's the hurt. I'll not abandon you to him again, Raoul. To any of them." He kissed him hard on the lips and crushed him close as the wind and snow battered them from all sides. Then, as quickly as it had blasted in, the storm collapsed. Blood-red snow stained the marble floors, melting into flowing rivulets and staining the gowns and shoes of the guests, turning them red. Rot bloomed on the walls. Dead ivy hung from dull chandeliers. Candles spluttered back to life, but so few that they bred shadow upon shadow. The masquerade had become a nightmare in the truest sense of the word.

The host's whip cracked.

Its tails looped around Raoul's neck. He gasped and reached for the strips of leather coiled around him. The host yanked, snatching him from Brice's arms.

"No—!" Brice dashed after him. "*Stop*!"

Another yank from the host and Raoul fell onto his side in the red slush. The whip choked him harder. He clawed at it, desperate to pry its lengths free.

Fury turned Brice's mind sharp, turned his thoughts vicious.

The host hauled Raoul up by the neck, dangling him as though from a noose. But Raoul wouldn't die. He'd suffer endlessly as he'd been suffering for decades. As they'd all been suffering under the cruel hand of one bitter, selfish, jealous fae.

"You monster!" Brice strode for the host but stopped when Raoul kicked out in an effort to force him back. Raoul's eyes blazed through his mask, pleading for Brice to go even now. The host tightened his hold so that even Raoul's choking sounds ceased. His mouth opened and closed in silence.

Hot blood burned through Brice's veins. He'd faced cowards, faced his father at the end of his rifle, and he was not backing down.

"You could end this at any time," Brice said with a snarl. "It's not even about love. It never was. You don't care she forgave you. It was never about her. It was always about *you*. Leon, my father, took her away, and it's *that* you can't stand. Nobody takes another's plaything. A mortal stole your mate. He loved her and she loved him. True love, not whatever obsession you felt. If you'd loved her, you would have let her go. You'd let them all go." He swept an arm out to encompass the shivering crowd. "I love Raoul, and by God, he loves me, and you can't stand to see it happen again. You can't stand to see happiness."

The host jerked on the whip handle. Raoul's face turned purple behind the mask.

"Love?" The host's lips tilted into a smile. "Is that what you think you have with him? The fae do not—cannot—love mortals."

"I know it. I'll prove it. Let him go and take your whip to my back. I'll take his pain a hundred times over."

Gasps echoed about the hall. The host eased his hold on

the whip, just enough for Raoul to slump against the floor and work some of the loops loose enough to breathe.

"Brice... no," he wheezed.

The hurt in his eyes was too raw, too painful.

Brice glared at the host. "Let him go, not just from this but from the masquerade. Let him leave. Take me. Because that is love. I give my life for his."

Titters simmered about the crowd.

The host scoffed. "You are mortal. You'll die for him?"

"Yes."

"You foolish, pathetic man. Love is a fantasy." He unlooped the whip. Raoul gulped air and clutched at his raw throat. "This isn't love," the host went on. "The masquerade fulfills your every want. Nothing you see here is real. Nothing you taste, you hear, you fuck... None of it is real. You're in a dream, Brice LeChoix, and that dream knows your desires, knows your every wish. You were lost. You sought a purpose. A soul to save because you cannot save your own. My masquerade gave you everything your heart desired. It gave you a reason to live." The host ventured forward. "You sought a reason to keep on living and the masquerade answered you. The fae you fell in love with is a lie. The fae you surrender yourself for is nothing but an elaborate mask. Raoul isn't real. What you feel for him, that desperation inside"—the host clutched at his own chest—"that savage ache to be loved? The masquerade is a mirror. It reflects only what you want to see, and you so desperately wanted love, Brice. A mother who wasn't yours. A brother who despises you. A father you could never please. A life you languished in." The host laughed again and backed away. "Ask him." He gestured at Raoul slumped on the floor. "Ask your precious love for the truth."

Brice held the host's gaze. He didn't need to ask Raoul anything. He knew the truth. "Lies, all of it. Lies you tell yourself. You cannot tell me who or what I love. My feelings are my own. I know what I feel, and I know it's right. Nothing has ever felt so right as this, as right as loving Raoul."

"Then get on your knees, fool." The host sneered. He tightened his hold on the whip and circled around Raoul toward Brice. "Bleed for your fantasy. If that is what you desire."

Brice swallowed. He believed in this, in love, in Raoul. As should everyone here. The masquerade's power came from fantasy, yes, but the fae and guests were real. He looked at the crowd, at their shining masks. Their makeup had run down their faces in streaks. Blood soaked into the hems of their clothing. The fae weren't laughing. They weren't smiling. But they were listening and hearing his words.

It began with love.

And only true love could end it.

Brice tore his mask from his face and dropped it in the bloody snow.

Everyone would see who he truly was, no more lies. Brice LeChoix. He'd come back to save them all. He'd come to save Raoul. He'd come to end their torment. "He has trapped you in his personal nightmare." Brice raised his voice, sending it over their heads to the far corners. "This isn't a story about love. It's one of obsession. There is no curse, just his selfishness. He keeps you here because he can. He can choose to release you. The only reason you all suffer is because he cannot stand to let you go."

The host's steely fingers dug into Brice's shoulder and drove him down to his knees. He tore Brice's jacket off, popping buttons. The pistol went next, its weight suddenly vanishing as the host pulled it free.

"Brice, no—don't." Raoul's voice cracked as he slumped forward onto a hand. "Look at me. Listen to me."

Teeth gritted, breathing hard, Brice met Raoul's pained gaze.

Tears swam in his eyes. "Don't do this. Not for me."

"They have to see. They have to know. Love exists. It's real."

Raoul crawled forward and clutched Brice's hand. "Please, Brice."

The host thrust his fingers into Brice's hair, yanking hard and hauling him back, out of Raoul's grip. "Tell him," the host growled at Raoul. "Tell him the truth and save him."

Raoul's gaze flicked up to the host and back to Brice's face.

"Tell him your truth, Raoul. Tell him your love is a lie or I will lash the skin from his back! You are but a player in *my* dream! *Tell him*!"

A small sob escaped Raoul. He bowed his head and his midnight hair unraveled from its braid, spilling over his shoulder. "I can't let you do this for me. I'm not worthy of your love."

Brice already knew the truth. There was nothing Raoul could say that would change their love. Raoul looked up and the sorrow on his face suggested he might deny his feelings.

He'd say it was all a lie to drive Brice away, to have him run, to *save* him. But while words could lie, the truth on Raoul's face did not. The truth in his reverent touches, the truth in his laugh when they'd danced in the snow, the truth in the fear of him losing this life, this love, to the truth, should the masquerade fall. Love. It had been there all along. Raoul had always loved him, before either of them had realized it. "You are worth everything to me," Brice said. "I love you, Raoul. I will save you."

The sorrow in Raoul's gaze boiled away. He got a boot under him and swayed to his feet. Chest heaving, hair askew, he lifted his chin and tore off his mask. Silver and black, he glittered like a star in the nightmare, drawing all gazes to him. His breathing slowed, and determination steeled his face for all to see. Only then did he stare back at the host. "Control us, punish us, make us dance to your tune until we forget our own names, but you will never deny us love. Our hearts are our own." He stared at the host. "You tried to control Anette. She forgave you. I do not. I love Brice and that's no lie. If there is a shred of compassion left in your hollow heart, let Brice go."

Fury burned through the host's golden mask. "You will both suffer for this!"

The hand vanished from Brice's hair. He snatched a gasp, reeling from the host's cruel grip, and reached for Raoul's hand. The first lashing tore across his back, ripping a silent scream from his throat and setting his skin ablaze.

Chapter Forty-Five

Pain was a firework exploding inside his head, robbing all thought and reason. Brice could only liken it to the time he'd accidentally fallen against the blacksmith's forge and burned his shoulder. Father had raged, but his words had been lost in the agony of the skin-tightening heat. The lash was the same but across his upper back. He'd barely registered that he'd been struck and what that meant before the second lash came on top of the first. The splash of agonizing heat doubled. He tried to gasp, but his body locked rigid, dropping him to his hands and knees.

Raoul shouted something that was lost beneath Brice's silent screaming. The pain... it was too much. But Raoul could not be allowed to stop this. The guests, the fae, they all had to see how lost the host was. They had to see that love was real. He tried to raise a hand to stop Raoul from coming closer, but the whip came down again, burning with such hatred that Brice could only squeeze his breath through gritted teeth and cling to the blood-red snow under his hands as though it could somehow save him.

Raoul said something, something vicious with weight behind it. A curse of his own, perhaps. "No." Brice ground out the word. He lifted his head, met Raoul's gaze, and said again, "No."

A flicker of Raoul's pain narrowed his eyes. "Let me bear the lashings. I am nothing. I am nobody, just a dream in this place. I cannot stand to see you suffer for nothing!"

The whip came down.

Wet fire blazed up his back.

He screamed.

Blood trickled down his hip.

Raoul spun as though to flee, made it two steps, turned again, and stood defiant with his hands clenched at his sides like the sentinel he was.

Brice blinked through sweat and tears. There were others behind Raoul. Fae watched on, expressionless, like dancers poised in their music boxes. But as Brice tried to focus on them, one reached up and removed her mask. Chantel. With her face suddenly exposed, she lowered the mask to her side and stepped forward. Unmasked, she was true, and she stood with him, for him. For love. Exactly as Raoul stood.

Blazing pain washed through Brice, racking his whole body. The lashes were indistinct now, just crescendos of agony in a symphony of hurt.

The female sentinel, dressed all in white, removed her mask and stood at Raoul's side. She dipped her chin, but then a lash robbed him of his sight for a moment.

When he looked up, Vine was there, Laurel and Claude too. Their handsome faces were unmasked, and it seemed for the first time they'd become solid and real, no longer faceless figments Brice had dreamed up. They didn't laugh or smile. They stood defiant alongside Raoul. Others stepped forward now, too, more fae. Perhaps all of them.

The host clutched Brice's hair and hauled him onto his knees. "Get a good look at your audience." The words burned against his flushed cheek. "Do you believe they care? They aren't capable. They are hollow—nothing but shadows cast by who they were."

"No." Brice forced the word through his teeth. Bitter tears squeezed from his eyes. "You are... the hollow one."

The host's body stilled. His rage quieted, turning from scorching heat to brittle ice. He turned his head, then threw Brice down. Brice braced for further lashings, his only relief the knowledge that with every lash, the host's control over the fae began to crumble.

"Stop!" someone called.

Just a guest. A brave soul.

The man stepped forward, and under the shifting light and the gaze of a thousand others, he removed his mask. Brice blinked though tears and focused on a face he knew. Frances... the hapless young man from whom Brice had stolen an invite. He had changed some, weathered a little with added years since they'd met. He bore the stance of a man full of confidence. A man who knew his own mind and knew wrongness when he saw it.

Another guest stepped forward. A short buxom woman with rounded features. She removed her mask and leveled her cold stare on the host. Brice knew her too. "Stop," Patrice said.

Brice's heart swelled as the guests all stepped forward, one by one, and one by one they removed their masks. He knew them all, knew every face, every person. Kris, the barkeep, his glare as frosty as it always was when a patron misbehaved, only now he stood dressed in his best attire and stared down a fae.

"What is this?" The host's grip twisted in Brice's hair.

"This," a proud male voice said, "is where it ends." The man who stepped forward removed his mask and lifted his gaze. Jonathon Brodeur, Sophia's father. He pulled from his pocket an invite, raised it in his hands, and tore it in two. The guests all did the same. Each invite was split down the middle and tossed into the bloody snow at their feet.

In front of them all, Raoul lifted his chin. His crooked smile said it all.

He'd sent them invites. Every single one.

He'd summoned the townsfolk here. ... save me... He'd called and they'd answered.

His gaze met Brice's and Brice's heart swelled. His clever, vulnerable trickster fae had turned the guests against the host.

Raoul stepped forward. "The masquerade and all its lies end now. Let Brice go. Let us all go, Sinclair."

Tremors racked the host and rippled into Brice. His hold on Brice's hair threatened to scalp him. The masquerade was all the host had left, and if these guests ended it, the host's whole world would fall.

Raoul took another step forward and offered his hand. "The time has come to face the truth."

The host's laughter bubbled out of him. He suddenly dropped Brice at his feet. "The truth? Oh, Raoul, are you sure that's what you desire? For your lover to know who and what you truly are?"

Brice looked up and saw doubt flicker across Raoul's face. *No, don't listen.*

"Do you think he'll love the truth of you once the veil falls?" The host staggered, plucked his mask off, and tossed it into the air. Its fine golden detailing unraveled. "Love is not immortal, Raoul. It changes with the seasons." The silken gold threads twitched outward, becoming larger. Where they struck at the walls and ceiling, the illusion of opulence rippled, blurred, and peeled away, melting, warping, twisting as though burned up by some invisible flame. Threads of gold unstitched the windows, the chandeliers, pulling the illusion apart at its seams. All around, the masquerade began to come undone.

The host smirked. "Have your truth, then. Have your precious reality. Rot among its folds and let us see if love finds you, Raoul, in the ugly light of day."

A heated wave of invisible power rolled over Brice, stealing his breath and much of his agony, leaving him numbed and dizzy. The ground shifted under his hands, bubbling between his fingers. Red snow melted, revealing rotted leaves and mulched earth. Damp, heavy air touched his lips, tasting of moss and dew.

The host walked away from the crowd and from Brice, and with his every step, the masquerade withdrew behind him, peeling back its dreamlike curtain, leaving stark, naked trees in his wake. Brice blinked. This was reality. In all its harsh, cold, beautiful imperfectness.

Was it over?

Was it done?

He reached a trembling hand to his back, expecting to find shredded skin and blood, but his hand came away clean. The pain was fading fast, like a bad dream on waking. It had been real, though, hadn't it? The pain had been, but the wounds were an illusion. He choked on something like a sob and kept the rest inside before he could be overcome.

The damp forest closed in with all its smells and tastes and noises: the breeze through the briars, damp earth and dirt under his hands and knees, the call of a fox somewhere in the night.

"Raoul?"

There. In front of the others standing dazed and confused in their disheveled finery, fae and human alike—Raoul was doubled over, hands on his thighs, hair spilling forward, the silver streak suddenly bright. He was all right. The masquerade was gone. They'd... won?

Brice clambered to his feet and stumbled closer. "Raoul... it's over." They'd truly done it. They'd ended the nightmare. The host was gone... where? Brice didn't know, but the masquerade was gone, and the fae and its guests had survived. They were all free!

Raoul straightened.

But his face... He did not look like Raoul. Fury pulled at this snarl. His eyes burned cold with it. So much so that he looked like a... stranger. "I remember," Raoul said. "I remember... We were wrong. So wrong."

Brice stumbled over some hidden root, almost falling in his haste to reach him. "Raoul, it's all right. Whatever it is... whoever you are, it doesn't change us."

"It changes *everything*." The words left him in a savage growl.

Brice's heart fluttered. This Raoul was different again and that look in his eyes was one Brice had never seen before. True hatred. "Don't... please." Raoul was about to run, and if he did, he might never return. "Raoul, you can choose who you are—"

The fury softened, but only because he'd made up his mind. Lips pressed into a firm line, he shook his head and strode toward the shadows in the forest.

"No! Raoul..." He staggered again, his body slow and heavy. The aches and agonies from too long lost to the masquerade weighed him down. "Please, wait..."

"Go home, LeChoix," Raoul called back. "Go home and forget we met!"

"No!" He slumped against a tree, furious with his body for failing him. "Raoul, don't let the host ruin us. Don't let him win. Whatever you remember, it doesn't matter. Please... talk to me. Tell me, damn you!"

Raoul spun with a swish of dark hair, marched back in two strides, and under the gazes of everyone still gathered, he glowered at Brice. "Damn me? I am a liar, a fiend, the creature we both should despise, not love. I am everything you thought me to be when we met. I've twisted the hearts of a thousand lonely souls just like yours. He was right. I don't love you. Our love is a lie. One of many I've spun." He paused, but only to breathe. "I wish we'd never met. I wish I had not seen myself through your eyes. I wish I could forget... Go home."

Brice's heart cracked, pieces of it falling away. He staggered toward him. "No. I refuse to believe you. You're telling me this to push me away. You think you don't deserve love, but you do. I know you. I know who you are and I love you." Brice caught his hand.

Raoul savagely pulled away. "You know nothing!" he

said with a snarl. "It was me. All of it. Everything. It was my dream. That prison was of my own making!"

The hatred he saw in Raoul's eyes, Brice had seen it before but not directed at him. He'd seen it in the strokes of a pencil when Raoul had drawn himself. Seen it in the way Raoul had carved out an image of himself as though he could cut it out of time and space. He despised himself. "I don't understand."

"You wouldn't because you're a good man. If you hand me your heart, I will tear it to shreds, that I promise."

"Who are you then?" Brice snapped. "Who are you really, that you hate me and demand I hate you?"

Raoul straightened and wet his lips, only now noticing the people around them watching everything unfold. Brice noticed them too. Fae, mostly. The guests were stumbling away, confused and disoriented. The fae lingered. They all had their memories back. They all knew who they truly were. And they all cowered from Raoul, hiding among the forest's shadows. Why?

Brice met Raoul's gaze. "Who are you, Raoul?"

"I am the host."

Chapter Forty-Six

BRICE HEARD the words but didn't understand them. Raoul wasn't the host. The host was jealous and wicked. He'd kept the fae in his cruel masquerade because his mate had escaped him. Raoul had nothing to do with it. He'd just gotten swept up in the host's game like all the rest.

Raoul stepped forward. Instinctively, Brice stepped back. "The masquerade was *my* dream," Raoul said. "My dancers, my cast. And with them, I tore mortal lives apart. Don't you see? I played your family like a child plays with dolls. I am the reason Anette lost her mind. Her madness was my creation. I brought your parents together and made them dance for me. I made them fall in love, knowing it would destroy them."

"What? No." No, not his playful Raoul. Not the vulnerable, gentle fae he'd come to love. He would never do such a thing. He was *not* that cruel. "Why are you telling me this?"

"Because it's the truth!"

"But... the host—"

Raoul's cool laugh chilled Brice's blood. "Just another

player in my game. Over time, the masquerade took even my memories. We forgot who we were supposed to be, who we really were, and fell into our roles. My lies became our truth."

It couldn't be like that. He must have been remembering wrong. "Raoul, no. You're confused—"

"Confused? Nothing has been clearer." He laughed cruelly. "It's all a beautiful lie and I am its master."

He fell quiet and turned his head toward a crowd of shuffling people. Unlike the others gathered, these people weren't clad in gowns and riches but rags. Murmurs passed through the guests. A woman cried out a name and rushed forward, sweeping a weary-looking man into her arms. The people from the rose garden—they were free.

Raoul suddenly framed Brice's face in both hands. His touch burned like ice. "The Raoul you love is a mask. One I'd forgotten I wore." He pressed his mouth to Brice's, thrust his tongue in, and Brice opened, needing, wanting. He clutched at Raoul, afraid to let him go. Then Raoul pulled back. His stormy eyes churned their magic, but the rage had vanished. And in its place, fear. "I am not the prince of this tale. I'm its villain." He leaned in and whispered, "Forget me, Brice LeChoix." Icy shivers spilled down Brice's back. Raoul brushed his thumb across Brice's lips. "Forget *everything.*" He shoved against Brice's chest, knocking him against a tree, and whirled away.

His name caught in Brice's throat—lodged there, unspoken. Raoul melted into the forest until the glint of silver upon his clothes vanished in the night.

Brice clutched the tree behind him. Without it, he'd already be on his knees. The ice Raoul's parting words had summoned continued to shiver through him, like ripples in a pond reaching farther and farther.

Raoul was the host, the master behind the game? He'd spun lies and illusions... he'd driven Anette mad?

"Oh God..." Brice choked on a sob. He was breaking inside. The foundations on which he'd built their love crumbled all around him.

"Brice!" a voice called. "Brice?"

Charon.

"Here," Brice croaked. He couldn't hear his thoughts behind the thumping of his heart, couldn't feel his body. Shock, perhaps. He wasn't sure. He wasn't sure of anything anymore. Was the ground at his feet real? Was the air he breathed truly filling his lungs? Was he free, or was he still in a dream somewhere? Because nothing made any sense.

A hand gripped his, and then Charon was in front of him, eyes pinched in concern. He looked... different. Bigger, somehow. Was this a trick too? He couldn't tell anymore. "Charon? Is it truly you?"

"Yes, brother." He hauled Brice into his arms. "You're safe. You ended it. It's over."

"I do not know..." he mumbled into Charon's shoulder and tightened his hold on his brother. "I don't know what is real."

"This is. I'm real." He grabbed Brice's hand and put it to his own warm cheek. "See?"

Brice stroked over the new lines around Charon's mouth. His fingers skimmed his brother's stubble. "You're so different."

Sadness softened his blue eyes. "It's been years, Brice."

"Years?" The thudding in his head grew louder. "How many?" he croaked.

"Two winters gone."

Two years with Raoul. Two years living a fantasy. Living a lie. They'd both lived it. They'd both loved. His heart constricted, stealing his breath. He had loved Raoul, and Raoul had loved him. That was the truth; that was real. And now it was over.

Brice had fallen in love with a lie.

"Charon, it hurts." He tried to breathe, tried to think, but his mind was a stormy ocean and his body at its mercy.

"Come." Charon crushed him closer. "Let's get you home."

They stumbled and staggered back along the forest pathway to a small closed horse-drawn carriage. Charon bundled him inside and closed the door behind them. The driver clicked to the horses and started the carriage into motion, and Brice slumped against Charon.

"We'll be home soon."

Charon's fingers stroked his hair. Brice listened to his own racing heart and his brother's soft breaths. Charon was real. The dream that had been the masquerade was over. And the Raoul he'd loved had vanished with it.

Chapter Forty-Seven

Like Charon, the house had changed. Every window blazed against winter's dark night, as though Latchly Hall were a glittering crown and the forest its bed of black velvet. The driver opened the carriage door and helped Brice step down. Another man opened the house's front door. "Welcome home," the stranger said.

"There are staff?" Brice muttered.

"Yes." Charon beamed. "Isn't it wonderful? I sold some land to Brodeur, which helped pay for extensive repairs—and Father's debts. We have tenant farmers on the eastern slopes now. Their rent goes a long way to maintaining the estate."

"Good evening, milords." A young lady curtsied in the drawing room doorway. Brice wasn't entirely sure she was real. They couldn't afford all this. He drifted by the housemaid and heard Charon call her Jeanine and ask her to draw a bath with lavender oil.

Charon chatted some more about land and farming and the old mill down in the valley that he'd begun to renovate.

His hand landed on Brice's back, igniting the ghost of the host's cruel lashings. Brice flinched.

Charon snatched his hand back. "Are you wounded? Shall I fetch some bandages—"

"No, no. I'm not wounded. Not on the outside," he muttered. The wounds inside were growing larger by the second. "I think I just..." He fluttered a hand toward his forehead. "Some rest."

"Of course." He led Brice up the stairs. "I'm sorry. You don't want to hear all this now. Some rest and a bath. I'll have Jeanine bring you some fresh clothes." His gaze trawled over Brice, taking in the disheveled shirt with its missing buttons, reading its meaning. He knew better than most what the masquerade did to people.

Tearing his stare away, he opened the door to a guest room. "I, er... I'm using the master room, but I'll move my things out tomorrow. I just... I wasn't expecting you to be alive. And I... when the invites came and they said... When they said they were going to go back and find you, I couldn't... I couldn't go. I wanted to—I did. I just... Everything has changed and if I went back—"

"It's fine, Charon. Really. You did as I asked. You kept the candles burning."

"Yes, but—"

"Please, go. It's all right." If Charon didn't leave soon, Brice feared the frayed line of tension running through him might snap and he'd lash out. "You've done enough. I need some time. Give me some time."

"Yes, of course." He backed away, his smile twitching between joy and concern. "Press the bell if you need anything." He gestured toward the bed where a button in the wall said *PRESS*. "We have bells now—for the staff."

Brice dragged what must have been a pathetic smile to his lips. "Thank you, Charon."

Finally, his brother left and clicked the door closed behind him. The lingering tension didn't dissipate. Tighter it pulled, tying his heart and chest in knots. He might scream. He wanted to. He rested his clenched hands in his lap and bowed his head. He couldn't think about it... If he thought about it all, about everything that had happened, he'd break apart. If he recalled Raoul's last kiss and how it had burned between them, not with hate but with love... Yet he'd thrown that love in Brice's face and gone. It was love. It was real. But if Raoul didn't want it...

The drawing.

He pulled a sketch from his back pocket and carefully unfolded it. Raoul hadn't known he'd taken it, slipped it into his pocket moments before leaving his cavern. The quill strokes, as before, held Brice's gaze enraptured. The image was of Raoul splendidly naked with the glint of mischief in his eyes. The trickster. Was he truly the mind behind the masquerade? Had it all been a dream as Raoul would have him believe, or did Raoul despise who he truly was so much that he believed he had no choice but to push Brice away?

Brice had taken the whip for him. Whether it had been real or not, it had *felt* real.

And he'd do it again.

He shot to his feet, tore off his shirt, and crossed the room to the dresser. The mirror was unkind, Brice's reflection so ghostly and distraught it was no mystery why Charon had treated him like glass. He twisted at the waist and examined his back—no wounds. Not even a welt. But they were there, branded into his memory if not his skin. The lashings *had* been real. Fantasy and lies, the masquerade wove both with reality. Raoul might not believe in himself, but Brice did. Their love had been just as real as those lashings, and Brice carried it with him still.

"You don't get to walk out on us," he told his haggard reflection, sending the words far away, hoping wherever Raoul might be, he'd hear them. If he could create the masquerade, then he had the power to hear him even now. "The truth is what we make it."

Silence filled the room.

The old house with its creaking boards and drafty windows sighed around him. He hated it suddenly, hated the harshness of it all, hated how time crept across his face, hated how the fire crackled in its grate, hated how his stomach rumbled and his body trembled. Hated it all. He wished Raoul were here. They'd lie together on the bed. Raoul would tell him fantastic tales of the missing prince and Brice would laugh because Raoul was no prince. But he wasn't the villain either.

Rage bubbled up and out of him.

He swept the mirror and its stand aside. Glass smashed across the floor. He shoved the dresser, and when it didn't move, he tore a drawer free and threw it at the wall. It wasn't enough. He wanted everything else to hurt like he hurt… inside. He ripped the curtains from their rods, sank his nails into loose wallpaper and ripped strips away. Everything hurt.

When there was nothing left to destroy, he fell to the bed and clutched at his head, twisting his fingers in his hair, making it hurt. Pain was good. Pain was real. *Sometimes you ache for the pain, just to feel again.*

He rocked and squeezed his hands into fists in his hair. The masquerade had not broken him. Vine had not broken him. The rose garden, the madness, Sophia's death, none of it had broken him. But Raoul's parting words had.

Forget me, Brice LeChoix.

A week passed in a blur. Brice drifted through a life he didn't recognize.

Latchly Hall was abuzz with staff and color and light. Charon had adopted Father's old office and made it his own. He hadn't yet offered to hand control over to Brice, but it was likely coming. Brice was accepted as the heir. The oldest. The lord. This life was all his, but he couldn't find joy at the thought of living it. Oh, he was proud of Charon and told him so. Brice should be happy but he didn't feel it. He didn't feel much of anything.

He dressed in his old clothes, shaved and combed his hair, ate bland food, spoke with the staff, visited the renovated mill, and did all the things expected of Lord LeChoix.

But with every passing of night into day, his heart ached for its missing piece.

The grand fire in the lounge roared and crackled. Most of the staff had retreated into their rooms for the night, leaving Brice alone. He braced an arm against the fireplace mantel and lifted the glass of whiskey to his lips.

"Are you all right?"

He stiffened at the sound of Charon's voice. "Yes, of course."

His brother poured himself a drink and drifted closer. With his golden locks tied back and his attire the very picture of a gentleman, he was quite the sight. Being the lord of Latchly Hall agreed with him. Or perhaps it was being without Brice that agreed with him.

"It will take some time to acclimatize after... that place," Charon said, sipping his drink while watching the fire.

Brice mustered a smile. "I suppose you are my older brother now, no?"

"I... well, no. Your time away changes nothing. You're the lord and you're back. So... we'll make it work."

It changes everything, the ghost of Raoul said in his ear. He was right. Brice was not the same man who had returned to the masquerade with grand ideas about ending it all. He'd lost parts of himself and shifted others around.

"Charon, I'm a bastard child, LeChoix in name only. You are more the lord than I am."

Charon turned his head. "The past doesn't matter," he said flatly.

"If only that were true."

He heard Raoul in almost every moment, felt his breath against his neck at night and his soft kiss brush his lips in the morning, and was haunted by his laugh.

"You're different this time. What happened?" Charon asked.

Brice slumped into a nearby chair and pressed the cool glass to his cheek. "I fell in love with a lie." He feared meeting his brother's gaze. He'd think him a fool. He *was* a fool. The masquerade had captured his heart and soul and torn out both. He'd known going in what it could do, but he'd let it happen. Because like the host had said, he'd so desperately wanted a cause, a way to prove himself. He'd ended the nightmare for everyone else but made his own.

Charon pulled an armchair closer to the fire and to Brice and sat on the edge of the cushion. "A fae?"

Brice swallowed hard. "Mother warned us. Apparently, I did not listen."

"They are beautiful and seductive." He trailed off, lost to his own memories. "We have no defense against them. I'm sorry, Brice. I wish I could have come for you sooner. I should have. I just..." He stopped and shook his head, going over the same ground again. "Tell me about her."

"Him."

"Him?" Charon blinked. "The fae you loved was male?"

"Yes, Charon. And it was my choice, before you begin to think I was coerced. I have always been attracted to men. Father forbade me to speak of my desires—another reason for him to despise me. Now I find I no longer care who knows."

Brice let him absorb the truth. It was almost a relief. His so-called wrongness had hung over him his whole life, like the sword of Damocles.

"All this time, you had no interest in women?" Charon finally asked.

"Not in an intimate way, no."

"But the marriage, with Sophia?"

"Father's wish, not mine." He chuckled at the madness of it all and sipped his drink. "And what a farce it would have been."

"God." Charon slumped back in the chair. "God," he said again. "Sophia knew, didn't she? She knew and didn't tell me."

"I asked her not to."

"Brice," he said on a puff of air. "I mean, I suppose I suspected... Some things I saw. That time one Christmas gathering, you and the carriage driver—I knew something had happened when Father flew into a rage, but... he was often like that."

Brice smiled despite the memory being unpleasant. "The maid tattled on us. Father banished him and then threatened to shoot me with his rifle if I did not resist my urges."

Charon winced. "He had a temper."

"Yes, and it was mostly directed at me." He finished his drink and crossed the room to collect the bottle, then returned to the fireplace and refilled his glass and Charon's. This quiet moment with them both seated in front of the fire, whiskey and words flowing... It felt good, finally.

"There was a time... at the... masquerade." Charon shifted uncomfortably in his chair. "Sophia and I and a third were engaged... intimately. A male... He was, er... quite thorough." A flush spread from Charon's usually pale neck up his face. "I hadn't known it could be so"—he plucked at some fluff on his trouser leg—"stimulating."

Brice tipped his glass to his brother with a grin and caught his shy smile. "The fae are wonderfully shameless."

"I hear same-gender couplings are quite the trend in Massalia."

"Not so much in our fair town or under Father's roof. My conflicted desires were rich pickings for the masquerade." Although he found he was no longer ashamed of his love. Just telling Charon things that would have terrified him before felt as normal as mentioning the weather. The masquerade had given him that. *Raoul* had given him that. *Fuck a tree if you wish... I can desire whatever or whomever I wish. And so can you.* God, he missed him.

He told Charon everything. How he'd come to care for Raoul, to understand the fae people, and somehow, inexplicably, to love one. It hadn't seemed like two years, not in his head, but while the masquerade lied to the eyes and the ears, it could not lie to the heart, and his heart knew the truth. "Raoul could not recall his life or who he was before. He thought it a blessing. I thought it didn't matter. I fear we were both wrong. The moment the masquerade fell, so did the lies. He said he was the host. He explained how he'd created it all, even going so far as to bring Anette and Leon together. He said I should hate him. But how can I?" Brice mumbled the next words into his glass as he drank. "The Raoul I love didn't exist."

Charon had no reply and they both fell into thought, the quiet broken only by the crackling fire. "The grief does ease."

"Then you think I should forget and move on?"

Charon rose and gripped Brice's shoulder. "In time." His fingers dug in. "Mother couldn't, and in the end it killed her. This house, the mill, the staff, the land, all of it... I did it for you, hoping you'd return to see it. I refused to grieve you. Without all this, I'd have walked into the woods and not returned. I can't lose you again, Brice."

His words jolted Brice's heart awake, making it beat again, reminding him of a different love—the love of a brother he still had and perhaps a life that awaited him. He squeezed Charon's hand. "Nor I, you."

After Charon retired for the evening, Brice watched the flames dance, trapped in their iron grate. Did Raoul watch a fire dance too, wherever he was? Did he think of Brice, and did he regret any of it? Such questions would be Brice's undoing. Taking the creased drawing from his pocket, he admired the naked sketch of Raoul in the shifting firelight. He should probably throw it on the fire. But instead, he rested his head back and closed his eyes.

Chapter Forty-Eight

*F*ORGET ME*, Brice LeChoix.*

Brice woke with a gasp. The bed beside him was empty. Of course. Just a dream. He'd been having them of late. Strange dreams that turned to mist on waking.

Spring sunshine poured though the gap in the heavy drapes at the window. He blinked at the line it made across the floor and for a moment, he thought he heard the swish of skirts and the delicate tinkle of a music box somewhere in the house. Its tune stuck in his mind. He hummed it as he dressed.

Descending the stairs, the maid dipped a curtsy and bid him a good morning. Charon was in the breakfast room. Brice thanked her and found his brother at the table reading the paper.

"That tune?" Charon lowered the paper. His frown cut so deeply it almost looked like despair. "Brice, please."

"My apologies." He pulled out a chair and sat, admiring the morning spread of toast, cereal, and fruit. "I'm not sure where I heard it. Do you know it?"

"I..." Charon folded his paper and set it aside. "You don't remember?"

"Perhaps I heard it in town?"

"Hm, perhaps."

Brice buttered some toast and caught his brother's long stare. "Apologies again for my tardiness. These dreams—I'm sure they will pass."

"Besides the dreams, are you feeling all right, brother?"

"I'm fine." He bit into his toast and ate heartily.

"You just seem... unlike yourself."

"Happy, you mean?" He snorted. "The sun is shining. The mill opens next week. Alongside the farms, the mill will see our finances recovering. There is every reason to be joyful, don't you think?"

"Well, yes." Charon's smile grew some. "I'm pleased if you're pleased."

"Indeed. I have a meeting with Jonathon Brodeur later today. He wants to invest in the mill."

They spoke about finances as they often did over breakfast. Charon was planning a trip for them both to Massalia, which would once again have the LeChoix name where it could be seen and heard. Charon believed a visit could open many doors that could help achieve his higher social ambitions. Brice was happy with what he had, but Charon had always wanted more. And a family. He'd find what he searched for in Massalia. And it would do him good to get away from Chamonet.

Brice joined Jonathon Brodeur at his home to discuss the mill and later left with a firm commitment. With Brodeur's investment, the LeChoix debts would be settled.

He and Charon would finally be free of their father's legacy. He walked the town and visited old friends, who were kind to remark on his family's change in fortune. It felt, for the first time, as though Brice had finally found his place.

He bid the carriage driver return him home near dusk, his purse somewhat lighter and his head a little fuzzy from Kris's fine ale. Strange how the barkeep had mentioned a few things. *That business with the fae,* he'd said, as though Brice knew them intimately. He'd even gone so far as to ask if Brice had seen anything of the fae. Apparently, some had caught glimpses of *others* in the trees and valleys. Brice hadn't thought the man prone to stories of the fae folk, but he clearly believed in it. And thought Brice did too.

He was lost in thought when the carriage jolted, the horse screeched, and the driver yelled an alarm.

"A wolf, milord," he said as Brice poked his head from the window. "Biggest damned creature I ever did see!"

"Well, where is it now?"

"Gone into them trees. Spooked the horse, it did." He made soothing noises at the animal.

It was early in the evening for wolves to be on the move. Farmers had mentioned a nuisance pack. Perhaps he'd better oil up Father's gun and hunt the animals down. "It won't bother the carriage. Carry on."

He found the rough sketch in his dresser drawer. A scandalous drawing of a male fae, his ears tipped ever so slightly where they poked through his long dark hair. For all his nakedness, the eyes were the most arresting part of him. The ink strokes had been rushed in places, messy in some areas while accurate in others, such as the lines making up his sumptuous mouth. Brice touched his own lips, skimming his fingers across them as though remembering... something. His cock, all but forgotten lately, warmed and filled. The picture really was quite stimulating. He could almost summon to mind the nameless fae standing by a moonlit pool, his member erect while his slanted smile beckoned Brice into the water.

He touched his lips again, unleashing a spur of lust that had him grasping the dresser top. He hadn't been so hard in months, not since the dreams had woken him breathless and spent on his sheets. The sharp arousal was familiar. His body demanded to be sated. A madness came over him. The taste of sweetness, the smell of jasmine, the murmur of *I love you.* Brice untied his trouser fastenings, took himself in hand, and roughly answered its call for release. He heard the laugh, could see the sweep of the fae's tongue across his lips, licking off his spend—

He stumbled against the dresser and ferociously climaxed. "God." The image of the fae subsided with his spent lust. The waking dream had been so vivid. It had felt not like a dream but more... a memory.

Brice was to be married. During his first trip to the wonder of Massalia, Charon had introduced him to Lady Blanchet.

He'd courted her as a gentleman should. She seemed the nice sort. Polite, pretty. A tad young. Charon was pleased with the match, and as his new hobby seemed to be who should be matched with whom, Brice was of a mind to trust him. Marriage seemed like the logical next step. So the summer had passed by, marriage negotiations had begun, and everything was splendid. At least, it should have been.

But he couldn't shake the feeling that he walked in someone else's shoes, and the path he took was wrong. The mill was a success, Charon appeared happy, the house thrived, but Brice found no joy in any of it.

He hauled the axe from a nearby stump and marched toward the forest.

"Milord? James can cut the wood, sir," Jeanine called, catching him leaving via the back courtyard.

"It's fine, Jeanine," he called back.

"But, sir, the sun be goin' down soon!"

He waved the maid's concern away. "I'll be back for dinner."

A stomp through the woods did little to soothe his rattling nerves. Marriage was... a daunting prospect. It was a paper exercise, of course. The joining of two families. Lady Blanchet would surely find a lover to satisfy the needs Brice could not. They would discuss it after they were wed, which was unfortunate timing, but if he told her before they were married how her honey pot was probably very lovely but he preferred to fuck men, he doubted her father would appreciate his honesty.

At the eastern clearing, he grabbed a log from a pile near a felled tree, arranged it on a stump, and brought the axe-head down with satisfying accuracy, splitting the log in two. Grabbing another log, he split that one too. Then another. Late afternoon heat beat down as he cut log after log, trying to quell the strange uneasiness in his gut.

He hadn't felt shame in a long while.

But talk of marriage and children, and how he'd have to lie to make it work... He despised lies.

Tearing off his jacket, he pulled his necktie free, rolled up his shirt sleeves, and murdered another log with gusto.

Anger bubbled from all its hiding places. He hadn't been aware he'd been harboring it until now, with an axe in his hand and nothing but forest all around.

If all else fails, we will burn it down together.

The voice in his head staggered him. He missed his swing and the axe-head *thwunked* deep into the stump. "Curses!" He tugged, but the axe's cutting edge was truly embedded.

God, these voices in his head! He was surely losing his mind. He yanked and heaved the handle. "Come on, you wretched thing! Let go!" His grip slipped, slick with sweat. He reeled, tripped, and fell on his ass in a bed of dried pine needles. Stunned, he stared at the sky and laughed. If Lady Blanchet saw him now, she'd probably reconsider their match. Perhaps that wouldn't be such a bad idea...

A growl simmered to his right.

From Brice's position on his back, the wolf loomed large. Gray, with mangy fur and gray eyes. *Just a wolf*... If he could get to the axe, he could easily fend it off. Slowly, he pushed upright and reached for the axe handle.

Another growl rumbled nearby from just behind him.

Two wolves.

And he was sprawled on the ground, easy prey.

The farmers had complained of attacks. He'd meant to deal with it, but with the trip to Massalia and the marriage and the mill, he'd forgotten. And now the problem was here, staring him in the eyes, about to tear out his throat.

He shifted onto his knees and stretched his hand toward the axe. A third growl resonated around the clearing. Three wolves. A pack. And his damned axe was stuck in the stump. Perhaps he was about to continue the tradition of the LeChoix family having the most pathetic deaths. The thought summoned an ill-timed huff of a laugh.

The pack leader burst forward, teeth bared. Brice scrabbled backward against the stump. He wrapped his hands around the axe handle. The wolf leaped. He raised his arm to protect his face—and a beast of silvery white struck the wolf in the side, knocking it clean out of the air. The animals tumbled in a flurry of teeth and claws. The larger wolf clamped its jaws around his victim's throat and ripped skin and fur apart. The huge silvery beast tossed the smaller wolf from side to side in its jaws, then dropped it limp and silent among the pine needles. With a growl, it turned its attention on the remaining two.

The beast, even on all fours, was easily the size of a man and like no wolf he'd ever seen. Once done with its smaller prey, would it turn on him? He clutched at the axe and frantically pulled the handle back and forth, trying to work it free. Wet sounds of tearing flesh and high-pitched yelps filled the air. If he could just—The axe surrendered to him. He grabbed it in both hands and froze.

Silence.

The wolves were either dead or gone.

But he wasn't alone. The heat of the predator's gaze burned between his shoulders. It was still there, behind him. He had the axe. He could defend himself. His heart thumped. Sweat stung his eyes and dripped down his back. He just had to turn slowly and face the animal.

Slowly, carefully, he turned.

He'd been right—*as big as a man*—with claw-tipped paws the size of dinner plates. It lowered its head, raised its upper lip, and snarled.

Brice flexed his hold on the axe.

The dead wolves lay scattered about the clearing.

There was no doubt—this beast would kill Brice.

The animal lifted its nose and sniffed the air. Its snarl softened. It snuffled the dirt near its feet and when it lifted its head again, pine needles speckled its damp nose. It sneezed, shook its head, and swiped a gigantic paw at its muzzle. Then, with a huff, it sat back on its haunches and...

Brice's vision blurred, unfocusing.

The beast's fur rippled. Its outline shifted and warped, its body moving in a way that wasn't natural. Shudders ran through the beast, doubling it over. Its back arched, and as it reared, all of it shimmered, like moonlight on water, and there in a blink stood a man. Naked. Fading sunlight touched his exquisite body, sweeping gold down his smooth chest, pooling at his hips, and then stroking down his thighs. He whipped his long black hair back, ran his hands through the thick locks, and parted his lips on a gasp. Fae-tipped ears poked through his hair.

Brice's mouth fell open.

The naked fae from the sketch. It was him. He was here. He was... real. And the artwork, although stunning, was a shadow compared to the splendid male in front of Brice.

The male turned his head, smirked, and said, "I'd kiss you, but your axe is sharp, and I'm rather exposed."

Chapter Forty-Nine

"I... WHAT?"

In two sweeping strides, the naked fae closed the distance between them, cupped Brice's face in his hands, and pressed a kiss upon his lips. A surge of desire sparked ablaze in Brice. And as though Brice's body knew him, he kissed him deeply in return, struck by sudden, ferocious familiarity. Lust scorched away the impossibility of it all. And Brice kissed him like his soul had found its missing half. Like together, they were whole.

The fae pulled back and rolled his lips together, tasting. Dark lashes fluttered downward, resting gently against precious pale cheeks. "I see you have not forgotten how to do that."

"Do I know you?" Brice whispered. He was sure he did. His body sang under the stranger's kiss, coming alive under his touch. The world around them, outside of them, melted away.

"It's complicated."

Of course, it would be. He'd just kissed a shapeshifting

fae in a clearing in the woods. Wasn't that exactly what the tales said *not* to do? Was this even real? Had he hit his head when he fell?

The fae sighed and looked up. "Will you show me your home?"

"I, er..." This was a trick, surely? But the picture... The picture was real and inside his dresser at home. So he did know this creature from the past? "I don't think that's—"

The fae flicked a hand near his head and a glittery flutter of light softened the tip of his ear, turning it rounded. "Nobody will know." When he spoke, his sharp fae teeth had vanished. He suddenly looked human.

"That you're fae? No. But they'll certainly notice you're naked."

"Ah, yes." He turned on the spot, searching, then looked up. "Your shirt?"

"What?"

"Take it off."

With no other means to cover him, Brice began to unbutton it. "You can't have my trousers."

A quirk of dry humor lifted the fae's lips. "Smuggle me in the back door, like you did the carriage driver."

"How do you know about that?" Brice held out the shirt. It was stained some and damp from his fall, but the fae didn't appear to care and threw it on over his shoulders.

"You told me." His quick fingers fed the buttons into their holes. "There is much to explain, and not much time to explain it. Trust me?"

"Trust you? You were a wolf. You're fae! And you want me to take you to my home—no, I can't do that. The staff, Charon! He despises fae."

"Yes, I imagine he does. And do you know why?"

"Well, yes, I—"

The fae raised an eyebrow and Brice found he couldn't recall exactly why Charon despised the fae so much. He just always had. He tried to summon some past memories that might help, but it all swirled like fog in his head.

"You forgot. Of course you did. Brice, *my lord*." The fae turned his voice to syrup while standing so thoroughly proud in front of Brice, somehow still mystifyingly beautiful even in Brice's filthy shirt. "If you dare not trust me, then trust your heart. It will not guide you wrong."

He did trust his heart, and his heart beat with a passion he hadn't felt in... forever. "Who are you?"

"I've told you once before. If I tell you again, you'll not thank me."

"I don't understand."

"I know." He offered his hand, fingers delicately poised for the taking. "But you will. Take me home, Brice LeChoix?"

He was surely dreaming because the man—*fae*—pleading with him with the most remarkable soft dark eyes had been a wolf moments ago, and such things did not happen in the realm of reality. He'd fallen and struck his head. But it felt real. And when he took the fae's hand, that, too, felt real and solid, familiar... and safe, as though he'd held the very same hand a thousand times before. Brice didn't understand any of this, but he did trust his heart. And his heart said he knew this creature.

"Come then, before darkness falls." He led the fae back along the path. The fae moved so silently that Brice had to glance behind him to check he hadn't dreamed him up, and every time he did, the fae lifted his gaze with a slight smile. The smile didn't reach his eyes. He was nervous—Brice's heart told him that too. If they truly knew each other, then where had this fae been? Why had Brice forgotten him?

"I will answer all your questions, my lord."

The way he said *my lord,* purring it, as though there was irony in Brice's title. He almost sounded as though he mocked Brice, but it wasn't meant as an insult, more like a... tease.

They approached Latchly Hall. Its windows glowed against the dark. Brice led the fae through the rear courtyard, past the coal store, and in through the pantry corridor. Staff bustled in the nearby kitchens. Brice took one of the narrow service corridors, bypassing the staff, and beckoned the fae on. If they were discovered now, his near-naked state and tousled hair would be impossible to explain away. Brice just had to get him up the small spiral staff staircase to the second floor and into a guest's room—

Boots clipped the floor, approaching. Door hinges creaked.

Brice's heart dropped through his stomach. Charon. The staff didn't wear boots about the house. God, how was he going to explain this?

The door at the end of the corridor swung open and Charon breezed in, head buried in several slips of paper. Another step and he began to lift his head.

All the excuses rushed to Brice's lips. The trouser-less man was lost. He'd found him in the woods. He'd given the man his shirt, as was the charitable thing to do. "I can explain—"

The fae—somehow impossibly dressed in a hunter's

jacket and trousers, complete with boots—stepped forward and offered his hand to Charon. "Pleasant evenin', sir," he drawled in a country accent.

"Oh." Charon smiled, switched the papers to one hand, and shook. "Hello, I..." He frowned and glanced at Brice. His frown deepened at Brice's bare chest.

"Just 'ere to fix your wolf problem, eh," the fae said. His clothes and the accent weren't the only things to have changed. His pale, whiskerless skin had turned golden and rough. His long hair had miraculously shortened itself and now hung in scruffy tails about his face. He was still young, still remarkably handsome, but a different person altogether.

"Oh yes," Charon remarked, lowering his hand. "Terrible business. Did the, er... did my brother summon you?"

"Aye." The fae smiled as though he wasn't lying through his teeth.

"Uh-huh." Charon's brow creased again. "Have we met before?"

"Oh no, sir, I don't think so. This is my first winter 'ere. Just passin' through, you see."

"Hm."

Any moment now, Charon would ask why Brice was shirtless. "I was just taking him to the parlor."

He beckoned *the hunter* to follow him and made it a few paces when Charon asked, "Through the back door?"

"I, well, yes—" If he asked about the shirt, Brice had no excuse. He'd set it down somewhere in the woods before chopping wood?

Some glint of knowing sparkled in Charon's eyes. "I see."

It took a few heartbeats for Brice to realize his brother's smile suggested he suspected Brice had smuggled the hunter in for a more personal reason that had nothing to do with hunting wolves and everything to do with why Brice was shirtless.

"Dinner's at six, I believe." Charon bid the hunter goodbye with a nod and continued on down the corridor, disappearing out of sight around a corner.

"How did you do that?" Brice whispered.

"Glamour, darling." The dull brown of his eyes melted away to reveal their hidden sparkle. "This level of detail is difficult to maintain for any length of time, especially outside my native territory. Wolf is far easier to fake than—"

"If you can do this, why borrow my shirt?"

"I rather fancied wearing it."

"Fabulous. Now my brother believes I'm screwing a huntsman." He turned on his heel and marched down the corridor, passing through the dark dining room.

"You seem more concerned by that notion than he is," the fae said, following quickly behind.

They strode through the dining room into the entrance foyer. Looking behind him, Brice stumbled into Jeanine, the maid. She tripped, and he swooped in and caught her.

"Oh, milord! You startled me!" Jeanine said.

"My apologies, I wasn't looking."

"No, no." She brushed down her skirts. "T'was my fault. Goodness, did you lose your shirt? I'll bring another one..." She trailed off, openly staring at the hunter standing hip cocked, a smirk on his lips. "Oh, sir. I didn't see you there."

"Hm." He took her hand and raised it to his lips. "You do now."

"Oh my."

A spike of ugly jealousy shortened Brice's patience. That was quite enough of that. "Jeanine, do you not have dinner to prepare?"

"Oh yes, milord." She pulled her hand from the hunter's, curtsied, and hurried off with a glance over her shoulder directed wholly at the fae.

"Well, she's lovely." The fae grinned, then caught Brice's glare. "Jealous, my lord?"

"My chamber," Brice growled. "Now." With every step they climbed, the swirl of strange emotion tightened around his heart and lungs. His feelings didn't make any sense. He didn't know this creature, but ever since the kiss in the clearing, he'd felt as though a small part of him had begun to unravel, and the more he reached to catch its end, the more it sped away from him. It felt like panic, like fear, like everything was about to change.

They entered his chamber. Brice locked the door behind them. "You need to tell me who you are and why you're here."

In three steps, the illusion the fae had cast to make himself look like a huntsman fell away like dust in the air and once again he was the dark-haired, elegantly muscular male from the clearing wearing only Brice's shirt. And the shirt barely covered his ass. Barefoot, he padded across the chamber floor. His silken black hair with its silver streak swished down his back. He rested a hand on the bed's corner post. "Yes, I do."

Brice couldn't help but draw closer to him. His body

sought him out. Even now, the sight of him in Brice's filthy shirt had Brice distracted by images of gathering him in his arms and kissing him so deeply that he'd look up at Brice as though he were his whole world. He'd missed that look. Hadn't he?

"If this were my choice, I would not be here at all," the fae muttered.

"Enough." Brice opened the dresser drawer and plucked the picture from inside. It was creased and torn in places but its image undeniable. He tossed the picture onto the bed. "Your name? Begin with that."

The fae's eyes narrowed on the naked image of himself. "You weren't supposed to have that. It was supposed to be a clean severing, like amputating a limb to save the body."

"What does that even mean?"

"It means I'm sorry."

"What for?"

"This." He stepped up to Brice as though to kiss him, and Brice's hands fell to the fae's waist as though they naturally fit. He'd have kissed him then, wanted to—but the fae tilted his head, brushed his cheek against Brice's, and whispered, "*Remember*."

The sudden kiss that followed burned with desperate fervor, and Brice might have fallen into it with his heart and soul if the memories hadn't begun to tumble forth. They trickled at first, then flooded in at once, blinding him with the past, making him deaf to the present. He staggered, braced against the bed, and grabbed at his head. So much... the masquerade, the music, the whip at his back. He gasped, feeling it all again. Shock lashed him. Fear at seeing Raoul walk away when it had all crumbled. They should have won, but Brice had lost the only thing he cared about. Raoul.

He lunged, caught Raoul by his slim neck, and slammed him against the bedpost. "You bastard! You wretched, lying bastard!" Madness and chaos clawed at the inside of his head and trembled through him. "You took us away!" Raoul —wide-eyed—dug his fingers into Brice's hold but didn't fight. He didn't fight because he damn well knew he deserved it.

Brice pressed his forehead against Raoul's and made him look—made him see the hurt in his eyes. "You tore out my heart. You made me *forget*!" Brice squeezed. "I hate you," he said. Raoul's face crumpled, and damn him, that hurt too. "You goddamned prick, I hate you..." Those words he said against his lips, and he meant them. If it weren't for the sudden blinding, fiery love, he'd have killed him then and there. Instead, he let go and slammed a kiss against his mouth. "You made me forget *us*." He'd forgotten his only true love. He'd vowed not to, but he had because Raoul had taken it away. But it was back and back with a furious vengeance.

Raoul tore his mouth free, gasped, and grabbed at Brice's hips as though afraid Brice would let go of his neck. Brice wasn't leaving. To hell with that and to hell with Raoul. He'd vowed never to leave Raoul, and he'd meant it. Whatever the fool fae did, Raoul was his and always would be. Why couldn't Raoul see that?

"Brice?" Raoul's fingers skimmed Brice's jaw and he looked at him, Raoul's face so raw and full of hurt that all Brice could do was kiss him again and again and more. Raoul's hands skimmed up his naked chest, the touch so damned familiar yet so startlingly new. "I deserve your hatred."

A growl of frustration had Brice half out of his mind. He clutched Raoul's hips, pulled him away from the bedpost, and shoved him onto the bed. "You deserve what I give you."

The fae's eyes flashed, first with hot anger, then with lust. He parted his knees, and in only Brice's shirt, he lay exposed and erect and ripe for the taking.

Brice grabbed the oil from the bedside cabinet drawer, dribbled some on his fingers, and quickly swept his fingers between Raoul's buttocks. Raoul gasped and arched his back. "Hurt me. I deserve it."

Taking Raoul's cock in hand, Brice swept his oiled fingers up and down the shaft, applying the right amount of pressure, exactly how Raoul liked it. He wasn't going to damn well hurt him; he was going to make him remember what Raoul had foolishly ripped away from them both.

Brice roughly and unforgivingly pumped his cock. Raoul's moans filled the room. His fingers clawed at the sheets. When he was writhing, his cock jumping in Brice's grip, Brice let go, grabbed Raoul's thighs, and yanked him to the edge of the bed. Freeing himself from his trousers, he slicked his aching erection, spread Raoul's cheeks, pressed himself against the tight hole, and thrust so damned hard he immediately buried himself to the balls. Raoul arched his upper back and opened his smart mouth in a silent gasp. Brice captured his hip in one hand, his thigh in the other, and worked into a fast, desperate rhythm. He never took his eyes from Raoul. The way Raoul's eyes shone, his snarl riding up over tiny sharp canine teeth, his hand scorching

Brice's arm, the way his hard cock bounced against his navel —he committed it all to memory. Every tiny line, every small twitch, every gasp, his whispered name falling from Raoul's lips. He gorged himself on new memories, needing to live them and feel them and breathe them and taste them all over again because he was so damned afraid of how he'd almost lost him, and he never would have known it.

Tears wet his face.

The snarl on Raoul's lips twisted, turning downward as his own eyes sparkled with tears for everything they'd almost lost. He hurt, too, and seeing them slip down Raoul's cheeks, knowing that? It was good. Brice needed him to hurt, to feel, to fear and grieve for everything he'd cost them.

Brice thrust harder, faster, chasing the end, but his tears made him a liar. He fell forward to hide his face in Raoul's shoulder and buried an arm beneath him, holding him so damn close there was nothing between them, just the slide and slap of skin on skin. Raoul's thighs locked around him, sealing him close, never letting go.

Pleasure crackled, building, rising, about to tip over. He clutched Raoul's face in his hand and made him see it all on his face. All the hurt and pain, the love and fear, the grief and loss. He came blindingly hard, buried in Raoul. Raoul threw an arm around his neck and held him so tightly he trembled. They both did.

"I missed you. Even when I didn't know it, I missed you." He sobbed against Raoul's neck, breathing in the smell of jasmine and magic and Raoul.

"I know..." Raoul whispered.

He knew. And he'd still done it. "I missed us." Brice encircled his fingers around Raoul's cock, delighting in its leap. "I missed this." He withdrew, dropped to his knees, perched Raoul's legs over his shoulders, and buried his face between Raoul's buttocks, sweeping his tongue around the sensitive hole as he worked Raoul's cock in his hand.

The fae twitched and bucked, breathless and free and in Brice's bed, and damn him, he was going to come at Brice's mercy. His writhing became tighter, his breaths sharper, and Brice gave a last flick of his tongue, then rose up, switched Raoul's cock to between his lips, and tongued around his smooth head, swallowing him deep. Raoul freed a growling shout. Hot seed spurted the back of Brice's tongue, and Brice pumped him between his lips and tongue until he writhed and gasped and moaned for Brice to stop.

He swallowed, wiped his lips, and prowled up Raoul's flushed body until he braced himself over the prone fae. "Promise me one thing, Raoul. Promise you'll never take my choice from me again."

"I meant to save you the pain of our ending."

"Promise me, damn you."

"I did it for you."

"Raoul, I know my own heart and mind. And I know whom I love, albeit right now, that fool is testing my patience—"

"But you don't know me."

"I know you don't want to be who you were. I know you were trying to be better. You were trapped in a nightmare of your own making, and you fought against it. I understand that. You are not the host, not anymore. You were. I know you were. And that is who you fear. That is who you tried to protect me from. But you're changed. The masquerade changed you, as it changed me and every other soul within it. Deny it, and I'll relent. Look me in the eye and tell me you haven't changed. Do that, and I'll believe you."

He breathed in, faced Brice, and said nothing.

Brice studied the face of his soft, troubled fae. "The host would not have come back."

Raoul sighed and stretched an arm above his head. "I promise, Brice LeChoix, I will never take your heart or mind from you again. It was incredibly wrong of me. Forgive me?"

Brice rolled onto his side and propped his head on a hand. Raoul mirrored him. He was sex-bruised, glassy-eyed, and tousled, and it took everything Brice had not to kiss him and begin again. He'd spend all night with Raoul in this very bed if he weren't so mad at the fool. "Ask me that again when I am less enraged."

"I missed us too," Raoul said, sweeping his touch down Brice's face. The grandfather clock in the hallway began its six chimes. Raoul's gaze slid to the door and back to Brice. "Dinner at six?"

He climbed from the bed but lingered to admire Raoul sprawled atop the tangled sheets. "Are you truly here?"

He stretched shamelessly like a cat in sunshine. "Touch me some more and find out."

Dinner would have to wait.

Chapter Fifty

They'd made love again, slower this time so Brice could savor the taste of Raoul's trembling skin. When the maid knocked on his door for dinner, he sent her away, claiming sickness. And then there was just Raoul beneath his hands, his lips, his tongue, bathed in gentle candlelight and kisses. His fury at what had been done still simmered between them, but he set it aside to focus on knowing Raoul again, loving him. And when Raoul kissed him and sucked him between his lips, his sultry eyes so full of raw need, Brice surrendered to every shudder, every gasp Raoul pulled from his lips, and every spark of blinding ecstasy.

All through the night and into the next day, they lay together. Sometimes frantic, sometimes leisurely, sometimes with Raoul dozing as Brice stroked his hair, or Brice halfway asleep with Raoul's breath tickling the back of his neck, his fingers tracing lazy circles on his hip or thigh.

There was no denying Raoul's bitter words had left their mark between them. But this was not the time for it.

Brice needed to love him again as much as Raoul needed to *be* loved.

"Come to dinner with me," Brice said, the idea new but gaining appeal. The clock had already struck five. The maid would be knocking again soon, and Brice was so damned tired of lies.

"Are you sure?" Raoul asked, lifting his head from Brice's chest.

"Yes. I'll not lie to Charon, and we can't stay in bed forever." He rose from the bed and set about searching for suitable clothes, then caught Raoul's arched eyebrow and knowing smile. His gaze roamed Brice's naked body, pricking his skin. "Raoul, will you come?"

"I believe I did, multiple times."

Brice threw a shirt at the fiend, hitting him in the face and muffling his laughter. "Get dressed."

He dug out some of Charon's old clothes that were more likely to fit Raoul than any of his own, and they dressed.

All wrapped up in gentlemanly finery, his lithe faeness still shone through, but Brice had no wish to hide him like a secret to be ashamed of.

Raoul tugged at his borrowed necktie in front of the dresser mirror. "How much does your brother know?"

Brice pulled on his shoes. "Most everything."

Raoul arched an eyebrow and glanced over his shoulder. "You told your brother?"

"Before your words faded my memory," Brice grumbled, "yes."

Raoul turned, folded his arms, and leaned back against

the dresser, curious. He looked carelessly seductive but sly with it. Like he could charm the knickers off a man of the cloth. "How much did you tell him?"

"That I love a fae." He loved how it sounded and how he felt no shame in saying it. He'd have shouted it from the roof if it wasn't past sundown. "That you said you were the host. He knows it all."

"Hm." He faced the mirror again and fiddled with his tie, checking his reflection. He'd braided his hair but kept the silver lock loose so its silver stream spilled over his shoulder and down his back.

"He'll listen. Might even understand." Brice shrugged on his own dinner jacket. They hadn't always dressed for dinner, but with staff came the need to maintain appearances. Raoul's ass clad in tight pants drew his eye and his thoughts. "And while we dine, you can tell us both why you've come here, as I'm sure it wasn't merely to warm my bed." He straightened his shirt cuffs and headed for the door but Raoul wasn't following. Instead, he stared at himself in the mirror. "Raoul?"

He spread his hands on the dresser top and peered more closely at his reflection. "I never did like my eyes. I would look into them and see someone else."

Brice sighed. "Now you know the truth. It's a good place to start."

Raoul breathed in and straightened. "For the sake of clarity, my lord." He straightened his sleeves with a tug at each cuff. "I am responsible for Sophia's death. The masquerade and its games were my design. Through it, I drove your mother to madness, which resulted in your father's social descent. My players also trapped Charon, almost breaking him."

That was all true but missed several pertinent facts. "You didn't kill Sophia. She killed herself. And you *saved* Charon."

Raoul pressed his lips together. "Your brother is within his rights to shoot me."

"By that reasoning, so am I."

Raoul crossed the room and looked Brice in the eye. "You hate me."

"I do, but not for the reasons you think. Fortunately, I love you more. But I'll not readily forget what was done."

"You know I can remedy that?" His lips twitched.

Brice glowered, then for something to do, he straightened Raoul's necktie. "Do not jest. The wound you dealt is a sore one."

"Or you'll punish me again?" He leaned in and whispered, "Please do, my lord."

With a laugh, Brice brushed a kiss upon his lips. "After dinner and the truth as to why you're here, hm?" He still didn't quite believe Raoul *was* here, in his chamber, solid and real. He pressed his hands to Raoul's chest, marveling at his firm warmth. This wasn't the masquerade, wasn't some twisted fantasy realm. Just Latchly Hall, and Charon, and the staff, and bills, and... Oh. The proposed marriage.

"What?" Raoul asked, either seeing him tense or catching some flicker of emotion crossing his face.

"Nothing." Of course, Raoul heard the lie and narrowed his eyes. Brice lifted Raoul's hand and kissed the backs of his fingers. "Later. First, we speak with Charon. No more lies."

They left the chamber and hurried down the stairs. Brice's nerves rattled. He'd put on a brave face to keep Raoul from leaving, but Charon's reaction to having Raoul here could go either way. He might be reasonable and listen, or his past trauma could flare up. Raoul's presence was never a subtle thing.

"Ah, Brice, I did wonder if..." Charon, standing by the lit fireplace, trailed off as his gaze flicked from Brice to Raoul. Shock widened his eyes, then anger turned his glare sharp. He grabbed an iron poker from the set beside the fireplace and lunged across the table.

"Wait! Don't!" Brice raised a hand.

"Him!" Charon barked. "How is he here?"

Raoul lifted his chin, standing defiant, although Brice saw how his fingers trembled behind his back.

"Let me explain."

"Explain?" Charon scoffed. "There is no explanation for why there is a liar and a deceiver in our home."

"Raoul is here with only good intentions."

"Did he tell you that?" Charon tossed the poker onto the table. "Of course he would. The truth never leaves his lips. Whatever his reason, it's fantasy, made up to seduce you. He'll trick you and fuck with your head, Brice. It's all he knows!"

"Charon! Damn you!" Brice slammed a fist down onto the table, making the crockery and cutlery jump. "Listen." Charon glared but stayed quiet. Brice cleared his throat. "Raoul, tell him."

Raoul met Charon's murderous stare. "Your brother is not wrong."

"But he's not right!"

Charon grabbed the back of the chair nearest him and said with a snarl, "He's fae."

"Darling," Raoul purred, "so are you."

The words hit Charon like a slap across the face. He gasped and stepped back.

"I knew your mother, Anette. It was I who introduced her to your father, knowing full well she was the host's mate. Leon had come to the masquerade to escape the pain of his reality—as many do. His first love died in childbirth."

Childbirth.

Oh God.

Brice's real mother.

The truth barreled through Brice, staggering him on the spot. He grabbed at the nearest chair to keep himself steady.

"Racked with grief, Leon was the perfect plaything," Raoul went on, his voice level. "My masquerade and its players took Lord LeChoix away—he wanted it. Craved it. We only ever give the guests what they desire. LeChoix returned again and again—abandoning his motherless newborn babe, *Brice*, to nursemaids. He always returned to Anette and she to him. The masquerade became his reality, and this house, this life, his son, became his nightmare."

Brice opened his eyes and found Raoul's quick glance. Father had hated him, and now he knew why.

"They fell in love, wrapped in fantasy and dreams. I believed their love a fantasy, too, but their hearts were always their own." Raoul paused. The fire crackled. Charon breathed. "Anette's mate, Sinclair, is formidable. Already playing the role of the host at my behest so that I might move freely among the guests, he assumed Anette was playing the same games as the rest of us until she confronted him with the truth. She loved a mortal man, and she wished to leave."

A small choking sob escaped from Charon. He slumped against a chair.

"The host did not react well and with the powers I'd given him, he sealed us all inside the masquerade forever, making us all forget. Until Brice confronted him with the truth, thus unravelling the curse. And here we are."

Raoul's fingers touched Brice's at his side, then encircled his. "I am the true host of the masquerade. Its beautiful lies are my stitches in time. Its bounty and its abundance are equal parts desire and seduction. I created it as an escape for human and fae alike. It was never meant to become a prison, but such is the way of magical things. It took on a life of its own. The tragedy of the LeChoix family is not of my design. And, I fear, it is not yet over..."

Charon fell into the chair. Planting his elbows on the table, he bowed his head and threaded his fingers into his hair. "It doesn't change what was done. Sophia, me... even Brice—you stole his mind." When Charon looked up, his blue eyes sparkled. "If it is forgiveness you want, I am not able to give it."

Raoul pulled out two chairs from the table and beckoned Brice to sit beside him. "No. I cannot forgive myself, so why would I expect anyone else to forgive me? That's not why I came. I had walked away, given Brice the gift of forgetting—" Brice opened his mouth to protest but Raoul raised a hand. "The masquerade fell. It was over but for Sinclair. As Brice has noticed, the curse touched us all. We forgot our lives and crafted new ones. The masquerade changed us. For some, it changed us for the better. Others did not fare so well. Our lives outside the masquerade went on without us. We returned home with the same faces as lost lovers and kin, but we are not the same inside. Sinclair... is changed, but not for the better." Raoul fell silent and leaned back in the chair. "Sinclair will not rest, I fear, until he has you, Charon."

Raoul reached into the air, and with a flick of his fingers and some sleight of hand, a square cream envelope appeared between his fingers. He set it down on the dining table. Gold letters swirled on the paper in unfamiliar, jagged penmanship.

Charon...

The masquerade awaits.

Charon sat bolt upright. "No."

"Raoul?" Brice asked.

"I did not write this invite."

Brice picked it up and turned it over in his hand. "Where did you get this?"

"I've been watching you both for some time. Intercepting messengers and the like... glamoured while in Chamonet, of course. Quite the delightful town. Albeit it's somewhat... lacking in flair. This invite is the tenth I've discovered making its way to Latchly Hall in the past three weeks."

"But the solstice is over two months away," Charon said. "This is not my masquerade. This is something else."

"Sinclair," Brice said.

"Well, then." Charon lifted his chin. "I'll just not go."

"I fear it will not be enough. Sinclair is no longer trapped in an illusion. He is free to do as he pleases."

"Meaning?" Brice asked.

"Meaning, if you do not go to him, he'll come to you. Here, at Latchly Hall. This is why I've returned. The host is not done with either of you, and outside my masquerade, my rules no longer apply."

Chapter Fifty-One

"He stays for one night. Then he returns to wherever he comes from." Charon leaned an arm against the mantelpiece, fingers tapping his chin. "I don't trust half of what he said. It's likely more lies. When has a true word ever left his lips?"

Brice swirled the wine in his glass. They'd forgone dinner, with nobody in the mood to eat, and Raoul had left the room, suggesting they talk without him. They'd sat in silence for what felt like an age until Charon had poured the wine and propped himself against the mantel. And here they were. Fantasy and reality had collided. Sinclair was out there, his invite in front of Brice, and the summons mocked them all.

What had happened within the masquerade, as terrible as many of the events were, was mostly fantasy. People walked away from it, albeit some broken. But death had no place there. However, death was very real in Latchly Hall. It had stalked the halls twice before. If the host were angry enough, vicious enough—as Brice had already seen of him—

then death might stalk the halls again. And he couldn't let that happen.

Brice downed his wine.

"Send him away and we'll forget this nonsense ever happened," Charon said.

"What?"

"Have you heard anything I've said, brother?" Charon whirled and strode to the table. "He can't be here. His being here will bring more of them. More chaos. It follows him. He *creates* it. He said so, probably the only true thing he's said in years. For all we know, his being here will *bring* the host."

That last part Charon had whispered, as though saying it too loud would summon the host to their door.

Brice picked up the invite and brought it to his nose. It didn't smell like Raoul. He hadn't really expected it to. It did smell like mulched earth and wet leaves, like time and decay and rotting things.

"Brice, God, are you listening?"

Brice held the invite over the lit candle in its holder and let the flame lick at its corner. That little flame bloomed, crawling over the paper, quickly devouring it until he could hold it no more and dropped it into a bowl. Seconds later, the invite was ash.

"Send Raoul away or I will."

"No."

"He took your memories, or have you forgotten that too?"

"Careful, brother—"

"Someone needs to tell you how it is. He will ruin you. It's what they do!"

Brice lifted his eyes, finally meeting his brother's gaze. "He's not going anywhere."

Charon's cheek pulsed. "We have lives. The land, the farms, the mill. You're to be married, for God's sake!"

Brice winced and hastily poured more wine. "Lower your voice."

"Why, so your lover doesn't hear? Tell him, or I will."

"Charon, stop... Just..." His stomach churned. This was too much. Charon's words made sense. He was probably right, about all of it, but Brice wasn't letting Raoul go again. He'd just gotten him back. "If the host comes here, what do we have to fight him? A fire poker? We don't know who or what we're dealing with in this world. Raoul does. He is our best chance at surviving."

"Surviving? Do you think the host means to kill us?"

"Me, certainly. You... I'm not sure what he wants with you. To take you away, hold you captive—I've no idea, but none of it will be good. We need Raoul."

Charon snorted. "He has you bewitched."

"No—"

"Is his cock so wonderful a thing that you can't see or hear his lies?"

Brice shot to his feet, knocking his chair backward. "That's enough! Do not make me choose, Charon."

"Choose?" He laughed bitterly. "I am your brother. I am your blood. You would choose a fae trickster over me?"

"You are my *half*-brother, and I am the lord of this house, by God. Raoul is staying."

"You haven't been the lord of this house since you left for the masquerade years ago. I am its lord in all but name. You are nothing but a ruined man lusting after dreams. Just like Father. It killed him, it killed Mother, and it will kill you, and I'll not stand by and let that happen!"

Charon's parting words rang in the air as he left, slamming the door behind him.

Brice dragged a hand down his face. Where had it all gone wrong? Perhaps from the moment his real mother had died birthing him. He'd struggled his whole life to somehow make things right, to make himself better, and nothing had changed.

"He has your father's temper." Raoul's smooth voice at least soothed some of Brice's anger. He propped his ass on the edge of the table and laid his hands on his thighs. "And his mother's passion. A volatile combination."

"How much did you hear?"

"A marriage?" Raoul crooned. "Will I receive an invite?"

He'd heard all of it then. "It won't go ahead. I'll write her—"

"Let it." Raoul's soft smile almost broke Brice's heart right there. "Charon's right. You have lives that would be far better off without me in them. Once Sinclair is dealt with, I'll leave—"

"No." Brice rose to his feet, set his glass down, and slotted himself neatly between Raoul's parted knees. "If I am to marry, it will be for love." He skimmed his fingers down Raoul's jaw and tipped his chin up. Fae eyes sparkled with unknown truths. Perhaps one day, Brice might know them all. But for now, he was content with just knowing Raoul. He skimmed a kiss across his lips.

"Hm, you taste of wine and fury," Raoul murmured. His fingertips skipped down Brice's neck, then yanked his necktie away from his throat. Raoul tossed the tie over his shoulder and grabbed Brice by his jacket lapels, hauling him close. "Would you believe me if I told you no one has ever fought for me as you do?"

"Apparently, I am bewitched. I'll believe anything you say." Brice dropped his hands down Raoul's back, caught his hips, and jerked him tight against him, body to body. "Who were you, before the masquerade?" Brice teased a kiss at his lips and when Raoul sought to steal it, Brice withdrew, holding back.

"Nobody."

"Hm, I don't believe that."

Raoul leaned back some and swallowed. "It's true." His gaze fluttered downward. "I prettied up the winter court. A wallflower, full of color and life, outshone by others above my social station. I am born to lowly kin, destined for the background. Overlooked and ignored. So I made my own court of dreams and convinced others to join me. We would play games with mortals. And that's how it began. At the masquerade, I had control. I had power. I could do anything. Create and shape worlds, make dreams come true. Until I made the mistake of temporarily handing that power to Sinclair and donning a mask so I might frolic with the guests. It seemed like a good idea at the time. Mistakes... as you know, I am not immune to them."

Brice caught his chin. "You're not my mistake." He slowly sealed the kiss, relishing the soft feel and taste of Raoul opening under him, remembering it—remembering this, and how his heart had swelled to feel Raoul love him in return. Raoul smiled and tilted his head back.

Something like a hungry growl rumbled out of Brice.

He suckled at his neck, drawing the soft flesh between his teeth. Raoul chuckled and made a pathetic attempt to separate them with a hand. "Unless you want to give the staff something to titter about, perhaps we should take ourselves somewhere other than the dining table?"

"I would marry you," Brice blurted. He meant it with all his heart. But Raoul's sudden stillness—as though he might be finding the right word to deny him—had him doubting his words. He couldn't take them back, so he plowed on. "I'd marry you tomorrow if the church allowed two men to wed. Perhaps, they will... Times are changing, and—" He cut himself off, afraid he was rambling.

Raoul's eyebrow arched. "Is this a proposal or an observation?"

"I suppose that depends on your answer." Brice could pretend his heart didn't race or that he hadn't meant to say such things, but it would all be lies. He wanted Raoul by his side. He wanted him in his bed, wanted to watch the seasons pass with him, taste the rain with him, dance in the snow with him. The more he thought of marriage, the more the notion clutched at his heart and made it race. Yes, it was right, damn the church and his brother and anyone who would think it wrong. None of them mattered. Only Raoul.

"Aren't you betrothed to another, my lord?" Raoul folded his legs around Brice, locking them at the ankle to keep him close. "So scandalous."

"When has the risk of a scandal ever stopped you? You adore drama."

Raoul grinned. "That is true. You are a good man with a good soul. I admire your strength, your passion, your willingness to do what is right against the odds. The nothing person I was before, he would not have come here to you. I have changed, but I am still that fae. I belong to a different world, a different people."

"We could belong together?"

Color touched Raoul's face. He glanced away and did not reply, and that was answer enough. "And all along I thought I was the dreamer."

It didn't matter. Perhaps it was foolish to ask Raoul to commit to such a human thing as marriage. Their love was enough. "Tell me how your kin show their love?"

"I can do more than that. Take me to your bed, and I'll show you."

Brice had barely made it back to his chamber before Raoul was kissing him. He struggled to kick the door closed, then fell back against it with Raoul's hands pulling up his shirt and his mouth scorching his neck. Their kisses turned messy, desperate breaths shared. Raoul had Brice's cock freed in seconds and went to his knees, leaving no time for Brice to prepare before warm, slick tightness enveloped him.

He thumped his head back against the door and rolled his eyes closed. "God, yes." Raoul's talented tongue swept away all the concerns Charon's reaction had summoned. Then Raoul slipped off and rose to his full height.

Pressing his hands against Brice's chest, he smirked. "I promised to show you how we love."

Brice knew that look. It was mischief and spice all rolled into one. Raoul was planning something.

He pushed off and walked backward, his body a symphony of teasing. He pulled off his necktie and flung it aside, then worked his jacket buttons undone with quick, precise flicks, reminding Brice of how those fingers could be both delicate and firm. Everything about him was a tease, one Brice couldn't resist and didn't want to. He swallowed, heard his own heart racing, felt his body burning up in anticipation of all the things Raoul promised. He loved how free he was to feel these things without shame.

With his clothes half undone, Raoul crossed to the door, flicked the lock, and nodded toward the bed.

Brice made it there in three strides, tearing off his tie and jacket and starting on his shirt. He'd barely touched the sheet when Raoul's heat plastered against his back and the soft, light flutter of his lips brushed his neck just behind his ear. Brice tilted his head, and Raoul's mouth skimmed lower at the same time his hand stroked over Brice's hip and eased down, finding his proud member again.

"The oil?" Raoul whispered and for a moment, Brice stumbled over his meaning. Then it hit him. Raoul meant to take him from behind. The idea set his nerve endings ablaze. The last person to enter him had been the trio, one or all three—he couldn't remember for certain and didn't want to. But this he wanted.

"Bedside drawer."

Raoul vanished and Brice used the time to unbutton the rest of his shirt. Trepidation dried his throat. With the trio, he'd been hidden behind a mask. This was altogether more personal. He turned his own thoughts over while removing his shirt and caught Raoul looking at him from the side of the bed. His interested cock upset the flatteringly tight trousers.

Brice dragged his gaze upward, over Raoul's smooth chest to the quirk of his lips and finally his arched eyebrow.

They didn't need words. None seemed worthy anyway. Brice burned for Raoul, stronger and hotter than before after having his feelings stolen from him. That wasn't ever happening again.

"Do it," he told Raoul. "I want to feel you inside."

"It will be my pleasure. And yours, I assure you."

Raoul came around behind him and placed his hands on Brice's hips, beginning a new kind of dance.

But it had to be more than that. More than a charade or a game. "Raoul... Do this because you want to, because I want you to. For no other reason. Nobody is watching. Just us."

"I'm doing this because I love you." He stroked down Brice's neck, over his shoulder, and skimmed his fingers down his bicep—the touch so light, it made Brice shiver.

Brice wet his lips. "What happened before, with... *them*... they mean nothing to me. It meant nothing."

"I know, darling." He flicked his tongue over Brice's ear, hooked his fingers over Brice's trousers, and levered them down over his hips. Cold air wrapped around his thighs and ass. Then Raoul's warm hands spread over his buttocks. His nails dug in suddenly. Brice gasped. Reeling from the sudden needling, he melted against Raoul as his touch softened. Raoul spread him again and brushed an oiled finger over his hole, teasing what was to come. He gently urged Brice forward.

Brice bent and spread his hands on the bed. Raoul's touch danced down his spine, then his tongue followed, strong and wet, then his lips, and it was all Brice could do not to rub his heavy, sensitive member against the sheets.

Raoul's finger eased to his hole again, and this time

slipped inside. The sensation of being entered, even with just a finger, crackled through him, pleasant but at the same time not, as old feelings of shame came crawling back to him. Then Raoul's mouth suckled his shoulder and his hair tickled Brice's back, and when a second finger eased in, with their angle and width, they expertly skimmed over that special gland.

Brice could no more silence his grunt then he could calm his heart. He groaned out something that barely resembled words and clutched at the sheets as Raoul mercilessly stroked into him. When Raoul withdrew, Brice almost whined like a wounded animal, but the heavy press of Raoul entering him again silenced him. Thickness spread him wide and filled him up. He panted, twisting the sheets in his fists, and moaned Raoul's name. He wanted this, wanted more. And told Raoul so.

Raoul captured Brice's hips with firm hands and impaled him over and over, each new stroke another splash of fireworks inside his veins. He lost all inhibitions, lost himself somewhere in the moment, and turned his head, needing to see. Raoul's fiery eyes locked on his. The contact set his soul ablaze. He was going to come and could do nothing to stop it. Then—because he always knew—Raoul gripped Brice under his arms, hauled him upright so his back was arched against Raoul's chest, and captured Brice's cock in his fingers. Three strokes and Brice came with a strangled shout the maids would surely hear. He twisted and buzzed, heart and soul on fire as he spilled over Raoul's fingers.

Teeth sank into Brice's shoulder. The bite was so fast and deep, its pain added to the ecstasy of orgasm. Raoul growled and bucked, spilling into him. And all at once, they were joined. Brice was Raoul's, and Raoul Brice's. Words weren't enough. He just knew. Raoul had promised to show him how the fae loved, and he'd marked him to prove it.

Mate.

Raoul swept his tongue over the weeping bite. "It will heal. Does it hurt?"

Brice could only smile at him, fearing his voice might break and give away how he was choking on a great swell of emotion he hadn't expected.

"Brice?"

"No," he croaked. "It doesn't hurt."

Raoul swept a hand up Brice's chest and hugged him back against him. "Mine," Raoul whispered into his ear.

"Yours."

He'd found his place. He belonged with Raoul. His mate.

Chapter Fifty-Two

Raoul was introduced to the staff as a family guest and with his tipped ears glamoured away, he played his part well enough—for a month. It didn't take long for a few of the staff to question how much of a gentleman Raoul was when he insisted on helping with their daily chores, or juggled with fruit, or delighted the maids with his sleight of hand. He cared little for etiquette or social norms. He particularly enjoyed helping the farmers. On several occasions, Brice found "Master Raoul" helping herd the sheep, or fixing a fence, or loading grain at the mill—gloriously shirtless in front of the mill-hands. He was a flirt and a tease, and the staff expressed how much of a joy his company was.

Brice often heard Raoul's laughter on the walk down to the orchards and would find him with an arm slung around one of the tenants, the both of them filthy from a day's work and chatting like lifelong friends. His charisma brought life and color and laughter to Latchly Hall in a way that hadn't been present since Anette's death.

He was a delight to be around, a delight to know, and in

the evening when the chamber door clicked closed, he was a delight to love.

They'd been caught more than once *in flagrante delicto,* startling Jeanine. Rumours swirled of how his relationship with Raoul was intimate. Brice ignored them. Latchly Hall was his. What he did in his own home was his business. And if that included thoroughly *doing* Raoul on the grand piano in the music room, so be it. Luckily, Raoul had become so loved that word hadn't spread much beyond idle gossip.

Charon said nothing, not even when Brice's engagement was called off. Which was perhaps worse than if he'd ranted and raved. He buried himself in work. The mill flourished. The estate was readied for winter, and the first storm of the season rolled in, dumping a foot of snow overnight, muffling the forest at dawn.

Brice found Raoul in the lounge standing by a fogged window, looking exquisite in a moss-green morning jacket and black trousers. "The solstice is in two weeks," Raoul said. "Jeanine found this." From his pocket he took an invite, but this one was different. The name was written in red ink:

Raoul

"Read it." Raoul handed it over.

"I'd rather not." Brice opened it anyway.

They are mine.

A chill licked down Brice's spine. *Mine*. The fae did not say such things lightly. He marched across the room and tossed the note into the fire, then watched it burn. Sinclair wasn't going to stop. There would be no reasoning with him. The masquerade's sweet illusions had gone, leaving only Sinclair's ugly infatuation behind. Brice feared for Charon, who was more fragile than he looked, and for Raoul, who would throw himself on a blade, believing his own life worthless.

"Promise me," Brice said as he looked up from the flames at Raoul, who was still staring out the window watching more snow fall.

"Promise you what?"

"You won't do anything foolish."

He turned his back on the snowfall and leaned against the sill, folding his arms. "I suspect we disagree on the definition of foolish."

Brice couldn't think about losing him. Not Raoul. And not again. He crossed to the window and as Raoul loosened his stance, Brice folded him close, breathing in the soft smell of jasmine in his hair. He captured the silver streak and ran it through his fingers, marveling at how it glittered against his skin. "You blame yourself for all of this." Raoul opened his mouth to argue. Brice pressed a finger to his lips. "Don't deny it. You made a mistake. We all make them. You don't need to punish yourself forever because of it. "

"Hm, think you finally know me, do you?"

"I know who you are now. I'm beginning to think I know you better than you know yourself. When Sinclair comes, please, don't do anything... Raoul-like."

He chuckled. "Raoul-like? And what would that be?"

"This isn't the masquerade." He pressed his forehead to Raoul's and fell into his eyes. "Blood is real here."

"I am more concerned with your habit of leaping into heroics without a second thought, LeChoix."

"I had nothing to lose before. Now, you are my everything." He entwined his hand with Raoul's.

"Truly?" Raoul whispered.

"You doubt it?"

"I do not doubt you, Brice. Never you."

"You are half my heart, Raoul. You are my color in a bland world. Don't throw yourself away to right a wrong that wasn't your fault."

Raoul's face turned serious. He frowned and grasped Brice's face in his hands. "Then make me the same vow. You're the light in the dark, Brice. You're the beat of my heart. I'd surrender time itself to spend every moment with you. You make me worthy. You make me someone I can admire, someone I can love. You're my mirror and through you, I see all the good I could be."

Brice choked on a sob. "You don't need to be anyone but yourself."

Chapter Fifty-Three

RAOUL

Lavender.

Just a hint of it.

Raoul stroked his fingertips over Brice's naked shoulder and down his arm. He didn't stir. Brice always slept like a fallen tree. Raoul rather liked that about him. He smelled slightly of lavender. Calming. Soothing. Raoul had lost count of the times he'd lain awake beside him breathing him in, admiring all of Brice's tiny human imperfections. Like the way his cheeks dimpled sometimes, mostly when he smiled in a way that suggested the opposite of what a smile should say. He'd never known someone to smile when they were angry before, but Brice did. Combined with the man's penetrating stare, it left quite the impression.

Of course, Brice had no idea how Raoul hung on his every word. He had no idea how Raoul watched him as he slept, and he had no idea the lengths to which Raoul would go to protect Brice and his life at Latchly Hall.

He'd considered taking him back to the winter court, but after the glamour of the masquerade had fallen, revealing Raoul's name at court to be mud, he could offer no real life for Brice. The fae played with mortals; they did not invite them home to live with them. Raoul wasn't even sure the court was still his home. Nothing had felt real after walking away from Brice. The masquerade was over, but without Brice beside him, all the light and love and joy had been bleached from his reality. After leaving Brice and returning home, he'd hated every passing second. He'd watched the seasons turn and felt nothing. The winter court, so full of splendid light and glittering wonderment, had lost its luster. His kin, the life he'd forgotten, none of it had mattered, just like the masquerade hadn't mattered. What was the point of such wonder if he had nobody to share it with?

He would have walked away from Brice for good, though. Let his whispered words to forget lie where they had fallen, giving Brice the gift of unknowing. After the masquerade's fall, he'd drifted back to Brice, watched him from afar, glamoured among the townsfolk, despite such magic being exhausting outside the masquerade. Several times he'd almost interfered. Brice had clearly been miserable, but once Raoul's spell had begun to sink in, Lord Brice LeChoix had become the talk of the town, and not because of his family's curse. With the gift of forgetting, Brice had slowly broken free of his trauma, and Raoul couldn't ruin that. So he'd watched from the background, as he had always been destined to do, until catching sight of an invite intended for Latchly Hall.

He should have known Sinclair wouldn't give up.

The fiend had always looked upon Raoul with jealous eyes. Raoul had foolishly thought him harmless. But Sinclair had lain in wait like a spider in his web, poised for the right moment to strike, and Raoul had gleefully handed him that moment, so blinded was he by the wonder of the masquerade and his role within it. One mistake—handing control to Sinclair—and the purpose of the masquerade had fallen like a house of cards.

Sinclair had remembered.

He remembered it all.

Raoul's games had taken Anette from him.

Bitter and twisted, Sinclair knew only jealousy. He'd take Brice because he could. He'd take Charon because nobody could stop him.

Raoul would.

He had to.

He couldn't lose his mate *or* his mate's brother.

He tucked Brice's scruffy hair behind his ear and admired the line of his jaw. Raoul had once laughed at those in love, thinking them fools for narrowing their world. He'd played and fucked and lied and danced, teased and laughed and lived a shallow life, thinking it had meaning. He'd laughed at Anette when she'd come to him for help in leaving Sinclair. Why would she do such a thing for a mortal? It didn't make any sense. Madness, he'd told her, then downed another glass of wine and fallen into bed with some masked mortal.

That was the last word he'd said to her. *Madness*. He

wondered about that too… if he'd accidentally given the word power.

He'd treated it all like a joke.

All the laughs had been lies.

Only Sinclair was left laughing now.

He slowly rolled onto his back so as not to wake Brice and blinked at the ceiling. The room was dark, the fire low in the grate, the house quiet. Nothing was every truly silent in the real world like it had been at the masquerade. The air was never frozen. Time leaked into every facet of life. He could feel it now, gnawing at his body and bones. Every second, Brice aged and so did Raoul. Brice didn't know. He thought Raoul immortal, untouchable, and Raoul would let him think it. Of course, he could go home and live forever in a gilded cage or stay and wilt with age. Wasn't that what he'd always craved? What was the point of eternal life if that life had no meaning? The masquerade had taught him that even the brightest of stars must expire for them to truly shine.

A thump sounded distantly in the house. It was too early for the staff to be moving about. Old houses creaked and settled, but the sound had been too abrupt for that.

Brice continued to slumber, breathing heavily.

Raoul climbed from the bed, threw on breeches and a shirt, and padded from the room. Avoiding the patchwork of creaking floorboards along the landing, he made his way down the stairs into the dimly lit entrance hall. The heavy quiet had thickened. The candles in the floor-standing candelabra near the front door, the one the staff kept lit, had burned low. The small flames danced in the stirring air.

Instincts chimed a warning. Nothing appeared out of

place, but it was the kind of nothing Raoul knew well. An illusionary nothing—*don't look here.* Vine had used it to hide the pleasure rooms. But Vine was unlikely to be here. He'd fled back to court with the others.

Raoul spotted an unlit candelabra on a sideboard. He lit the candles from those already burning and ventured down the hallway, lighting the lamps in their sconces along the way.

Music tinkled ahead. Raoul stilled mid-step. He knew the tune well, having lived with it for an eternity. The masquerade's unmistakable lullaby spilled out into the hallway from behind a closed door, as did the shifting candlelight. The tune was tinny, mechanical. A music box?

He switched the candelabra to his left hand and reach for the door handle. He had to know, had to see before the rest of the house awoke. The handle creaked under his touch. The door clicked open, and in that moment's gasp, the music and the light vanished.

There was nobody in the room. No lit candles. But he'd heard—

A flash. A candelabra swung into the corner of his eye too late to stop. Heavy iron cracked across his head, rattling his thoughts. He reached blindly for the wall with one hand while swinging his own candelabra in a wild arc, driving his attacker back. Blood ran into his right eye, blurring the room red. The second blow almost knocked his consciousness out of him. He fell but barely felt the floor rush up to greet him. And there was the music box sitting inches from his fingers, its lid open, the dancer motionless on her stage. He *had* heard it. The entwined initials shimmered: A & S.

Hands gripped Raoul's shirt and hauled him onto his

back. He blinked through blood, clearing his vision but not his thoughts. A figure stooped over him, candelabra raised. "Sophia didn't get to love, so neither do you," Charon said with a snarl.

Raoul gasped and tried to bring an arm up, but his body was slow, his thoughts broken. The candelabra came down a third time.

Chapter Fifty-Four

Brice

Raoul wasn't beside him when he woke. It wasn't unusual. They'd only recently begun sharing a chamber after Jeanine had made it clear the staff all knew Raoul and Brice were intimately engaged and they had no interest in telling tales outside of the household. He'd warned her all the same—gossiping would risk their employment. He'd had to. Not all the staff were as loyal as Jeanine.

Still, he'd become accustomed to waking with Raoul close so they could indulge every morning. Perhaps Raoul had woken early to visit the farms.

Brice dressed and made his way downstairs. Jeanine bustled around the breakfast room table, clearing Charon's plates away. "Sleep well, brother?" Charon asked, taking a sip of water from a glass.

"Hm. Have you seen Raoul?"

"No..." Charon said. "Perhaps he had an early start in the valley?"

"Hm." Fixing his shirt cuffs, Brice took a seat at the table and poured himself some tea. Raoul always told him if he was going to be visiting the farms. The days were short and the snow brutal. It was unlike him to leave without a word, especially so close to the solstice. He might have told Jeanine. Brice would ask her when she returned with his breakfast.

Brice idly buttered some toast and drank his tea. "The solstice is in three days."

"I can hardly forget." Charon's hand trembled as he reached for his glass. He sat stiffly with his back upright and his gestures wooden. This time of year was always hard on him. Hard on them both. The solstice marked too many anniversaries they both wished to forget.

"I was thinking of asking the staff to stay indoors, just for the next week," Brice said. "For their own protection. If the host—"

"I won't let the host dictate my actions—our actions. We should continue as though all is well and hopefully the solstice will come and go without event."

Considering Sinclair's invites, the chances of him not making some kind of statement were slim. Charon was usually more careful than this. "We are responsible for the people we employ. They could be in danger." A rustle from the outside corridor hushed Brice.

Jeanine entered with a tray of food. "Breakfast, milord. Raoul not joining you this morning?"

"No... I was going to ask if you've seen him but you've answered that query."

"Not since last night with you, milord. We were expecting him in the kitchens, actually. He'd promised to share his apple-and-cinnamon pie recipe. We was rather looking forward to it. He's a delight. Has us in stitches, he does. Did you know he can juggle like them fancy troupes that come through town? Can keep five apples in the air at once and take a bite from each!"

Brice smiled at the image. "I did, yes. And I'm sure he'll be pleased to hear your kind words—"

"Perhaps he forgot," Charon said, butting in. "He's good at that. Easily distracted."

Jeanine cut Charon a wary look. "Yes, milord. Perhaps he did." She curtsied and left.

Brice glared at his brother. "We've talked about this. Raoul is staying."

"Talked, yes. Agreed, not even close." Charon rose. "I'll be at the mill."

"Charon, with the solstice so close, I'd really prefer it if you stayed indoors—" Charon left the room, leaving Brice frowning after him. He'd be fine. They'd all be fine... as soon as the solstice passed.

Chapter Fifty-Five

Raoul

The mill's gears and wheels hung motionless in their monstrous iron frame. Great iron rods and chutes jutted from the ceiling and dove beneath the floorboards. Raoul's thumping head beat hotter and harder in time with his heart. He'd at least managed to work the strip of cloth from his mouth, but the bindings tying his wrists to the chair wouldn't loosen. Illusionary magic was of no use here. Lies could not undo restraints.

One small window hinted at daylight outside.

His breath clouded in the cold air.

The stomp of boots was almost a welcome relief to his own company, although the wrong LeChoix emerged from the stairs. Raoul swallowed all the vicious accusations, waiting instead to see where this led. Charon could have killed him but clearly hadn't. He didn't seem the type for torture. So his attack served anther purpose then.

"It will not be much longer now," Charon said. He stamped snow from his boots and blew into his cupped hands. The cold had nipped at his cheeks, flushing them red.

"When Brice discovers what you've—"

"You left. Returned to your people. You thought it better to let him live his life without you. He'll get over you."

His lie was so damned accurate, Raoul had no reply. Although Charon was also wrong. "It will break his heart."

"Yes. *You* will. Like you broke mine when you took Sophia."

Breathing in, Raoul waited for a reply to come but found he had no defense. Or excuse. He had done exactly that. Although it was Sinclair that had spotted their young love and cruelly cast her out. Still, it was all because of Raoul's design. "Brice won't thank you."

"I don't really care whether he thanks me or not. I'm doing this *for* him."

"For him?" Raoul snorted. "What a fine liar you are. This is petty revenge. Don't insult me by dressing it up as anything else."

"All right, then it's revenge. For ruining my *fucking life!*" Charon marched forward, grabbed Raoul by the shirt collar, and yanked, lifting him and the chair. "You are the curse that must be stopped."

"Kill me then. Make it final."

He snorted. "If only it were that easy."

"It is. Outside of my court, I'm as vulnerable as you. How do you think your mother was able to take her life?"

Charon swallowed hard. "If it weren't for my brother's

obvious love, I would." He dropped him and backed away. "He'll take you. And it will be over."

He could only be Sinclair. Raoul gaped at the foolish man, then let his smile crawl onto his lips. "Is that what he told you? And you believed him?"

"You'll never set foot in Chamonet again. That's all I care about. Brice and I can live our lives and put this madness behind us. We almost had it until you returned, dragging the masquerade and its nightmares back into our home with you."

"Did you forget who Sinclair is?"

"I have forgotten *nothing*!"

"He is the host—"

"No, *that is you*."

"Well, yes and no. I gave him the power over the masquerade. Temporarily, until it wasn't. Before Sinclair, I was the host, yes. But he twisted my game. He made it what you saw. His madness will not be sated just by me."

"*You* betrayed him. You conspired to ruin him, too, like you ruin everything you touch."

Raoul couldn't help but laugh. Charon wasn't wrong. He had betrayed Sinclair, cruelly wrecking his love, although it could be argued Anette would not have fallen for another soul if theirs was so fine a match. "I don't suppose it will matter if I tell you how your brother changed me? How, even now, I think of him and what will happen when he realizes I'm gone? I don't care what happens to me. I am not who I was. The masquerade is gone. It exists only in our memories. And Sinclair's desperation. You're playing into his hands, Charon. Can't you see?"

"I see in you, Raoul, a creature who will eventually

break my brother's heart. Whether it's now or later doesn't matter. It's inevitable. It's all you know to do."

"If you truly understood love, you wouldn't make your brother suffer like you did."

Charon's mouth tightened into a snarl. "She didn't deserve to die."

"No, she did not."

He moved to the window and wiped the condensation away, revealing fat, messy snowflakes bumping against the glass. "My mother didn't deserve it either."

"Your mother's death was her choice, as terrible as it was."

"She never forgave herself."

"Will you forgive yourself when you look into Brice's eyes and know you took his love away or will you take a pistol to your head, years from now?" Raoul's voice cracked. He tightened his lips against their quiver, but damn him, Charon turned his head and saw anyway. "I love your brother, Charon. And he loves me. Whatever you do here cannot change that. Did you stop loving your mother after she died? Have you stopped loving Sophia?" Charon looked away. "Then you know you're about to wound Brice forever. Don't do this. If you love him, if you truly want to protect him, let me go."

He sighed and stared out of the window, then looked at Raoul. "You stole Brice's heart and soul, and when that wasn't enough, you stole his memories. You'd do it all again in a heartbeat. It's over. Prepare yourself." He headed for the stairs. "Sinclair is here."

"Charon, wait..." He had to stop him, to stop this.

Outside the court, outside the masquerade, a deal was nothing but empty words. Charon was walking into a trap.

Charon glanced back over his shoulder.

"He wants you, not me," Raoul said. "You're his mate's son, his last connection to Anette. He'll say and do anything to get to you and to hurt Brice—the man he believes keeps taking what is his, just like Leon took Anette. Please... listen to me. You're making a mistake."

"No. The only mistake here is you."

Chapter Fifty-Six

Brice

The wind had gotten up, rattling the windows. For the middle of the day, it was as dark as night outside. Snow fell in earnest. And Raoul had not returned.

Brice shrugged on his thick coat and pulled on heavy, fur-lined boots. Something was wrong. The cold bite in his veins told him so.

"Forgive me, milord." Jeanine wrung her hands and dallied at the foot of the stairs. "But the paths to the mill be knee-deep by now. Are you sure you want to venture out in this?"

"I don't want to, Jeanine. I must."

"Masters Charon and Raoul probably be safely holed up at the mill, like master Charon said."

"That's just the thing..." Raoul's absence and Charon's behavior at breakfast niggled his instincts. "Charon said he'd be at the mill, Jeanine."

"Aye, he did."

"But the river is frozen. The mill wheel hasn't turned in weeks. Why would he go there now? During such a storm?"

"I don't rightly know, milord. But the storm don't feel right. It has teeth. I don't like it." As though to hammer her point home, the wind chose that moment to roll against the door and puff the thick curtain aside. Cool air slipped into Latchly Hall's warmth and down the back of Brice's neck.

"No, neither do I." He flicked his collar up. The storm did indeed have teeth. "Fetch my father's rifle."

Jeanine hurried off and returned moments later with the rifle. Brice checked it wasn't cocked, then tucked it inside his coat to prevent it freezing. "Keep the fires burning in every room and the lamps lit and make sure the rest of the staff stay indoors. Do not leave the house." He drew in a breath and sighed it out. Hopefully, it was all for nothing. Raoul would be holed up in one of the farmers' cottages avoiding the cold, and Charon would be at the mill, just as he'd said.

"Master Brice, milord?"

"Yes, Jeanine?"

She was a young thing, no older than Brice, he supposed. But she had the kind eyes of someone more wizened with age. "Come back to us," she said.

She'd heard of the curse. Of how Leon had walked into the forest and never returned. Of how Lady Anette LeChoix had taken her own life. And they'd all heard whispers of the masquerade and the fae. Terrible things happened on nights like these.

"I will," he said, then opened the door. A blast of cold,

snow-blinding air rolled over him and he stepped into the dark.

Chapter Fifty-Seven

Raoul

Sinclair emerged on the mill's second floor in his gold-laced black suit and golden filigreed mask as though he'd just stepped from the masquerade. The effect was ruined somewhat by snow melting in his otherwise perfect hair. His attire was an illusion... probably. It was good, especially outside the masquerade and the court, but he'd had plenty of practice.

He surveyed Raoul tied to the chair and Charon standing near the window. Bottomless dark eyes gave nothing of his thoughts away.

Raoul shut his eyes, surrendering to the inevitable, and bowed his head. He pulled again at the ties, but the knots held. When he opened his eyes again, he found Charon staring at the host, trying to fight his fears. Charon had spent months dancing the masquerade's music, and in those months he had likely indulged in more than just dancing.

The host knew it all. His being here probably reminded Charon of those long debauched nights, all those things he'd tried to forget, all the times he'd lain in their arms, mind and body fucked to oblivion. He'd enjoyed it. Mortals always did. Until the truth made itself known and the joy soured.

Raoul despised his part in it, in Charon's pain, in all of it. He despised who he'd been and what he had done. He deserved this.

Charon gestured at Raoul. "As you wished, he's here."

Tall, imposing, unrelenting. The host—Sinclair—carried a menacing air about him. Raoul felt the sting of Sinclair's lashings again as their memory crowded the room. In the confines of the masquerade, Sinclair could only go so far. Everyone hurt and healed. But out here? Out here, wounds bled and tears fell until hearts and breaths stopped. Raoul had ached for that finality. He'd sought time and age and decay. But suddenly he faced the threat of his own demise, and he wished he had more time. He'd never feared death before, but now he feared leaving Brice behind and all the things he'd left undone. Brice was strong, but so was his love. He showed it willingly, held nothing back, and Raoul feared another love lost might destroy Brice's heart and soul.

Vengeance burned in the host's eyes.

Raoul readied to beg. Not for himself but for Brice.

"Such a rare sight, seeing you so afraid." Sinclair crossed the dusty floor and peered down his nose. "How does it feel, knowing your fate once again rests in my hands?"

"Rather uncomfortable, actually. Could you loosen the ties?" Raoul couldn't make his twitching smile stick.

Sinclair reached down and flicked a blood-matted lock of hair from Raoul's forehead.

Raoul jerked his head away. "You have me, Sinclair. So end this but leave Brice alone."

Sinclair bit into his own bottom lip and smiled. "Without the masquerade, you really are just a lonely, pathetic fool. You tried so hard to be seen, and when that failed, you crafted your own little parade." He stroked Raoul's jaw. "Every time I brought the whip down, I saw how you loved it. Just so long as you were the center of attention. It was all about you."

Raoul's insides writhed. He could not deny it, although the very notion of his own selfish desires sickened him now.

"It's over?" Charon approached with confidence but froze the second the host's glare turned to him. "You'll leave my brother and me alone?"

The host took a step back and raked his gaze over Charon. "That really would be a fitting end for you. The LeChoix family free to do as they please. But I am owed far more than Raoul."

Charon's panicked glance found Raoul before darting back to the host. "But you said—"

"I said bring me the fool and I'd settle our debt." Sinclair's smile slithered onto his lips.

Sinclair's turning on Charon was all woefully predictable. Charon glanced again at Raoul but not in hatred. In desperation. He'd made a deal with the host in a world where deals meant nothing. He'd handed Sinclair the only weapon he had and only now did he understand the gravity of his mistake.

"Run," Raoul said.

Sinclair stepped toward the stairs, blocking Charon's exit. Taller than Charon but slimmer, he didn't look like a challenge, not physically. But the fae didn't fight fair and as Charon lunged for Sinclair, the host grabbed Charon by the neck as easily as plucking a chicken off the ground, walked him backward, and pinned him bucking and writhing against the wall. "*Get off me!*"

Sinclair lifted Charon off his feet and pushed in. He bowed his head and inhaled. "You smell like my love, like sunshine and light." He stroked a lock of Charon's golden hair between his fingers.

Charon's writhing stopped. He breathed hard through his nose but hung still, held aloft by Sinclair. Sinclair teased Charon's golden locks between his fingers, then brought them to his nose and sighed.

Raoul twisted his wrists at both corners of the chair. If he could just loosen the ties some more, he might be able to slip free.

"We would have had a family," Sinclair whispered, stroking Charon's hair. "She was my mate. Mine for eternity. Frivolous mortals do not understand such love."

"You're wrong." Charon spat. A globule of glistening spit struck Sinclair's mask and time froze still. Even the wind outside no longer howled. Sinclair had turned to ice. If he breathed at all, Raoul couldn't tell.

"I u-understand love." Charon trembled. "Anette loved my father, not you. I saw it every time she looked at him. I was born of that love. She chose him—*not you! I am their son—not yours!*"

Sinclair roared and threw Charon to the floor. Charon scrambled backward, trying to get his feet under him. Sinclair snatched his hair and shook him like a doll. A vicious slap tore across Charon's face like a whip's lash. He gasped, stunned, then struggled, trying to wrestle Sinclair off.

Raoul tugged harder at the ties wrapped around his wrists, yanking and writhing.

"No! Don't!" Charon cried.

Sinclair wrapped his fingers around Charon's throat and squeezed. Charon kicked uselessly at the air and clawed at the fingers locked around his throat. His face turned scarlet.

"Stop!" Raoul barked. "Sinclair, stop. He is all that is left of her. If you kill him, she's gone."

Sinclair leaned in, placing his face an inch from Charon's, and squeezed so hard his fingers turned white. "He's right—he's not mine!"

Charon's mouth opened and closed in silent pleas. His twitching slowed.

The tie at Raoul's left wrist snapped. He twisted, tore at the remaining knot, and loosened it enough to pull his hand through the loop. He sprang forward and launched himself at Sinclair, knocking him away from Charon. Sinclair reached for Charon, but Charon scrabbled free, and that was all Raoul needed to know—just that Charon was free. He landed a punch across Sinclair's jaw, knocking the mask off, and grabbed Sinclair's face under his hand and slammed his head into the floorboards. Once. Twice.

A vicious punch cracked Raoul's cheekbone, toppling him over. He caught sight of Charon as he reeled—the fool wasn't running. Why wasn't he fleeing? "Run, damn you!"

Charon finally bolted for the stairs.

Sinclair lunged toward him.

Raoul grabbed Sinclair's ankle and yanked. He went

down, twisted, and kicked, catching Raoul's chin with his heel. Skin split, and he hissed with pain. But in those moments, Charon was gone—vanished down the stairs. He'd go to Brice at the house. They'd have warning. They'd prepare.

Sinclair whirled on Raoul, snagged his hair, and slammed his head face-first into the splintered floorboards. "You wretched fiend!"

Pain rattled Raoul's skull. His vision spun. Blood wet his tongue. He spat at Sinclair's unmasked face, dashing his pale skin with scarlet droplets.

Sinclair's hand came down over Raoul's mouth and nose. Raoul opened his mouth to gasp air but nothing came. Sinclair straddled his chest, his weight suddenly crushing him, smothering him. He couldn't breathe. His lungs heaved, burning for breath. He tore at Sinclair's sleeves and shoved at his chest to pry him off. Nothing worked.

"All those times I whipped you for insolence, punished you for defying me—with every lash I wished you'd die and every time you smiled. Now—in their world—you will die, Raoul. Even the most beautiful of things must end. You'll be forgotten. Nobody will remember your name. I'll make sure of it. That bastard Brice will be next. And Charon... Charon I will take and make mine until he's forgotten all this. Until he believes he is *my son*. The son we should have had. *He will be mine*."

Raoul still shoved and writhed, but the hand over his nose and mouth grew heavier, and Sinclair's weight crushed his ribs. The heavy thumping in his head slowed. He wasn't surviving this. After so long a life, so many games, so many mistakes, he'd finally found the one true thing that made him worthy—a man who saw through all the masks and still loved who he was inside. It didn't seem fair that it should end like this.

Tears squeezed from his eyes.

He wished he'd told Brice everything he meant to him, told him how he'd already surrendered his soul to him. He wished he could say he was sorry, just one last time.

Chapter Fifty-Eight

Brice

Snow swirled and spun. The wind tugged at his clothes, trying to rob him of warmth. He might have lost the path. He couldn't be sure anymore. He was a damned fool to venture out in the bone-chilling storm. Even his horse had refused to leave its stable. "Raoul, you'd b-better be safe in a cottage somewhere," he stuttered through chattering teeth.

A figure loomed ahead. The snow swept in, then pulled back, then swept in again, but there was definitely someone stumbling toward him. Raoul?

"Ho!" Brice shielded his eyes from the battering snow.

"Brice!"

"Charon?" He quickened his pace, plowing each boot through heavy snow. "Charon—good lord!" Charon all but fell into his arms, gasping and pale. Brice tore his gloves off and cupped his brother's cold face in warm hands. "You're freezing. Let's get you home."

Charon grabbed Brice's coat and stared, his eyes wide and full of fear. He hesitated as though torn between thoughts. Ice sparkled on his lashes. He lowered his gaze and pulled his coat tighter around him. "Yes—h-home."

The wind shoved at them. Snow danced. And something gave Brice pause. The way his brother couldn't meet his gaze, or perhaps it was some voice carried to him on the wind, a voice that sounded so like Raoul's. *I'm sorry,* that voice said. Those words clutched at his heart, made it race, made him look again at Charon. His behavior that morning. The cold bed beside Brice... Raoul's sudden absence.

And he knew.

He gripped Charon's shoulder. "What did you do?"

Charon lifted sorry eyes. It wasn't ice on his lashes, but tears. "He's at the mill."

No... no, what had he done? Raoul. Brice had to get to Raoul. Brice shoved Charon aside and followed his brother's rapidly filling tracks in the snow.

"Wait! The host is there! He tried to kill me—"

The storm howled and moaned, and inside, Brice's rage matched its fury. "Go back to the house," he yelled over the wind. "Lock the doors and windows."

"Brice, wait! He'll kill you."

He spun. "Go back or *I'll* damn well kill you ."

Charon's face crumpled. "I'm sorry, Brice. So sorry..."

"Go!"

He couldn't look at him, couldn't stand to think that his own brother would hurt someone he loved. He had to get to the mill.

He stumbled and trudged and fought for every step. *Get to the mill. Get to Raoul.* Raoul would be there. He'd be safe. He'd be all right. Because he was Raoul, and no matter the hurt, the pain, the masks he wore to hide, he smiled and laughed and always found the joy to be had from the smallest of things. He always survived. He had to. He was all Brice cared for, the light in his life. He couldn't stand to lose him.

Raoul would be there. *Get to the mill.*

The wind pushed him back, bore down on him with heavy hands, but he fought on. One boot in front of the other. *Get to Raoul.* The wind battered him. Snow blinded him.

Get to Raoul. He needed him. Brice would always be there for him. He'd vowed it. Meant it. He'd never leave him. He'd chosen Raoul, the other half of his heart.

The mill loomed ahead like a giant headstone. Charon's footprints had almost vanished now. Brice followed the divots in the snow. The wind had eased, the snow just gentle flurries. All around, the forest held its breath.

"Raoul?" He shoved through the half-open door, letting in a curtain of snow. Old half-empty bags of grain filled the ground floor, stored for the winter. The rickety timber staircase beckoned. "Raoul?" If he was here, why wasn't he answering? Maybe he wasn't here. Perhaps he'd already left. But there was only one set of tracks in the snow leading out of the mill. Nobody else had left. Just Charon.

He gripped the banister and climbed the steps. His breath misted. His heart pounded in his chest and ears. With each step, more of the second floor came into view. The iron cogs took up much of the back wall. He tasted damp, cold iron in the air, so like blood. A chair, frayed ropes dangling from its corners.

Raoul lay on his back on the floor, arms spread, one leg bent.

Brice's heart stopped in his throat. He gagged.

No.

After sprinting up the last few steps, he dashed to Raoul and skidded to his knees. Was Raoul breathing? His eyes were closed, dark lashes against pale skin. Cuts and scuffs wept blood, his face battered. "God, no." Not dead, no. Not his beautiful fae.

He tugged off his glove again and reached for Raoul's face. Cold. So cold. "Raoul?" His heart might shatter and tear him asunder. His vision blurred through tears. "Please... Raoul. No."

The cold, hard nudge of a pistol pressed against the back of Brice's head.

"Hurts, doesn't it," the host said. "Like your heart and soul and mind have been ripped out. Hurts more than any physical wound. Know that hurt, cherish it. It's how I felt when Leon took Anette from me, how I felt when I learned she'd taken her own life in this wretched world."

The tears in Brice's eyes made the room shift and warp. He straightened, pushing back against the pistol. Anette's pistol. The host had taken it, and here it was, pressed against his head in some cruel fated irony. "Do it. Shoot me then!" What was there to live for if he couldn't share his life with Raoul? He had nothing.

"And end your suffering so quickly?" The host's fingers slipped around Brice's neck, the pistol skimming his cheek, and the host whispered in his ear, "No. You will feel this agony for eternity, Brice LeChoix. Your father took my chance at vengeance. So I will have my vengeance through you." As he spoke, the mill's walls and its gears rippled as though caught behind tears but with a silvery shimmer that could mean only one thing: illusion. A curtain of fantasy spilled over them, brightening the rusted reds on the iron cogs and sharpening all the edges, lending everything a polished sheen Brice hadn't seen since the masquerade. Somewhere distantly, familiar music played, ebbing and flowing like waves on a beach. And all at once, the raging storm outside fell silent, suffocating reality.

The host's hold on his throat shifted downward. He yanked at Brice's collar as he dug the pistol into his cheek, exposing his shoulder and its mark. "You are mated?" Sinclair scoffed. "That only makes this sweeter. Take a long look at the trickster you loved, at your *mate*. Because soon, you will not remember why your heart pains you so. You'll not remember his face, or his touch, or his voice in your ear, but you'll remember the ache of loss, the grief of letting him go. That agony will torture you for eternity."

No... The host was going to take his memory of Raoul. Never again. He'd rather die than lose him. Falling forward, he sobbed a kiss against Raoul's cold lips and whispered, "He can take my memories but never our hearts."

Raoul's eyes opened.

Brice gasped. Purple and blue eyes glittered and fixed on Brice. He winked. Raoul's hand thrust inside Brice's coat, dislodging the rifle. He cocked it, pulled it clear, and, aiming over Brice's shoulder, pulled the trigger. The rifle boomed. The muzzle flash burned Brice's cheek. He whipped his head away from the noise and heat, and twisted, catching Sinclair clutching his face.

Sinclair let out a cry. Blood ran between his fingers. He

took a step back, then a second, and bumped into the guardrail. Wood creaked, snapped. Sinclair reeled, and the rail collapsed. He fell backward, plunging down the gaping stairwell with a crash of splintering wood.

It had all happened so fast, in less than a breath, and now Brice wasn't sure what to believe. He blinked and turned his gaze back to Raoul. Raoul smirked, and that damned smile on his face put all the pieces of Brice's heart back together. He lunged for Raoul, wrapped him in his arms, and crushed him tight against his chest. "You fiend! I thought you dead!"

"That was rather the point."

He hated him and loved him. And kissed him. Until Raoul winced and hissed, and Brice eased off.

"While I am assuredly not dead, I am not far from it." His smile cracked and he grimaced in Brice's arms.

Brice stroked his blood-matted hair from his face. "Can you walk?"

"Yes, but check Sinclair." When Brice didn't move, Raoul's smile grew. "I'll be fine for a moment. Check the host."

Brice reluctantly left Raoul's side and peered over the edge of the exposed staircase down to the floor below. The timber stairs lay in pieces, but there was no sign of Sinclair. "He's not there," he growled.

Brice swept back over and helped lift Raoul to his feet, tucking him in close against his side. He was so cold still and seemed so small suddenly.

"He'll go to the house—for Charon."

"Damn my brother."

Raoul swayed on his feet and Brice folded him close

inside his arms, trying to embrace his shivering away. All around them, the mill's artificially rusted reds and sharpened edges rippled, the illusion warping for a moment.

"Some of this is real, some not," Raoul said, lifting his head and gently easing from Brice's hold. "It's a blur. Unrefined. Sinclair can't sustain it for long without my architecture supporting it—he has not the knowledge to make the masquerade a new—but he'll use it as camouflage and a means to get inside Latchly Hall." He peered down the broken stairwell. "We must go after him."

"Perhaps I should let Sinclair have him," Brice muttered.

"No." Raoul stiffened. "He is grieving. He tried to protect you."

"You are far more understanding than I." Brice still might kill Charon if he got his hands on him. Raoul could have died because of his selfish actions.

Raoul gave a splintered cough.

"You're hurt?"

"Yes," he wheezed. "Mostly—everywhere." He gestured roughly at his chest. "It will heal. Eventually."

He was in no condition to trek through snow. Without winter clothes and boots, he wouldn't last. "Take my coat." Brice began to shrug it off. "I'll carry you home—"

"No." Raoul took his hand. "I'll shift. As a wolf, I have my own coat."

"You're well enough for that?"

"We'll see."

Chapter Fifty-Nine

Raoul

Sinclair's bitter, decaying scent led Raoul toward Latchly Hall and its blazing windows. Blood mingled with the smell of fae too. Sinclair was hurt but it hadn't slowed him down. As a wolf, Raoul snuffled about the snow, finding a pair of single tracks leading around the house and huffing for Brice to follow.

Being a wolf had dulled the pain from his wounds and had given him enough clarity to think. Not about the absolute grief on Brice's face as he'd cried over his motionless body—he could not dwell on that or he might take Brice and hide him far away from the world. He thought about Sinclair and how broken he was, how lost. His madness knew no boundaries, no limits. And now he'd cast an illusion upon Latchly Hall's lands, there was no knowing what they might find waiting inside the house.

He shifted back from a wolf on the house's rear doorstep, instantly shivering and wishing he could stay as a wolf for longer. But the effort of appearing in a form that wasn't his natural state had taken its toll, leaving him numb and spent. Brice handed him his clothes, and he dressed.

"Are you well enough for this?" Brice asked, his concern making him pale.

Raoul nodded, and Brice rapped on the door.

Moments passed with no sound coming from inside. The silence was the hungry kind, the same silence Raoul had walked into before, only to have Charon assault him.

The lock snicked over of its own accord.

Brice turned the handle and shoved open the door. A blast of light and sound and laughter spilled out. Unmistakable sounds of a gathering but it was too loud and sharp. The illusion was stretched, turning brittle. Sinclair was losing his hold.

Brice ventured down the hall and Raoul followed. Music tinkled through the air. A kitchen maid swept from one of the rooms, plates in both hands. She didn't see them and hurried on by. The house had changed too. Old had become new. Wallpaper gleamed, wooden floors had been polished. There were no soot stains above the lamps, and the windows were all cobweb-free. The stilted perfection reeked of lies. Sinclair never had learned how to perfect tiny imperfections to make the illusion feel real.

"This isn't right," Raoul whispered.

"I know."

A tall, slim boy wearing lordling clothes bolted from the room ahead, golden ringlets bouncing.

"Charon!" a woman's voice rang out. "I'll count to ten!" True to her word, the woman counted down as the young Charon disappeared up the stairs, grinning from ear to ear. He hadn't seen them. Perhaps Brice and Raoul were the illusions? With lies and reality so neatly intertwined, it could be difficult to tell what existed where.

Raoul slipped his hand into Brice's, startling him. "He wants you distracted."

Brice swallowed and squeezed Raoul's hand. "Living this again will break my brother," he whispered.

That was probably Sinclair's plan: break Charon down, then rescue him and build him back up again in his own image. Sinclair was undoubtedly watching nearby somewhere. This was *his* illusion. He controlled its strings.

"Can you change this?" Brice whispered. "Do you have that power?"

"No... I gave it all to him."

Two more guests wandered from the lounge, chatting animatedly. Strangers to Raoul, but from Brice's flat expression, he clearly knew them. His soft eyes widened.

"—Ten! Ready or not!"

The woman who stepped from the room was a vision in blue silk and white lace. She turned her head, glancing toward them—through them. Raoul sucked in a breath. Anette had hardly aged a day since he'd last seen her and laughed her off for foolishly falling in love with a mortal. Brice's grip on Raoul's hand turned to stone. Brice reached toward her, instantly bespelled, but this Anette was a fantasy. She gathered her skirts and climbed the stairs after Charon.

Brice's sigh shuddered through him.

Raoul pulled him closer. "I'm here. I'm real."

"This is harder than it should be."

Raoul skimmed his fingers along the back of Brice's hand, distracting him. The fraught lines around Brice's mouth and eyes faded. "The past cannot hurt you, my love," Raoul whispered. He wished for this to be over, for all the games to end and the lies to come crashing down. He'd make it so. But for that to happen, Sinclair had to die.

Raoul pressed closer still and brushed a kiss over Brice's lips. Brice opened, then pushed his fingers into Raoul's hair and kissed him back, tongue teasing.

"Brice!" a man bellowed, and Brice jerked away as though suddenly burned. He tore his hand from Raoul's as a thousand furious memories of his father's disgust and disappointment assaulted him.

Leon LeChoix entered the hall. Tall and imposing, Leon bore all of Brice's features, only harder and colder than his son's.

An older boy entered the hall, back straight and chin up. His dark eyes dazzled with intelligence and pride. "Father, forgive me, I was just—"

"What did I say? It's as though you deliberately do not listen!" Leon stalked toward his son.

The young Brice stood firm. Only his eyes betrayed his fear.

Leon towered over him. "These are your guests. You might not want to be here, but you must. Much to my dismay, you carry the LeChoix name." Leon adjusted the young boy's necktie, tightening it so hard the boy winced.

"I cannot watch this again." Brice pushed from the wall, heading for the lounge.

"What if I don't want the name?" the boy said, his voice cracking on the last word.

Raoul didn't see the slap but heard it resonate behind him as he followed Brice into the drawing room. Brice paced beside the bookshelves.

"Sinclair is doing this to hurt you."

"Oh!" Anette slowed as she entered the room. "My apologies, sirs. I did not realize the room was occupied."

"Mother?" Brice straightened.

"Yes, my dear?" Her smile warmed the room.

Brice blinked and drifted toward her. "You see me?"

"Why wouldn't I?" She laughed and the sound danced about them, so very like the masquerade's magic. Because it was that very same magic, the very same lies. "Have you seen Charon? We were playing and—"

"Sinclair! Stop this!" Raoul said.

Rich, syrupy laughter rolled through the house.

And then the music began. Past Anette whirled—hair and dress swirling—and ran from the room.

"Mother, wait!"

Raoul threw out his arm and blocked Brice. "Don't."

"But she saw me." He pushed at Raoul. "She was real! Let me go."

Raoul blocked his every shove then caught his face, freezing him in his hands. "Look at me. It's a lie. All of it."

The music went on, growing louder, a whole band of piano and string instruments, building, growing, *breathing*, like a thing alive. The masquerade was here in all its power of illusion and wonderment.

"Raoul... I have to know why she did it. If I can ask her that—"

Raoul gripped his shoulders. "She made a mistake. That's all. There is no mystery, no answer you haven't yet found. Don't let him lure you in. You must resist. Don't go to her."

"Brice... Brice... Where are you? Help me..." Charon. Or so it sounded. But Raoul was not so easily fooled. This illusion was no different to those he spun to smooth out the wrinkles in his clothes or mend his masks. But here it was souring, turning vicious.

"Don't listen."

"Brice, God..." Charon whimpered. "The pistol. He shot me..."

Brice roughly shoved Raoul aside and ran into the hall.

The young Charon stood at the foot of the stairs, his hand pressed over his heart. Blood dribbled between his fingers. He lifted his head. "Brice?" He sniffed, eyes full of tears. "You were supposed to keep me safe. Mother told you to keep me safe."

Brice recoiled but grabbed the stairs' newel post and stared past the image of his bleeding brother. "Sinclair, you bastard! Show yourself! Or are your pathetic lies all you have left?"

Charon the boy wisped away to dust. The laughter and light crackled, stuttered, and fell silent. But the music played on and on and on, a relentless torture that poured in through the ears and tried to curdle their thoughts.

"You don't believe my lies, but your brother does." Sinclair stood atop the half landing like he had as the host of the masquerade. His mask was gone, revealing his fine, sharp face. Fae-tipped ears added to his angular features, and sharp teeth glinted as he spoke.

"What have you done with him?" Brice asked.

"Just showed him what he needed to see." Sinclair rolled a hand in the air. "His memory did the rest."

"Memory of what, *damn you*?"

Sinclair sighed and flicked his dark-eyed gaze to Raoul. "I should have expected your death to be a lie too. It is all you're good for."

"You cannot hide yourself in fantasy forever," Raoul said. "Nothing you do here will bring her back. Charon won't bring her back either."

The illusion, or memory, chose that moment to pour into the hallway like a storm in the form of Anette and Leon. Leon chased her past Raoul and toward the stairs. She whirled on him, her face so full of fury it twisted her lightness into something darker, and like Sinclair, her tipped ears and sharp teeth revealed her as fae. "They will take him away, Leon! Our boy!"

Leon tried to capture her hand, but she shook him off. "Anette, please. See reason. The host will not come for Charon. Our son is safe with us."

"He'll come..." Horror blanched her face. "He'll come and he'll twist him and make him dark like he is. Like I am afraid I did to him." Her fury softened. "I shouldn't have come here. We shouldn't have... we shouldn't have done this. Charon must not be made to pay for my mistake. We must hide him, Leon." Madness widened her eyes. The madness of regret and knowing and fear. "We can take him away. Perhaps if I am not here, then... then Charon will be safe. It's me he wants... If I go back, he will be safe..."

"Anette, please, listen..." Leon touched her face in the same reverent way Brice so often touched Raoul's. "I love you."

Anette ran up the stairs, her ghost passing through Sinclair. He staggered, gasping, and both Leon and Anette fizzled to dust, the past vanishing. Sinclair rocked and grasped the banister.

Raoul knew what happened next and only had to look at Brice's face to know he remembered. The fateful shot. The taking of her own life to protect her son.

Leon blamed himself, Brice blamed himself, and now Charon—having been shown this truth—likely blamed himself too.

But none of them were to blame for Anette's fatal decision.

"You showed him that?" Brice growled. "You showed him his mother's final moments, wishing herself gone to save him?" He placed a boot on the bottom step. "She feared you even then, Sinclair. *You* killed her. Nobody else. Her madness was your doing. You were never her mate. You were her nightmare."

Sinclair drew the pistol from inside his coat and aimed at Brice. "Silence!"

Panic clutched at Raoul's heart and mind. *No... by the stars, no.*

"You killed her as surely as you hold that pistol now," Brice growled, ignoring the pistol. "Her fear of you drove her to try and protect her family in the only way she knew how. To make it so you never had reason to leave the masquerade. She surrendered her life for her son. That is love. Not whatever twisted, poisonous thing you think you had for her."

"Love?" Sinclair laughed. "You know nothing of such things. A mortal's love is nothing compared to that of a fae's!" His finger slipped over the trigger.

Raoul burst in front of Brice, blocking Sinclair's aim and staring up at him. "You speak of fae love—then know Brice is my mate. Nothing you do will ever change that."

"You think I won't shoot you, Raoul? I already believed I'd killed you once. Step aside or die."

Raoul held the mad fae's gaze. "She asked you to forgive her. Her final words to you, and you crushed them. Your soul is empty because you know you drove her away."

Sinclair's finger twitched over the trigger. "She loved me."

"Yes," the real and solid Charon said. "She did." He began his descent down the stairs with a blue box in his arms. He simply set the box down on a step, turned its crank, and opened the lid. Thin, hollow music began to play. The masquerade's music. A & S—the initials glittered. And the tiny dancer twirled on her silk stage.

"She never forgot," Charon said. "Somewhere in all the madness, she never forgot, and she still loved you. It's why she kept it."

Sinclair stumbled down a few steps. He gaped at the box and its dancer. "How... how do you know this?"

"She told me." Charon wiped tears from his face. "The box was her secret. I was her secret, a half-fae boy. And so were you, the mate she left behind. She didn't hate you. She was sorry, in the end. Sorry for everything."

Sinclair lowered the pistol. As his arm came down, the

sharpness of his illusion fell with it. Candles fluttered. Latchly Hall groaned, breathing back to life as time thawed.

Brice's fingers slipped into Raoul's. So strong and firm, like the man he loved. Soon it would be over.

Raoul's gaze fell to the pistol.

There was just one last thing that had to be done.

Chapter Sixty

Brice

Brice held his breath. Sinclair still gripped the pistol, and now he was closer than ever to Charon, who stood beside the music box. If he chose to shoot him, he couldn't miss.

If Charon would just step away...

Brice tried to catch his brother's eye, but Charon just stared at the host, suddenly so defiant on that step.

Sinclair knelt and watched the dancer in the music box twirl. The music played on, its melody hauntingly beautiful. Sinclair reached for the dancer with his free hand, and his fingers hovered close, not touching. "I miss her with my every breath."

Brice drew Raoul close to his side, feeling the host's words as though they were his own. A love lost was a terrible thing. A mate lost could sunder a man's soul.

The hand crank slowed and the music began to fade.

The dancer dipped and twirled until she came to rest. And then there was only silence. Silence in which a thousand memories lived and where a love never died.

Sinclair tilted his head up to meet Charon's gaze and sighed. "Forgive me." He raised the pistol, pressed it under his own chin. And pulled the trigger.

The shot rang through the house and boomed straight through Brice's soul, so like the shot from the past that for a moment he was here and there, a young man again, desperate for his mother to wake. He choked on a gasp and took a step toward Sinclair.

Sinclair slumped forward onto the stairs, falling still at Charon's feet. He was motionless on his side, his eyes open and unseeing.

Charon's moan snapped Brice into motion.

He raced up the stairs and pulled his brother into his arms. "It's over." Charon collapsed against him. "It's over. He can't hurt us anymore." Charon's sobs shuddered through him too. "It's over," he said again and again, then caught Raoul's gaze.

He stood alone on the stairs, his trickster fae, his mate. And a small sad smile lifted the corner of his lips.

Raoul nodded. It *was* over. Finally and forever, the curse of the final masquerade was done.

Solstice, the longest night and shortest day, came and went at Latchly Hall. No invite appeared beneath the door, no masquerade summoned the townsfolk into its charms. Life went on uninterrupted. Winter's snow melted, darkness turned into the light of spring, Charon left to spend the summer in Massalia, and Brice watched Raoul flourish. He was beloved by the staff and farmers alike, and when he didn't have his hands buried in flour from the mill, kneading dough, he rode the farmers' horses and helped corral the sheep. Even the townsfolk had become accustomed to the LeChoix family friend who entertained the children with his quick hands and juggling tricks on market day.

Brice hadn't thought it possible, but with every passing day, his love for Raoul blossomed. Spring gave way to hot summer days, and even the forest swelled with lush life once more, like Brice had only heard of in tales. Whispers reached him of how the fae folk had returned to the forest. That explained the abundance of color in the meadows, the plentiful births of newborn lambs, and the goodwill throughout the town.

Raoul made no mention of it and merely smiled when Brice repeated the tales. It wasn't all his doing. Brice was fairly certain of that, although he did light up every room he walked into. There were other fae folk among the townsfolk, he was sure of it, but they hid themselves, like Raoul had hidden behind the last of the lies.

As time marched on and summer faded into autumn, Raoul's wonder at the cycle of the seasons, the ebb and flow of life, had Brice seeing his own life with fresh eyes. But a tiny thread of fear remained. Would Raoul stay with him or would he grow bored of a mortal life and return home?

He met Raoul in the meadow returning from the mill. White mill flour had smudged across his face. His jacket hung open, thrown carelessly on after the day's tasks. Disheveled and chaotic was where Raoul shone. And for a moment all Brice could do was stop among the fading flowers and stare. Amber sunlight caught in Raoul's silver streak, setting it ablaze. Dandelion fluff and butterflies flitted between them, and for a moment the sight of his fae ambling through the meadow stole Brice's breath.

Then Raoul saw him, stopped on the winding path, and planted a hand on his cocked hip. "Why, my lord, your gaze deflowers me."

Brice closed the distance in a few steps but stopped short of embracing him, even as his fingers itched to. "I've been thinking."

"Oh? Sounds terribly dangerous."

He eased an arm around Raoul's waist and drew him close. "It's time we told Jeanine and the others who you really are and what you are to me."

"But I am nothing, my love." Raoul tilted his head for a kiss.

"You're everything," he whispered against his lips, "and I want the world to know it."

Raoul huffed and pulled from Brice's grip but kept hold of his hand. He backed away, pulling Brice with him along the path. "Tell them what, that I am fae? They'll never look at me the same again. I like who I am with them. It's enough."

"But... is it really?"

"Yes."

Brice yanked Raoul back into his arms, and suddenly they were together, poised like dancers in the long grass and wilted flowers. Brice stepped, and with a soft, growing smile, Raoul stepped with him. God, he loved this—loved him, the way Raoul was always beside him, the way they talked without words. He never could have dreamed a love like this would be his. They danced in the meadow among the butterflies, and it didn't feel foolish or wrong. Nothing had felt so right.

Brice stopped suddenly. This was right. And nobody could stop them. There was no masquerade haunting them, no curse hanging over them, no host stalking them, and no father to disapprove.

Raoul's smart mouth tilted sideways. "Hm, what are you plotting?"

Brice tipped his chin up. His veins buzzed, his heart soared. "Marry me."

Raoul's lips twitched. "And who would I be then? Lady LeChoix to your Lord?"

"If you like. Especially if you'll wear the lace garter for me."

Raoul's sudden bark of laughter scattered a dozen nearby butterflies. He flung his arms over Brice's shoulders and peered into his eyes. "Who are you proposing to? Raoul the family friend or Raoul the trickster fae?"

"Whoever you want to be." *God, please say yes.* He wouldn't beg, despite wanting to. This had to be Raoul's choice. *Marry me, you wonderful, impossible dream.*

"What will the staff say?"

"I could not care less."

"The townsfolk... Lord LeChoix is to marry a male? Imagine the scandal."

"I really don't care."

"Hm." Raoul nudged his nose against Brice's. "What of your brother?"

"My brother has no say in any of this. The only person whose opinion I'm interested in is yours."

"Well, then..." Raoul teased an almost-kiss at Brice's lips. "It took you long enough. I feared you'd never ask."

His heart might burst. It beat against his ribs as though trying to escape. "Say it..." he whispered. "I have to... I have to hear the word."

Raoul's resonate purr rumbled through him. "How long can I drag this out for?"

"You cruel, cruel fiend." Brice teased the kiss some more but pulled away when Raoul chased it, delighting in the way Raoul's eyes narrowed.

"Well, I am fae. Did you expect a straight answer?"

"Don't make me beg. I will."

Raoul arched an eyebrow. "There's an idea, my love."

Brice dropped to a knee, captured Raoul's hand in his, and looked up at the male who had captured his heart and held it for ransom. "Be my other half in all things. Be the light in my dark. I cannot promise it will be easy, but together we'll prevail. I was told I was wrong, told I wasn't good enough, told to be the person I did not want to be, and that was to be my life. Until I met you. You showed me who I really am. You taught me true love and freedom. I love you, Raoul. Marry me, be my husband, my lover, my mate in all things."

Raoul's throat moved as he swallowed. He briefly glanced away at the meadow in the fading sunlight and then back to Brice on his knee. Emotion made his fae eyes glassy, and his bottom lip quivered. "Yes. Of course, yes. A thousand times yes."

Brice shot to his feet and wrapped his arms around him, hauling him close.

Raoul laughed in his ear, then crushed him close. "Forever yours," he whispered.

"Forever mine," Brice said, and gave him the kiss he so deserved.

Chapter Sixty-One

Raoul

Latchly Hall had fifteen staff, and Raoul knew them all better than he knew his own kin. Jeanine ran the house with a firm but friendly manner—just minutes ago she'd chased Raoul out of the kitchen after catching him stealing a few finger-sized appetizers. He'd loitered there to gauge their mood. All were suspicious of Lord LeChoix's invite to dinner. Rumors were flying. Some *big announcement*, they suspected. Something to do with Charon's imminent return? They'd tried, in various ways, to get Raoul to hint at the reasoning behind the invite, and as Raoul delighted in gossip, he made an easy target, but this time he'd merely smiled and stayed quiet, creating more whispers. They'd discover the reason soon enough.

And might not look at him the same again. A touch of glamour here and there had made sure none recognized him from the masquerade, but really, it was all another mask and he'd grown quite tired of wearing them. He found, with fear, that he wanted these people to know him and to welcome him, as they would a friend.

The staff had readied the food and then quickly changed into their best attire, leaving two of the newest members to serve. Excited chatter bounced around the table. Brice's chair beside Raoul's was empty.

He didn't really do nerves. Confidence ran in his blood. But for this occasion, he could barely hold a smile.

"Are you all right, Raoul?" Jeanine discreetly asked.

"Yes, fine."

She heard the lie. His talent for deception had slipped of late.

Brice finally entered the room, resplendent in his gentleman's clothes. Raoul's heart leapt at the sight of him and thudded harder when he pulled out his chair and sat. "My apologies for making you all wait. Please, eat, we can't have this wonderful spread getting cold on my account." He sat, and while the others helped themselves to various starters, Raoul slid his gaze to Brice.

"Sorry." Brice grimaced. "I was waiting for a delivery."

What kind of delivery could delay such an important announcement? "It's fine, really."

"Not hungry?"

"Oh, absolutely..." Hungry, but he dared not eat.

Brice leaned in. "Liar." He slipped his hand under the table and captured Raoul's. "All will be well."

He wasn't so sure. Myths about the fae had percolated in the area since the masquerade had kept his kin away from Chamonet, and in a vacuum of knowledge, rumors had swirled, turning into superstition. Talk among the townsfolk swung wildly from intrigued to afraid. The older generations remembered the fae and their court and sometimes playful, sometimes deceptive ways. The younger generations knew only of the masquerade and the memories it had left behind. *Raoul's* masquerade.

With the dinner eaten—Raoul having pushed his around his plate—and the mood jovial, Brice stood and chinked his knife against a glass, silencing the room. "You all know me well enough by now, and I like to think we are more than employer and employee. Events of the past few years have been... difficult. It's time this house finally celebrated good news, so with that, I'd like to announce my engagement to someone we all hold dear to us." The staff tittered. "He has touched all our lives." The tittering abruptly stopped. The staff's collective gazes fell to Raoul. "And brightened our hearts. Raoul and I are to be wed."

"Like... together, milord?" Jeanine asked.

Brice's smile cracked a little. "That is generally what marriage alludes to, yes, Jeanine." He smiled down at Raoul and produced a small velvet box from his pocket. Fingers trembling, he opened it. Inside sat two golden rings. The lines around Brice's kind eyes tightened.

It seemed as though Raoul should perhaps take those rings. But if he did that now, his life would still be a lie.

"Raoul?"

Raoul breathed in and stood. Fifteen friends looked up at him. "There's something else. I find myself lacking in the words to describe any of it, so I'll just show you and beg your forgiveness in such a deception." He swept a hand over his face, unravelling the glamour—the eyes, the ears, and a somewhat toning down of his general faeness. He'd removed his final mask, laid himself bare, and had never felt more naked. It was done.

A few gasps broke the silence.

He could only hope they didn't despise him.

"Well… I don't know what y'all are gaping at. It ain't really a surprise," Jeanine said in her matter-of-fact way. "He be clearly fae right from the beginnin'."

Raoul frowned at the wily woman. "You knew?"

She shrugged, as did most of the others. "You ain't as good a liar as you think, Master Raoul."

Raoul mock-gasped. "You wound me, Jeanine." Relief lifted a weight off his shoulders. A weight he hadn't known he'd been carrying. He'd feared they might not accept him, the real him. His kin had cared little for him, so why should this family be any different? But they *were* different, and that meant everything.

Jeanine stood and raised her glass. "A celebration is in order. To his lordship and his lordship, may their love be a blessing upon us all."

"Here, here." The staff raised their glasses. "To Master Brice and Master Raoul!"

Brice smiled his smug smile, like he'd known all along this would be the outcome. "Take the ring, Raoul, please… if you will. Before my heart stops."

Raoul took up both rings and slid Brice's on his finger, then Brice slid Raoul's on his. A cheer went up and Raoul absorbed its warmth. Yes, this was where he wished to be. No dream or fantasy could compare to having Brice beside him, and these people he'd come to call friends.

Chapter Sixty-Two

Brice

The solstice.

Brice fiddled with his necktie.

He hadn't seen Raoul in eighteen torturous hours, as was customary. And it was killing him. The only thing keeping him from rushing to the Laughing Crow, where Raoul was being prepared for the event, was the thought of the lace garter and stockings Raoul had promised he'd be wearing beneath his trousers.

God, his stomach was racked with nerves.

"Milord?" Jeanine rapped on his chamber door. "The carriage is ready. It's time, milord."

"I'll be right there." He admired his reflection and recalled seeing his father in a similar suit the day he'd wed Anette. He sighed and tried to swallow the knot in his throat.

"He'd be proud, you know," Charon said.

Brice jumped. He hadn't even heard the door open. Or known his brother was back from Massalia. "Charon... I thought... You didn't reply to my invite." He'd assumed Charon wouldn't be coming. His opinion of Raoul, and the marriage, too, likely wasn't good. The past was not so easy to forget without the aid of magic.

Charon swept his hair back and smiled. "I wouldn't miss my brother's wedding. I thought perhaps I might surprise you." He offered the crook of his arm. "Allow me to escort you?"

"If you like."

They left the house, accompanied by a flurry of staff and Jeanine, who fussed over Brice's clothes until the carriage door was finally closed and the carriage rattling down the road.

Charon wore a startling blue suit, and with his golden hair, he gleamed, probably outshining Brice as he always had done. "It's good to see you," Brice told him. "We missed you at the house."

"My apologies, brother, for my silence. I've been rather busy with business affairs and time got away from me."

He'd probably delayed his return as long as possible. They hadn't parted on the best of terms. Rather, Charon had left one night and only later written from Massalia to say he was safe.

"Congratulations," Charon said stiffly. When Brice opened his mouth to explain, Charon lifted a hand to stop him. "Allow me, please... to speak. I am sorry, brother, for my actions last year. Deeply sorry. There is no excuse. I harmed you and Raoul, and I will regret it for the rest of my days. I can only aim to do better. To be a better brother to you both. I want you to know, I wish you no ill will, truly. I see you're in love. I saw it before and... I was jealous and angry, and a terrible fool." He swallowed, breathed in, and asked, "Forgive me?"

Those words.

They had haunted the LeChoix line for far too long.

The carriage trundled along the road toward town and Brice swayed with its motion, trying to organize his thoughts around a reply. He had no wish to push the man away, but the things that had been done were difficult to move past. "You are my brother, Charon. You will always be my brother. We are blood, and I will always love you. But I love Raoul too. Please, never make me choose between you."

Tears swam in Charon's eyes. "I won't. I'm sorry, for all of it."

"I know. That is why there is nothing to forgive."

Charon sighed hard and blinked the unshed tears away. "Raoul is so right for you."

Raoul would have some smart, razor-edged comment for Charon, no doubt. But he had understood Charon's mistakes, perhaps better than Brice. "Yes, he is."

"Father would have come around, eventually. Mother... she once spoke fondly of a fae who could charm the stars from the sky. She called him shallow, back then. I think she spoke of Raoul before he changed. She would have loved this for you. I hope, one day, I can find someone I love as much as you love him. I met someone in Massalia. You'll like her. We're... taking it slowly. *I* am taking it slowly."

"That's good." Brice could think of nothing he wanted more than for Charon to finally find happiness.

"She's heard of the LeChoix family curse and about our

rumored connections to the fae." He chuckled. "She thinks it exotic, country fantasy."

"Hm." Brice smiled back. His lady would be in for a surprise when she learned her beau had fae blood. "Isn't everything fantasy until it becomes real?"

"I suppose it is."

The carriage rumbled into town and pulled up alongside the central fountain. Ice had encrusted its edges, and it sparkled in sunlight. Its waters still flowed. Chamonet wasn't yet in winter's full grasp.

Charon moved to open the door. "Ready, brother?"

He brushed his trousers down and cleared his head of all things. He twirled the ring on his finger. "Yes."

Charon opened the door. Brice stepped down into a crowd of what seemed to be the entire population of the town. They all wore heavy coats to keep them warm but also their finest hats and outfits beneath their furs. Faces full of smiles greeted him. Friends, all.

"Best wishes, milord!" they called.

"Best wishes, LeChoix!"

"Happy days, Lord Brice!"

Snowflakes dallied here and there, and in amongst the crowd, he saw others he knew. Chantel, her head tipped down but her eyes up and her smile made for mischief. She nodded her blessings and Brice's heart gave a stutter. He skimmed the crowd, looking for others.

Then the crowd parted, and there he stood.

Raoul wore a suit of midnight black laced with the finest silver thread. Heeled boots propped up his natural height. Silver was braided through his hair. Kohl darkened his eyes. A fine silver choker graced his neck. And he had to be the most magnificent fairy tale to ever come to life. There were no words, just a great heartfelt swell of emotion.

Raoul began to walk the pathway made by the crowd, every step a showman's display. Snowflakes melted in his hair. One touched his perfect mouth, and he licked it free, little sharp teeth hinting at his true self. He offered his hand and Brice kissed his ring as he fixed his gaze on the most precious thing he would ever hold. "Marry me."

Raoul laughed. "I rather planned to."

He drew him close and whispered, "Did you wear the garter?"

Wicked delight shone in his eyes. "That is for you to discover."

He could resist no longer and kissed Raoul beside the fountain with snowflakes in their hair and the townsfolk watching on. Raoul, the trickster, the player, the dancer in the music box, was finally free to choose his path, and he'd chosen Brice. Brice's heart soared far and free.

No dream, no fantasy, could ever compare to his heart's true love.

It began with love, the tales tell. And love ended its curse. But love never truly ends, and neither does the masquerade. Listen on the wind on the longest night, listen hard, and you might hear its call. Come, it beckons, take my hand, come with me, to the masquerade ball...

Also by Ariana Nash

Please sign up to Ariana's newsletter so you don't miss all the news and get a free ebook!

www.ariananashbooks.com

Want more amazing gay fantasy?

Award winning Ariana Nash, has everything from a star-crossed elf assassin and dragon prince pairing, to the infamous and epic enemies-to-lovers story of Prince Vasili and his soldier, Niko Yazdan. There are even demons in disguise as angels!

Search for:

Silk & Steel

Primal Sin

Prince's Assassin

About the Author

Born to wolves, Ariana Nash only ventures from the Cornish moors when the moon is fat and the night alive with myths and legends. She captures those myths in glass jars and returning home, weaves them into stories filled with forbidden desires, fantasy realms, and wicked delights.

Sign up to her newsletter here: https://www.subscribepage.com/silk-steel

Made in the USA
Monee, IL
06 December 2022

19835267R00301